Sophie King is the author of

Second Time Lucky

'An absorbing, feel-good novel – I really enjoyed it.'
Penny Vincenzi

'Over one eventful summer, four people make friends, share
each other's pain and fall in love in this light-hearted read.'
Heat

'A feel-good, entertaining read.' *Essentials*

The School Run

'A lovely debut – warm and engaging' Catherine Alliott

'There is a lot for women to relate to here' Katie Fforde

'A funny new novel' *Mail on Sunday*

and

Mums @ Home

'Fascinating reading' *My Weekly*

'Entertaining' *Closer*

'Funny and moving . . . captures the love, pain, humour and
guilt of being a parent.' *Bella*

By the same author in Hodder paperbacks
The School Run
Mums @ Home
Second Time Lucky

About the author

Sophie King is a pseudonym for journalist Jane Bidder, who contributes regularly to national newspapers and women's magazines. She also writes short stories for *Women's Weekly* and *My Weekly*. She was runner-up for the Harry Bowling Award in 2002 and the winner of the Romantic Novelists' Association's Elizabeth Goudge Award in 2004. Sophie also teaches creative writing and is Writer in Residence at Grendon Underwood Prison. She grew up in Harrow and now lives in Hertfordshire with her three children.

You can find out more on her website:
www.sophieking.info

The Supper Club

SOPHIE KING

HODDER

First published in Great Britain in 2008 by Hodder
An imprint of Hodder & Stoughton
An Hachette Livre UK company

2

Copyright © Sophie King 2008

A CIP catalogue record for this title is available from the British Library

ISBN 978 0 340 93539 2

Typeset in Plantin Light by Palimpsest Book Production Limited, Grangemouth, Stirlingshire

Printed and bound in the UK by
CPI Mackays, Chatham ME5 8TD

Hodder & Stoughton policy is to use papers that are natural, renewable and recyclable products and made from wood grown in sustainable forests. The logging and manufacturing processes are expected to conform to the environmental regulations of the country of origin.

Hodder & Stoughton Ltd
338 Euston Road
London NW1 3BH

www.hodder.co.uk

This book is dedicated to:

Giles, who would – if he could – live on bacon and egg
William, who barbied his way across Australia
Lucy, who could run my kitchen
My sister, who inherited our mother's culinary skills
My friends and our girly lunches (all right, just one
more then . . .)
My father and those special childhood breakfasts
All the Agas I have ever owned
Memories of Jane and Friday coffees

This book is not dedicated to:

Children who sneak snacks into their bedroom/insist on
eating supper in front of the television ('all my friends
do it!')/won't eat the same food/aren't hungry when
supper is ready/are hungry when it isn't

ACKNOWLEDGEMENTS

Many thanks to:

Betty Schwartz for giving me a taster
Carolyn Caughey for cooking up a dish
Penny Vincenzi, Catherine Alliot and Katie Fforde for choice
reviews

Charisma Magazine

AUGUST ISSUE

Bored with dinner parties? Too broke to eat out this month? Revolutionise your social life with the latest vogue – mystery supper clubs! The ingredients are simple. Take two friends and get them to bring along another guest. (This is more fun if you don't know him/her.) Or, if you want to play safe, simply ask friends/acquaintances whom you haven't seen for a while or want to know better. Then take it in turns to hold a supper party at individual houses once a month.

Bon appétit!

AUGUST

*Goat's cheese tartlets with spinach and
sunripe tomatoes*

Lamb baked with apricot and prunes

*Optional vegetarian quiche with peppers
and mushrooms*

Pavlova

One

'OhmyGodwhoputthepavlovainthetopoven?Look!It's burnedtoacinderandIcan'tevenscrapeitoffthebakingtray. Mike,didyoudothis?'

It was at times like this, thought Lucy as she heard herself screaming, that she missed the security of being married for a long time. Missed the old comforting familiarity when it didn't matter if you yelled like a fishwife because dinner was burned or if you accidentally farted in bed.

But now, as she looked up at Mike's surprised face, with his ruggedly handsome jawline contrasting with his soft blue-grey eyes, she suddenly wondered if she was doing the right thing in getting married again. Mike had always put her up on a pedestal. The Lucy he thought he knew, was the kind of woman who wouldn't dream of shouting at the children or swearing if someone cut her up in the car. Of course, that was the Lucy she wanted to be, too. But all it took was for the kids to be rude – or a domestic disaster like that wretched pavlova which she'd put in the bottom, cooler oven until someone had moved it – and she turned into someone whom she didn't like either.

'Not me, pet,' he shrugged. 'I don't know one end of your Aga from the other. There's no way I'd have gone near it, let alone interfered with anything inside.'

'I'm sorry.' How could she have lost it like that? Moving closer, she wrapped her arms conciliatorily round his neck. 'It's just that I spent ages making it and I wanted to be prepared for Saturday.'

Pulling her towards him, he stroked her hair in a way

guaranteed to melt her knees. 'But you've got loads of time. Another five days. You can make another.'

His calm rational tone instantly made her feel better. Luke would have lashed out at her unfair accusations or sharply reprimanded her for wasting ingredients. It still made her feel slightly sick to recall how he'd hit the roof when Kate had spilt hot chocolate on the cream sofa. Her husband had hated mess; hated anything in fact when things didn't go right or he wasn't in control.

Now, as she snuggled into Mike, feeling his warmth envelop her, the ruined pavlova didn't seem important any more. What was it about him? Ever since they'd been introduced fifteen months ago, she'd felt this incredible chemical pull towards him which she'd never experienced before. Nor, he'd assured her, had he.

'Let's go upstairs,' she murmured.

Mike's hand slid down her back towards her bottom, gently squeezing it. 'We haven't got time, Luce. Doesn't Jon need picking up from the station about now?'

'We've got ten minutes,' said Lucy, suddenly deflated and somewhat embarrassed. Since meeting Mike, she sometimes didn't recognise herself. When Luke had been alive, sex had been something that had to be done once a week or fortnight. Occasionally, she used to worry that she might be frigid but now she knew better. You only melted under the right touch. With Mike, it also lasted a lot longer than ten minutes. There was, she thought dreamily, nothing like a man who really loved your body. A man who spent time kissing each of her bits in turn and telling her how beautiful she was, even though she was just another ordinary middle-aged mum with a slightly baggy, post-kids tummy and blondish hair that was, right now, badly in need of its four-monthly highlights. Something else for her Must Do list.

Mike brushed her lips with his before picking up his car keys from the side. 'I'll collect Jon. You make another batch of those meringuey things.'

'Sure?' Even after a year, she still found it hard to believe her luck. Not many men would take on a 'single muddle of three' as her sister patronisingly called her, let alone offer to chauffeur teenagers from the station or help them with homework.

'Absolutely.' He paused at the door, grinning at her, before coming back for another brief cuddle. The smell of his warm body – sort of lemon aftershave mixed with something indefinable – was so tempting that she pulled him towards him again. He laughed. 'We've got all night for that. It's not fair to keep Jon waiting. And look, if you want to do that pudding stuff again, why not use my oven? The temperature's more constant than yours. There are plenty of free-range eggs in the fridge and the caster sugar's in the dry ingredients cupboard.'

Briefly, she considered his suggestion. Mike's house was only a fifteen minute drive from here and it was true. His oven was more reliable than her Aga which was due for its annual servicing. In fact, so were a lot of his things. Despite those rugged looks that were more in keeping with a handsome rugby player than a property developer, he had his own ways when it came to running a house. Not many men actually had a 'dry ingredients' pull-out storage unit, instead of simply shoving everything in to whichever cupboard or drawer it would fit in, as she did.

Years of living on his own, punctuated by long-term relationships which had never quite reached the status of 'live-in', meant Mike was far more domesticated than Lucy. Although he was five years younger – something else that niggled – he seemed more grown up somehow. Look at the neat row of socks that he would peg onto the dryer in the utility room! She just sandwiched theirs behind radiators where they inevitably fell down the back, only to be reclaimed, dusty and squashed, several months later. Yes, it might well be an idea to cook at his place.

'I'll go over tomorrow,' she said, 'when there's more time. I've got to walk Mungo now before Jon gets back.'

'That reminds me, pet. There are dog hairs again, all over the sofa. You might want to do something about them.'

Mike wasn't keen on dogs but that would come, she was sure, with time. Lucy held up her face to be kissed and watched him through the window as he strode towards his car, a gleaming silver Alfa Romeo. Immaculate inside and out. Completely different from her own untidy Volvo which was littered with old car parking tickets, squashed, empty juice cartons from the kids, overdue library books and a rather smelly dog blanket which ought to be washed. Maybe tomorrow, if there was time.

'Hi, Mum.' Kate swept past, heading for the fridge. Her purposefully-slashed jeans, thought Lucy ruefully, contained more oxygen than denim.

'Don't eat anything! It's nearly dinner.'

'Chill out, Mum,' said Kate emerging with what Sam called 'half a boob melon'. She glanced, eyebrows raised, at the tray of black gooey mess sitting on top of the cooker. 'I'm starving. Anyway, looks like you've burned supper.'

'That wasn't for tonight. It was for the weekend.' Lucy proceeded to scrape the muck into the bin which needed cleaning out as Mike had gently pointed out that morning. 'By the way, did you move my pavlova to the top oven?'

'Blast.' Kate neatly sliced the melon in half and spread a thick layer of peanut butter on it. 'Sorry. I only meant to do it for a sec because I needed to dry my trainers in the bottom oven.'

'But I've told you loads of times not to do that. It smells it out.'

'Well they were damp.'

'And you made me blame Mike for spoiling my pavlova.'

'Chillax, Mum.' She helped herself to more peanut butter. 'I didn't make you. You did it yourself. No, Mungo, you're too fat already. So what is it with the pavlovas. Having someone round, are you?'

'Kate, please don't talk with your mouth full. And yes, Antony and his new girlfriend are coming over and Jenny's bringing someone too.'

Kate raised her eyebrows and Lucy winced again, still unused to that awful gold ring which her daughter had had inserted above her left eye the other month.

'Antony's bringing his new girlfriend?' repeated Kate, giving her one of those 'Are-you-sure-you-know-what-you're-doing, Mum?' looks that always made Lucy feel like a kid instead of an adult. 'Wow! Have you told Maggie?'

Lucy felt a twinge of guilt. 'Not exactly.'

'You mean no.' Kate sucked the knife before putting it back into the peanut butter and spreading it on a slice of bread, this time. 'You ought to ask her too. That would really be fun.'

'No, it wouldn't. And stop eating. You won't want supper.' She sighed. 'To be honest, I wasn't sure about Antony bringing her either. But there wasn't much I could do about it.'

It was true. Antony was Mike's best friend and it was him and Maggie she had to thank for introducing Mike to her. Maggie was her closest female friend after they'd been at school together locally. Two years ago, Maggie had confided that she and Antony really weren't that happy but had agreed to soldier on for the sake of the children. Lucy had presumed they'd just continue rather as she and Luke had. As Maggie said, it wasn't as though there were any awful arguments; merely an under-current of just-about-bearable dissatisfaction.

Then Antony had met Patsy – a model! – and almost overnight, he left a twelve-year marriage and two children. Maggie had been, and still was, inconsolable. Their other friends, like Chrissie, claimed not to understand that but Lucy could. It was all very well knowing your marriage wasn't great but it didn't mean you weren't upset when it ended.

'Who's Aunty Jenny bringing?' demanded Kate, noisily sucking peanut butter off her fingers.

Lucy flushed as she weighed out the soft granulated sugar

for an apple crumble, accidentally spilling some of the floor. 'Er, she doesn't know.'

'What do you mean, she doesn't know?' Kate's eyes glinted with amusement. 'You're hiding something from me, Mum.'

Damn. Now she'd gone and trod in the sugar and it would get walked all over the rest of the house. 'If you must know, I said I'd invited that new chap who's moved in opposite to look after his father.'

'A blind date? That's so uncool.'

'I know, I know. But it's better than being on her own.'

'I dunno.' Kate tossed back her hair defiantly. 'If I hadn't found the right person by Aunty Jenny's age, I'd have a baby from a sperm bank.'

'It's not just a baby she wants,' began Lucy, wondering if she should have this kind of conversation with a sixteen-year-old.

'Sure. It's the company.' Kate mimicked her mother's voice. 'Whatever. I just hope you know what you're letting yourself in for. You know Aunty Jenny. If she doesn't like him, she'll say so.'

Lucy felt a wave of unease at the prospect of falling out with a new neighbour. 'You're probably right.'

'What's he called anyway, this bloke?'

She tried to remember. What was it about middle age and memory loss? It seemed that as soon as she'd turned forty, her brain had turned over and gone to sleep. Names, numbers – especially mobiles – and dates simply floated away out of reach when she tried to recall them. And the gingko tablets, which Jenny had got from one of her health clients, didn't seem to be doing anything.

'Gary, I think.'

Kate snorted. 'Well you'd better remember before he arrives or you'll have fun with the introductions. By the way, you know you and Mike were talking about going to the Lake District? Don't take it the wrong way but Sam and I really don't want to go. It's just not our thing.'

She gave Lucy a brief 'sorry' hug and then sprang back. 'Shit, is that the time? *Big Brother*'s started.'

'What about your homework?' called out Lucy as the door banged and the noise of the television filtered through. Too late. Sitting down at the kitchen table, she felt Mungo's wet nose in her lap as though sensing her mood. A small part of her had really hoped the two youngest would come on holiday with them, even though Jon would be at uni. It might, she and Mike had agreed, help bond them as a family. But that was the trouble, wasn't it?

However much she tried to pretend with cosy suppers round the kitchen table and wet holidays in the Lakes, they couldn't be a family. Not a proper one. Not without a real blood-related father. And as she was beginning to learn from her children's cool attitude to Mike, a future stepfather simply wasn't the same. Especially when, in the kids' eyes, he had to live up to the memory of a dead hero.

A hero who should never have died in the first place.

Two

Violet. Very lightly on the upper eyelid with her thin sable tapered brush. Violet set in place with Crème Brûlée Brown. That's what was needed.

'Sandwich, girls?' asked the photographer's assistant, putting his head round the door.

'No thanks,' said Patsy shortly, deftly working the brush across the model's right eye without pausing. 'We're working.'

What a cheek! She knew his game. He'd hoped to catch some flesh in the middle of changing. Stuff that. Patsy scrutinised the bare face, sitting in front of her, poised expectantly, still in her flimsy dressing robe. The violet looked good. Now what? Tawny Gold foundation, a dash of Illuminated Silver Concealer and soft brown Kohl pencil. After that, she'd think on her feet. She always did. And somehow it always worked.

'Cool,' said the girl, holding up the hand mirror while Patsy applied the Tawny Gold.

'Thanks,' she said in a tone which was meant to imply 'Stop looking until I've finished'. But the girl – who looked as though she should still be at school instead of being the latest 'discovery' to be signed up by Model Models – was so clearly entranced by the whole procedure of being made up for her first shoot, that Patsy didn't have the heart to be cross with her.

Besides, she knew what it was like. She hadn't been much older than this girl when she'd first walked into that tacky little model agency just off the docks, long before the new theatre was built. Patsy hadn't realised then how lucky she'd been to be taken on. Tacky or not, the agency somehow had good links with a local designer who used their models for his catalogue.

A scout for a leading London model agency had then spotted her 'unusual face' and within a week Patsy had been signed up and moved down to the bright lights.

'I usually use black eyeliner,' said the girl, interrupting her thoughts.

'Trust me,' said Patsy smoothly. 'Brown suits your colouring better.'

She'd soon learned what suited her own pale looks once she'd got to London. The agency had looked after her; she'd give them that. Looked after her, in fact, far better than her own parents. From the day her mother had died, Patsy had never touched a drop. It had been one of the things that had made her stand out from the other models. She'd watched them lose control at parties and quietly congratulate herself for knowing exactly what she was doing and who with. At least if she did make a mistake with men, she only had herself to blame and not the bottle.

'Do you drink?' she asked the young girl suddenly.

The child's eyes opened wide. 'Sure. What have you got?'

'I'm not offering,' said Patsy shortly. 'I'm asking if you drink and what.'

The girl laughed. 'Anything. I had this great vodka cocktail the other night. Got really smashed, I did, with my mates.'

Patsy frowned. 'I can tell.' She ran a finger over the girl's complexion. 'You can get away with it for a bit but after a while, it ruins your skin. You need to stop, right now. Drink water instead. Don't bother with the bottled stuff. You can just filter your own with a squirt of lemon juice.'

'Don't drink?' The girl was staring at her incredulously. 'But everyone does.'

'Then be different,' said Patsy simply. 'In this business, you need to be in control; understand what you're doing.'

The girl's eyes narrowed like a beautiful gazelle. 'Were you a model yourself, then?'

Patsy nodded.

'What were you called?'

'What I'm called now. Patsy Jones.'

'And what kind of modelling did you do?'

'All sorts,' said Patsy vaguely.

Teracotta blusher. Blended with Apricot Sunrise.

'*Tatler*? *Vogue*?'

The girl was persistent. Might help, providing she used it in the right way.

Patsy nodded.

'So what made you become a make-up artist, then?'

Patsy laughed hoarsely as she outlined the girl's lips in Mauve Meringue. 'I reached the magic age of thirty. We all do eventually. And although there are some mature models around – like Twiggy – there isn't always the work for the rest of us. So save your money and keep drinking the water.' She took another look. 'I think we're ready now.'

The girl slipped off her robe and smiled into the mirror. 'Cool. Ta very much.'

'Off you go then.' She patted the girl lightly on the shoulder, feeling as though she was sending her off to the slaughter. Briefly, a look of nervousness flashed across her face. 'You'll be fine,' said Patsy. 'Just pretend you're somewhere else. Think of the nicest place you've ever been to and put yourself there. Cut the photographer out of your head. He doesn't even exist.'

The girl was looking at her now as though she was insane. 'Whatever.'

Reluctantly, Patsy watched her trip across the floor in her high heels and swimsuit. Where was her mother? Who had allowed her to enter a dangerous world like this? For one crazy moment, Patsy wanted to drag the girl back and . . . and then what? What else did life hold for her? A till job behind the cosmetic counter at Selfridges. The parties where men paid for . . .

Patsy shuddered. No, she wouldn't allow herself to think of that now. The past was the past, as Dan always said. Gathering up all her pots and potions, she began to put them into her large make-up holdall. Glancing into her jewelled mirror, she automatically smiled with approval. People never believed her when she said she was thirty-five, insisting she had to be younger, but she had her mother's naturally youthful genes to thank for that. Babs had inherited them too but much good it had done her.

Right. Done now. Putting the mirror safely in the side pocket of her bag, she glanced at her watch. The session had taken just over an hour but she could just about bump that up to an hour and a half in her invoice. Switching on her mobile (golden rule: never keep it on when working), Antony's number immediately flashed up on the screen. Should she take it or make him sweat?

'I've been trying to get hold of you, love.'

Patsy smiled. Another golden rule: be mean, keep them keen. 'I've just finished a shoot.'

'Anyone famous?'

'Not today.'

He sounded disappointed. Antony almost took a childish delight when she 'did' celebrities. It was such a different world from his, he told her. Too bloody right. More different than he could ever realise.

'Just ringing to check you're still all right for Saturday.'

Patsy laughed brightly. 'Absolutely fine. Can't wait.'

Sometimes her lies were so convincing, she even believed them herself. Saturday. She'd thought of little else since he'd mentioned it. A casual kitchen supper, whatever that meant, with his best mate and wife plus some of their friends. Patsy, who was used to meeting people, still felt sick with worry. Supposing they didn't like her? Suppose they put Antony off her?

It had been a long time since she'd met anyone like him and even now, if someone had asked her what the attraction was, she wouldn't have been able to put her finger on it. 'He's got class,' she might have managed. 'He walks on the right side of the road. He makes me laugh. He's intelligent. And he's got money.'

She hadn't asked him to leave his wife for her but when he had, she'd been silently pleased. Excited even. No one had ever done that for her before and no, before anyone could ask, she didn't feel guilty. Men who left their wives generally did so for a good reason.

'I'll pick you up around 8 p.m. then if that's all right.'

'Great.'

'Are you all right?'

He'd picked up on her nerves. 'Fine,' she said crisply. 'I just can't talk much at the moment. I've got the next one to do now.'

'Bye then.' He hesitated. 'Love you.'

He'd been saying that for a while now and she knew he expected her to say it back.

'Bye. Speak later.'

She clicked her mobile shut. It wasn't true of course, about having someone else to make-up but she needed to get off the phone. To have some time to herself. That girl had unnerved her by reminding her too much of the past. There was only one person who really understood that. And he wasn't Antony.

Three

'*Layout ready. Shall I cm into office 2morrow 2 show u? Steve.*'

'*Yes pls,*' Jenny put down the wire basket at the newly-furbished M&S at Euston, so she could text back. '*9am?*'

'*OK.*'

It didn't stop. Texts, emails, phone calls. Exactly the way she liked it. You're always so busy, her mother used to sigh. But what was wrong with that? Jenny couldn't think of anything worse than having nothing to do. Besides, if you owned a successful company like Eventful Events, deadlines and pressure came with the job.

Now, what did she fancy for dinner tonight? Jenny picked up a packet from the chiller. Supreme Solo Microwave Chicken Kiev? Maybe. Or should she text Steve back and suggest they discussed the layout tonight over a friendly bottle of Chablis? No. Too pushy.

Jenny turned over a Supreme Solo Microwave Stir-Fry packet and ran her eye over the instructions. Three minutes! Their mother used to spend hours making an evening meal. She could remember it so clearly. They'd all sit up round the table when dad got back from work. Liver and bacon on Monday nights. Lamb casserole on Tuesday. And so on. The monotony had put her off cooking when she'd left home, although Lucy – ever the home-maker – had been different. That reminded her. Saturday. Lucy's supper party.

Why the fuck had she agreed? She'd been swayed, that's why, by that patronising article in last month's *Charisma* which advised readers to accept all invitations. Bridget Jones had given singletons a bad press! Of course it was nice to have a date but only if it wasn't the UPVC version. Frankly, if there wasn't anyone nice around, she was quite happy sitting down in front of the telly on her own with a good DVD, ready-made meal and a glass of cool white Hardy's on a Saturday night.

On the other hand, rather against her better judgment, a supper club as described by Lucy, sounded quite intriguing. Different people every time yet with a core of familiar faces and all in the same area so she didn't have to stay over.

Her stomach began to rumble noisily, reminding her that if she didn't hurry up, she'd miss her train. Flinging the Stir-Fry into her basket, she joined the queue for one of the express checkouts behind a mother with a kid, whining for sweets. No! The mother (as soft as Lucy) was actually giving in, allowing her kid to open them before she'd even paid. Now if she had children of her own . . .

Not the phone again! Plonking the basket down on the ground, she rifled through her bag for the slim silver handset.

'Jenny Macdonald speaking.'

'Hi. It's me.'

No need to ask who. As they'd got older, she and her older sister had not only begun to look more alike (though Jenny had always been blonder and thinner since Lucy had had the kids) but also to sound similar. Their mother, she thought with a pang, would have liked that.

'Is this a bad time?'

When wasn't it? She and Lucy had this unhappy knack of ringing each other exactly when the other one was busy. Irritably, Jenny moved forward in the queue. 'Not great. I'm in the super-market. Can I ring you back?'

There was the sound of shouting from Lucy's end and Jenny had to hold the phone away from her ear. 'Can't you tell the kids we're talking?'

'It's not that easy,' said Lucy tightly. 'No, Sam. You've got to ask Kate's permission before you can borrow her iPod for the school trip tomorrow.'

Almost at the front of the queue now. 'Look, I've got to go,' said Jenny shortly. 'I'll try you later.'

'Hang on. Mungo, down. There's something I've got to tell you first.'

'What?'

'It's about dinner on Saturday. I just wanted to tell you who's going to be there.'

Jenny crooked the mobile between her ear and shoulder as she lifted the basket onto the checkout. 'Go on, then.'

'Mungo! Sorry. We've got Antony and his new girlfriend who's a model, apparently.'

'Great. So she'll show the rest of us up.'

Lucy continued as though she hadn't heard. 'And then there's Chrissie and Martin Richards, plus Gary who's just moved in over the road to look after his dad.'

Jenny stiffened. 'Is that it?'

'Well, yes.'

Jenny withdrew a crisp £10 note. 'So he and I are going to be the only singles there? A bit obvious, isn't it?'

The woman on the other side of the till was eyeing her curiously.

'Well not really,' said Lucy haltingly.

'I thought there were going to be several people on their own.'

'Well, I did ask some others but they were busy . . .'

'Forget it. I'm not coming. It's too obvious.'

'But I've already asked him.'

'Then un-ask him.'

'You've got to come.'

Jenny felt an inexplicable pleasure at the desperation in Lucy's voice.

'I've already started making the food.'

Oh, God. Lucy's track record for over-cooked food or recipes that didn't turn out right was legendary.

'I'm sorry but I'm not being set up like this. Ring you later.

OK?' Jenny grabbed the change from the woman and, teetering on her heels, half-ran across the concourse to platform 8. Why did Lucy always make her feel such a failure? Everything always went right for her. Well, not everything, obviously, because of Luke. But now she had Mike while she, Jenny, couldn't find one man who fitted the bill, let alone two.

Only two minutes until the Watford train left! Tucking her slim black briefcase under her arm, Jenny broke into a desperate jog down the slope to the platform. Ouch. Her ankle turned, causing her to stop momentarily before shooting through the barrier and into the train, just seconds before the doors closed. No seats of course but at least she was on it.

Phew! Leaning back against the partition by the door to catch her breath, Jenny noticed that a rather good-looking man was looking at her. Her eyes travelled downwards to the wedding ring which gleamed dully from his left hand. Inwardly sighing, she pulled out a copy of *Charisma* from her briefcase. The magazine was running a profile on one of her new clients which she really ought to read before their meeting tomorrow.

Sneaking a look over the top, she caught the man looking at her again. Pointedly, she looked away. With that blonde floppy fringe, he looked a bit like Luke. Instantly, Lucy shot into her head. The differences between them were so vast that sometimes she caught herself thinking that if they weren't sisters, they might not even have been friends. Still . . .

'Lucy? It's me again. I'm on a train so I'll be quick.' She lowered her voice, conscious that the good-looking man with the wedding ring and striped grey suit was still staring. 'Sorry about just now. It's just that I get embarrassed about that sort of thing. You know.' She whispered fiercely. 'Blind dates.'

Turning away, she tried to shield the mouthpiece with her hand. 'But I'd still like to come. Would it be all right if I brought someone with me? No. Tell you more about him when I can talk properly. Bye.'

Leaning back against the partition which was shuddering

with the movement of the train, Jenny closed her eyes. 'Who are you bringing?' Lucy had asked, not unreasonably. God knows. That was who. But one thing was certain. She'd find someone, even if it was the kid who delivered the office sandwiches.

Slowly, Jenny half-opened her eyes to check. Yes. That man was still looking. Quickly, she shut her eyes again, pretending to be asleep while upright. Married men! Sod them. All of them. That was one mistake she was never going to make again.

Four

It looked like a slightly larger version of the new television remote control, except that it had two wires coming out of it, leading to a white plastic fish-shaped loop.

'Just insert it inside you and press the On button,' Sandra, the health visitor had brightly explained. 'Start off at the number I've set it on – let's see, 29, wasn't it? – and increase it when you feel able to.'

Chrissie looked at her Battery-Operated Super Pelvic Floor Toner doubtfully. She simply had to do something. It wasn't just that she couldn't even feel Martin floundering around inside her like a slice of raw, damp, filleted plaice. It was also that every time she ran after George, she became aware of a warm, wet patch below, suggesting that it wasn't just George's nappy that needed changing.

Sandra had given Chrissie this contraption the other week and she still hadn't got round to using it. 'Do it every day,' she'd chirped. 'Get into the habit. Like cleaning your teeth.'

Well now was as good a time as ever. George, thankfully, was riveted to some children's presenter who hadn't been taught to say his 't's and Martin was safely at work. If she did it here, in the kitchen, she could hear if her son did anything awful like pulling over the glass cabinet which he'd done last week. 'Keep away from children', the instructions had advised. If only.

Tentatively, Chrissie pulled down the kitchen blinds, followed by her XL knickers from Marks. Gingerly, she squirted some gel round the white plastic loop and gingerly pushed it up herself. No, that didn't feel right. Maybe it should be horizontal like a little fish. Maybe not. This was getting sore. Right. That wasn't too bad.

Volume 29. That's what Sandra had said, wasn't it? Oooo. Oh. That felt weird. Rather like someone beating an electrical drum inside her. 'Walk around,' Sandra had advised. 'Some of my ladies just get on with their housework while it's attached to them.'

How on earth did they do that? Holding the box with one hand, rather like a Victorian heroine holding the hem of her skirt, Chrissie waddled to the sink to start transferring the contents into the dishwasher. Was it possible, she wondered, to get an electric shock if she accidentally splashed herself? For a minute, she envisaged Martin coming back to find her slumped on the floor with a wire coming out of her insides. He'd think she'd invested in one of those stimulators. And suppose George came in and touched her. Would he get an electric shock too? And . . .

'Wah, Wah, Wah.'

'OK, George, I'm coming.'

Chrissie lumbered towards the screaming in the television room. God, she was fed up with things inside her. Martin's persistent fumblings. The cap which the GP had fitted because Martin hadn't wanted her to go back on the pill ('It took you long enough to conceive George after you came off it. Supposing we want another?') The cracked nipple chamomile cream that smelt of thick antiseptic which she'd stupidly tasted to see what it was like for George (Ugh!). And now this.

'What's the matter, George?' How on earth had he reached that pot pourri? 'You haven't eaten any, have you?' Swiftly, she lunged at her son's clenched fist, tripping over his pile of bricks as she did so. 'Ow. Ow!'

OmiGod! She must have pressed the Increase Volume button on the box by mistake when she'd got down on the floor. 54! 54! Her entire nether regions were rocking, making it almost impossible to pull the white loop out of her. For a few seconds, it stuck in the flabby fleshy folds of whatever was left down there. Yanking it furiously, the plastic fish finally flew out at the same time as her index finger finally located the Off button. Sinking down on the ground, she couldn't stop shaking. What had she done to herself?

'No, George, no. Don't suck. Not nice.'

Chrissie grabbed the white loop from George but his fists gripped firmly. She gave an extra pull and the wires came out. 'Now look,' she yelled, 'you've broken mummy's Super Pelvic Floor Toner. How am I going to get myself back to normal now? It's all your fault, you know.' Her arms grabbed little George's shoulders and for a moment, she felt she could throw him across the room. 'All your fault!'

'Everything all right?' asked Martin when he rang at lunchtime for his usual brief call.

Fine, she wanted to say. I nearly killed myself in an attempt to reacquaint myself with my vagina and George might or might not have eaten Marks & Spencer's finest pot pourri. 'Yes, of course it is. Why?'

'You sound a bit quiet.'

'I think George might be getting a cold.' Impatiently, Chrissie tucked her hair behind her ear, wishing, not for the first time, that she hadn't had it cut to 'make it easier'. Now it made her look boringly mousy compared with her previous layered office bob which had demanded four-weekly trips to the hairdresser.

'Martin, I'm not sure if we should go to Lucy's on Saturday. If George is sickening for something, it won't be good for him to take him out. And it will upset his routine, too.'

'He'll be OK. Besides, it will be good for us to go out.'

'What do you mean by that?'

'Nothing.' He sounded irritated. 'But we haven't done much since George was born, have we? At least this way, we can take him with us and know he's all right. It's a great idea. And then, when it's our turn to have everyone here, he's in his own environment.'

'I'll see. Got to go. I can hear him crying.'

He wasn't but she couldn't bear it when Martin got so smug and self-assured. He didn't have the responsibilities she had. From the minute the midwife had put George on her chest, soaking wet and screaming lustily, she realised amidst an unexpected rush of love and terror, that it was her job – and her job alone – to make sure this baby grew up safely and healthily.

But it was so difficult! Especially with a child like George who was always bumping into everything, refused to sleep for more than three hours on the trot and hated solids, even though she did everything she could to ease the heavily sterilised spoon into his stubborn little mouth.

What was he doing now? Good. Still standing in his baby-walker, riveted by the *Teletubbies* video. If she was quick, she could just nip up the stairs and try on a couple of outfits to see if anything fitted for Lucy's supper party which Martin seemed determined to go to.

Grabbing the baby monitor, Chrissie limped up the stairs, still feeling the after-effects of her battery overdose, and flung open the wardrobe doors. This might do. After all, it had an elasticated waist. Forcing herself to look in the mirror, she groaned out loud. Either it had shrunk in the wash or else her stomach had been secretly given building permission for a single-storey extension.

It didn't help that she was short ('petite', Martin had called her before George) so couldn't hide any post-baby flab. Even worse, her body seemed to have grown back in different places. Look at her wrinkled stomach! It reminded her of the face in Munch's 'The Scream' from the days when she had time to go to art exhibitions. As for her boobs . . . how could they have sagged into rabbit ears so fast while her thighs almost rippled like a giant lilo bed with what Sandra brightly called 'water retention'?

Looked like the only thing that would fit her for this flipping dinner party was this fuchsia pink late-stage maternity dress. And she wouldn't, she just wouldn't, wear that. In fact, she'd rather not go. Perhaps she could . . . Oh, my God, what was that?

Later, Chrissie couldn't even remember flying downstairs. What she did remember – as she told Lucy later – was seeing George's highchair on the ground with her son, still strapped inside, yelling with a face as pink as that bloody maternity dress.

'George!' Her fingers were shaking so much she could hardly undo the buckle. 'George, darling,' she wept, clasping him to her and feeling, at the same time, a lump the size of an egg on the back of his head.

Where was the phone? Chrissie picked up the Super Pelvic Floor Toner by mistake, flung it across the room and looked wildly round for the real thing.

'Ambulance,' she managed to yell above George's screams. 'Number 3, Lavender Drive. Please come quickly. Something awful's happened to my baby.' She burst into tears. 'And it's all my fault!'

Five

'Don't touch!'

Lucy tapped Jon's hand playfully as he dipped a finger into the bowl. She'd always loved his long artistic fingers; so like Luke's. Sam and Kate's were stubbier, like her own.

Her eldest son made an appreciative face. 'Wicked, Mum. What is it?'

'Goat's cheese. And mind your elbow. You're about to put it in the pastry.'

Jon picked up the packet. 'What's this ready-made puff stuff? You always used to make your own.'

Lucy began rolling it out before pressing down with a glass tumbler (where was her pastry cutter?), to make circlets for the baking tray. It had been like this before, she remembered, when Luke was alive. She'd enthusiastically suggest having people around and then panic at how much there was to do.

'Yes, well I've run out of time. Look, do me a favour, can you, and fill these cases with the cheese as I go along.'

'Honestly!' Jon pretended to sound disgruntled but she knew he was teasing. 'The things I do for you.'

Lucy snorted. 'You mean the things we do for you! Running around after you, picking you up at all hours, giving you free accommodation . . .'

He put his arms around her from behind and she leaned her head back on his shoulder, wondering how her little boy could have grown up so fast. Sometimes she felt guilty for loving him in a different way from the others because he'd seemed hit hardest when Luke had died. No wonder he was so sensitive.

'Well, I'll be gone next month, Mum. Then you'll only have two of them to nag.'

Her chest tightened with apprehension. 'Don't say that. You'll still come back some weekends, won't you? Oxford's not that far.'

'I can't come back too often, Mum. There'll be things going on and I don't want to miss out.'

Of course he didn't. She still wasn't sure that the course he'd chosen to read – social anthropology – was right for him but, as far as Jon was concerned, it was Oxford and that was all that mattered. Not because it was prestigious but because Luke had gone there, all those years ago, before she'd even met him.

'This all right?'

It took her a second to realise Jon was talking about the tartlets. 'They look great. Thanks. Oh, no, is that the time? They'll be here in less than an hour and I still haven't decided what to wear.'

'You always look lovely in whatever you're in, pet.'

'Mike! You're back. Did they like it?'

He gave her a warm kiss. Over his shoulder, she could see Jon's back stiffening as he carried on spooning in the goat's cheese mixture.

'Seemed to, although you can't tell. Look at the couple last week who said they loved it and didn't even bother returning the agent's follow-up calls.'

Mike had been showing some people round his house which still hadn't sold. It was the market, said the estate agents glumly. They weren't desperate for it to sell, thank goodness, like some couples. But when they did, the plan was to sell Lucy's house and buy somewhere together. Somewhere, as Mike said, that they could do up together, although Lucy knew that what he really meant was somewhere that didn't resound with Luke's memories.

'I've finished now, Mum.' Jon was talking to her as though Mike wasn't there. 'I'm going out now, OK? Peter's picking me up.'

She didn't like Peter, who had been at school with Jon. He drove too fast and he smoked too. There was something about him that she couldn't put her finger on, even though he was always polite – almost obsequiously so – to her. 'Where are you going?'

'To some pub. And maybe a party.'

'Make sure your friend doesn't drink and drive,' inserted Mike.

Jon gave him a withering look. 'He's not that stupid. See you later.'

The door slammed. 'Don't worry,' said Mike, drawing her to him. 'Get away, Mungo. Jon will be all right when he goes to uni. It's a difficult stage; he's probably nervous. And he's still upset after his driving test.'

She nodded. In one way, she'd been pleased about Jon failing last week. The idea of her son driving was one more thing for her to worry about. But on the other hand, it meant he was in the hands of someone else at the wheel; someone like Peter.

'Look, I'll keep an eye on these things while you get changed. How long do you want them in the oven for?'

She forced herself to concentrate. 'Ten minutes max. I'll set the timer.'

'Want me to lay the table?'

'Kate said she'd do that. KATE!'

No reply. Kids, she'd often thought, ought to have some kind of 'Message Received Safely Even If I Don't Answer' gadget like you got on the computer to confirm your email had been opened.

'Typical.' Lucy ran her hands through her hair. 'Why did I bother organising this in the first place?'

Mike kissed her forehead. 'Because it's fun and it's what couples do. Now cheer up. Jon will be fine. He's a big boy. I'll lay the table and take the tartlets out of the baking oven. See, I'm even getting the hang of your Aga. Anything else to do?'

Lucy consulted her list. 'Nothing much at the moment. The lamb's cooking nicely and the vegetarian quiche is done.'

'Who's veggie?'

'Someone's bound to be, so I made it just in case.'

He gave her a playful slap on the bottom. 'Upstairs with you or they'll be here. Come on, Mungo. You'd better go in the utility room so you're out of everyone's way. I said "Come on!" Honestly, Lucy, I thought this dog was meant to be trained.'

'He was,' began Lucy. She'd got Mungo, a loveable black and white refuge mongrel, after Luke had died in an attempt to provide a distraction for the children. But after six years, he still didn't always come when he was called.

'There's the door.' Lucy whipped off her blue and white striped pinny with egg yolk stains down the front. 'Quick, you do drinks while I change.'

She'd intended to work out what to wear beforehand. But it had been so many years since she'd given a dinner party – a proper dinner party – that she hadn't given herself enough time to get ready. Lucy pulled out her long green skirt from the wardrobe. It always looked good with the cream top and it was easy to wear. Bother. It had a stain at the front. Why hadn't she checked it before? Frantically, she leafed through the rail. The pink dress was too smart and the blue skirt, an old favourite, was a bit tight. After Luke's death, she'd lost nearly two stone but in the last couple of years, she'd slowly begun to put it back on. She'd have to start being more careful.

Lucy stood in front of the mirror critically. If she twisted the green skirt round so the stain was at the back and if she made sure the label, which was at the front, didn't show, she might just get away with it. Downstairs, she could hear voices. The green, it was. Quickly, she slapped on some matt foundation on her nose – whoops – and then some powder. Mascara, a dab of gloss and her favourite lipstick. Not bad. Lucy smiled unsurely at her reflection. Sometimes, she felt it was someone else standing in front of her in the mirror. Someone who had lived a completely different life from her; a woman with an unblemished past and an uncomplicated future to look forward to.

Bother. Her mobile. Please don't let it be Jenny pulling out. It had been so embarrassing cancelling that nice man over the road, telling him that they'd had to postpone dinner but that she'd hoped he'd come another time.

'Hello?'

'Hi. It's me.'

'Maggie!' Lucy's heart sank. Had she found out Antony was coming round? Mike had thought it best not to tell her but she'd had her misgivings. 'Are you all right?'

She spoke dully. 'Not really.'

Lucy could practically taste the fear. 'Why?'

'I'm lonely.'

So Maggie didn't know about Antony coming over! The relief made her babble with shame. 'Mags, I'm sorry. Look, why don't you come over for lunch tomorrow?'

There was the sound of Maggie blowing her nose at the other end. 'Actually, I wondered what you were doing tonight.'

No! 'Tonight? Well, tonight's not great, I'm afraid. Mike's got an old friend coming over and I've got to take Kate to a party and . . .'

'It doesn't matter.'

Yes it does. It does! 'Come over tomorrow,' pleaded Lucy. 'Mike's going fishing. Bring the kids; Kate loves looking after them. You know she does.'

Maggie sniffed. 'If you're sure I wouldn't be in the way.'

'Of course not.' Heavens, she felt guilty! 'Can you watch something on television tonight?'

Maggie was speaking so quietly she could hardly hear. 'There's nothing on. I rang Antony – yes, I know I shouldn't have – but his answerphone was on. I rang the bitch too but hers was on as well.'

'I didn't realise you've got her number.'

'Not only that, I've got her address too.' Maggie sounded almost triumphant.

'How?'

'I wormed it out of the kids. Do you know, Lucy, I can't even dream any more. I used to dream all the time but they always had Antony in them. Now he's not here, I can't dream any more.'

'Oh, Maggie . . .' She could hear the door going; someone else had arrived. 'Look, I'm sorry, Mags, but I have to go. I'll ring you in an hour or so to check you're all right. And Mags . . .'

'Yes?'

Lucy swallowed, thinking of that black time after Luke when she never thought she'd be all right again. 'Take it from me. It will get better. I promise you.'

Still feeling treacherous, she made her way down the stairs just as Mike came out into the hall. 'Wow, pet. You look great.'

'Thanks.' She nestled into his shoulder as they went into the sitting room. Luke would never have noticed how she'd looked. Luke would have got cross that she was late in greeting their guests. Luke would have . . .

'Hi.' Antony kissed both her cheeks lightly. He was wearing pale blue designer jeans, as though trying to look younger although the effect was marred by his paunch which stuck out, iceberg-like, through a white silk shirt still bearing its packet creases. Holding his hand, was a very tall, extremely skinny and impossibly beautiful girl with cat-like eyes and ebony hair cropped close to her head, elfin-style, with pink feathery bits at the nape of her neck. In the corner of her nose, was a tiny sparkly diamond stud.

Her legs went on for ever in shiny ladderless ten denier and she seemed to be wearing – Lucy was trying not to stare too much – a black leather skirt which ended some way above her knees. Despite those fragile arms which looked as though they might snap any minute, she had to be at least a 38B. In fact, her chest probably experienced a different atmospheric temperature from the rest of her body! As for that perfume – which was pervading the room – well, it reminded her of an expensive brand which she'd tried once in Selfridges but made her feel sick.

'Lucy,' said Antony with indecent excitement. 'I'd like you meet Patsy. Patsy, this is Lucy.'

Six

Foundation too pink. With her colouring, it should have been terracotta-based. Eyebrows needed shaping (Possibly never done?). Mascara-clogged eyelashes. Kind smile. Terrible pale pink lipstick. Stain on back of her skirt, suggesting their hostess might have peed herself.

Patsy knew what that felt like. Ever since that time as a little girl, when she had wet herself with shock the first time she'd seen her dad beat the daylights out of her mum, she always needed a wee when she felt scared or vulnerable. She felt like that, right now. From the minute Antony had pulled up outside this elegant detached white house in a chocolate box village near Watford, called Little Piddington or something – a million miles away from her council flat in Highbury – she'd been desperate for the toilet.

A widow, Antony had said. Her husband had been killed in some kind of tragic accident a few years ago. That explained the house. There had probably been insurance to pay off the mortgage and maybe put the kids through some posh school. And she was getting married again apparently. Lucky bitch.

Lucy didn't seem like a bitch, though. 'Hi,' she'd said, running down the stairs to greet them, clearly flustered. Patsy, who'd reprimanded Antony in the car for being too early, almost felt sorry for her. 'So nice to meet you, Patty.'

'Patsy,' she corrected firmly.

'Gosh, I'm so sorry. I'm always getting names wrong. Middle-aged memory loss, you know. I mean, you probably don't of course but . . .'

Patsy watched her getting even more flummoxed. Go on,

say it, she dared. Yes, I'm younger than Antony but not as much as you think because I've got good age genes and I know how to hide the wear and tear.

For some reason Lucy seemed quite cool with Antony as she greeted him, barely thanking him for the bouquet he'd bought her from the Harrods flower hall. Mind you, Patsy thought smugly, they weren't as lovely as the stargazers he'd given her when he'd picked her up tonight. They were still sitting in her kitchen sink, waiting for a suitable vase which she'd have to pinch from the studio on Monday.

'Come on through,' said the Mike bloke, leading them into the sitting room. Antony put his hand ever so gently on the small of her back as they went through. She liked that. It was the right mixture of chivalry and familiarity in a setting where everything seemed so utterly different from her own life. Patsy looked around, taking it all in. Mahogany coffee table with turned legs. Thick blue and pink Chinese rug on top of wool cream carpet. Deep expensive chintz chairs that cushioned your bum when you sank into them. Paintings – not posters – hanging on the wall. Music (hotel reception stuff) in the background. And something good smelling from somewhere.

'What would you like to drink, Patsy?' asked Mike. He had hands like hams, she noticed. A big man with a slightly northern accent. A capable man who was honest through and through. Patsy prided herself on being able to suss out personalities from the minute she met them. It hadn't always been like that, of course, or she wouldn't have got into such a mess in the past.

'Vodka and lime, please,' she said smartly.

Mike frowned. 'Do we have any lime, pet?' he said to Lucy who was handing round a bowl of nuts.

Pet? People used to call her that in Liverpool but somehow it seemed all wrong for a posh woman like this. Yet Lucy seemed to think it perfectly natural. 'Gosh, I don't think we do. Terribly sorry. We've got orange or tonic.'

'Go on then, I'll have a g and t.'

As she spoke, a large black shape bounded into the room. Patsy let out a small scream.

'Mungo!' The Mike bloke grabbed its collar. 'How did you get out?'

'It's all right, love.' Antony had his arm around her but Patsy couldn't stop shaking.

'I don't like dogs.' She tried to recover herself. 'When I was a kid, one chased me.'

'Mungo's fine,' said Lucy. 'Just a bit bouncy.'

Blimey! If it had got any closer, it might have snagged her stockings, if not worse. They'd taken it away now but Patsy felt distinctly wobbly. 'Is there a toilet round here?'

Antony sprang to attention. 'I'll show you.'

It was exactly as she'd thought it would be. Small cream-coloured china basin with pretty blue and pink flowers painted inside; posh soap in a dispenser; clean neatly folded towel on the little bend under the basin. And a toilet that wouldn't flush first time. Shit. She sat on the downturned seat while waiting for it to refill itself so she could try again.

If she left it like this, they'd think she didn't have any manners. Nervously, Patsy clicked opened her bag and lit a cigarette. This was an important evening for Antony. Mike was a good friend; she needed to make the right impression on him and his partner.

Urgently, Patsy sucked in the taste. It calmed her down to watch the smoke billowing out. Christ what was that noise? It sounded like a siren. Someone was pounding down the stairs which felt as though they were above her; voices were raised in alarm; there was a loud knocking at the toilet door. 'Patsy?' It was Antony. 'Are you OK?'

Shit. There was no alternative but to come out. 'I see.' He looked down at her ciggy. 'That's why the smoke alarm went off.'

A horrible hot flush spread over her body as realisation dawned. 'I'm sorry.'

'It's all right, everyone,' Antony called out over his shoulder. 'False alarm. Patsy's been a naughty girl and lit up in the loo.'

To her embarrassment, Lucy appeared behind him. 'Oh dear. Never mind. I'm afraid our sensors are very sensitive.'

'Who's been smoking in the bog?' A pretty fair-haired girl with a ring through her right eyebrow put her head round the door. Any more, thought Patsy, and they'd be having their bloody tea in here.

'Kate, darling, leave our poor guest alone. Don't worry about it, Patsy. Mike's stopped it now.'

The terrible ringing had indeed finally ended. Everyone else trooped back to the sitting room, leaving Patsy red-faced and Kate who was hovering. 'I did that the other day when Mum was out,' said the girl grinning. 'Luckily she never found out.'

'You shouldn't smoke at your age,' said Patsy severely. 'It will ruin your skin.'

Kate's eyes turned cold. 'Oh, yeah? Then why do you smoke?'

'I don't much. Only when I need to.'

The girl's face softened again. 'I know what you mean. But you'll be fine when Aunty Jenny arrives. She's cool. Here, I've been told to give you one of these. No, don't look. I've got to stick it on your back.'

Patsy stepped back. 'What is it?'

The girl rolled her eyes. 'It's one of Mike and Mum's stupid games. Everyone wears a celebrity's name on their back so they can't see it and after dinner, we take it in turns to ask each other questions and guess who we're meant to be.'

It was only when she was desperately trying to think of something to say to the bloke on her left (Tony Blair, according to the label on his back), that Patsy remembered she hadn't flushed the chain a second time. Too late now. She could hardly get up when everyone was chomping their way through lamb.

'How long have you been vegetarian for?' asked the man

whose name she couldn't remember but who was married to the short plump woman (smudged eyeshadow, shiny nose and a Charlotte Church label on her back) with a kid climbing all over her.

Patsy looked away, unable to watch the gravy dribbling down his chin. 'Eighteen years and eleven months.'

'Wow. That's precise. Any particular reason?'

She pushed a piece of burned quiche to the side of her plate. 'Yes.'

Go on. Ask me. He might have too if the kid hadn't started to grizzle. 'Oh dear.' The woman frowned. 'I think he needs feeding.'

'Again?' Her husband seemed almost proud. 'We're trying to wean George, you know Patsy, but he doesn't like his solids. He'd much rather have my wife, if you get my meaning.'

He gave her a large wink. Gross.

'Does anyone mind?' The plump woman was looking round the table questioningly. 'I think he still needs a bit of comfort after what happened.'

I don't believe it, thought Patsy. The woman was unbuttoning her frilly top at the table and there was an almighty flash of vast white skin and a tube map of blue veins, before the kid's head obscured the Piccadilly Line.

'More beans anyone?' asked Lucy brightly.

How come their hostess managed to get herself a Penelope Cruz sticker? Patsy began to sweat. Supposing she couldn't guess her own identity. They'd all think she was stupid. Were these the kind of games that Antony had played with his wife? Were they all measuring her up against his ex?

Fear always made her talk too much. Without meaning to, she started gabbling to her neighbour. 'That's some bruise your kid's got.'

Martin nodded and she edged away from the sweet smell of beer on his breath. 'Earlier this week, George was in his high-chair and managed to tip himself over by kicking the table and pushing backwards. He's got a massive egg on the back of his head. We had to get it checked out at Casualty.'

'I remember Kate doing that to me,' chipped in Lucy. 'She fell off the swings when she was five and had to have five stitches.'

Great. The conversation was degenerating now into a 'Do you remember?' and 'Aren't kids a worry' mixture that she simply wasn't able to enter into. Patsy stifled a yawn and as she did so, caught the eye of Lucy's sister; a pretty woman called Jenny who'd arrived so late that Patsy had had to break her no calorific-ridden-peanut rule through sheer hunger.

'Do you have kids?'

Jenny – or Margaret Thatcher according to her label – shook her head while running her hand through her expensively layered blonde hair. She was wearing a flimsy top to reveal her cleavage and looked as cold as Patsy felt. Why didn't they turn up the heating? It might be August but it was freezing.

'Do you?'

'No.'

'What do you do?'

Patsy was suddenly aware that the rest of the table had fallen silent, as though waiting for an answer. 'I'm a freelance make-up artist.'

'Thought you were a model,' said the man next to her disappointedly.

'I was but now I make them up instead.'

'Anyone famous?' asked the woman who was breastfeeding.

Trying to look her in the face (difficult with those massive boobs on parade), Patsy mentioned a few well-known names which clearly impressed the other guests.

'Who did you model for when you were younger – I mean when you modelled?' asked Lucy.

'Oh, magazines mainly.' She was deliberately vague, as always.

'So not Page Three, then?' joked Jenny's companion who had to be at least ten years younger.

'I did actually.'

There was a brief silence. 'You know,' said the man next to her, 'I always wondered if they did something to make you a bit bigger.'

'Martin!' said his wife sharply.

'Well,' began Patsy slowly, 'some of the agency girls continued when they were pregnant and . . .'

'Nice lamb,' interrupted Jenny.

How rude!

'It was one of mummy's recipes.'

'I didn't know you had that cook book. The one where she wrote down all her recipes?

'Yes. You can borrow it if you like.'

'OK. Can you pass me the salt, please.'

'I didn't think it needed it.'

'I'm not criticising you, Lucy. I just think it needs a bit more flavouring. I'm sure mum put more salt in it.'

Those two really didn't like each other, did they?

Lucy stood up, her mouth tight. 'If anyone doesn't want any more, I think I'll bring out pudding. Actually, there might be a slight delay.' She looked round the table, pushing back a strand of hair which looked a bit damp, probably from stress. 'You don't mind, do you?'

Half an hour later, she still hadn't come back, although there was a distinct cluttering and muttering of low frantic voices from the kitchen. Patsy wondered if she should offer to lend a hand. She wouldn't half mind seeing what it was like through there but she'd probably have to disinfect her hands and feet first before they'd allow a former Page Three to touch anything.

On the other hand, anything was better than sitting here, listening to that story again about little George and his high-chair. 'Just going to help.'

Antony looked up from pouring another glass. 'I'm sure there's no need.'

'I want to.'

Lucy was clearly surprised to see her. 'Gosh, thanks. Actually, I've had a bit of a disaster. I made this pav a few days ago but it's rock-hard so I'm having to whip up something else instead.'

Patsy frowned. 'Pav?'

'Pavlova. It's like a meringue but with a soft inside.'

Enviously, Patsy took in the designer-tiled kitchen. 'Why don't you just put out that fruit instead?'

She nodded towards the enormous bowl of grapes and apples and bananas that was sitting on the pale beech kitchen table.

'Just what I said,' chipped in Mike. 'Honestly, pet. Everyone's eaten masses anyway.'

Lucy looked doubtful. 'I don't know . . .'

'That will be Jon.' Mike, who'd already started to wash the grapes, turned at the sound of the door. 'Forgotten his key again, no doubt.'

'I'll go,' offered Patsy, glad of something to do.

'No, really . . .'

She opened the door. A tall, skinny older woman wearing baggy tracksuit bottoms, stood on the other side. No make-up. Black smudges under the eyes. Bright auburn hair, the wrong side of Nicole Kidman. She looked at Patsy blankly. 'Is Lucy there?'

Patsy nodded. 'I'll get her.'

The woman had already come into the hall with a familiarity that suggested she knew her way, just as Lucy was coming out of the kitchen wiping her hands on a tartan drying up cloth. 'Maggie!' she gasped.

Patsy froze.

'I didn't realise you had company.' The woman was slurring her words. Blimey, she was well trolleyed. 'I thought you were going out but I went for a drive and saw the lights were on and I was so desperate to talk that I just came in. I'm sorry.'

'No, no, it's fine.' Lucy was twisting the cloth round and round in her hands. 'Come . . . come on in. We can talk in the kitchen.'

Maggie looked towards the dining room. The door was half open and Antony was clearly visible, throwing back his head and laughing at something Chrissie was saying.

'He's here, isn't he?' She went pale. 'How could you, Maggie? How could you?'

Then she turned to Patsy, her eyes blazing. 'Who are you?' Patsy tried to find her voice.

'I said, who are you?'

'Now, Maggie, it's not what you think.' Mike was coming out of the kitchen now, assessing the situation. Maggie pushed him away, almost spilling the glass of wine he was holding. She was standing so close to Patsy that she could smell the wine on the woman's breath.

'Tell me.' She was almost growling. 'Tell me who you *are*.'

Patsy took a deep breath and stood up straight, facing Maggie fair and square in the eyes as she'd learned to do over the years when in trouble. 'I'm Patsy. Hi.'

Seven

There was definitely some kind of commotion going on out there in the hall. 'Back in a second.' Jenny patted Steve on the arm. 'Sounds like one of the kids is playing up.'

She felt a bit mean at leaving him alone with the others, including Martin who'd overdone it on the red and had sprouted a near-Pavarotti waistline since she'd last seen him. But Steve had done really well, considering. The idea had come to her yesterday when he'd come to the office to deliver a layout for the engineering conference programme. 'I don't suppose you're free on Saturday night?' she'd asked.

He'd flushed. 'Well, I do have a partner.'

Of course he did. Good-looking man like that.

'But he's away this month in Dubai for a shoot.'

Jenny mentally kicked herself. She'd been dealing with Steve for about a year now and she should have guessed, considering every good-looking bloke in London was either gay or married.

Steve lightly touched her arm. 'I could be free. It depends what you had planned.'

So she told him. Told him about Lucy and the supper party and not having anyone (at that particular time of course), to bring along. And to her amazement, he'd agreed. So far, it had been fine. He'd mixed in well with the others and even managed to raise her street cred by singing her praises work-wise. And, because he wasn't obviously gay, she could see that Chrissie and that so-called 'ex-model' with the tiny purple butterfly tattoo on her shoulder, had been quite intrigued, especially when Steve rather naughtily implied their relationship was more than platonic.

But what was going on here?

Maggie, Lucy's oldest and best friend, had that girl Patsy virtually by the neck. Mike was trying to pull her back. 'Maggie, come on, love. Calm down.'

Maggie let go of Patsy and pushed Mike away so he stumbled against the wall. 'Why should I? You asked Antony to dinner with his tart and you expect me to calm down?'

Poor Lucy was sitting at the bottom of the stairs, head in hands. 'I knew it was a mistake.'

'Thanks very much,' snapped Patsy, straightening her skirt even though there wasn't much of it to straighten. Jenny inwardly shuddered. Black leather was so tarty even when it was clearly an expensive design. 'Well, I won't outstay my welcome any longer.'

'No.' They all swivelled round as Antony strode in from the dining room. 'Hello, Maggie. Look, I'm sorry you're upset but you've got to accept the situation. Lucy might be your friend but Mike is mine. So he's bound to meet any new friends of mine.'

Jenny watched aghast as Antony put his arm around Patsy. Couldn't he see how upset Maggie was?

'Come on, Mags.' She threw Antony a filthy look. 'Let's go into the kitchen and find you something to drink.'

'I think she's had quite enough already,' said Antony sharply.

'That's none of your business. No, it's OK, Lucy. You look after your other guests. Maggie and I will be in the kitchen for a while.' Jenny glared at Patsy. 'And as for you, you ought to be ashamed of yourself. Any decent single woman knows that married men are strictly off-limits. Especially when they tell lies about their wife not understanding them.'

'Well at least we didn't have to play that stupid game,' said Jenny as Kate made them all coffee in the kitchen.

'What game?' sniffed Maggie.

'The Guess Who one. Sam, you look really miserable. What's up?

Her nephew broke off a piece of pavlova, scattering crumbs

all over the kitchen floor which Mungo promptly vacuumed up with a wet floppy tongue. 'Mum said she'd write me a note to get me off school for this concert I want to go to. But Mike won't let her.'

'Why not?' Maggie was calmer now, although it had taken a large brandy to do it. Someone would definitely need to drive her home.

'Because he's so bloody proper,' butted in Kate. 'Fuck. This pav nearly broke my tooth.'

'Don't swear all the time,' said Jenny evenly, 'or you'll do it without noticing. It's as difficult to give up as smoking. Trust me. I know.' She poured Maggie another coffee. 'At least you won't have to worry about the ghastly teenage stage for a few more years. How are the kids taking all this, by the way?'

'I've told them daddy's working away during the week.' Maggie blew her nose. Some women, thought Jenny, could cry in an attractive way. Poor Maggie wasn't one of them. 'I know I've got to tell them some time but I keep putting it off. And they're young enough to accept it when Antony sees them on Sundays and then leaves.'

Sam cut himself a large slice of cheese. 'I told him,' he said indistinctly, his mouth full of cheddar, 'I told them both just say I've got a ruptured spleen. Then they couldn't expect me at school, could they?'

'What do you want to see anyway?' asked Jenny.

'The Wattevers.'

'I'll see if I can get some press tickets if you like, providing it's during the holidays. One of my clients is an agent in the entertainment business.'

'Cool. And can you have a word with Mum about sex?'

'Sorry?'

'She's always going on about what I do at these concerts and parties. I've told her but she doesn't believe me. I don't drink much and I don't do drugs and I only have sex with my right hand.'

Jenny spluttered over her drink.

'I can see the party's definitely in here!' said a voice.

'It certainly is. How's Miss Ex-Page Three doing in there?'

Steve pulled up a chair. 'Strutting her stuff. Declaring to the table at large that it was nothing to do with her. Did anyone notice her label by the way. The Duchess of Windsor. Pretty apt, don't you think?'

'Bitch,' sniffed Maggie. 'What I don't understand is how he could go for someone like her. She's so completely different.'

Exactly, Jenny wanted to say. Your husband wanted someone different and it wasn't surprising. Maggie had really let herself go since the kids. Really, there was no excuse for not wearing make-up or getting your hair properly cut. And just look at what she was wearing. If that's what marriage and kids did for you, she was well out of it.

'He's not worth it, darling.' Steve took Maggie's hand. 'Anyway, when you get close, as half the men at the table were trying to do, she doesn't look so great. In my opinion, it's down to that clever bra she's probably wearing.

'I could do with one like that,' said Lucy lightly, coming in. 'After three kids, it's all downhill.'

'Mum! You're so embarrassing. Here, have some coffee.'

'That little blue jug,' cut in Jenny, watching her niece pour out the milk. 'I didn't realise you had that.'

After their mother had died, they had divided her things between them. There was little that was valuable in monetary terms but plenty in emotional.

'You said I could have it if you had the coffee cups.'

She'd forgotten that. Now she'd made herself look mean.

Maggie looked up mournfully. 'Shouldn't you be with your guests?'

Lucy sat down next to her friend. 'They've gone now. Well, Chrissie's still here but she's gone upstairs to change George.'

'For another baby, I hope,' shuddered Steve. 'I've never seen such an ugly kid.'

Jenny stifled a smirk. 'Shhh, you naughty boy or you'll get Lucy into even more trouble.'

'I'm really sorry about Antony,' said Lucy in a low voice to Maggie. 'But Mike wanted him to come over.'

Maggie looked away. 'Couldn't you have said no?'

'Hey.' Jenny put out her hand, keen to make up for her mistake about the jug. 'I told you just now. It's not easy for Lucy in the middle.'

Maggie sniffed. 'I know. But it was awful coming in and seeing you lot having fun. I used to be one of you and now I'm an outsider.'

This was Mike's fault for insisting on asking Antony. 'Of course you're not.'

'It's so difficult being on your own with the kids.'

'Who's got them now?'

She rubbed her eyes. 'One of next door's girls. She's nearly fourteen but my lot were asleep and I only meant to pop out for a bit and I'm just round the corner . . .'

Jenny leapt to her feet. 'Isn't there a law about under-age baby sitters? Come on, Steve, we'll drive Maggie home.' She could do with getting out of here.

Maggie rose unsteadily to her feet. 'I don't usually leave them,' she protested. 'It's just that I really needed to get out and talk to someone.'

'We understand.' Steve put his hand under Maggie's elbow. 'Thanks for a great evening, Lucy.'

'Yeah, thanks, sis.'

Lucy went with them to the door. 'It's been the worst dinner party of my life.'

'Oh, I wouldn't say that. Whoops, hold on to me, Maggie. It's been really entertaining, hasn't it, Jen? Wow, who does that piece of junk belong to?'

They all watched as a dirty, old-style red Mini braked sharply in the drive. 'That's Peter,' said Lucy tightly. 'A friend of Jon's.'

Two tall youths, each with a guitar, clambered out, laughing loudly. It had only been a few weeks since she'd last seen her nephew but he seemed to have grown even taller. How she envied today's generation of teenagers who spent more time planning gap years than CVs.

'Hiya, Aunty Jenny.'

She felt herself being embraced by a long pair of arms. In vain, she tried to reach up and ruffle his hair. 'Hi, my amazingly tall nephew. Just like your father.'

'Peter, this is my Aunty Jenny and . . .'

'A friend of mine,' said Jenny smartly. 'Steve.'

Steve was looking at Peter oddly.

'Do you know each other?'

'No.' Steve's voice had a Keep Off tag. 'Why do you think that? Well, guys, nice to see you but we must dash. Come on, girls. We ought to make sure those kids are all right.'

Eight

Chrissie sat on the chair in Lucy's bedroom, wriggling herself into a position that was comfortable for both herself and George. It wasn't easy now he was getting bigger.

Ouch. 'Don't bite!' Automatically, she jerked backwards, causing her nipple to slip out of George's mouth while he yelled indignantly.

'All right, all right, there it is,' she said pushing it back. He guzzled hungrily and Chrissie, grateful for the peace and for the relief (her aching breasts had started to flood during coffee), leaned back and closed her eyes.

Frankly, it was nice to be away from everyone. Funny. When Martin was at work and it wasn't a mother and toddler day, she desperately craved adult company. So much so, that she'd even started listening to *The Archers*. But when she did find herself with other adults, like tonight or even at mother and toddler, all she wanted to do was run. No one, wherever she was, was like her. The women – and one man – at mother and toddler were all younger and none had given up high-flying jobs. Actually, there had been one but she'd scooted back to work before her maternity leave had been up.

Every now and then, Chrissie still wondered about doing that herself but when she thought about someone else looking after George, she felt sick. No one, no one apart from herself, could be trusted. Just look at that story in the papers the other day about the au pair who had let a toddler play unsupervised in the garden only to find it dead in the neighbour's swimming pool.

Automatically, she stroked the back of her son's downy head

where that terrible bruise-egg had been. It was amazing how it had gone down in just a few days but it still made her feel ill to think of it. If someone else had been looking after him, they might not have run down the stairs so fast or called the ambulance that quickly even though the doctor at Casualty had said it wasn't necessary.

'But it might have been, mightn't it?' she said to George. His eyes were locked firmly on hers; it was clear he knew exactly what she was saying. Downstairs, she could hear voices. Raised voices. It almost sounded like an argument, except that she could hear Martin's deep throaty laugh which always got deeper the more he drank. He was probably having one of his verbal spars with Mike. She liked Mike. He was good for Lucy, although she needed to get over this guilt thing about Luke. Having her dead husband's picture in the bedroom was hardly the most tactful thing to do.

'I mean, what must Mike think when he stays over?' she asked George. His eyes were drooping now and his grip on her nipple was loosening but she kept on talking, knowing that he found her voice soothing, just as she found it reassuring to talk to him. She glanced at the picture of Luke again. It showed a young, blond man with a baby in his arms (Jon?), laughing with his head thrown back as though he didn't have a care in the world. 'That sort of thing must make a man feel pretty insecure,' she added. George's head, heavy with imminent sleep, nodded in agreement.

If Martin died, she would never marry again. She'd dedicate herself to George although it would mean that she wouldn't have any more children. Still at forty-one, the chances of that happening anyway were probably small and besides, how would George cope with a rival?

George had slumped away from her now, his little rosebud mouth still open with milk dribbling down and his eyes firmly shut. She ought to put him against her shoulder and burp him so he didn't get wind but she couldn't bear to disturb him. It might wake him too, if she went downstairs and she really didn't want to put him in the travel cot which Martin had put in the corner of Lucy's bedroom. It seemed too impersonal and cage-like. Besides, he'd be traumatised if he woke up in a strange environment. Chrissie had brought the baby monitors but she wasn't convinced they were working properly. The manager of the shop where she'd bought them, had changed them twice at her insistence, even though he claimed they were perfectly all right.

The voices downstairs were getting louder one minute and then quieter the next. Up and down, up and down, rather like one of the songs on George's Fisher Price musical carousel. There was barking now and footsteps running up the stairs followed by a door slamming and loud music from next door's bedroom. Chrissie looked down with concern at the sleeping George, hoping it wouldn't wake him up.

They could both go downstairs but it was so nice up here away from that ghastly girl Antony had brought and Martin's lewd remarks. Besides, Lucy's bedroom was calm and restful with its pink and green colour scheme. Pretty chintz curtains; antique patchwork bedspread on a brass bed; the nice dull kind instead of shiny new. There were a couple of Mike's things, scattered around the room to mark his presence. A pair of his jeans draped over another chair. His brown leather wallet on the pine dressing table.

Idly, Chrissie reached over for the pile of women's maga-zines on the ottoman at the end of the bed. Gosh! The one underneath was a different kind of magazine altogether! Surely Mike didn't read this kind of thing?

Stunned, Chrissie turned over the pages. She'd never actu-ally looked at a men's magazine before and what she saw now shocked her. Not that she was a prude but somehow she hadn't thought Mike was the kind of man who was into pictures like this. Maybe they used them to spice up their sex life. She'd often noticed how tactile they were with each other; at times she could almost feel the chemistry between them.

'I never really felt like that with your father,' she whispered to George. 'I mean, I love him, don't get me wrong.' She glanced down at the magazine. 'But it wasn't ever like this.'

Sex, when they had it, was — in her mind, at least — something that was way down her list after her exhausting day with George. And Martin, too, was often shattered after a gruelling week in the office. How any parent had mid-week sex was beyond her. 'It was different before your father, although, to be honest, there was only one person who really turned me on.'

She smiled at the memory. It had been a long time ago and, mentally, they hadn't been suited at all. But no one, since him, had ever had the same effect on her body; never been able to turn it to water below her waist as he had done. 'Sometimes,' she whispered to George, 'I pretend it's him and not your father. I know it's naughty but it gets me there so much faster.'

George stirred at the music from next door which was getting increasingly louder. Why didn't Lucy get the kids to turn it down? Now George was waking up! Angrily, Chrissie stood up, clasping the screaming George to her shoulder and stormed out of Lucy's room, to knock on the adjacent door. No answer. Well, they wouldn't be able to hear her above this racket, would they? The noise was almost deafening. This was ridiculous! Chrissie pushed open the door which seemed to have something blocking it.

'Can you lot turn that music down,' she began. And then stopped. Lucy's eldest son Jon was standing in front of her, a towel draped round his waist. And in the bed behind him was someone else.

SEPTEMBER

Smoked salmon and crispbread

Tuna salad

Garlic bread (remember to de-frost)

Fruit salad?

Fortune cookies

Nine

Everyone, apart from Mike, seemed to be finding fault with her. Even her BT answering call service had reprimanded her that morning, with its automated voice sternly warning her that it was 'completely full'. Well that was because she hadn't had time to delete or answer messages.

The autumn fair was the last thing she needed right now but she'd done the cake stall for so long that there was no way Lucy could have got out of it. Not that she wanted to. She enjoyed the market town atmosphere and the easy chat and banter with neighbours, many of whom she'd known for years. But there was so much going on with Jon going off to university this week, not to mention the office.

A year after Luke had died, Maggie had suggested she took a part-time job. 'I know you don't need the money but it will get you out of the house,' she had urged. 'The agency needs another pair of hands. Don't look like that; it's not taxing. Someone to answer the phone and sort out the odd problem.'

Lucy still smiled when she remembered Maggie's job description. Odd problem! The problems never stopped. Right Rentals, for which Maggie was deputy manager, specialised in renting out houses in the area, mainly for owners who were going abroad or hoping to make money with buy-to-lets. Simple. Or so Lucy thought. But the reality was that there was always something wrong either from the tenant's point of view or the owner's. She'd lost count of the times she'd been phoned up by an irate tenant because the shower was flooding or because the trip switch had gone or because Mrs Thomas, a new tenant, insisted she could hear noises in the attic.

All the staff were on a rota for out of hours emergency calls but in fact, this had been no bad thing, especially in the early days of her widowhood. There was, she told herself ruefully, nothing like a poor woman panicking at the other end of her mobile because she'd lost her front door keys. Once, Lucy had driven down to the office at 11 p.m. to collect the spare (they always kept duplicates) and the woman had written an effusive thank you note to the manager, which had not only boosted Lucy's office standing but also made her realise she was capable of thinking about something other than Luke and the children.

Not all men would have relished their future wives having to answer nocturnal calls but Mike, bless him, was really supportive. 'It must be very hard for people who have to live in houses that aren't their own,' he commented when she'd added that the key woman had been forced to rent after her husband had left her. That's what she loved about Mike; his ability to step into other people's shoes.

The only person he did find hard to understand (apart from Mungo), was her mother-in-law, Eleanor and, in particular, her habit of turning up unexpectedly. Lucy still blushed to recall the first time this happened. Mike had stayed over – he hadn't done so before – and the children had all been away at various sleepovers. They had woken up in that lovely post-night haze, wrapped in each other's bodies when there had been a loud knocking at the door and a 'Cooeee, it's only me!' through the letter box.

Eventually, when it became clear Eleanor wasn't going away ('I can see your car in the drive, dear. Are you all right or shall I call the police?'), Lucy had had to put on a nightdress and answer the door. Her mother-in-law, who'd arrived with a suitcase for an impromptu visit, was most unimpressed to find Mike in situ. 'Personally, dear, I feel that when you've been married once, you can never really repeat the experience.'

Lucy, who had often wondered how much Luke had confided in his mother about the state of their marriage, had restrained herself from commenting that she sincerely hoped her experience would never be repeated. But as Mike had said, it couldn't be easy for her. Luke had been her sole child. Lucy and the children were the only family that Eleanor had left.

But first she had to get Jon off to uni.

'There are shops in Oxford, you know,' her eldest had protested when she'd tried to take him shopping to replace those terrible jeans he lived in. 'I can buy some more when I'm ready. 'Sides, these are my favourites. And yes, Mum, the holes are fashionable. If you darn them, I'll go mad.'

He'd been particularly snappy that week. When Lucy had said Chrissie was coming round for a coffee, Jon had stormed out saying he was pissed off with strangers in the house. Mike, who'd thought the comment was directed at him, suggested it was nerves.

'But it is odd, considering he was so excited when his results came through,' Lucy pointed out. 'And he's always saying he can't wait to get out of this place and live his own life.'

Mike gave her a comforting hug. 'All teenagers say the same but they don't mean it. Probably like poor old Chrissie and her ramblings on the baby alarm.'

'Don't,' said Lucy. 'It makes me feel hot and cold just to think of it.'

'Have you said anything to her?'

'I'm too embarrassed, frankly.'

'I hate to imagine the row that must have happened when they got home.'

'Well, if they did have one, they must have made it up. Chrissie sounded all right when we chatted last week.'

Meanwhile, Lucy was trying terribly hard, during Jon's final days at home, to make it easy for him. But whatever she said, was wrong. 'Stop fussing, Mum,' he said irritably when she'd tried to run through practicalities like how much he'd have to live on and whether he'd got all his books on the reading list that had been sent to him.

Even Kate, who normally sided with her brother, was getting fed up. 'What's got into your Calvins, Jon?'

'Fuck off.'

Lucy winced. Jon never used to swear and sometimes she thought he did it to annoy Mike who hated bad language. Just as well he wasn't there today. In fact, he'd already called to say he'd be late after seeing a site in Plymouth. 'I'll probably spend the night at my place as I'll be late but I'll come round in the morning to take Jon down,' he had added.

'I've already told you; I don't want him there,' said Jon firmly, squatting down on the floor to cuddle Mungo. 'Can't the two of us go together, on our own? I just want it to be family.'

So Lucy had had to tell Mike who, though he'd pretended not to be, was hurt. How, she wondered as she set off the next morning after finally squeezing everything into her car, how did other stepfamilies manage? And what would happen when she and Mike finally got married?

It took under two hours to drive there during which time Jon, plugged firmly into his iPod, hardly said a word. For her part, she tried to sound jolly as though this was nothing, this trip. Just a little jaunt to Oxford instead of the end of an era. When the children had been little and older mothers had said they'd grow up 'all too soon', she hadn't believed them. But now in the last couple of years, all three of them seemed to have shot up both emotionally and physically.

Glancing in the rear mirror at the large trunk on the back seat – containing countless CDs, the stereo, the books, the clothes, the posters – she found herself glad that Mike wasn't here to intrude on these precious moments with her son.

Desperately, she floundered for something positive to say. 'I know it must be difficult starting somewhere new.' Silence. 'And I know it's hard leaving your friends behind.' Still more silence. Could he hear through his iPod? She touched his arm. 'I also know it's tough doing this without Dad. But he'd be really proud of you. Just like I am. You'll be fine when you get there. You'll see.'

It was a relief when they arrived and Lucy didn't have to make any more small talk. In fact, it all happened so fast after that that Lucy barely had time to say goodbye. A tall spotty youth was already waiting at the porter's lodge for Jon and introduced himself as a second year who'd been designated as his 'shadow'. Together they heaved Jon's trunk out of the boot of the Volvo while Lucy's offers of help were waved away. Any hopes she'd harboured of a quiet word of goodbye were instantly dismissed.

'Bye,' she said, kissing his cheek. He barely responded. Poor kid. He was scared stiff, clutching his beloved guitar like a teddy. 'It will be fine,' she managed to whisper in his ear, hungrily inhaling his smell and willing herself not to burst into tears. 'Ring me tonight if you can, or tomorrow. And keep your mobile on.'

She cried all the way home; so much so that she didn't even pick up when Mike rang on the mobile. She knew what he'd say. It would be all right. Jon was just nervous. He loved her really, and yes, of course he – Mike – understood about Jon wanting his mum to take him down.

Sometimes, Lucy thought, Mike was just too nice for a woman like her.

Whatever she'd thought earlier, the autumn fair that Saturday helped take her mind off the empty place at the dinner table. Last night, she had stupidly started laying it for five instead of four and then, realising what she'd done, had burst into tears. 'He'll be back soon,' said Kate matter of factly. 'They only have eight week terms, lucky sods. Wish our school term was that short.'

Despite her plea for help in the parish mag, Lucy still needed cakes for her stall, so at the last minute she'd had to make some extra Victoria sponges. In the old days, she remembered, setting up the cakes on the rickety wooden table at the fête which was held in the old vicarage (now owned by a family who'd moved down from London but who lent their grounds out for occasions like this), the kids would have come too and had a go on the tombola or coconut shy. But Kate was out with her friends and Sam had gone into town after getting a lift from Mike.

'Hello, Lucy,' boomed one of her neighbours, wearing a huge lilac hat studded with plastic strawberries. 'How nice to see you.' She picked up a slice of cherry cake. 'Goodness, what a price!'

'Do you think so?' Lucy had fretted over the pricing but last year's, everyone on the committee had agreed, had been too low.

'I do, my dear, although I must say, it looks quite delicious.' She sighed, opening her purse with large podgy fingers. 'Oh well, I suppose it's all in a good cause. Is your handsome fiancé back now?'

Lucy counted out the change. 'He should be. He's just running Sam into town.'

'Oh, so he is back.'

Lucy fumbled for a 20p bit at the bottom of the float. 'Back from where?'

'Manchester, of course! I happened to spot him at a restaurant. Such a coincidence as I was telling the niece I was visiting. I thought he recognised me. He certainly looked at me as though he seemed to but then again, maybe I was mistaken.'

'I think you must be,' said Lucy confused. 'Mike was in Plymouth yesterday.'

The woman shook her head. 'I don't think so. Not unless he has a double. Oh well, give him my regards, won't you? I shall enjoy the cake, although I do think your prices are definitely too high this year, dear.'

Lucy felt uneasy until she got home. Mike, who had a key to the house, had clearly been back since taking Sam into town but then gone out again. She got him on the mobile. 'I just needed a few things from my house, pet. Home within the hour. How did the show go?'

'Fine.' She hesitated. 'But an odd thing happened. One of my neighbours thought she'd seen you in Manchester yesterday. I thought you'd gone to Plymouth.'

There was a brief pause at the other end of the line. Such a brief one that Lucy wondered if she'd imagined it. 'I did. Go to Plymouth that is.' He laughed. 'She must have seen my double.'

'That's what I told her.'

'By the way, pet. The phone rang a couple of times when I was back. I didn't get there in time to pick up so you might find some messages. Want me to pick something up for supper tonight? I could get a DVD too, if you like.'

People did have doubles, she told herself as she pressed the answerphone machine. It happened all the time. Maybe not exact doubles but people who looked like them.

Play.

'Hi, Lucy. It's Antony here. Thanks for supper the other week. I'm sorry it's taken us so long to get back to you. And I hope you understand about us leaving early but it was very awkward for Patsy when Maggie turned up like that. Anyway, Patsy really liked the idea of your supper club and she wants us to hold the next one. At her place. She's already asked Jenny – as a sort of peacemaking gesture – so I hope you can come too. Ring us back and we can run through some dates.'

Play.

'Hello? Hello? Is that the emergency number for Right Rentals? This is Mrs Thomas here again. Look, I'm sorry to bother you. But there's something in my roof again. And this time, I'm absolutely certain it's not a bird.'

Ten

Concealer. Definitely concealer; the type for mature skins. A very mature skin with lines that announced the owner was extremely cranky; a double combination of arrogance and too many years in the sun.

Patsy, who for years had protected her own skin with a home-made yoghurt mask, gazed down in distaste at the television presenter sitting in the make-up chair before her. The woman had once been a household name and was now the kind of person of whom viewers said 'Oh I wondered what had happened to her' when she occasionally made an appearance on the screen. It had taken ages to remove the make-up which the woman had been wearing when she'd arrived.

'I'd avoid eyeliner if I were you,' said Patsy carefully, wiping away the last vestiges of black goo. 'It can look rather ageing.'

The woman bristled. 'What exactly do you mean by that?'

A long time ago, Patsy had made a rule that she would never allow self-professed divas to intimidate her. 'Only that we all get to a certain age when we need to rethink the way we do our faces.' Carefully, she dipped the edge of a sable brush into a palette of violet eyeshadow and then applied the merest hint to the underneath part of the eyes. 'What do you think of that?' she asked, handing the woman her lucky jewelled pink and silver Moroccan hand mirror.

She wasn't gracious enough to say how much better that looked – Patsy didn't expect that – but her softened expression was proof enough. 'Show me how you did that,' demanded the woman.

Why was it that some people's faces looked as though they'd

just stepped in shit even when you'd done something nice for them? But it wasn't worth her job to be rude. She'd seen other make-up artists, tired of difficult clients, dismissed for less. 'You only need a tiny bit of powder and it's also essential to use a sable-hair brush,' she explained. 'Then you make tiny dots or, if it's easier, brush strokes along the bottom.'

'Why not the top?'

'You can if you're going out in the evening but it looks less natural during the day.'

The once famous presenter snorted. 'I'll see. What's that you're putting on me now?'

'Concealer,' said Patsy carefully.

The woman had flared nostrils which would have made her look haughty even if she hadn't sounded it anyway. 'But I don't have anything to conceal. My skin is flawless. Look, not a blemish on it.'

'We all have lines.' Dipping the foam applicator into the bottle, Patsy turned away and quietly spat on it while her client was looking in the other direction. 'It's good to have lines; they show that we've lived life,' said Patsy smoothly, wiping a satisfactory mixture of spit and concealer into the woman's face. 'Laughter lines. Crying lines. They're part of us. But the camera can be cruel, as you know, so sometimes it's nicer to cover some of them up.'

The woman sniffed. 'Maybe.' She held up the mirror to see the results. 'What's that stuff called? I've got a girlfriend who could use some of it.'

'Take this bottle, if you want. I can get some more.'

'Thanks.' She spoke as though she'd expected it as a freebie anyway. Still, if it kept the bitch quiet, it was worth it.

'Ready everyone?' said the director impatiently.

The woman rose majestically. A definite boob job, observed Patsy. And she'd had her eyes done too.

'Where would you like me?' she demanded in a deep gravelly voice. And off she went without even a goodbye to Patsy.

Still, that's what it was like sometimes, especially with television. It was a different world. A world as far flung from Lucy's Little Giddington, or whatever it was called, as possible.

Patsy hadn't been able to get that weekend out of her head. It was one thing feeling flattered because Antony had left his wife for her, but another actually seeing Maggie in the flesh. The despairing look in her eyes, which no concealer could ever disguise, still haunted her. It was all very well Antony telling her that his marriage had been over for years and that they hadn't had sex since the last kid had been born. But she'd heard all that kind of stuff before.

'Perhaps we'd better have a break,' she'd said to Antony after they'd left early at her insistence.

He'd pulled in when she'd said that and turned to face her under the light of a streetlamp. 'Is that what you want?' he'd demanded huskily.

She'd wavered. Antony did something to her that very few men had done before. If she wasn't such a cynic, she might have said that from the minute she saw him, she'd fallen for him. 'No,' she'd said, tracing the outline of his lips with her finger. 'No, it's not what I want. But we have to think of other people here. Your wife,' she'd said the words with difficulty, 'seemed so upset.'

'She still needs time to accept it,' he'd said before taking her finger into his mouth and sucking it.

Patsy had withdrawn her finger. 'If it hadn't been me, would it have been someone else?'

Antony had slid his hand under her white silk t-shirt. 'There could never be anyone like you.'

She wasn't allowing him to get off that lightly. 'But if you hadn't met me, would you eventually have found someone else while you were still married?'

He had shrugged. 'Maybe. Does that make you feel better?'

'Yes.' She'd snuggled into his arms, her back towards him so his hands could explore her breats. His hands began to go further down, stirring her, making her wet inside.

'Let's go back,' he'd murmured.

Patsy had briefly thought of her one-bedroom flat which had been small even before Antony had moved in.

'What's wrong with the back seat?' she'd said, unbuttoning his shirt fiercely.

Now, as Patsy sat at the back of the television studio, ready to run on set with concealer and whatever else was needed to make the former presenter look her best, she reran that scene in her head. If it was up to her, she'd never see those people again although, despite that awful outburst, she couldn't feeling an affinity with Jenny and there was something vulnerable about Lucy that she couldn't put her finger on. But Mike was Antony's best friend. And as she knew from experience, a woman needed to get the best friend on her side. That was why she had insisted that she'd like to host the next supper party in this daft club idea that Lucy had dreamt up. It was just the kind of thing that suburban couples did to alleviate the boredom. But if I want Antony, thought Patsy, I have to play his kind of game.

And she'd make sure that dinner at her little place would be something that no one would forget.

The session went on much longer than she'd allowed for, partly because the former presenter had definitely lost her knack. She was being interviewed as part of a series called *What They Did Next* and the woman kept fluffing her lines or saying things that had to be beeped out. By the end, Patsy almost felt sorry for her.

Was this what it was all about, she asked herself as she finally gathered up her things and headed for the tube. You work hard for what it is that you think you want in life and then, at some point, before you know it, you're past the peak of your career and no one wants you any more. Someone ought to stick a flag up when you're at the top and say, 'This is it! Make the most of it because from now on, it's all down hill.'

She knew what that was like all right. Ten years ago, she'd

been quite famous; not as big as Jilly had been but still well-known in the business. It would be all right if she could do a Twiggy come-back but the opportunity had never arisen. She was lucky to have her make-up artist job but it wasn't enough. And that was where Antony – or if not him, someone else – came in.

Patsy pushed her way through the crowded tube to a minis-cule gap where she could find somewhere to hold onto. By the time she'd got to Edgware, she should with any luck have got a seat. She needed it. It had been a long day. And this evening would be even harder.

The mobile rang just as she got out of the station. 'It's me.'

She tingled with pleasure. When men started saying 'It's me', in a relationship, you were almost there.

'Are you going to make tonight?'

''Fraid not.' Patsy carried on walking briskly down the high street towards the house. 'I'm still stuck in the session.'

She turned into a side road, full of houses with To Rent signs outside, cupping the mobile with her hand in case Antony could hear the traffic.

'That's a real shame.' He sounded petulant like a little boy. 'Anyone famous?'

She named the presenter she'd just done and he sounded impressed. 'Wow, she was really big.'

'Well she could do with losing a bit now, to be honest, especially round the jowls.'

He laughed and she felt easier. One of the things she had first liked about Antony was his deep, extremely sexy laugh.

Nearly there now.

'Look, I'm sorry but I've got to go. Ring you later. OK?'

She cut him off before he had a chance to say anything. Be mean, keep them keen. That had been her motto ever since she was twelve and there was no reason to change it now.

Patsy's mouth had gone dry. It always did when she came here. It had been a fortnight since the last visit although, with any luck, he might not have noticed that she'd skipped a week. Her heart beating, Patsy pressed the intercom button.

'Yes?' said a sharp voice.

'Patsy Jones,' she said, wondering why it was that her own name always sounded so ordinary to her, almost as though someone was taking the piss out of it.

There was a buzzing noise and the door swung open. Instinctively, Patsy glanced behind to check no one was looking, and slipped inside.

Eleven

Jenny woke up that morning, as she did every morning, with the same two questions ringing round her head. Why was I so stupid? Will I ever find anyone else like him?

Since there wasn't, and never would be, a satisfactory answer to either question, she eventually – prompted by the soothing encouragement of *Magic Radio* – swung her legs out of the bed and padded her way, over cream wool bedroom carpet, to the shower. That was better! There was nothing, she thought as she soaped her breasts, like the comforting force of warm water cascading down her body and blinding her face to wake her up both emotionally and physically.

Pouring herself a black coffee and idly flicking through their mother's collection of hand-written recipes which Lucy had reluctantly lent her (even though Jenny had no intention of using it, she didn't see why her sister should hog it), she reflected on the gruelling day in front of her.

'What exactly does an events organiser do?' that silly girl Patsy had asked at Lucy's dinner party. It was a fair question but she had answered it curtly, disliking Patsy before she'd even met her because of what she'd done to Maggie.

'An events organiser organises events,' she had said coolly. 'I have all kinds of clients ranging from engineers to fashion firms. I'll organise the speakers, find a venue that fits the budget and the size of the conference; organise the catering; sort out security; and make sure everyone is generally happy.'

'Do you like it?' Patsy had asked, twiddling her pink feathered fringe with one hand and placing the other on Antony's knee as if to establish sitting rights.

'If I didn't, I wouldn't be doing it.'

Even so, the question had troubled her in the two weeks since the dinner party. Yes, Jenny quite liked her job. And it had earned her enough to buy a maintained flat not far from Lucy and afford nice things like holidays and smart cars. But there were times when she wondered just how long she could keep it going for. Companies were cutting back on budgets and she'd already lost two big clients in the last year. Besides, she was nearly forty. If she wasn't careful, she'd end up like one of her competitors who would be retiring soon to her little weekend cottage in Swanage. There had to be more to life than this and there would have been, if things had worked out differently.

Shut up, Jenny told herself crossly. Get dressed instead. Put on make-up. Set alarm. Go out of flat and make way to station. It was the only way to keep going. To shut out what might have been.

'Thanks for the other week,' said Steve on the mobile. 'I meant to ring earlier but Duncan got back earlier from Dubai and it's been all go.'

'It's me that should be thanking you for bailing me out.' Jenny peered anxiously out of the taxi at the traffic. If they didn't get a move on, she'd be late for her own conference.

'I'd no idea these suburban dinner parties could be so entertaining, what with exes turning up out of the blue.'

'It got better. My sister was telling me that after we left, Chrissie started talking about her sex life on the baby alarm!'

'Fantastic! Shame we missed it. Listen, there's something I need to mention. That boy . . . Peter . . . well he goes to some of our clubs. I couldn't say anything of course but I just thought you ought to know. Your nephew and all that.'

She knew it.

'Don't say anything, will you?' Steve sounded worried. 'You have to be so careful at that age. My mum really messed it up.

It's why I don't see her now and, of course, just because your nephew's friend is gay doesn't mean he is too.'

'No. Exactly.' She barely noticed the traffic was moving now. 'Thanks.'

Should she tell Lucy? Jenny still hadn't decided by the time the taxi finally got to Bankside Buildings at just after 9 a.m. The conference was due to start at 10 a.m. but she'd arranged to meet the client earlier to run over final details. Already, some over-eager delegates had begun to trickle in.

Engineering wasn't Jenny's thing. She had hated anything technical at school. But when she had first started off in this business, working for someone else, she had soon discovered that not only was there a gap in the market but that engineering firms were always putting on conferences to keep members abreast with the constantly changing workplace and technical developments.

It had, she had stated crossly when Lucy had once gently asked her, nothing to do with the fact that their father had been an engineer. But every time she came across an engineering client, she asked if they knew a Jim Macdonald. Sometimes she wondered about tracking him down, using a private investigator but Lucy had always been dead against it. 'He left because he didn't want to be with us any more. And Mum didn't want us to find him. You know that, Jenny. We ought to respect her wishes.'

Today's client was almost old enough to be her father or perhaps a youngish uncle. Jenny had met Alan ('That's spelt with one 'l', lass, not two') twice already and established his type. Good-looking in a rather heavy Robbie Williams way. Warm infectious belly laugh. Terrible taste in ties (today's had purple spots!). Director of an engineering company based in Newcastle which was keen to forge links with the south. Jenny wasn't even sure where Newcastle was except that it was somewhere up north, on the west or maybe the east coast. Wedding ring. Great sense of humour which clearly wasn't evident today as he paced up and down the vestibule waiting for her.

'You're late, lass.'

Jenny never allowed herself to get flustered. It sent out the wrong signals to the client. But there was, however, a place for contrition. 'I'm terribly sorry but there was a security scare on the tube.'

His expression immediately softened and she felt bad about the white lie which had slipped out so easily. 'Nothing happened?'

'No. At least I don't think so. But it was impossible to get on so I had to rush back up and get a taxi.'

He patted her on the shoulder. 'Can't be helped. Let's get cracking now, shall we? There seems to be a problem with the caterers. They say they're waiting for the china to arrive for the coffee break. Apparently they want a word with you about dinner too.'

Jenny resisted the temptation to point out that in her circles, it was called 'lunch'.

'There's another difficulty, too.'

She couldn't wait.

'It's the Gents, lass. One of our lads went in earlier. There's no nice way of putting this. 'Fraid he's caused a bit of a blockage.'

A bit of a blockage? The bloody man had virtually incapacitated the entire system single-handedly. Actually there was probably a far ruder way of putting that but Jenny would leave that to Sam when she saw the kids tonight – if there was ever going to be a tonight with the way this was going. Alan was right about the china not arriving. The caterers had explained, as though it was her fault and not theirs, that it hadn't been delivered as promised last night but would arrive at some point during the morning.

'Too late,' Jenny had said tightly. The catering manager had shrugged. 'We're doing our best. Unfortunately, the vegetarian options have also failed to arrive.'

'What?' Jenny glanced at her list. 'But we've got fifty-six fucking veggies to cater for.'

'If it hasn't arrived, there's nothing we can do. I've made phone calls and there seems to have been some kind of confusion about numbers.'

Jenny eyed the girl steelily. 'If, and I repeat if, you wish to work for me or anyone else I know again, I suggest you sort this problem out immediately. If necessary, you can make a vegetarian option yourself in the kitchen.'

'Sorry.' She didn't look it. 'There aren't the facilities.'

'What do you mean?'

'There isn't an oven. Only a microwave.'

'For Chrissake!'

'Everything all right, lass?' asked Alan coming in behind her.

'Fine.' Jenny smiled brightly. 'Just a few last-minute hiccups but nothing I can't handle. Excuse me but I just need to take this.'

She turned to one side, cupping her hand over the mobile for some privacy. 'Yes?'

'Blimey, Aunty Jenny. You sound stressy.'

'I am. Look, Kate, this is a really bad time. I'll have to ring you back.'

'What's wrong?'

She ducked behind a screen for more privacy. 'There's no bloody coffee for the delegates for this sodding conference I'm meant to be organising. Some heavy handed engineer has bust the Gents. And there's no vegetarian food for lunch so I'm going to have to buy some in from somewhere.'

'I can make you some veggie lasagne.'

Jenny's heart lurched. She adored her niece who was far more like her than Lucy. She recognised the girl's inbuilt ambitious energy; her determination to succeed which unfortunately sometimes came hand in hand with impatience. 'Darling, that's really nice of you but you're too far away.'

'When do you need it by? And how many for?'

'For fifty-six; by 12.45 at the latest.'

'Leave it to me.'

'No. Honestly. I'll get something from somewhere.'

'Aunty Jenny.'

'Yes?'

Kate's voice was tearful. 'No one thinks I'm capable of doing what I promise. Mum's always having a go about it. Please. Let me.'

Jenny glanced across at Alan who was talking angrily to the caterer, his brow furrowed. What was more important. Her career or family? Silly question.

'OK, Kate. But I'll be relying on you. If you're late, I've really had it.'

She must be crazy. Which was why, to be on the safe side, Jenny had made a few phone calls. It might have been all right if there had only been a handful of veggies. But fifty-six was, it appeared, too many for outside caterers to cater for at such short notice. She even tried ringing up the local M&S stores but although she could have got various different veggie meals, no one had enough of the same.

Still, at least she had given Kate the wrong time. She actually needed the food by one o'clock. So if Kate didn't arrive by 12.45, she'd run next door to Marks and make do with a hotch-potch. If she was sensible, she'd do that now. But something inside her wavered. Give the kid a chance. Show her you believe in her, just like their mother – who had always favoured Lucy – had never really believed in her. It wasn't, Jenny told herself, a question of scoring over Lucy who was constantly squabbling with her daughter. It was just an aunt supporting her niece.

The pre-conference coffee crisis was easier to solve. Jenny's young assistant Lily had arrived by now – she'd had 'trouble with the tube' too – and she'd promptly despatched her to Costa Coffee. She'd also spoken to the health and safety officer in charge of the building who was sorting out the Gents. In the meantime, she'd arranged for the delegates to use the Ladies which caused a few chuckles. There were in fact, eight women engineers at the conference. If they weren't thrilled at cosying up in adjacent cubicles, that was just too bad.

'Jenny!'

Alan was striding towards her, plastic cup of coffee in one hand. She was expecting him to say 'Well done'. If she said it herself, she hadn't done a bad recovery job, even if she was still extremely nervous about lunch.

'Can you come over here?' He was close up now so she could see his unnaturally even teeth. Probably false. 'The projector isn't working.'

Thank God she had contingency plans for this kind of thing. Projectors had gone in the past but they hadn't come in tandem with no coffee, no veggie lunches and blocked loos. Somehow she got her emergency supplier to deliver a substitute within half an hour. It meant the conference started late but at least it had started. You'd think that with all these bloody engineers, there would be one who could fix a sodding projector!

Now all she had to worry about was lunch. As the minutes ticked by towards lunchtime, Jenny was beginning to sweat. Kate's mobile was switched off. Did that mean she was on her way? How would she have time to make enough lasagnes? What were fifty-six beefy engineers doing being veggie anyway? And how would her niece get them here on time. 12.25 p.m. Sod it. M&S, it was.

'Aunty Jenny!'

The car pulled up outside the offices just as she was coming back with Lily, laden with carrier bags. Her niece was leaping out of the car, her face beaming. 'We've got them. They're in the back. And they're still warm. You did say you could heat them up, didn't you?'

Jenny nodded. 'Who's the driver?'

Kate blushed. 'Peter. You know, Jon's friend. You met him at mum's the other night.'

A tall boy with dark skin and long eyelashes, wearing a crisp white shirt and jeans was already unloading from the boot. 'Come on, Kate, or I'll get a ticket.'

Jenny felt a prickle of unease. 'We'll give you a hand.'

Kate looked at the M&S bags suspiciously. 'You've got food already?'

'What. This? No it's for another conference tomorrow.' Jenny hugged Kate. 'Honestly, darling, you've got me out of one hell of a hole.'

Kate's eyes were shining at her praise. 'I said I'd do it, didn't I? I even made a couple of extra portions but Mungo nabbed one, naughty boy.'

It had been a long day. The conference seemed to go down well; possibly because lunch had been so delicious that many of the veggie delegates had passed their compliments to the caterers. One had even asked for a card.

'I have to hand it to you, lass.' Alan clamped a large, somewhat clammy hand on her shoulder. 'You kept your cool. Had my doubts this morning, I did, but you saw us all right. That lasagne was nearly as good as my wife's. We'll use you again, I promise. Now, how about a bite to eat to celebrate?'

Jenny hesitated. She'd really rather go home and sink into a long, hot bath. But one of her other golden rules, made when she'd first set up Eventful Events was to network, network, network. And that included socialising with the client even when you were knackered. 'That would be lovely,' she said. 'Can you just give me a minute to freshen up?'

'Sure, lass.'

'By the way,' she couldn't help herself, 'I used to have a . . . a friend in engineering. Actually he was a friend of my dad's. Jim Macdonald. I don't suppose you know him, do you?'

Alan frowned, as though thinking. ''Fraid not but it's a massive industry. What kind of engineering was he in?'

She felt stupid. 'I'm not really sure.'

Thankfully the Ladies was empty; the delegates had all gone home by now. She rang Kate to thank her – the girl's answerphone was on – and then checked her messages. The first one took her by surprise. How did Patsy get her number?

'Hi, Jenny. It's Patsy. Antony's friend. We're having some people to dinner on the 27th and wondered if you'd like to come. If you don't want to bring anyone, that's OK.'

Bloody cheek! If you don't want to bring anyone, that's OK. She wasn't having anyone feeling sorry for her. And she wasn't going to some bloody dinner party held by a woman who couldn't keep her mitts and tits off someone else's husband.

Angrily, Jenny deleted the message, redid her make-up with the essentials she always carried in her bag, and braced herself for an evening with an overweight client who probably called dinner 'tea'.

Twelve

'How old are yer other kids then?'

Chrissie swallowed her mouthful of undrinkable instant coffee from a Kids Are Fun chipped mug and looked at Tracey who was in charge of the squash table. She was stick thin, looked only slightly older than Lucy's Kate, had three earrings in one lobe, tight jeans and a skimpy t-shirt with sequins round the neckline.

'He's my first, actually.' Chrissie looked worriedly across the hall to where George was fiercely pushing a gaudy pink ladybird-shaped pram, even though another toddler (dressed in a Dolly Mixture-lilac top with the slogan 'If you think I'm cute, you should see my mum's partner') was trying to wrench it away. She only hoped he didn't pick up germs either from the kid or the pram.

'Your first? Blimey. Been trying for a long time then, have you?'

'A while.' Chrissie felt the heat rising up her neck at the tact-less reference to the glaring fact that she was at least fifteen years older than everyone else in this sodding mother and toddler group. 'But I chose to concentrate on my career first.'

No need to mention that it had also taken her a very long time to find the right man who was not only single, interesting, sexy and stimulating but found her that way too – and was prepared to have a baby. Honestly, if you put all those object-ives on a marketing projection plan, this ignorant girl would know how well she'd done to get this far.

'Oh, so you're a career girl.' There was a slight sneer to Tracey's lips, accentuated by the ring on the upper lip. 'Go on then. What did you do?'

'I was in HR.' Even as she said it, it felt like a lie. Had she really been in HR – known as Personnel when she'd first started – for over ten years?

'Isn't that what they give you when your hormones go funny?'

'No. It's . . .'

'Oy, Kylie. Wait till it's your turn or you'll go in the naughty corner.'

Chrissie glanced at her son's competitor. She should have realised that the child belonged to this woman; they both had the same pale, pinched determined expression. 'I thought Sting was yours,' she said, looking across at another skinny toddler with hair that was cut short at the sides but was long and feathery down the middle like a juvenile punk rocker with a mini Mohican.

'Yeah, he is.' The girl took one of her nose earrings out, wiped the end on her jeans and put it back in again. 'Fourteen months between them, that's all there is. Fucking nightmare. Bloody sore.'

Chrissie shuddered, remembering her own experience. 'Labour usually is.'

'I mean me earrings. Bought them from Carole, I did. That woman over there. She sells them at craft fairs but me ears have been itching ever since.'

'Oh dear.' Chrissie was aware she was sounding like her mother. She was about to ask if Tracey had disinfected them first as a precaution when her new acquaintance cut in.

'Yeah, and I've got another kid in school, thank Christ. I've got to wait a whole sodding year and two months till they'll take Kylie and another year for Sting.'

'Then will you go back to work?'

Tracey giggled. 'Might be a bit difficult. My bloke's not that keen.'

'What did you do?'

'Sort of tele-sales.' She put her head on one side coquettishly.

'What did you sell?'

'Me!' She giggled again. 'I did one of those chat lines. You know. You see them advertised in the local paper. These poor lonely blokes ring up and I make them fell better.'

Chrissie wasn't usually at a loss for words. 'Did you, er, ever meet them?'

''Course not. Kylie, tell the little boy it's your turn now. Nah, I just spoke to them. My boss wants me back cos I've got a knack. Been doing it for years, I have. You can do it from home, see, although you've got to make sure the kids are quiet. It puts the callers off if they think they're talking to a woman with children.'

'And, er, you say your husband isn't that keen?'

The girl was taking her earring out again and inspecting it. ''S'not my husband. He's my partner.'

'And how did he find it to have two children in such quick succession?'

'What?'

Chrissie knew she'd been too inquisitive but she needed to know. Martin was still going on about having another baby but she wasn't sure if she could cope. 'I mean, did he find it hard to have two children so fast, especially as you've already got an older one?'

'Dunno, really. Never asked him. 'Sides, Kylie's dad takes her out at the weekends which gives us a bit of a break.'

Chrissie was beginning to get the picture. 'So Kylie's dad is different from Sting's?'

'Yeah.' The girl was looking at her as though she was stating the obvious. 'And my older kid – Bryn – he don't know who his dad is.'

'Do you?' Chrissie couldn't help herself.

'If I did, I'd be able to get some money off him, wouldn't I? Hey, you'd better go and see what's happened to your kid. Looks like he's hurt himself.'

★　★　★

'What on earth happened to George's face?' asked Lucy when she popped round unexpectedly between calling in on tenants, later that afternoon. She'd brought a push-along toy which had belonged to Sam years ago although Chrissie privately planned to take it to the dump later. Anything second-hand was bound to be rife with disease.

Chrissie, still agonising over whether she should tell Lucy what she'd seen in Jon's bedroom, poured the coffee. 'His face? Awful, isn't it? Some ghastly kid at mother and toddler beat him up over a toy they both wanted and he fell against a table. Want some chocolate cake?'

'No thanks.' Lucy smiled ruefully. 'I'm trying to lose weight.'

'Why? You look amazing after three kids. I wonder if it's worth even trying.' She tried to pull in her stomach, horribly aware it was lolloping over her elasticated waistband under the disguise of one of Martin's sweat shirts. 'This,' she said patting the blob ruefully, 'still seems to think it's pregnant.'

'You'll lose it eventually, especially as you're still feeding.' Lucy pulled George onto her knee. 'I must say, poppet, you've got a real shiner on your forehead, haven't you?'

Chrissie watched with envy as George nestled into her friend. 'He doesn't do that with me. He's always squirming and trying to run off unless there's boob on offer.' Her eyes filled with tears. 'Sometimes I wonder if he even likes me.'

'Of course he does.' Lucy released George and reached out for Chrissie's hand. 'He's just interested in me because he doesn't see me that much. Children can be very cruel and you're still feeling vulnerable. All new mothers do.'

'I haven't got postnatal depression if that's what you think,' said Chrissie stiffly. Was that why Lucy had come round unexpectedly; to check up on her? 'Anyway, George is fourteen months now. It's too late for that.'

'I'm not suggesting that, although actually you can still have it some years after the birth. I'm just saying that it's not easy, adjusting to a different way of life.'

Chrissie stood up, under the pretence of pouring the coffee so Lucy wouldn't see her tears. 'Did you find it difficult?'

'I did. And so did Luke. In fact, he found it harder than I did.'

Chrissie thought fleetingly of Martin who had been strangely quiet in the last few weeks for no apparent reason. 'Why?'

Lucy sighed behind her. 'He felt restricted. Suddenly we couldn't go out as much. And I must admit that I was quite a panicky mother. I worried about everything.'

There was that lump in her throat again. 'So do I.' She kept her back purposefully to Lucy so she couldn't see the tears rolling down her cheeks. 'I'm so scared something is going to happen to George. When he's asleep, I stand over him and check he's breathing. The first thing I do when I wake up, is run over to his cot to make sure he's all right. And he still isn't talking.'

Suddenly Chrissie became aware of Lucy standing behind her, putting her hand on her shoulder. 'He will be all right. He's a lovely, healthy little boy.'

'But supposing something suddenly happens!' Chrissie couldn't hold the sobs back now. 'There was a terrible story in the *Mail* last week about a little boy, exactly George's age, who was fine one day and then was a bit off colour the next morning. By evening, he was dead from some awful rare virus. His poor parents! And you know, the awful thing is, the really awful thing is, that sometimes – just sometimes – I might almost be relieved if George did die because if he did, I wouldn't have to worry about him any more. I could live a normal life again. I could sleep without having to wake up. I could read a book. I could go back to work . . .'

Lucy was looking at her with an odd expression.

'Of course, I don't really mean that.'

'I know you don't.' Lucy was hugging her now. 'You're just exhausted and that makes everything muddled.'

'It's so bloody difficult!' Chrissie couldn't speak now through the sobs. Clinging to Lucy, she cried, just as she had wanted to cry at mother and toddler when she'd run over to George and, for one frightful moment, thought he had been unconscious or worse. When he had then opened his eyes and begun to yell – loud angry yells that proved his lungs were working at any rate – the relief had been intense.

'Shh, it's all right.' Chrissie allowed herself to be soothed by Lucy's hand that was stroking her shoulder rhythmically. 'It's all right. Honestly. Let it out. You'll feel better.'

Fleetingly, Chrissie wondered if Lucy had cried like this when Luke had died. She'd met her friend shortly afterwards and often wondered what he'd been like. Poor Lucy had had so much to cope with but now she'd finally found happiness. How could she spoil all that by telling her about Jon? Besides, it was up to him to do so in his own time.

'You know, it might help if you put some arnica cream on that bruise.' Lucy was fishing in her handbag now. 'I think I've got some. Yes. Here it is. It'll bring the swelling down.'

'You're such a good mother. I don't know how you do it. I'll never be as capable as you.'

'Yes, you will. We all feel like that when we start out. Remember your first day at work?'

Chrissie nodded.

'It was all very new and strange then, wasn't it?'

She smiled, remembering. 'It certainly was.'

'And you got to grips with that. You went right to the top.'

It was true.

'Have you ever thought about going back?'

'I couldn't leave him with someone else,' said Chrissie trying to pull George onto her knee. He resisted, pummelling her with his small fists and charged off into another room. There was a crash. Chrissie leapt to her feet. Lucy pulled her back. 'It's all right. Listen. He's not yelling. I can hear him playing with his toys. If you're always following him, he won't learn to be independent and you'll always be on edge. Why don't you leave him with me or Kate for an hour or so while you have a break, one day? Kate's very sensible when she wants to be.'

'I couldn't. Not yet. I'm sorry. Don't be offended. But I find it so hard to leave him with anyone, even Martin. Besides, what if he wants feeding?'

Lucy gave her the kind of look that the others had given her in mother and toddler when she had given poor George a comfort suck after his fall. 'I don't want to interfere, Chrissie. But have you thought about when you're going to stop? I know he has solids as well but it's going to make it even more difficult for you to have an independent life if you're still feeding him.'

She'd been crazy to think that Lucy, whose own kids were virtually grown up, would understand. 'He's still a baby. If I want to spoil him a bit, I will.'

'I know. And you're entitled to.' Lucy put her cardigan on. 'I didn't mean to offend you. Look, I'd better go. I've got to sort out a tenant's leaking roof, an overflowing drain and a landlord who keeps going round to his house to make sure the tenants are keeping up the garden, instead of leaving it to us. And all by lunchtime.' Lucy smiled. 'Feel like swapping places today?'

Chrissie laughed hollowly. 'You'd make a better job of looking after George than I have. I bet he wouldn't have so many accidents if you were around.'

'Toddlers are always falling over; it's part of their job description. Changing the subject, are you going to Antony and Patsy's next week?'

'I don't like taking George out in the evening. It spoils his routine.'

'Kate might be able to babysit.'

'No. Thanks. Anyway, my mum said she could come down but . . .'

'But you don't like leaving George,' finished Lucy kindly. 'And you're entitled to think that way. Well, I do hope you do come. Jenny's refusing to go – she didn't take to Patsy. And I don't particularly want to be stuck there.'

'You'll have Mike.'

'Yes, I know. But he doesn't really seem to understand that it's difficult for me with Maggie. Because Antony is his friend, he expects us to carry on as normal.'

Chrissie had never heard Lucy criticise Mike before. 'It can't be easy for any of you. How is Maggie?'

'A bit off, to be honest. And I don't blame her. What did you think of her, anyway?'

'Patsy? I thought she was an intelligent tart.'

'Exactly.' Lucy laughed gaily. 'And you know, the awful thing is, that part of me couldn't help admiring her because she didn't try to hide any of that Page Three stuff. She was just herself. Come on, Chrissie, do come. We really don't want to be the only ones there. Besides,' she reached out and touched Chrissie's arm lightly, 'it would be good for you both to get out.' She seemed to hesitate. 'Everything all right between you and Martin?'

'Yes. Why?'

Lucy went pink. 'It's just that Mike overheard . . . well he said that . . .'

'What?'

'Nothing really.' Lucy was getting pinker. 'But it's normal for couples to have problems after babies, you know. Children are a great blessing but they can also wreak havoc on relationships.' She kissed Chrissie on the cheek. 'See you soon. Bye.'

Why did she have to go and spoil her visit by asking nosy questions, thought Chrissie crossly. It was all right for Lucy, driving off without even having to check someone was strapped in the back or that there were enough nappies and juice and spare training mugs. When would she ever be able to get into a car again without having to make enough arrangements as though they were going on a trek to the Sahara instead of Ikea? No wonder things were strained with Martin.

Peeping round the door of the playroom, she could see George sitting quietly for a change, putting one brick on top of another before knocking it to the ground and starting again. Maybe Lucy was right about leaving him alone a bit more. Going back to the kitchen, Chrissie made herself another cup of coffee, found herself cutting another large slice of chocolate cake and opening her professional magazine which had arrived that morning in the post.

Sometimes, she didn't open the post for days because there wasn't time. 'You're at home all day,' Martin would say. 'What do you mean you don't have time?' She'd given up trying to explain.

Now as she leafed through the journal, she felt a strange sense of detachment. She knew so many of the names and pictures; people who had moved jobs; people who had improved sales figures. People who belonged to a world that she had once known so well and which now felt as far removed as another planet. A planet without babygrows or sore nipples. Chrissie stopped at the appointments page, her heart beating. So they had finally done it.

'*We are pleased to announce that Jessica White has been appointed head of HR. She has been acting head during her predecessor's maternity leave but has now accepted a permanent post.*'

'Predecessor's maternity leave'? They hadn't even had the decency to mention her name. Eyes stinging, Chrissie stuffed more cake into her mouth. It was as though everything she had done for the company for all those years, had been negated with that single sentence. She was no longer Chrissie Richards, head of HR. She was Chrissie Richards, reluctant member of the mother and toddler group. Mother of . . .

Crash.

'George?'

He'd be screaming in a second. Screaming lustily to prove he was all right. But, as she sprinted from the kitchen to the play room, there was a terrible, ominous silence.

Thirteen

'And now, our No Fuss Cooking slot! Australian chef Bruce Sydney is going to show you how to knock up a tuna niçoise salad in six and a half minutes flat!'

Patsy sat down in front of *Breakfast TV* with a mug of hot water and lemon, her usual morning drink to stimulate her complexion, and tried to concentrate. Mmmm. Not bad looking! Blond. Tanned. Hyacinth blue shirt. And she liked his method of tossing the tuna bits carelessly into the bowl with some other stuff which she didn't quite catch the name of.

If people made less fuss about food, she thought, sipping the water, they wouldn't be overweight and they'd find more interesting things to do. Frankly, her favourite meal was smoked salmon (providing there was someone around to buy it) on Ryvita with chopped raw green and red peppers. Took five minutes to prepare and left time to do other things.

Patsy switched off the television (next week Bruce was apparently showing viewers how to cook a salmon in the dishwasher!) and picked up her new book, *How to Learn Spanish in Six Weeks*. She'd always fancied learning a language but had presumed it was beyond her capabilities until making up a relatively unknown Spanish actress the other week. The girl had told her how she'd been to crammer classes to learn English for her minor part in a well-known soap. 'You must be bright then,' Patsy had commented.

'If it will help me, I do it.' The girl (Sparkle Cheekbone Fairy Dust with Tangerine Tart lipstick) was oozing determination. 'How do you say? It sharpens my mind.'

Patsy was all for that. It wasn't fair the way some people

categorised her. Just because she'd been a model, didn't mean she was thick. She still bristled when she thought of that chap at the dinner party – the bull-dog neck one who was married to the plump woman with the baby. Cheeky bugger had barely been able to keep his eyes off her breasts. When he and his wife came round tonight, she'd leave the *How to Learn Spanish* book out, clearly on display.

'Are you sure you want to have them all round here?' Antony had asked when she'd first voiced the idea. They were lying on the bed, facing each other in that post-sex period (she'd always shied away from the term 'making love'), with Antony tracing the outline of her nipple with his forefinger. Slightly to her surprise, her nipples began to stiffen.

She'd moved away. 'I know I don't live in a place like your mates but I'm not ashamed of it.'

'I didn't mean it like that, darling. Your flat's great.' He looked around at the lilac wall behind him, softened by the cream woodwork and huge pink ostrich feathers that were draped over the antique pine dressing table left behind after a shoot for a posh country home magazine. 'It's got atmosphere.' He sank back on the duck feathered pillows. 'I can really relax here.'

'Couldn't you relax in your old house?' Patsy had asked casually. She had often wondered what Antony's home had been like inside. Probably like Lucy's. Nice road with drives so the owners' posh cars didn't get bashed. Detached. Oldish. Classy.

'Not without you,' Antony had said, moving onto her other breast.

Now, as Patsy searched for the tin opener for the tuna, she recalled the conversation. She often wondered if Antony found her flat cramped after a great big house. If she and Antony were going to continue, they'd have to think about getting somewhere bigger. But to do that, she needed to know that he was committed and – more importantly – that he was worth it.

What about Maggie? asked a small voice inside her as she

mixed together some mustard, vinegar and sugar before pouring it over the tuna. (That bloke on telly had used virgin oil but she didn't have any.) Antony was also paying Maggie a monthly sum which, in her view, was unnecessarily generous. So the woman was OK, wasn't she?

Patsy slopped some lemon squash on top of the tuna salad (Bruce had said real lemon but surely this would do?) and put it in the fridge. But it's not just the money, is it? insisted the small voice. Remember her face . . .

Patsy slammed the fridge door shut. It was hard enough getting rid of Maggie's distraught face in her dreams let alone in broad daylight when she had more control over her mind. Antony's marriage was over, she reminded herself, before he'd met her. He'd told her that, shortly after they'd met at some huge cocktail party that one of her clients had asked her to and to which Antony had also been invited.

'I've been thinking of going for years,' he had said defensively when she'd said she didn't want to be responsible for breaking up a marriage. 'We were never right. I've just stayed because of the kids.'

That's where he was now. With the kids. He had left at lunchtime, although it was really breakfast because they'd stayed in bed all morning. The plan was, he had said, to pick them up from the house and take them to an outdoor adventure playground before taking them back. She'd wanted to ask if he'd see Maggie or if the kids would be waiting on the doorstep, but hadn't liked to. After he'd gone, she had walked around her flat, savouring the peace. But then, after about an hour, it had seemed strangely empty.

'I'm used to being on my own,' she said out loud as though to reinforce the point, while unwrapping the salmon slices. 'You can't afford to go all soft now.'

Shit! That recipe had said three eggs and she only had one. She'd just have to do her usual trick and gently tap the only egg with a teaspoon so it cracked. Then she could take it back to the shop; complain the others had been the same and get a full re-fund.

When you were hard up, you had to think of everything.

Two hours later, the table was laid with soft lavender-coloured woven mats, 'borrowed' from a shoot, and candles in the middle. She'd tidied up the magazines that had been scattered around the flat and picked up a jumper of Antony's which he'd left carelessly on the back of a chair. The salmon starters were already on the mats, covered with yellow toilet paper squares, as was the tuna salad. The fruit salad was in a bowl and the wine, for those who drank, was in the fridge. At the last minute, she'd realised she didn't have enough plates and cutlery and had to dash out to get some.

Meanwhile, she'd weighed herself twice as a sharp reminder not to eat any of the garlic bread she was defrosting. 'You're so thin,' someone had said to her at the studio yesterday. When you were a model or even an ex-model, you couldn't be too thin otherwise you'd end up like those women at the party.

All she needed now was Antony. He'd rung, finally, half an hour ago to say he was on his way, sounding harassed. When she'd asked what was up, he'd curtly said, 'Nothing. See you later.'

If he didn't buck up, he wouldn't have time to change, thought Patsy admiring her backless black silk t-shirt that the 'Spanish-in-six weeks' actress had left behind. It clung nicely, she noted approvingly in the mirror and, not for the first time, she mentally congratulated herself for taking large bags to shoots. Those high heels looked good too and the top hinted at the outline of her breasts. She could have worn something slightly less revealing but why not make Antony's friends jealous? It might make him keener.

Impatiently, Patsy looked out of the window as a gang of youths sidled past, bent towards the pavement, their heads obscured in black hoodies. This was the time of night when, if you were over fifty-five, you stayed inside. A car pulled up. Not his.

She felt tempted to ring his mobile but it wasn't her style to nag, push or cajole. Men had to do the running or it never worked.

Finally, came the sound of the key in the lock. About bloody time! Patsy headed swiftly for the sofa, crossed her legs and pretended to be reading a magazine. She looked up as Antony came in.

'Hello, darling . . . What?'

Clutching their father's hand, one on each side, and glaring at her, were two small children. Patsy gathered herself quickly. 'Hi,' she said smoothly, getting up. 'You must be Matt and Alice.'

Two pairs of green eyes, exactly like Maggie's, glared at her. Same colour hair too. Orange. Corkscrew curls. Freckles. Wow! She could really do something with the girl.

They were already diving for the salmon as though they were starving. Antony nuzzled her neck and whispered into her ear. His touch, coupled with relief that he was back, was electrifying. 'Maggie's not well so she's asked me to have the kids for the weekend. You don't mind, do you?'

Fourteen

Lucy was still in her peach-coloured silk underwear set – Mike had bought a size 10 for her last birthday and she'd quietly had to swap it for a 14 – when she decided to ring her sister just one more time.

Cupping the phone between her ear and shoulder, she squeezed some foundation out onto the palm of her left hand and dabbed it on with her forefinger down the centre of her face. Bother. She'd spilt a blob on the silk knickers. She was still furiously rubbing it off with a towel when Jenny finally answered.

'Hello?'

Did Jenny realise how abrupt she sounded at times? Or did she just presume that because they were sisters, she could say what she wanted?

'It's me, Lucy.'

'I know. Your name's come up. What is it?'

'I just wondered if you'd come to Antony and Patsy's after all to keep me company.' Lucy glanced briefly behind her to make sure Mike hadn't come into the room. 'I'm really not looking forward to it on my own and I feel horribly guilty about Maggie. She doesn't know I'm going.'

'Then tell her. And no, I'm sorry, but I'm not going for two reasons. First I can't stand that bitch because she's ruined poor Maggie's life. And secondly, I don't have a date.'

'You don't need one. Lots of people go out on their own nowadays. Besides, it's a supper club, remember? We said we'd do it every month.'

'You said that. Not me.'

When Jenny was in a mood like this, there was no reasoning with her.

'OK.' Lucy had given up sponging off the stain on her flimsy knickers. 'What are you doing tonight, anyway?'

'Sitting in a bar, if you must know, waiting for my date to arrive.'

'I thought you didn't have a date.'

'Well I don't, do I, if he's half an hour late?'

'Who is he?'

'I don't know.'

Lucy felt a sisterly wave of intuition. 'You've got him off the internet, haven't you?'

'You make it sound like a Tesco delivery. No, I haven't. He's a blind date, if you must know. Except that he isn't, because he isn't here. Shit. This looks like it might be him. I'll ring later.'

'Jenny!'

Too late. She'd rung off. What had she meant by her expletive? Was it because he looked different from her expectations or because he was a madman wielding an axe? All the horror tales Lucy had heard about blind dates came back to her. Had Jenny taken precautions? Had she told anyone where she was going? Fingers shaking, Lucy keyed in her sister's number. *'Hi, this is Jenny. Leave a message.'*

Damn, damn, damn.

'Pet!' Mike slapped her bottom playfully. 'Seen the time? We're going to be late.' His hand slid down the back of her pants. 'And gorgeous as you look, I don't think you can go like that!'

Lucy hastily drew a wobbly line of brown Kohl pencil under her eyes, followed by a flick of mascara. She really didn't feel like going but it was important to Mike. He'd integrated into her life so she owed it to him to do the same by having dinner with his old friend. 'I'll just be five minutes. Has the sitter arrived?'

Sam was at that awkward age when he insisted he was too

old for a sitter. But neither Lucy nor Mike felt comfortable about leaving him on his own unless the older two were in. 'Ah. Bit of a problem there. Sam says he's going out. One of his friends rang to ask him to a gig in town. You were on the phone so I said he could go if you said it was all right.'

'What kind of gig?' Lucy began to say and then stopped as her youngest came into the room.

'MUM. Put something on, will you?' He shielded his eyes with his hand.

'This *is* my bedroom,' began Lucy, pulling on her dressing gown hastily. 'Hang on. What have you done to your hair?'

Her youngest shrugged nonchalantly. 'I've put it up.'

'But it's a . . . what do you call it, a Mohican! And it's orange.'

Sam preened in the mirror. 'Burnt orange, actually, according to the packet. Chill out, Mum. It's wash in, wash out.'

'But what about the Mohican?' demanded Mike.

'I can comb it out. I had it cut that way, this afternoon. When it's down, it just looks short at the sides with a floppy bit in the middle.'

Lucy sat down heavily. Sam always lived life on the edge, just as Luke had done. 'Takes up less room,' he used to joke. What would he say if he could see Sam now?

She tried another tack. 'School won't allow it.'

'It's nearly half term.' Sam clearly had all his answers ready. 'We get ten days off, don't we? It'll be back to its usual colour by then. Look, Mum, I've got to go. Someone's dad's bringing us back but I need a lift there. I'm late.'

Mike picked up his keys from the dressing table. 'I'll take you. Your mum's still getting dressed. Lucy, can you be ready by the time I get back?'

He was always so considerate, thought Lucy. Luke would have moaned and groaned about going out last minute, as indeed might she have done if she'd still been on her own. 'I want you back as soon as the gig ends. And take your mobile so I can nag you!'

She shot him a conspiratorial smile and he grinned back. However naughty he was, she couldn't help having a soft spot for him. Besides, all the parenting books and articles said you needed to keep communication channels open with your terrible teens.

After they'd gone, leaving the bedroom door wide open, Lucy slipped into the pair of black silk, wide-bottomed evening trousers she'd decided to wear this evening. Brushing off the dog hairs (how had they got there?), she examined herself in the mirror. The elasticated waistband made her look reasonably slim but she still wished she was a size 10 again. After Luke, she had lost a lot of weight but happiness, she'd learned, made you more comfortable. Then again, what right did she have to happiness, after . . .

The phone! Maybe Jenny had changed her mind after all. Or maybe it was a tenant. They all had to take turns to man the phone out of hours and this weekend was hers, unfortunately.

'Hello?'

Her initial relief that it wasn't Mrs Thomas about her attic again instantly evaporated. 'Eleanor? What's wrong? Sorry. Can you say that again?'

'Sorry we're so late,' gasped Lucy as Patsy opened the door. She was panting after the climb; Patsy's flat was three floors up, past identical chipped pale blue doors, some of which had their numbers scrawled on the wall together with unidentifiable brown marks. 'Mike had to take one of the children somewhere at the last minute and then my mother-in-law rang and . . .'

'It's fine.' Patsy, dressed in thick-ribbed, bright pink tights below a black silky-looking t-shirt that ended some way above her knees, waved her in. Her cigarette, which she was waving in her right hand, would have burned Lucy's trousers, had she not swiftly moved out of the way. 'Relax. We don't stand on ceremony here, do we, Antony?'

'We?' Until only a few months ago, Antony had been part of a Maggie and Antony 'we'. Now, Antony, whose newly-acquired tan suggested he'd been on a sunbed, had changed partners in a seemingly effortless manner and everyone else just accepted it. If it wasn't for Mike, she wouldn't be here at all.

They'd discussed it in the car on the way over. With Luke, it would have been a row. Mike was far more reasonable. 'I don't know how you can have a best friend who leaves his wife and kids,' she had said.

'It doesn't sound good when you put it like that,' agreed Mike. 'But you know, there are always two sides to a story. Antony hadn't been happy for years.'

'It's still no excuse to abandon your responsibilities.'

'He hasn't. He sees the kids every day and I know he's being very generous towards Maggie, financially.'

Lucy had snorted, making a remark that money wasn't everything. But she couldn't criticise Antony when it came to the kids. Even Maggie had always said how good he was with them. And now, here they were at Patsy's.

'Aunty Lucy!'

Alice came running up in Patsy's tiny corridor of a hall, eyes shining and jumped up at her, pulling on her arms. 'Is Kate here?'

Alice adored Kate, seeing her as an older role model. 'Sorry, darling, she's out tonight. I didn't know you were going to be here. How lovely.'

'Mum's not well.' Matt spoke with all the gravity of a twelve-year-old who knew more than he should at that age.

Lucy glanced at Antony. 'Really?'

He brushed the air as though to dismiss his son's comments. 'Just a migraine. I told her to go to bed and that I'd have the kids. Now, Lucy, what would you like to drink?'

'A glass of white wine would be lovely.' Lucy took in the

glass-topped circular table which looked too small for a dining table with a paper plate of smoked salmon and dried parsley on top.

'Help yourself.' Patsy was nibbling on a carrot stick. She ate daintily and her teeth were surprisingly small, very white and neat. 'Grab a seat if you can find one.'

Clearly this wasn't going to be a sit-down meal. Passing on the two remaining slices of curled-up smoked salmon, Lucy made her way to a beige two-seater sofa in the corner where Chrissie was sitting on her own next to the television. Why didn't someone turn it off? There was also a *How to Learn Spanish in Six Weeks* on a small chrome coffee table. Antony was obviously making the most of his new life. 'Where's Martin?'

Chrissie rolled her eyes. 'Late . . . Something came up at work.'

'And George?'

Chrissie looked uncomfortable. 'In Patsy's bedroom. Or should I say Antony and Patsy's bedroom. He zonked out on the way so I've put him in the travel cot.' She lowered her voice. 'The bedroom stinks of cigarettes and incense sticks. Babies don't like strange smells, you know. There was an article in *Bella* recently about a child who got a terrible allergy to his mother's perfume.'

Lucy touched her arm lightly. 'I know you don't believe me but George will be all right, you know. My mother-in-law once said to me, when my lot were little, that when you worry, just think of all the babies that are brought up in really awful conditions and still survive.'

Chrissie smiled wanly. 'You're probably right.'

Lucy took a large gulp of wine. 'Just wait until baby George grows up to have his very own orange Mohican haircut.'

Chrissie's eyes widened. 'Not Kate?'

'Sam.'

'But he's only fifteen.'

Lucy took another gulp. 'I know. And it's probably all down to lousy mothering.'

'Don't say that.' Chrissie spoke indignantly. 'You're the most conscientious mother I've ever known. It's just a phase. They all do it.'

Lucy nodded, scattering a pile of Ryvita crumbs all over her lap. 'That's what Mike says.' She looked across at her future husband, uncomfortably perched on a black and white checked beanbag next to Patsy, cross-legged on the carpet talking animatedly. 'This is different, isn't it?'

'I know.' Chrissie giggled. 'She's got some more friends coming over apparently. I'd rather hoped Jenny would be here.'

'She wouldn't come.'

'Why?'

Lucy sighed. 'She doesn't approve of Patsy "taking someone else's husband", as she puts it. And she doesn't want to come on her own.'

'Well I don't like the Patsy set-up either. In fact, I'm not sure why we're here but Martin said it would be good for us to get out and yet he's late and . . .'

'What's wrong?'

Chrissie's eyes were watering. 'Martin's been really off ever since . . . well ever since your dinner party actually. He's become distant and cold. I know work's really busy – that's why he's late – but he won't seem to open up to me. When I talk to him about it, he accuses me of imagining it. Weird, isn't it?'

Oh, lord. So Martin hadn't told her about the baby alarm. Why not? And should she do so instead? She'd nearly done so last time when she'd called in but had chickened out, feeling too awkward.

'Why don't you talk to him?' she began tentatively. 'Ask if anything's the matter.'

'Maybe. So tell me. Why are you so late?'

'Sam needed a lift somewhere and then Eleanor rang. She

just wouldn't get off the phone, even though I said we were going out.'

'She's lonely.'

'I know but it's difficult.'

Chrissie nodded. 'You've got a new life now.'

'But . . .'

'Hi, everyone.' Antony, walking awkwardly in what looked like stiff new jeans, was coming up with a bottle of wine to replenish their glasses. 'Just help yourself, won't you?' He jerked his head towards the small table and Lucy saw that a large plastic bowl of tuna had been put there, next to a candle which was dripping wax onto the paper tablecloth along with the 'serviettes', paper plates and flimsy beige plastic cutlery. She almost felt sorry for him. It was all so different from his previous life. Or was that what he wanted? Something that was as far flung from Maggie with her warm cosy smile and fan-shaped dinner party napkins, as he could imagine.

'Thanks. Where are the children?'

'Oh, in the kitchen, I think. There's the doorbell. Patsy?' He looked around. 'Do you know where she went?'

'Would you like me to open the door?' asked Lucy.

'Thanks. I need to check something in the microwave.'

Chrissie made a face at Lucy. 'He never checked any ovens or microwaves when he was with Maggie. And what's this with the fake tan? Patsy's put him on a diet too, you know. By the way, whatever you do, don't have any of that so-called tuna salad. I swear it's got sugar in it and the garlic bread hasn't defrosted.'

Lucy, hoping no one else had heard, was already fumbling with the unfamiliar door catch. On the other side, stood a very tall man clutching a bunch of garage chrysanthenums. He was wearing a phone piece in his ear and stared straight at her with very bright piercing blue eyes. Something about him made her feel deeply uncomfortable but, at the same time, dangerously unable to look away.

'Dan Green,' he said, making a mock bow. 'Friend of Patsy's. And you are . . . ?'

'Lucy. We're friends too. Well, sort of. Antony asked me to answer the door. Come on in.'

Fifteen

Jenny dipped her finger into her cocktail, pulled out the cherry with her thumb and forefinger and sucked it meaningfully in front of her audience of one.

'Not turned up then?' asked the barman.

'I could report you for being cheeky,' giggled Jenny.

'Or I could buy you a drink when I finish work.'

Jenny looked at him quizzically. Pluses: tall, dark in a rather edgy attractive way with a good sense of humour. Negatives: couldn't be more than twenty-three. Not much older than her eldest nephew, for pity's sake. On the other hand, no wedding ring . . .

'Thanks but no thanks,' she replied in a softer tone than she normally used for invitations like this. 'Shouldn't you be getting back to your mum anyway?'

He grinned. 'She lets me out in the evenings. What about you then? No hubby or kids waiting for you at home?'

She drained her glass. 'Well since, as you've already pointed out, I've been stood up by my date, that seems highly unlikely.'

'You could have kids.'

An unexpected wave of sadness washed through her. 'Yes,' she agreed quietly. 'I could. But I don't.' Nearly nine o'clock now. Too late to have kids unless she was very lucky and too late for her blind date. Not that she was particularly bothered. He was a friend of a friend of Steve's (straight, he'd promised) and when he'd spoken to her briefly on the phone to arrange where to meet, he'd sounded very up himself.

'Say.' The sexy barman was looking behind her. 'Are you sure that's not your date over there? He can't take his eyes off you.'

'Where?' Jenny sat where she was, straining to look in the mirror behind the barman instead.

'An older chap. Terrible purple spotty tie. Not much hair. Overweight.'

Jenny pushed her glass towards the barman. 'If that's who I think it might be, I'll need another.'

'Jenny!'

Quick, put on your business smile. A client was a client even when it was after hours. Offend them at your peril or you might not get another booking. But don't get too friendly. She knew more than a couple of other event organisers who'd made that mistake.

'Alan!' She treated him to a warm smile. 'Thought you'd gone home by now.'

'I would have, lass, but then I asked myself, why rush back? So I've been to a couple of West End shows and done some shopping. I'm flying back up tomorrow. What a coincidence seeing you here.'

'Yes, isn't it?' Jenny glanced at the mirrored walls and dim lighting with the small drinks tables scattered round, together with big squashy sofas. It was one of her favourite bars in London and not just because she had been here with . . . Stop right there.

'I like it.' She was gabbling now to hide her nervousness. 'It's one of the few places around where you can talk above the music.'

'Ah well, lass, if it's atmosphere you want, you ought to come up to the Quayside.'

'Where?'

He pulled up a high-backed metallic stool next to her. 'Don't tell me you haven't heard of Newcastle's finest dockside development.'

Jenny caught the sympathetic eye of the good-looking barman and began to regret turning down his invitation. 'Can't say I have, to be honest, Alan.'

'Well you're missing out. We've got some great places up in my neck of the woods, you know. You ought to come up some time.'

Jenny smiled politely. 'Thank you.'

'No, lass. The thanks is all mine. You were great in that conference. Really great. I couldn't believe how much went wrong. First the projector and then the toilets overflowing . . .'

The barman raised his eyebrows again. 'Oh that was nothing,' said Jenny quickly. 'I've had to handle far worse.'

'Really? Like what?'

'Well, last year, I was booked to organise a sixtieth birthday dinner for the chairman of this huge company. It was going to be on a Friday at 8 p.m. But the printers made a mistake with the invitations and no one turned up. They thought it was the following week.

'Flipping heck,' said Alan impressed. 'What did you do?'

'Sued the printers – it was their mistake – and took the unwanted food round to a centre for the homeless. Then we did it all again the following week when this time everyone turned up. At least it was that way round. If they'd come a week early, it would have been disastrous.'

'I must say, lass, you're resourceful.' Alan pulled out his wallet. 'Can I buy you another drink?'

'Thanks. I'll have a vodka and lime.' She looked straight at the barman. 'Then I'm afraid I might have to leave you. I'm meeting someone shortly.'

A flicker of disappointment flitted through Alan's eyes. 'That's a shame. I was wondering if you fancied some dinner with me.'

'That's very kind of you.' Jenny gave the barman a meaningful look. 'But I'm meeting someone in half an hour.' She looked at the barman again. 'By the entrance.'

'Well, we'll just have to make the most of the time we've got then, won't we?' he gesticulated towards one of the squashy sofas. 'Shall we make ourselves more comfortable?'

She hadn't noticed his limp before.

'It's nothing,' he assured her, seeing her look. 'Just an old injury. Par for the course, really.'

She tried to focus through the haze of three vodkas. 'So you hurt yourself playing golf?'

'You're a smart one.' He rubbed his leg ruefully. 'It's still sore but Doris says I'll live.' He patted the place next to him on the sofa. 'Now why don't you come and sit here and tell me a few of your own life stories.'

Half an hour later, she made her excuses and went to the Ladies. Alan Browning was a far more interesting man than she'd led herself to believe. Or maybe it was the drink. Either way, she was wondering if she could really be bothered to meet up with the barman and the blind date was definitely a no-show. Suddenly, an early night seemed far more enticing.

'Thanks for a great time,' she said, returning to the sofa to get her jacket.

Alan leaped to his feet, holding out his hand. 'Your date's arrived then, has he?'

'Yes.' She hesitated slightly. 'He's just texted to say he's waiting.'

Alan was still holding her hand and she didn't like to remove it in case he was offended. She'd read somewhere that northerners were a tactile lot; it went along with their friendliness. They probably needed to hug everyone just to keep warm. 'You know, Jenny, you might be a resourceful events organiser but you're one hell of a bad liar. Your date isn't coming, is he?'

Jenny sighed. 'That obvious, is it? All right, I've been stood up.'

'Happens to me all the time. Well, just once actually. But I was bloody annoyed. I'd driven all the way from Newcastle to Carlisle to see this lady.'

Jenny was intrigued. 'Did you ever find out why she didn't turn up?'

He smiled wryly. 'It's a bit complicated. But I could reveal all if you care to have dinner with me.' The smile faded and now he was looking at her more intently. 'Providing you don't have any other plans apart from waiting for a DNA.'

'A what?'

'A DNA. Did Not Attend. It's what they said in the hospital when I took my wife in and people didn't turn up for appointments.'

She hadn't realised his wife was ill. She must have got better or he wouldn't be wearing his ring still. But that story about the woman who'd stood him up . . . was that before or after he was married?

'So are we on for dinner, lass, or not?'

For one crazy moment, she almost felt like inviting him to Patsy's. Alan was different enough to surprise them all but then again, he'd get the wrong idea. Besides, even if she did like him, which she didn't, he was out of bounds.

'I'm not sure. To be honest, I feel terribly tired. It's been quite a week.'

He nodded. 'Well, at least let me get my driver to take you back.'

'I thought you said you were flying home.'

'I am. But I have a driver in London for when I'm down here.'

She tried not to show she was impressed.

'Please don't worry. I'll just get a cab.'

'Absolutely not. I insist.' Alan whipped out his mobile. 'It's no trouble at all. And besides, I'd sleep easier tonight myself if I know you're home safe.'

'That's very kind. I'll just get my coat.'

She felt a twinge of guilt as they passed the bar. Someone else was on duty so perhaps he was already waiting outside. Why could she only get the ones she didn't want and not the ones she did?

On her way to the Cloakroom, she passed the Gents. A stocky looking man with dark curly hair was going in. Something about the way he was walking, even from the back, seemed familiar. 'Mike?' she asked unsurely. The man faltered slightly before pushing open the swing door and half-stumbling inside without turning round.

Perhaps, Jenny thought, sinking into the back seat of Alan's car, she'd been mistaken. How nice to snuggle down into the warmth of the leather seats and know someone was going to take you back! There was still time for that new Hugh Grant DVD she'd treated herself to and the remaining quarter bottle of Jacob's Creek in the fridge. Perfect.

The car rounded the corner and as it did so, Jenny caught sight of the barman waiting, his hands in his pockets in protection from the cold. As she went by, he looked up. Jenny gave an apologetic wave. It was too dark to see his face but she could guess what it looked like.

'You're a no-good bitch, Jenny Macdonald,' she told herself. 'And frankly you deserve everything you get.'

Sixteen

'Take risks but don't go far.'

What did that mean, wondered Chrissie, screwing up the small piece of paper and chewing the fortune cookie slowly in the hope it would take away the taste of tuna.

'Anything interesting?' asked Patsy, handing her a mug of coffee. She was wearing some kind of hair extension (Chrissie always wondered how they worked) and her long hair brushed against the rim of the mug in a most unhygienic fashion. 'Mine said I was going to come into money. Fat chance.'

Chrissie smiled awkwardly, wishing there wasn't a candle on the table next to her. There must be at least six in the room. So dangerous! Supposing someone knocked one over? 'Mine wasn't quite so specific. Sorry, but I don't drink coffee. Have you got tea by any chance?'

'I'm out. Want me to run to the corner shop?'

'No, really, thanks. It doesn't matter.'

Chrissie waited until Patsy had moved on before opening another cookie. Of course she didn't believe in them but there was something irresistible about fate, especially when it was at your fingertips.

'Beware of strangers.'

She shivered. Ridiculous. It was like believing in horoscopes. Standing up, Chrissie was about to join Lucy when she saw Mike sitting down next to her, awkwardly balancing a paper plate of fruit salad on his knee. Lucy was frowning and Chrissie was pretty sure she heard the name Eleanor.

Personally, Chrissie thought Lucy's mother-in-law was an interfering old cow. Better leave them to it. Sidling into the tiny galley kitchen with its flecked formica worksurface, she tipped her half-eaten bowl of fruit salad into the bin. Those orange segments had been so stringy, they'd caught in the back of her throat.

'Hi, Chrissie. Enjoying yourself?'

She'd been caught! Antony and Patsy stood in the doorway, his arm around her bare back, stroking her shoulder. Chrissie never trusted women who dressed half-naked in mid-winter.

'Fine.' She glanced guiltily at the bin. 'Where are the children?'

'They went to find George in the bedroom.'

'What!'

Pushing past and catching her hip on the corner of the cheap formica work top, she raced towards the bedroom with its horrid little black plastic door handle.

Two small faces by the travel cot stared up at her.

'Hi, Aunty Chrissie.'

'You haven't woken George, have you?'

''Course not.'

Frantically, she put her hand on his back, feeling the re-assuring rise and fall of his chest. Thank God for that.

'Did you try to pick him up?'

'No way.' Two pairs of eyes stared at her indignantly.

She wouldn't have been indignant at that age. She would have been apologetic. Children these days were so knowing; so confident. She'd make sure that George showed respect to adults when he was older. Then she looked back at Alice. 'You've got make-up on!'

Alice giggled. 'Patsy did it for me. She did everyone on *Big Brother* the other month. Do you like it?'

Chrissie was appalled. 'You look very . . . very striking, although there's rather a lot of it. Make sure you take it off before you go to bed.' A thought hit her. 'Where are you going to sleep tonight?'

'Here.' Matt spoke sullenly. 'On the sofa when everyone's gone.'

'You can come back with me, if you like.'

'It's all right. Dad will be hurt if we don't stay. I just hope Mum's all right. I tried ringing her on my mobile but she didn't pick up.'

Poor kid! 'I'll call in on her on the way back, just to make sure.'

Matt looked relieved. 'Thanks.'

It still wasn't right that they were up so late. Alice looked exhausted with dark circles under her eyes. 'Why don't I ask Patsy if you can lie down on her bed until the grown ups have gone?' she suggested.

'No thanks.' Matt put his arm around his sister. 'We want to be where everyone else is.'

She wouldn't want to be left in this room on her own either. It just didn't feel comfortable with that feather boa draped on the bedhead, crystals hanging from the ceiling and little pots of potions and make-up everywhere, not to mention the piles of newpapers and magazines on the floor.

Idly she picked one up, only to find it was a sort of cuttings file. LOCAL MAN NARROWLY ESCAPES JAIL, read the headline.

'Auntie Chrissie, can we go back into the other room now?' Alice was tugging on her sleeve.

Reluctantly, Chrissie put down the folder. What kind of weirdo kept stuff like that? Really! She only hoped Antony came to his senses soon. And if not . . . well, surely it was their duty for one of them to help him.

It would have been nice to have had a drink, especially as Martin had reluctantly agreed earlier that it was his turn to drive back after supper. His usual 'couple of beers' had turned into at least four or five in one sitting recently and Chrissie jumped at any excuse to limit his intake.

But where was he now? His mobile had been switched off all evening. Before George, she would have been terrified Martin had had an accident. But now she couldn't help thinking that she would have been far more anxious if George had been in the car too.

Chrissie helped herself to an orange juice, leaning against a wall in the tiny hall. There were too many people in the little sitting room and Patsy had lit up another cigarette. Didn't Patsy realise how dangerous passive smoking was? It was the real reason why she had put George in the bedroom and not kept him with her.

Someone tapped her on the back. 'Chrissie? Chrissie Evans? Is that you?'

Swivelling sharply, she came face to face with a tall, very thin man with a floppy black fringe and piercing blue eyes. Something inside her spun madly over and over again as though her insides had turned into a centrifuge. Even worse, she could feel herself leaking through her breast pads.

It couldn't be.

'It is you, isn't it?' The man was laughing delightedly, his head thrown back revealing perfect white teeth and a slight thickening of stubble on his jaw line. He was wearing a Bluetooth which Chrissie always thought was very rude when you were in company.

'Bloody hell, Chrissie. It's been a long time. How do you know Patsy?'

'Do I know you?' She regarded him coolly.

He reached out for her hand. She pulled it away.

'Come on, Chrissie. Don't play these games with me.'

The centrifuge of fear inside, switched to anger. 'You've made a mistake. My name's not Chrissie Evans. It's Chrissie Richards. Now if you'll excuse me, I need to check on my baby.'

'Baby?' He looked slightly shocked.

Chrissie felt a wave of satisfaction. 'That's right.'

There was a knock on the door. 'Martin!' The familiarity of her husband's slightly chubby face filled her with gratitude, despite the sweet sickly tell-tale smell of his breath.

'Darling, I'm sorry. I couldn't help it. The bloody client insisted on taking me out for a drink afterwards at some club and if I'd said no, he'd have been offended.'

'You've missed supper,' she said tightly.

'I know. I'm sorry.' His eyes travelled to the man standing next to her. 'Hi.'

He looked at Chrissie as though expecting her to introduce them.

'Do forgive me.' She slipped her hand into her husband's challengingly. 'Martin, darling, this is Daniel. Daniel, my husband, Martin.'

'Please,' his eyes danced, 'call me Dan like most of my friends.'

His eyes were boring right into her, making her prickle with unease. 'And you're wrong about supper. It's more of an informal buffet, although I'd avoid the tuna unless you like sugar mixed with bullet-boiled eggs. Skip the fruit salad too. It's the only thing that our dear Patsy made herself and it's definitely on the stringy side. Still, you can't be good at everything, can you?' He winked at Martin. 'And I hear our hostess is rather good at other things instead.'

Chrissie made a beeline for Lucy. 'Something awful's happened,' she hissed.

'Poor you.' Lucy looked sympathetically at her leaking chest. 'The bathroom's over there.'

'It's not that. It's something far worse.'

'What?'

'See that man over there?'

'The tall dark one. Rather like Heathcliff crossed with James Nesbitt?' Lucy nodded. 'I let him in. There was something unnerving about him.'

'You can say that again. Well . . .'

There was a small cry at the other end of the room. It was difficult to see through the haze of smoke and people but it looked as though someone had fallen to the ground. Chrissie sprang up, followed by Lucy. Antony was kneeling on the floor next to Alice who was being violently sick.

'What shall I do?' he asked wildly, looking around.

Patsy was busy throwing towels down. 'She's going to ruin my carpet!'

Chrissie grabbed the fruit salad bowl, tipping the contents out onto the paper tablecloth and shoved it under Alice's head, holding back her hair. 'Just get it out, poppet.'

Matt began to cry. 'It's all right, kiddo,' said Antony wildly. 'She must have eaten something.'

'Are you saying there's something wrong with my food?' asked Patsy indignantly.

'I told her not to,' sobbed Matt, 'but she wouldn't listen.'

Chrissie felt cold. 'Told her not to do what?'

Matt clung to her arm. 'She wanted to know what vodka tasted like, Aunty Chrissie. So we had a bit. Then she just took the bottle before I could stop her and knocked it back.'

'What?' roared Antony. 'Where did you get it from?'

'In the kitchen,' said Matt. 'It was just sitting there. Next to the Ribena.'

'Hang on,' said Patsy. 'She's being sick again. Put the bowl under her, can't you? That carpet's new.'

'Alice,' shouted Antony. 'Quick. She's gone white. OmiGod, she's going to pass out. Call an ambulance. Now.'

OCTOBER

Wild mushroom tartlets

Lamb (spinach soufflé for Miss Fussy)

Home-made sorbet

Seventeen

'Alice, Matt, stop it right now or I'll have to take you home.'

Lucy wanted to put a hand on Maggie's thin arm and say, hang on, they're only kids. It's normal for them to be running round in an office where they were understandably bored stiff, despite the crayons and notepads and books that they'd brought with them.

Poor Maggie had been a bundle of nerves since Antony had left. When the local paper had run a recent advertorial on the agency (one of Genevieve's ideas to increase business), she had looked terrible in the local newspaper photograph. Lucy, who always froze in front of the camera had disliked her own picture too, although she personally put her pale pinched appearance down to the after-effects of Patsy's tuna salad. They'd all had queasy stomachs for three days and Martin, who'd been hit worst, declared he'd developed a sudden food intolerance 'to anything prepared by that woman'.

'Why don't you ask Antony to have them for the day?' Lucy now asked quietly, so the children didn't hear.

'After he got Alice drunk last time?' Maggie's eyes glinted almost madly. 'There's no way I'd allow that man or that crazy, stupid, irresponsible tart of his to look after the children. He's lucky I didn't call in the police or social services.'

Lucy sighed. They'd been through this so many times. It had been an accident, she'd told Maggie. Yes, it had been daft of Patsy to put the vodka next to a bottle of lemonade. But Alice hadn't actually passed out in the end, even though she had been violently sick. And although she and Antony had taken

Alice to Casualty, they'd been advised to take her back home and let her sleep it off.

'Lucky she didn't drink more,' said the duty doctor sternly as though it was Lucy's fault. 'Last week, we had a child in who was in a coma for three hours after knocking back half a bottle of wine.'

Lucy hadn't thought it wise to repeat this cautionary story to Maggie who now refused to let her ex see the kids unless he came to the old family home without Patsy.

'Matt, don't touch those papers! And Alice, leave the photo-copier alone!'

Was Maggie, with her dark eyebags, on the edge of a break-down? Her gaunt face, permanently lined with fear and hurt, reminded Lucy how she'd felt after Luke had died. It made her want to pick up the phone right now and tell Mike how much she loved him, especially after their silly tiff over the kitchen rules he'd put up on the wall last night. What were they now? Something about no eating in front of the tele-vision and putting their plates away in the dishwasher afterwards.

'They get away with too much, pet,' he'd pointed out. 'I'm only trying to help. It was meant to be a bit of a joke.'

But the children, especially Kate, had been really cross. 'He's treating us like we don't belong. I can't wait to get out of this place like Jon.'

She only hoped they weren't having another argument right now without her there to keep the peace. She and Maggie didn't normally have to work Saturdays but Genevieve, the owner, was on holiday and had asked them to help out. The phone hadn't stopped ringing; in fact, there it was again. 'I'll get it,' said Lucy quickly. Maggie had already upset one tenant this morning by saying that if she didn't know how to find the trip switch, she shouldn't be renting at all.

'Right Rentals, speaking.'

Lucy listened to the torrent of abuse that was hurtling down the line. Just as well she'd taken the call instead of Maggie who would probably have sent it straight back. No need to ask who was speaking. Mrs Thomas's angry tones distinguished her immediately from their other tenants.

'I do understand your concern, Mrs Thomas.' Lucy spoke soothingly in a way she would like to do to her children. Why was it always easier to be nicer to strangers than your own flesh and blood? 'But as you know, we sent our plumber up into your roof and he insists it's the noise of the cistern.'

She held the phone away from her ear. Alice and Matt were sufficiently intrigued to stop fiddling with the photocopier. 'No, I don't believe the house is rat-infested, Mrs Thomas, but we will get it checked out if you like.'

'Rats!' Alice was jumping up and down beside her, tugging at her sleeve. 'I want to see them.'

Lucy shot a 'Help me' look at Maggie but she was staring into space, oblivious of the chaos, hands cupped round a mug of cold coffee.

'No, Mrs Thomas, we don't have a crossed line. The office is rather busy today and there are, er, other clients here. Yes, I will contact you as soon as I get a reply.'

'How many rats are there?' demanded Alice just as she put the phone down. 'Can I have one as a pet?'

'There aren't any, Alice,' said Lucy in a sharper tone than she'd intended. 'And you mustn't interrupt, dear, when I'm on the phone. I'm sure Mummy's explained we have to be quiet in the office.'

'But it's so boring.' Alice sat on the corner of her desk, threading paperclips through her plaits.

'I know.' Lucy looked across at Maggie who was still in a daze. 'Suppose I ring Kate? She's only mooching around town. She might come in and take you with her.'

'Will she let me get my eyebrow pierced like hers?' demanded Alice.

'Absolutely not,' said Maggie dully.

'But you can look at the shops with her,' added Lucy encouragingly. 'Would you like that, Matt?'

He shrugged.

It was enough. Lucy dialled Kate's number on the mobile. 'Darling, it's me. Listen, can you do something for me?'

It was a long morning. By the time they had dealt with a number of problems, including a dripping tap ('I'm afraid that will have to wait until Monday, Mrs Hughes'); a tenant who refused to pay his rent because one of Right Rental's trusted handymen hadn't arrived to mend a cracked window; and an owner who wanted to know why his property still hadn't found a tenant even though he was asking far too much, both Lucy and Maggie were exhausted.

Still, thought Lucy, as she let herself into her unusually quiet house, at least Maggie had seemed to come out of her shell once the children had gone off with Kate. She'd even sorted out the over-optimistic owner by assuring him that the market was picking up thanks to a large American firm which needed to relocate some of its staff.

Lucy put on the kettle and sank down into the sofa in the family room. Bliss! Although she missed Mike's warm funny presence, it was nice to have a few minutes to herself. Besides, they'd all be back soon, slamming the door behind them, shouting and arguing, wanting to know what was for lunch. She only hoped they'd got over the kitchen rules business.

There was a slight ping from the kitchen, indicating the kettle had boiled. Lucy took the lid off the teapot to warm it with hot water. Typical! No one had bothered to throw away the old tea bags. Pulling open the kitchen bin drawer, she slung them in, tutting as they dripped on the floor. And then she saw it. Later, she wasn't quite sure what had made her look at the small, seemingly insignificant piece of paper, pull it out from the bin, straighten it on the draining board and take a good look. After all, it was only a petrol receipt which Mike must have thrown away since it wasn't one of hers. But it was the name of the garage that made her stomach turn to water. A garage in Manchester. Dated the same day that Mike had said he had been in Plymouth.

She was going to say something as soon as he came back, just before the kids. But Kate wanted to drag her back to town to show her a pair of jeans.

Sam should be doing his homework but was claiming he hadn't got any. 'Sure?' asked Mike sceptically. 'You need to work hard at school if you want to get anywhere, you know.'

Sam had given him a withering look. 'I've told you before. I want to be a *Blue Peter* presenter and you only need to be a runner for that. That's how the last one got his job. There was an interview about it in *Oi!* magazine.'

Lucy smiled ruefully. 'Well can you pack your sports kit for tomorrow and make sure you give back that rugby top to whoever it belongs to. It's not fair on the poor child's mother.'

'Everyone borrows stuff, Mum.'

'And stop stabbing your chop,' intercepted Kate in her bossy older-sister voice. 'It's already dead.'

'Piss off. 'Sides, I'm thinking of going veggie like Antony's hot girlfriend.'

Mike shook his head. 'Language, language. And hang on, before you all shoot off, put your plates in the dishwasher, can you?'

He waited until they'd left, before turning to her. 'Actually, pet, I think I'll go back to my place tonight to tidy it up for tomorrow's viewers.'

'Really?' Lucy had been steeling herself to discuss the receipt business with him. Well it would just have to wait a bit.

'And I was thinking . . .' He reached out for her hand. 'Why don't we go away for a couple of days? Just the two of us.'

A wave of alarm washed through her. 'But who'd have the kids? It's term-time so they can't go down to Eleanor.'

'Surely you can find someone?'

'Not really. I would have asked Maggie but I can't now. Not

in the state she's in. You do understand, don't you? Besides, I think the children need me.'

Mike stood up. 'We all do.'

'What do you mean?'

'We never have enough time together. There's always someone who wants you and there are times, Lucy, when I think we need to make more space for ourselves.'

'But you knew, when we met, what the situation was. I told you that the children – and Mungo – were part of me. And you were happy about that.'

'I was. But they're getting older now, Lucy. Jon's already gone and it won't be long before the others go too. If you don't mind me saying so, I think it's time you let go.'

After that, she did what she always did to clear her head. Mungo wasn't just great company; he was also a perfect excuse for going for a long walk and having time to herself. By the time she got back, it was dark. But the house was lit up like a beacon. Mike had promised, slightly coldly at the end of their conversation, to come round for supper. She'd tackle him then, she decided, about that receipt. In a funny way, she hadn't been that surprised when she'd found it. Ever since Mike had come into her life, she had hardly been able to believe how lucky she was. It seemed to make perfect sense, after everything that had happened with Luke, that it should all go wrong again.

As Lucy fished for her door key on the step, the door suddenly swung open.

'Lucy, darling. You're back. We were getting quite worried.'

She stared at the tall elegant woman in her pale green twin suit and grey-white hair. 'Eleanor!' Confused, Lucy tried to think straight. Had she made a terrible mistake? Had she forgotten that she'd invited her mother-in-law to stay?'

'I knew you wouldn't mind,' said Eleanor, leading her into the hall as though it was her house rather than Lucy's. 'Although I must say that your friend Michael didn't seem very welcoming.'

'He probably didn't realise you were coming.'

'Didn't you get my message?'

'When did you leave it?'

'Actually, come to think of it, I might not have bothered. I do hate those answerphones. Now I must tell you, Lucy, that I don't approve of Kate's earring. In our day, we wore studs in our ears not eyebrows. And as for Sam's hair. I really don't know how school allows it.'

'They don't. He only puts it up at weekends and in the evenings,' replied Lucy wearily. 'Has someone shown you to your room? I think the sheets need changing.'

They kept the spare room for Eleanor. Conscious she was the children's only remaining grandparent, Lucy always made an effort, keeping the same little china ornaments out on the dressing table with a robe on the back of the door and pink cosy slippers by the bed with its thick candlewick bedspread.

'Kate's already done it, thank you. Such a sweet girl, despite that awful earring. Sam tells me he's studying for his Asbos. Is that like Matric in our day? Your friend Michael has kept himself to himself in the kitchen. Mind you, the dog has improved, has he? Not so much jumping up. Now tell me, dear, how did Jon get on?'

She'd forgotten how her mother-in-law had an ability to play mental gymnastics with sentences that ran into each other with no obvious connection. 'He seemed to be all right.' Lucy swallowed the lump in her throat.

'You need to let him grow up a bit, my girl.' Eleanor tapped her hand. 'I agree with Michael on that one.'

So they'd been talking about her!

'Did I hear my name?'

Mike came out of the kitchen, tea towel slung over one shoulder. 'Hi, pet. Had a good walk?'

Lucy ignored the look of horror on her mother-in-law's face at the 'pet' endearment. 'Yes, thanks. Eleanor, why don't you make yourself comfortable in the sitting room with some magazines.'

'Actually, dear, I thought I'd carry on doing my address book.' She tapped it on her lap. 'I've had to do another, you know, because so many of my close friends have died. Still, I suppose that's our age.'

'You mustn't think like that,' said Lucy softly. She gave Mike a meaningful look. 'Can we have a quick chat?'

'Sure. By the way, before I forget. Chrissie rang. She wants you to call her back. Says it's urgent.'

Eighteen

Black with a vivid splash of crimson in the middle. That was how she always mentally pictured the second Monday of the month. The day when she always went to Edgware. Recently she'd been getting there increasingly later and today it looked as though she wasn't going to make it at all. Not the way the shoot was going.

'I usually wear pink blusher,' protested the model, whom Patsy had once worked with before at *Vogue*.

'I'd like to try this,' said Patsy firmly, applying Tahitian Tawn to the model's cheekbones. Francesca was dangerous. Married to the MD of her model agency (talk about nepotism), she usually got her own way.

'Excuse me.' Francesca waved over the stylist for the advertising company which had commissioned the shoot. 'This woman insists on putting this awful colour on my face. I want pink.'

The stylist wavered. 'All right, go with the pink. I think it's nicer too.'

Patsy bristled. 'Ready?' The photographer's assistant was hovering. 'We've only got another hour before we have to get out.'

The shoot was taking place just off the green and grey marble-floored foyer of a smart London hotel. They'd been given permission by the hotel's press officer, provided the hotel was credited. Patsy always thought these credits were such a con, especially when a fashion shoot took place at considerable expense in some far-flung exotic country. Surely the reader didn't give a fig as to whether the palm tree in the background was fake or not?

Still annoyed at having her judgment questioned, Patsy sank

back into her chair as she watched them pose by the lights. She was near enough to dash on set and adapt the model's make-up if necessary but far enough away to shut her eyes and wonder whether, if this session ended before 7 p.m., there was still time to get to Edgware. It would mean being back late, which wouldn't please Antony, especially as he was still mad at her.

'Why hadn't you put the vodka out of reach?' he'd demanded once the panic was over and Alice, the stupid girl, had gone back to her mother's.

'That's not the point. Don't your kids know they shouldn't help themselves to drink? Besides, if you remember, I wasn't exactly expecting them.'

He'd had slept at the far end of the bed that night, for the first time since they'd got together. By morning, they had gravitated towards each other again but even now, a good two weeks later, there was still an awkwardness between them.

'Patsy?' A tall pretty woman with blonde hair stood before her. 'It is you, isn't it?'

It took a few seconds to place her. She'd had her hair cut and it suited her, the way it fell in soft layers just below her ears. Nice make-up. Honey foundation with shimmery glints on those sharp upper cheekbones.

'Jenny.' Patsy stood up. She was considerably shorter than Jenny which made her feel unusually unconfident. 'Hi, how are you?'

'Busy.' Her tone was frosty. 'I'm here to check this place out for a conference. What are you doing?'

Patsy waved a hand towards the scene behind one of the Grecian pillars where she could still hear Francesca muttering something about pink. 'I'm here on a shoot.'

'Oh, yes, I remember. You're a make-up artist, aren't you? Who's the shoot for?

'A magazine. But it's an advertorial. That means . . .'

'I know what that is,' interrupted Jenny impatiently. 'What's it promoting?'

Patsy looked around to see if anyone else was listening. 'Pelvic floor toners, actually.'

'What? But the model's just sitting there, on the chair, looking smug.'

'Well they can hardly show her putting the bloody thing up her, can they?'

Jenny began to laugh and then stopped as though she'd just remembered something. Fine, thought Patsy, so you don't like me. I can live with that.

'Quiet, please,' said the photographer's assistant, putting his head briefly round the pillar with an admonishing look.

'Oh dear, I'm in trouble again,' muttered Patsy.

'I heard about the vodka party.' Jenny's voice was cool. 'Thank God the children were all right.'

'It was only one kid,' said Patsy defensively. 'And I don't see why everyone should blame me. If I'd helped myself to my dad's booze, I'd have got a clip round the ear. But now it's always the adults who are in the wrong.'

Jenny nodded. 'I know what you mean. I get really fed up with parents who assume the world should revolve around them just because they decided to bring kids into the world.'

'Exactly.' Patsy poured herself a glass of cold water from the water filter and offered one to Jenny. 'They moan about doors not being wide enough to get buggies through . . .'

'And they get all the prime spots in supermarket car parks.'

The two women glanced at each other with new-found respect.

'Ever been tempted to have kids?'

Patsy shrugged. 'Sometimes I think it would be quite nice to have a daughter. Not a boy. I wouldn't know how to handle one of those. But it's never been the right time and place or man to be honest.'

Jenny nodded. 'By the way, are you going to Chrissie's in a fortnight?'

Antony hadn't mentioned it. Maybe he wasn't planning on

going. Or maybe he wasn't taking her. Patsy felt a slight shiver of apprehension.

'Not sure. Are you?'

Jenny made an I-don't-really-care face. 'Depends what else is on offer, to be honest. And work. This job takes over my life.'

Patsy glanced at her watch. 'I'm meant to be somewhere right now but it doesn't look as though I'm going to make it. What's Chrissie like, anyway?' With any luck, this might lead onto Antony's wife and she could find out more about her.

'Nice. She and I used to hang out together until she met Martin.' She nudged Patsy. 'Mind you, did you hear what she was saying on the baby alarm at Lucy's the other month?'

Patsy didn't like being reminded of that awful time when Maggie had turned up so unexpectedly.

'No. What?'

'You must have left by then. Well, Chrissie was upstairs feeding her baby and had obviously forgotten that the baby monitor was plugged in. She started talking to George . . .'

'Who?'

'Her baby. Anyway, she was telling him that Martin didn't really turn her on any more and that there'd only really been one person who had done that and that was years ago.'

'But he's only a baby. How's he meant to understand?'

Jenny made a face. 'It's the kind of thing mothers do. Lucy was the same. Weird. Anyway, Martin was downstairs in the sitting room with Mike, and they both heard her! I'd love to have been a fly on the wall that night when they got back.'

'Actually,' said Patsy, 'she was behaving a bit oddly at my place. I overheard her being really rude to Dan.'

'Who?'

'A friend . . .'

'Patsy? Where are you?' Gael marched in, followed by Francesca who gave Patsy an I-told-you look. 'I need the model's make-up touched up. And I need her in an orange skirt – not this pink one. Why hasn't someone ironed it?'

She glowered at Jenny. 'Are you here to help?'

'Just passing actually.'

Patsy watched her rising languorously from the chair. In some ways they had a lot in common. Each was her own woman, unwilling to let anyone boss her around.

Patsy looked up from wiping off Francesca's make-up. 'See you at Chrissie's.'

Jenny slung her bag carelessly over her shoulder. 'Maybe.'

She'd be late but when she'd phoned and explained, they had grudgingly said she could still come, provided she left at the usual time. Honestly, you'd think they were doing her an enormous favour, thought Patsy crossly as she walked up Canons Drive.

How many years had she been doing this? Sometimes it didn't do to count. If it hadn't been for that stupid vodka incident, she might just have confided in Antony. Now she wasn't sure how he'd react.

The mobile rang just as she was about to turn into the street. Caller unknown which meant it wasn't Antony.

'Hello, gorgeous.'

She'd know that deep Green & Black's voice anywhere just as she recognised the tell-tale ring of gambling machines in the background. Would Dan never learn? 'Just ringing to thank you for dinner the other week. I'd have called before but I've been in LA.'

Daniel always threw in references to LA and KL as though he still felt the need to prove himself. He'd been like that when they'd been growing up; a period which neither of them cared to talk about. After he'd found her again in London, they'd clung to each other like wreckage, two misfits in an unreal world.

'That's OK.' She was nearly there now. 'It was nice to see you.'

'Was that kid all right?'

'Fine.' Was everyone going to go on about that for ever? 'What did you think of Antony's friends? I couldn't help over-hearing that girl – Chrissie – being rather rude to you.'

'Was she?'

'I heard her telling you to bugger off.'

'Oh, that. I think she'd just had too much to drink. Looks like you're well and truly into the suburban dining set, then. You'll be getting matching fish knives soon.'

'Fuck off,' she said agreeably. 'Look, I've got to go.'

'Somewhere nice?'

'Edgware,' she said shortly.

There was a brief silence. 'Good luck.'

'Thanks.' Dan knew how she was feeling; the only person who could understand. She must have been crazy to have thought of confiding in Antony.

Switching off the mobile, she pressed the doorbell of the faceless black front door. Upstairs, one of the grimy white net curtains twitched, as though he was up there, waiting. A vision of the usual black cloud that always came into her head, swam before her eyes. The small crimson blob in the middle got bigger and bigger.

Footsteps. The usual woman was opening the door. Squeezing her buttock muscles (a trick she'd learned years ago to steel herself for something difficult), Patsy forced herself to go in.

Nineteen

Chrissie turned over in bed and traced the shape of her husband's tummy button with her forefinger. In pre-George days, this had been the sign for him to stroke her breasts and they'd go on from there.

Since George had been born, however, it had been a huge effort to respond to Martin's overtures, let alone initiate sex. And as for the wild hungry and, let's face it, grateful sex in the early days of their relationship, forget it. The only person who was wild and hungry around here was baby George.

But tonight, Chrissie had decided, would be different. Somehow, by some miracle, she had managed to get George to sleep before midnight. She had also bought herself a long slinky silky nightdress from La Senza. And she told herself that even if all she wanted was to put her head on the pillow and zonk out, she would make an effort.

'I'm a bit tired,' mumbled Martin, rolling over.

Chrissie felt a nasty flutter in her soft flabby stomach. 'What's wrong?'

He spoke with his back to her. 'I can't turn it on and off when you feel like it, you know. There've been loads of times when I've suggested it and you just haven't been interested.'

Stung, Chrissie sat bolt-upright. 'Not interested? That's because I'm knackered. Do you know how exhausting it is to look after George all day. I'm drained. Absolutely drained.'

Martin moved further away. Any more and he'd fall out. She was almost tempted to push.

'And what do you think I am? I have to be out of here every day at 7 a.m. I can't go back to bed like you.'

'That's because I'm up half the night with George. And being at home isn't an easy option, you know. At least you're not responsible for making sure that one of your staff doesn't fall over and bump his head. You don't have to make sure that your secretary eats enough so she weighs what she's meant to at her next weigh-in. And when you go to the lavatory, you can do so in the confidence that someone isn't going to be yelling for you the second you've pulled your pants down.'

Martin switched on the bedside lamp. He looked cold. Older. Distant. A nasty chill shot through her. 'There's no need to be crude. You were the one who wanted a baby.'

'So did you!'

'Yes, but it wasn't as important to me.'

'Yes, it was. It was one of the first things we discussed when we got together.'

'Not exactly. I said it would be good if it happened but that at our age, if it didn't, we would just accept it and have a nice life together.'

Had someone, wondered Chrissie, entered them for *Husband-Swap* without her knowing? 'So we can't have a nice life with George?'

'Well, we could if you weren't so uptight all the time.'

'I'm not.'

'You've changed since George was born, Chrissie. You're tense and you're always worried. It's different between us.'

Her entire body felt like a pool of fear. 'But babies do change people. You read about it all the time.'

He shook his head. 'Not to this extent. It's made you say – do – things you would never have done before.'

'Like what?'

Martin switched off the light. 'I can't go into this now, Chrissie. I'm too tired and some of us have got to get up at 6.30 in the morning.'

'Some of us will probably be getting up at 4 a.m.,' retorted Chrissie. 'I never ask you to help, you know.'

'Well I've got a day's work to do, haven't I?'

'Tracey's partner does shift work and he still gets up in the night when their baby wakes.'

'Who's Tracey?'

'Someone from mother and toddler.'

Martin snorted. 'Well if this bloke does shift work, he can catch up on his sleep during the day. I'm going to sleep now. Night.'

She remained sitting upright against the headboard, mulling over the impossibility and unexpectedness of what Martin had just said. Was he cranky because he was tired? Work had been particularly worrying recently, in view of the recent spate of redundancies. Thankfully, they hadn't affected him but he had been told to sack members of his team which had been horrible.

Chrissie yawned. She felt exhausted but unable to sleep now after that horrible scene. Besides . . . oh, no. Oh, *no*. Don't get up, she told herself. It's only a murmur. He'll stop if you don't go in. But the murmur was getting louder. A whimper now. A whimper that was about to turn into a full blooded yell.

Martin burrowed his head under the pillow. He could hear it too but he wasn't going to get up. That was her job. Chrissie Richards. Once HR manager for Bicky Biscuits. Now full-time mother, on duty day and night.

Angrily, Chrissie stumbled out of bed towards George's room. She'd have liked to have had his cot next to them but Martin insisted they should have their 'own space'.

'All right, all right, I'm coming.'

She padded into George's bedroom with its expensive hand-painted frieze on the wall and boxes of toys all beautifully packed away from the day before. George had hauled himself up on the cot bars and was rattling them; an irate prisoner, tears streaming down his face and glaring at her for imprisoning him in this white designer cage.

God, he was heavy! As Sandra had said at the last check, she'd have to move George into a bed soon. But when that happened, how did you stop them getting in and out? George was so active, they'd never have any peace.

He was still yelling. 'Oh do shut up.' She hadn't meant to snap but it came out so easily. Her angry voice made George yell even more. 'I said "Shut up".' For a minute, she wanted to shake him until he stopped. It was so tempting. 'Stop it, stop it.'

For a blind moment, she considered slapping him. Only the sheer force of digging her own nails into the palm of her hand, stopped her. For pity's sake, what was she thinking of?

Shaking, Chrissie opened the flap in her blue flannel nightdress and George lunged for her right breast, his greedy mouth seeking her nipple. Peace. Horror flooded through her as she gazed down on her now contented son. She hadn't meant it. Of course she hadn't. She was tired, that was all. Upset after that argument with Martin. And disturbed, deeply disturbed, at having seen Daniel after all these years.

George was sucking noisily. 'I saw him,' she murmured. 'The person I told you about. I saw him. And do you know what? He hadn't changed a bit.'

Chrissie snuggled down in the chair, closing her eyes in semi-sleep as George sucked on. 'What would it have been like if Dan and I had stayed together,' she whispered out loud. 'Would we have had you?'

The thought was so preposterous as to seem almost real. Chrissie stroked the downy back of George's little head. 'I love you,' she whispered, 'so much.'

How would she feel, she wondered, if George turned out to be gay. Poor Lucy. Did she guess about Jon? Somehow Chrissie didn't think so. 'I'd love you just as much,' she said to the now slumbering George. 'But I might wonder if it was my fault.'

Perhaps Martin was right. Maybe she ought to stop mollycoddling George so much and start getting tougher.

Chrissie woke with a jolt. What time was it? 6.17 a.m. according to the nursery clock. She was still in the chair in George's room and George himself was slumped against her right arm which had gone dead with the weight. OmiGod, he wasn't breathing. Yes, he was. But so quietly she could hardly see his little chest rising up and down.

Stiff with the position she'd had fallen into, she stood up unsteadily and bent over the side of the cot to lower George in. He protested in his sleep and Chrissie waited in apprehension for him to open his mouth and yell. Instead, he turned over, eyes still shut. Chrissie felt a flood of relief followed by the nasty remembrance of last night's scene.

Maybe there was time to make it up before Martin left for work. But the bed was empty! He wasn't in the bathroom and nor was he downstairs in the kitchen and – what was this? – his BMW wasn't in the drive. Even worse, the mobile (always on) was off.

Numbly, Chrissie made herself a cup of tea and sat miserably at the kitchen table, cupping her hand around the mug for warmth and comfort. For a brief mad wonderful moment, she considered hurling it against the wall. Don't be so ridiculous, she told herself. It would make a horrible mess.

Crash.

Chrissie surveyed the broken bits of mug and stained wallpaper with surprise. Had she really done that? Tears welled into her eyes as she searched under the sink for the dustpan and brush. As she picked up the pieces of china, she cut herself. Good! She deserved to be cut after what she had done.

Her mobile! Martin to say he was sorry? It stopped and then started again. Still bleeding from the gash on the palm of her hand, Chrissie picked up the mobile. It stopped again. Caller unknown. The blood was still gushing. She ought to get a plaster; there were bloody finger prints all over the phone now. But somehow, she just couldn't be bothered. Besides, she had to get George up now or they'd be late for the baby clinic.

*   *   *

Sandra, the health visitor, was a plump round organised woman; the kind who'd know exactly where she was in her menstrual cycle as well as the location of the household Sellotape. She had, she'd frequently assured Chrissie, two teenagers of her own, so knew 'what it was like'. Chrissie doubted if anyone knew what it was like with George.

'So we're onto solids now, then!' beamed Sandra. 'What do you give him?'

'Oh, mashed vegetables and that kind of thing,' replied Chrissie airily, smoothing down her skirt. She'd taken great care to dress nicely and to put George in a clean outfit. Some of the mums round here were unbelievably scruffy in filthy trailing jeans and it was important to her that Sandra realised she was different.

'Mashed vegetables are good but they're not enough on their own.' Sandra eyed her beadily. 'That's something they don't tell you in the Mothercare catalogue, isn't it? Most mums find it best to purée whatever the rest of the family is having, like shepherds pie.'

'Well, my husband is home late because of his job and often he eats out with clients.'

'But you must make a meal for yourself,' Sandra persisted.

Chrissie thought of the slice of toast that she usually made do with in an attempt to get her figure back. 'Sort of.'

Sandra never gave up when she sniffed a rat. 'Are you still breastfeeding George?

Chrissie shifted uncomfortably in her seat. 'Every now and then.'

'He's getting a bit old for that now, you know. And it might make it more difficult for you to conceive again if you're breast-feeding. That is, if you're thinking of having another.'

She might as well have added the words 'even at your age', thought Chrissie.

'Possibly. But I find breastfeeding comforts him and helps him get to sleep.'

'Ever thought of a dummy?'

Chrissie shuddered. 'I'd rather not.'

'They can be very soothing, you know. I know some people are worried in case they affect baby's teeth but if you get the right design, they're fine.'

Chrissie thought of Tracey's kids who permanently had a dummy in their mouths.

'At least George's weight's on target,' observed Sandra approvingly as she looked at the scales. 'Do you have any more questions?'

Yes, Chrissie wanted to ask. How do I know he's all right? How do I know he's not going to pick up some horrid bug from all these snotty kids around them, including Tracey's who were behind her in the queue. Is it normal to throw a cup of tea against the wall for reasons which she still couldn't explain? Why did she want something awful to happen to George so she could go back to her old life? And why, at the same time, was she terrified of something dreadful happening to him?

'No, I don't think so.'

'Well, you know where to find us if you do, don't you? Come here, George, what have you been doing to your legs?'

'Oh they're just bruises.' Chrissie laughed. 'He's always bumping himself. I suppose that's boys.'

Sandra was still scribbling notes. 'Watch out for sharp corners on furniture. Some parents find it useful to tape them with sticking plaster so they don't hurt if toddlers walk into them. That kind of thing is on their eye level, you know.'

'I do know,' replied Chrissie sullenly. Did the woman think she was thick?

'And what about you and your husband? Are you managing to have some time to yourself?'

Had Sandra had been sitting at the bottom of their bed last night? 'Actually, we've got some friends coming round for supper in a week.'

Sandra nodded. 'Good. Well, make sure your husband does the washing up. Don't take on too much yourself.'

You couldn't win, thought Chrissie on her way out. Either you were accused of doing too much or not enough. Of feeding your baby the wrong thing or too much of the right stuff. How did anyone ever get as far as the teenage stage? She'd like to ask Lucy; she'd like to tell her about the broken mug. She'd rung to tell her about Daniel the other day but Lucy had been out and by the time she'd rung back, it hadn't seemed like a good idea any more in case it got back to Martin via Mike. Chrissie felt her bottom half go watery again with apprehension. She needed the loo.

'Hi.' Tracey was going past with Kylie and Sting. 'OK, are you?'

Chrissie nodded. 'You were quick.'

'Yeah. Sandra was pleased with Sting's weight.'

Why didn't mothers like Tracey worry, wondered Chrissie. Was it because they were too unintelligent to know about all the dangers in store? Or was it because they were more emotionally intelligent than her and knew that these dangers probably wouldn't happen?

'Can you look after George for a second, while I go to the loo?'

'Only if you're quick.' Tracey glanced at the clock on her mobile. 'I've got to get back to work.' She grinned. 'I've got a few phone calls to make.'

The trouble with having a baby, thought Chrissie when a cubicle was finally free, was that when you wanted to go, you had to go. This was taking longer than she thought. Just as she stood up, she needed to go again. Come on. Come on.

Washing her hands, she raced out of the doors exactly at the same time that she heard the yell.

'George!' she screamed.

His pushchair was upside down! 'OmiGodareyouallright?'

Hands shaking, Chrissie turned the pushchair the right way

up and unstrapped a screaming beetroot-red George, comforting him against her shoulder. Already, a large egg was forming on his head. 'Shhh,' she soothed, 'shhhh.'

'Oh dear, what's happened here?' Sandra was running up breathlessly, her plump little body rippling with effort through her uniform.

'I left George in his pushchair when I went to the loo – Tracey said she'd look after him – and when I came out, she had gone and George's pushchair was upside down.'

'I saw a toddler near him,' added a mother helpfully. 'He was holding the handles. Maybe he pushed him over by mistake.'

'Which toddler?' demanded Chrissie.

'That doesn't really matter,' said Sandra sharply. 'The point is, Chrissie, that you shouldn't ever leave a pushchair unattended. Now that's something they do tell you in the Mothercare catalogue.'

'But I didn't. Tracey said she'd look after him.'

'Well she isn't here now.' Sandra was feeling George's head. 'I think we'd better check him out. Those pupils look rather dilated to me. It looks as though he might have mild concussion.'

Twenty

'I've told you. I want a full-size crocodile. Not some kind of bath toy. If you can't come up with the goods, just let me know instead of keeping me waiting. I'll give you until Tuesday. OK?'

Jenny slammed down the phone in frustration.

'Problem?' asked Lily, her assistant, straight out of college with her media degree, Bond Street shoes and parents in Tunbridge Wells.

Jenny was frantically leafing through her address book. 'You could say that. If Gizmo Gadgets doesn't come up with the goods this time, I'm never using them again. In fact, I'm going to try and find someone else anyway in case they let me down.'

Lily leaned on the desk, admiring her own nails. 'Why does it have to be a crocodile anyway?'

Jenny regarded her with suspicion. She'd already explained this and although Lily might come cheap as a student without any work experience, there were limits to her patience. 'Because this is a very important party for Stunning Swimwear which, as you know, or should know, is a large swimwear manufacturer based in Liverpool. They are holding this party for their clients, most of whom are shopkeepers. And we are organising it for them at the Smooth'n'Spa Club in Kensington where there is a pretty amazing pool.'

Lily nodded as though she hadn't heard this before. 'And will they ride the crocodile?'

Dear God, thought Jenny. This girl has to go. 'No. It's going to be anchored in the middle as a theme piece. Just like the swimming waiters.'

'Swimming waiters!' Lily trilled. 'That's such a cool idea! What are you going to wear?'

What it must be like to be twenty years of age and worried about what one's going to wear!

'Nothing,' retorted Jenny.

Lily's beautiful grey eyes widened in concern. 'Are you sure that's wise? My sister stripped off at an eighteenth birthday in St Lucia and she got arrested. But then it got into *Tatler*, so she didn't mind.'

Jenny picked up the phone. 'I was being sarcastic. Of course I'm going to wear something. And so are you. We're both going to be wearing something by Stunning Swimwear.'

Lily's face fell. 'But it's for fat women!'

'Well-endowed,' corrected Jenny. 'We'll just have to get the smallest sizes and get them taken in. You know the score. We have to help promote the client's goods. It's all part of the show.'

Lily made a face. 'But I've just bought this gorgeous two piece from Harvey Nicks.'

'Well, you'll just have to save it, I'm afraid.' Lily looked hurt and Jenny felt slightly repentant. She shouldn't snap so much but it was hard not to under pressure. Besides, she wasn't always like that. Look how nice she'd been to Patsy the other day; too nice actually. She could almost like her if it wasn't for what she was doing to poor old Maggie. 'Hello, is that Toys for Big Baths? I wonder if you can help me. I'm looking for a full-size crocodile. No, not a real one . . .'

'Aunty Jenny!' Kate's beaming face at the door of her sister's lovely house with the wisteria clambering up the front and neatly-clipped bay trees in terracotta pots by the front door made Jenny glad that she'd made the effort. After all, it was the kid's birthday. She had to bring her present round in person, even though she was really up against it now with the bloody swimming party event.

'Hi, darling.' Jenny gave Kate a warm cuddle and felt a fleeing sense of regret. She'd have liked a teenage daughter like this one; sassy, feisty, opinionated. More like her than her sister.

'Happy birthday.' She handed her an envelope. 'Hope you like this.'

Kate was already opening it. 'Cool! A voucher for River Island! Thanks so much!'

No need to mention it had been Lily's idea. The look of pleasure on her niece's face was the only thing that mattered right now.

'Mum around?'

'She's on the phone to Jon. I've been cooking – you've got to try these new brownies I've been working on.' She dropped her voice. 'Mike's in the kitchen with me, getting in my way.'

Reluctantly, Jenny went through. Ever since they'd met, Jenny felt that Mike quietly disapproved of her. Occasionally, he'd make a comment, suggesting life was easy for her since she only had herself to please. He could talk! Even now, he was still living a bachelor life when he chose to scuttle back to his own home.

Frankly, Jenny wondered if he'd ever actually commit to Lucy. They still hadn't set a date. But there was no denying that he adored her – quite sick-making sometimes. And her sister had positively bloomed

'Jenny! Do come and sit down. Would you like a drink?'

He was always the perfect host, even in someone else's house.

'No thanks. Just a flying visit, I'm afraid. Got to get back to the office to sort out some final details for an event this week.'

Mike looked at his watch in an exaggerated fashion. 'At this time of night? I don't know. You career girls . . .'

'Us career girls have to make a living,' interjected Jenny swiftly. 'Nice jumper by the way. Unusual colour. No it's fine, honestly. Shows you're comfortable with your sexuality. Hi, Lucy. Great. You're off the phone. I just popped in to give Kate her present.'

'Thanks.'

'What's wrong?' Jenny eyed her sister knowingly. They might be like chalk and cheese but she always knew when something was up.

'It's Jon.'

Lucy sat down on the sofa and Mike immediately took his place next to her, putting his arm around her concernedly. 'Is he still miserable, pet?'

Lucy nodded.

This was the first Jenny had heard about it. 'Doesn't he like Oxford?'

'Not really. He's not sure if he's chosen the right course and he hasn't made any real friends yet. Pete went down last weekend to be with him.'

Jenny felt a prickle of unease. 'Pete? I thought he'd gone to York.'

'He's having a gap year first, working to save some money,' interrupted Kate eagerly.

Should she tell Lucy about Steve having seen Pete in a gay bar? Maybe later when they were on their own.

Mike patted Lucy's knee reassuringly. 'Just give him time. He'll be OK. I only wish I'd had the opportunity to go to uni myself.'

'I hadn't realised you didn't go to university, Michael,' said a voice from the door. 'Of course, Luke went to Oxford which is why we were all so delighted when Jon got in.'

'Eleanor! I heard you'd come to stay. How are you?'

Eleanor kissed her warmly on both cheeks. 'Very well, dear, thank you. And how are you? Met any nice young men recently?'

Jenny smiled brightly. 'Several. But no one special.'

'Dear me. Well, you could always become a Latte.'

What had coffee got to do with her non-existent sex life?

'You know, dear. Living Apart Together, I believe they call it. Like Lucy and Michael here.'

Jenny tried not to laugh. 'I think it's called Lats, actually.

Sorry, Eleanor, but I really have to dash. I've got a big event to sort out this week and I'm still trying to find a crocodile.'

Eleanor raised her elegant grey eyebrows. 'You young things lead such exciting lives! Why on earth do you need a crocodile?'

Jenny groaned. 'Don't even ask. Lucy, I'll give you a ring. And try not to worry about Jon. I'm sure he'll be fine.'

Platitudes. So many of them in life. Jon will be fine. The event will be all right in the end. 'I'll be fine,' poor Luke had assured everyone when he'd been called out to some remote spot in Brazil to deal with yet another crisis. Why did they say these things when no one knew if they were true?

Still, thought Jenny, surveying the pool, at least the crocodile had come up trumps. There it was, floating in the middle, a fantastic 'table piece'. Talking of tables, the staff had finished laying up now. All round the pool were little round tables with blue tablecloths imprinted with little yellow fish. She'd already checked with catering and there weren't, for once, any problems or at least any foreseeable problems.

The only hitch was her bloody swimsuit.

Lily had been right. Both their costumes were ghastly, even though she'd had both hers and Lily's altered so they suited their size 10 and 8 figures respectively. Even so, they were made in this hideous blue and yellow polyester fabric in a pattern reminiscent of London Underground upholstery circa 1980. Jenny shuddered. Still, only another five hours to go and she could get out of it, receive her cheque and never have to wear another Stunning Swimwear swimsuit in her life.

'Jenny!'

Lily came running in.

'What?'

Irritated, she gazed at Lily's perfect figure. Even though her swimsuit was just as horrendous as Jenny's, the younger girl looked gorgeous in hers.

'The client's already here!'

Fuck. They were early. Just as well that everything was all ready.

It was, Jenny thought halfway through, one of the best events she had ever organised. Everyone was impressed by the crocodile, especially when he spouted champagne out of his mouth, courtesy of a clever little gadget supplied by Toys for Big Baths who had really come up trumps. At this point, everyone dived in, including Lily who was clearly much in demand with several of the client's guests.

Jenny watched her worriedly as her young assistant dived down under the crocodile and out the other side. She'd warned her about the fine line between being friendly to a client and over-friendly. But in a situation like this, where horseplay was the order of the day, it was difficult. Unless of course, you were approaching the wrong side of forty in a swimsuit that was bright enough to be seen on the other side of the Channel.

'You've done very well.'

Jenny hadn't even noticed Alicia King coming up. She was one of those large stately women with the ability to walk like a cat. Silently and dangerously. Alicia had inherited the business from her father but had only recently branched out into larger sizes for the fuller figure, partly, Jenny suspected, because she possessed one herself.

'Thank you. It looks as though your guests are enjoying themselves.'

'They are. Of course, a lot of them have had a long journey.' She surveyed Lily who was flicking back water at a good-looking young man with a black floppy fringe. 'Now they're letting off steam, rather like your assistant.'

Jenny decided to ignore the reproof. Lily had worked hard; she was young. She'd have a word later when the client had gone. 'Have they all come down from Liverpool?'

'Most of them are north of Watford.' Alicia's lips tightened. 'I don't suppose you venture up there, do you?'

'Actually, I know someone from your neck of the woods. A model, although she lives in London now. Someone called Patsy Jones.'

Alicia's eyes narrowed. 'The Patsy Jones?'

Jenny felt uneasy. 'You make it sound as though she was famous.'

Alicia laughed hoarsely. 'Well, the family made headlines.'

'In what way?'

'I'm not sure I should go into that now. It's in the past really although I remember it well as I grew up nearby. Gosh, that's a clever idea.'

Jenny frowned. 'What is?'

'Green water.'

'Green water?'

Alicia was frowning. 'Is it meant to come off on people's bodies like that?'

'Oh, shit!'

Jenny watched aghast as a mass of green bodies scrambled out of the pool, shouting and screaming. They looked like a cast from some sci-fi film; even their hair was green.

'Where's it come from?' she gasped.

'There's only one other object that's green around here,' said Alicia coldly. 'Tell me, Jenny, where exactly did you get that crocodile? I just hope you've got some good lawyers.'

Twenty-one

'Mum, can I get my ears pierced?'

'Absolutely not.'

'Why not?' Sam was dancing round her, the way he always did when he wanted something. He'd go on and on until she gave in. Well she wasn't doing so this time even though she felt like banging her head against a wall. A vision of Luke's angry red eyes flashed into her mind. He'd never been able to take it when the children played up.

'Why not, why not, why not?'

'Because I said so. Stop it, Sam. You're driving me mad and if you were me, you'd drive yourself mad too.'

If Sam had been up for adoption – what a terrible thing to think! – he'd have one of those 'Difficult to Place' notes on his file. No wonder Mike found him hard to handle. But he was her son and she could never stop loving him, however impossible he was. Even so, she was glad they were going to Chrissie's tonight. Anything to get out of the house, especially now the rental agency had cut her hours because business was slow. Home didn't seem like hers any more. It wasn't just the kids who were hyped up with pre-Christmas fever. It was also Eleanor.

Her presence was overwhelming. The radio in the kitchen which she had turned to Radio 3 without asking Lucy's permission. The sitting room, where her mother-in-law's complex tapestry took up half the sofa. ('Don't let Mungo near it, dear.') The bathroom where the shelf was dominated by anti-ageing potions and vitamin pills. Even the downstairs loo where Eleanor had turned the lavatory paper roll round so it faced the wall.

A simple gesture but one which spoke volumes. Eleanor was here to stay. At least for as long as she deemed fit.

'How long is Gran going to be here for?' demanded Sam as she plonked a bowl of steaming macaroni cheese in front of them. 'She keeps telling me to turn my music down.'

'And she interrupted me on my mobile the other day, telling me to use the landline instead,' added Kate indignantly.

'Well, she's right,' began Lucy, smugly noting that her daughter, who'd been so pro-granny before, was now beginning to get fed up too. 'Look, I know it's difficult. But she's lonely and we owe it to her.'

'Why?' insisted Kate.

'Because she's Dad's mum and she misses him too,' sang out Sam, mimicking the phrase she always used. 'Mum, if you won't let me get my ears pierced, can I go to a concert?'

'When?'

'December 9th.'

She checked her diary. 'That's a Sunday. It's school the next day.'

'But it starts at 5 p.m. And it's the Wattevers, my favourite band. You made me miss the last one but luckily they're doing some extra dates.'

'You won't be back until after ten. It's too late.'

'Please. I've got to buy my ticket online now or they'll sell out.'

'No.'

'Please, please, please, please . . .'

'Stop now.'

'Pleasepleaseplease . . .'

'What's going on here?' Mike had come in. 'Sam, stop talking to your mother like that. And Kate, don't text at the table. It's rude.'

'We've just finished.' Kate scowled at Mike. 'Thanks for supper, Mum. What time are you getting back, Mum?'

'I'm not sure.'

'Mum.' Sam was standing close to her, wrapping his arms round her waist and looking up at her, pleadingly like he did when he was little. 'Please let me go to the concert, Mum.'

It was so tempting to say yes and keep the peace but Mike was looking at her. He was right. Kids needed boundaries.

'Sorry,' she said, looking away. 'Now put your plates away. I have to get ready. By the way, Sam, I've been meaning to ask. How did you get Tippex on your blazer again?'

Sam grinned. 'That's not Tippex. That's sp . . .'

'Shut up, Sam.' Kate was pulling him off the chair. 'Let's go and wash up to keep them quiet.'

After Mike had come into her life, Lucy had allowed herself to think that life was getting more stable. But now it seemed to be going all wrong again. Lucy had thought she'd get used to Jon's absence by now; it had been a few weeks, after all, since he had gone. And it wasn't as though he had 'gone' gone, like some of her friends' children who'd gone off for a year travelling. Jon would be back well before Christmas. Besides, he was at one of the most prestigious universities in the country. How could she be so selfish as to miss him?

Still, at least he seemed to be settling down more now, Lucy told herself, scrabbling in her jewellery box for the onyx earrings that went well with this dress. She hadn't had any more tight phone calls, suggesting he was hiding his emotions, just as Luke used to do.

Mike patted her bottom playfully, interrupting her thoughts. 'Great dress, pet. You've got a gorgeous bum, you know.'

If that compliment had come from anyone else, Lucy would have been deeply embarrassed. Luke would never in a million years have said anything more than a cursory 'You look nice'. But somehow Mike made her feel different. Sexy. Not her.

Yet ever since she'd found that receipt, she had felt uneasy. When she'd finally asked him about it, he'd airily claimed it was a petrol receipt that one of his employees had given him for expenses. It could be true. It had to be. She knew Mike. He was totally straight. Totally honest. Otherwise she wouldn't be with him.

'How did your meeting go this morning?' she asked, trying to fasten her necklace in the mirror.

'Here. Let me do that.' He trailed his fingers against her neck and her skin tingled. 'It was all right, thanks. I didn't get exactly what I wanted but I managed to get some concessions too.'

Not for the first time, Lucy wished she knew more about property development. 'This was for the Ringer site, right?'

He nodded.

'So are they going to sell it to you?'

He began to unzip her dress.

'Maybe. If the price is right.'

'Mike!' She gently pushed him away. 'There isn't time.'

His hands were already on her breasts, stroking caressing.

'Spoilsport,' he murmured. 'Chrissie won't be ready for us; you know that.'

Lucy's resolve was weaking. 'But the children . . .'

Swiftly, Mike moved across to lock the door before coming back and taking her in his arms.

'The children are busy downstairs arguing over television channels with Eleanor.'

'They'll hear us . . .'

Mike turned on the radio. 'No they won't.' He bent his head down to her breasts, nipping her nipples in reply. At the same time, he slid his hand down her pants. Lucy let out an involuntary groan. Mike always did this to her. Reduced her to liquid. Took away any rhyme or reason. He was looking down at her now, the light still on by the bedside table. He liked to see her face, he always said, when he entered her.

'God, I love this bit,' he said stopping as her body gently resisted. Slowly and carefully, he pushed again, this time sliding in.

Lucy wrapped her legs around him. They were such a perfect

fit. A better fit than she had ever been with anyone else, even though her experience had been limited.

'I love you, Lucy,' whispered Mike as he thrust against her.

Her body arched like a cat against his. 'I love you too,' she moaned.

'Mum. MUM!' Someone was knocking on the door which, thank God, they'd locked. 'Is there anything else to eat? Yes, I know we've had supper but I'm starving . . .'

'Sorry we're late,' said Lucy, still flushed, as Martin ushered them in.

'No problem. We've only just got George down anyway so we're running a bit late ourselves.'

Mike squeezed her hand as though to say 'Told you so'.

Lucy could still feel him inside her; like an internal footprint. Until she'd met Mike, sex had been something she had just done because, well because you did it and because she had wanted babies. But now she could see what all the fuss was about, it made her re-evaluate her life. Why hadn't she felt that way with Luke? Why hadn't they talked about it? And if they had, would that have stopped him from . . .

'Hi, Lucy. What kept you two?'

Her sister was looking at them knowingly. 'Oh, we got delayed by Eleanor. Then the kids decided they needed a second supper.'

Jenny snorted. 'You shouldn't let them run rings round you, especially that woman. Mike, can't you tell her that?'

Mike put his arm around Lucy's shoulder. 'Lucy must do what she thinks is right. Besides, it's not easy for Eleanor. She's old and lonely. It will happen to us all one day.'

Lucy nestled into Mike's shoulder. She loved his ability to see things from others' perspectives, although she wished it could apply to the children too. If Mike had his own kids, he might understand better.

'Meanwhile,' continued Mike, 'you're looking pretty stunning tonight, Jenny. Who's the lucky man then?'

'No one. I'm perfectly capable of dressing up to please myself,' replied Jenny stiffly.

Lucy groaned silently. Why did those two always rub each other up the wrong way? 'Just going to see if Chrissie wants any help in the kitchen.'

Her friend was spooning mushroom bits into a tray of pastry cases.

She eyed them doubtfully. 'Want any help?'

'Bloody tarts,' hissed Chrissie. 'The recipe made out they were so simple! I should have bought them ready-made. Just look at them! Half of them have collapsed. I'd need to do plastic surgery to put them back together again.'

'They'll probably be all right when you've put the filling in.' Lucy put on a spare apron that was hanging over the chair. 'Look. This one's not so bad.'

'Thanks. Can you do that while I sort this rack of lamb out? Oh, God, and then there's the spinach soufflé for Miss Vegetarian.' Chrissie's eyes sparkled. 'You'll never believe this but she's coming without Antony.'

'Really? Why?'

'Apparently Maggie asked him at the last minute to look after the kids until the babysitter came but she wouldn't let Patsy in the house.'

'And he went along with that?

'I suppose he wanted to see the children. He's coming on later and Patsy's announced she still wants to come, although I don't know how she's going to get here. She doesn't drive, you know, though she could probably steer with those boobs alone. Oh, I nearly forgot. Eleanor rang just before you arrived. Wants you to ring her.'

Lucy closed her eyes while Eleanor fired off questions at the other end of the phone. They were all things she'd already gone over but which Eleanor had (intentionally?) forgotten. Where was the trip switch in case the lights fused? Should she feed the dog or had he been done already? And when would Lucy be back?

'I'm not sure but don't wait up for us.'

'Us? Surely Michael isn't staying the night?'

'He might.'

'Is that wise, with the children in the house? It will send out all the wrong messages?'

'I'm not sure I'm with you,' said Lucy carefully.

'Well it's not as though you're married, is it dear? He has had rather a lot of girlfriends in the past, hasn't he? How do you know he's committed to you, especially given the age gap?'

She really was the limit! 'Eleanor, I know this hasn't been easy for you to accept but we are engaged.'

'Maybe.' Eleanor sounded smug. 'But that's very different from being married, isn't it, dear?'

She'd ignore that. 'Is Sam behaving himself?'

'He is now, dear, I gave him a little drop of my Bach's Rescue Remedy. Just squirted it into his orange juice. Works a treat. You should try it.'

By the time she had gone back into the sitting room, Mike was talking to Patsy who was wearing a very striking rainbow-coloured silk shift dress with long dangly jade earrings. She looked, Lucy had to admit, absolutely gorgeous and for a minute, she felt a pang of jealousy. Then Mike looked up and drew her to him.

'Everything OK at home?'

'Fine. Eleanor's drugged Sam and she and Kate are playing Dirty Scrabble.'

'What's that?'

'It was Luke's . . . I'll tell you later. Hello, Patsy. I hear Antony's coming on later.'

Patsy shrugged prettily. 'It's nice for him to see the kids, even though it was short notice. Your friend Maggie was going out.'

She hadn't known that.

A tall dark man came up with a glass of white wine in each hand. Lucy vaguely recognised him from Patsy's dinner.

'Hi.' He shook her hand firmly. 'I'm Dan. We met briefly

before. Lucy, isn't it? You're a friend of Chrissie's, aren't you?
Like me.'

She hadn't realised that. 'Did you work with her?'

Dan shook his head. 'No, but we go back a long way.'

Lucy would have liked to have asked more but Martin was
clapping his hands. 'Right everyone! Dinner's ready. Would you
like to sit up?'

She followed everyone into the dining room. Chrissie had
laid it beautifully with a white tablecloth and name places with
calligraphy lettering. In the middle, were a pretty pair of pear-
shaped crystal dropped candelabras. Only the brightly coloured
toddler toys in the corner gave away the fact that this was a
family room too.

'Very posh,' she heard Patsy muttering.

'Lucy, would you like to sit here? And, Dan, I'm afraid we
didn't know you were coming so you're under Antony.'

Martin tried to cover his snigger by reading out the list of
names. 'Right. Boy, girl . . . Mike! You're here.'

'Lucy!' Chrissie came out of the kitchen, clutching the phone.
'It's for you.'

Jenny groaned. 'Bet it's Eleanor again.'

'Shhh.' Lucy made a face. 'She'll hear you.'

'Actually, it's Jon.' Chrissie handed her the phone but it slid
out of her hands. 'Bother. I've cut him off. Well, he's bound to
ring again or you can call him. Sorry everyone. You've caught
me in my pinny. Dinner's almost ready.' She caught sight of
Dan and turned an unflattering shade of puce.

'Hello, Chrissie,' said Dan smoothly.

'Dan gave Patsy a lift here, love,' said Martin, grappling with
the corkscrew. 'So I asked him in. We can manage one more,
can't we? Besides it looks like Antony's going to be quite late.
You remember Dan, don't you? He was at Patsy's.'

'Actually, Chrissie and I have met before,' said Dan smoothly.

For a minute, Lucy thought Chrissie was going to deny it.
Then she slowly nodded her head. 'Yes,' she said. 'We have.'

Martin frowned. 'Really? How?'

At that point, her mobile rang again and Lucy missed Chrissie's reply. Instead, all she could hear was a terrible sobbing down the phone. A sobbing that got louder and louder like an animal cry.

'Jon!' she cried. 'Jon? What's happened?'

Twenty-two

'Charades anyone?' slurred Martin happily.

It was the kind of gaiety, thought Chrissie grimly, that was induced by too much wine followed by a large brandy, coupled with a guest who was having a domestic crisis in the kitchen. Lucy had been on the phone to Jon for nearly an hour now so Chrissie had had to dish up without her. Still, at least she'd managed to avoid talking to Dan.

'Not charades, darling,' she said firmly. 'We agreed we wouldn't subject everyone to that.'

Martin gave her a sullen look. 'You're just cross because your sorbet was all soggy.'

'Nonsense.' Mike's calm, even voice cut in. 'It was delicious.'

She shot him a grateful look. 'No, it wasn't, Mike. It tasted of polystyrene.'

'Oh, God.' Martin pretended to fall backwards. 'You didn't put any of your milk in it, did you?'

Dan cleared his throat. 'Going back to charades, I can remember a time when Chrissie was game for almost anything.'

There was a short, scary silence during which Chrissie tried to remember how to breathe. 'Ah yes,' said Martin slowly, 'you were going to tell us, I believe, just before Jon rang, how you know my wife.'

'We were at Durham,' said Chrissie quickly. 'Hardly knew each other actually.'

'I wouldn't say that.' Dan grinned. 'We were on the same corridor in hall. Chrissie was a very keen hockey player. Still at it, are you?'

He was taunting her. She'd never played hockey in her life. 'I don't have time.'

'What did you read, Dan?' asked Mike.

He said it with a tinge of envy, noticed Chrissie. She'd seen that before. They all had degrees apart from Mike and it clearly made him feel different.

'PPE.' He said it as though it was the only subject worth reading. Arrogant bastard.

'And what about you, Chrissie?' Mike wasn't going to let this go.

'English.'

'I'd have liked to have done that myself.' Mike sat forward on the sofa. 'Did you specialise in a particular period of literature?'

'Victorian and contemporary.' She didn't want to be talking about this; she needed to steer the conversation away from Dan. Maybe charades wasn't a bad idea after all.

She glanced at her watch deliberately. 'Shall we play then? Martin, you divide everyone up into teams while I check George.'

Martin groaned, topping himself up with another brandy. 'You'll wake him. It always happens but you never listen.'

'I just want to make sure, that's all.'

'I understand that.' Patsy's voice piped up unexpectedly. 'The kid's just little.'

Chrissie found herself feeling grateful. 'By the way, you never told me how you two knew each other.'

'We're from the same neck of the woods,' said Dan smoothly.

'Was that during Patsy's Page Three days?' slurred Martin. Any more and she'd kick him!

'Way before that. Back home in Liverpool when we were kids. When I came to London some years ago, he looked me up.'

'And down, I'd say,' slurred Martin.

Damn, she missed.

'And you've kept in touch all this time?' asked Mike curiously.

'Only above the waist, I hope!'

'Martin!'

'Sorry, love. It just slipped out.'

Patsy laughed uncomfortably. 'We're good friends. Aren't we, Dan?'

Chrissie stood up, uncomfortably aware of her post-baby tummy bulging under her elasticated skirt. 'Just going to look in on George before we start. Martin, why don't we have a girls versus boys team?'

He nodded. 'OK.'

At least that way, thought Chrissie as she tiptoed into George's room, she wouldn't have to be on Dan's side.

'Film!' said Mike.

'What?'

'I said FILM'.

They had to shout to drown out George's own extremely persistent voice.

'I said you'd wake him if you went in,' grumbled Martin.

'And I said you'd drunk too much,' retorted Chrissie, juggling a wide-awake George on her knee. 'That's your third glass of brandy.'

'So what? It's not as though I'm driving home, is it?'

'Three words!'

Mike was clearly enjoying this, even if no one else was.

Patsy was shaking her head; an action which triggered off other parts of her body too, much to Martin's obvious pleasure. Even Mike was finding it hard to look away. How anyone could wear a flimsy top in weather like this was beyond Chrissie.

'First word, three syllables,' called out Dan.

Patsy nodded vigorously, holding up one finger.

'First syllable!' yelled out Martin.

Patsy got down on all fours and began panting like a dog.

'Sex,' called out Dan.

She shook her head.

George began to yell even louder. Chrissie jiggled him on her knee.

'Horse,' she called out.

'You're meant to be on the same side,' said Martin snidely.

Idiot! This was what motherhood did to you; addled your brain so you couldn't remember the simplest of things. That, coupled with meeting someone whom she'd never expected to meet again, had rendered her incapable of doing anything except holding George. Chrissie tightened her arms around her son, hungrily breathing in his smell. He was so comforting; her buffer from the real world. How could she both love and hate someone with such equal intensity?

'Dog,' suggested Dan.

'What?'

George's cries were making this almost impossible. She'd have to take him out.

'I said "dog".'

Patsy shook her head in exasperation.

'Do "sounds like",' suggested Chrissie.

Patsy looked puzzled. 'What's that?'

They'd already had to explain the basic rules since Patsy had never played charades before.

'You cup your hand to your ear to indicate you're miming a word that sounds like the one you're trying to get across,' slurred Martin. 'You know. Like cat and rat.'

Patsy appeared to think for a minute. Then she threw herself on the floor, next to Martin and, to everyone's amazement, did a handstand.

'Blimey,' gasped Martin. 'That's pretty athletic.'

Chrissie couldn't even look. Did Patsy realise how much she was revealing? The men's eyes – including Mike's – were out on stalks. Only Dan seemed unfazed. Perhaps he'd seen it all before.

George began to yell even louder as though in disapproval. Chrissie agreed. 'Let's go into the bedroom,' she murmured. If Martin wanted to ogle over that sort of thing, that was up to him. Frankly, all she wanted to do was lie down on the bed with her baby, away from all these people. Once upon a time they and their lifestyles might have meant something to her but now it all seemed so irrelevant. The only important thing in this world was bringing up children. If only George would stop crying . . . If only Patsy hadn't brought Dan.

Chrissie wasn't sure how long she had been there before the door opened. The others were clearly enjoying themselves because she could hear raucous laughter downstairs. 'Who is it?'

'Me. Lucy.'

Her friend spoke dully as though someone had died. Chrissie felt a wave of fear pass through her. 'What's wrong?'

'It's Jon. He wants to leave Oxford. He doesn't like it.'

'But he can't! It's such a fantastic opportunity.'

'That's what I told him. But he says he hasn't made any friends and he doesn't like the course.'

'Can't you go down and see him? Make him see sense?'

'I am. I'm going tomorrow.'

Chrissie reached out for Lucy's hand and patted it in the dark. They were talking in whispers; Lucy instinctively knowing baby George had fallen asleep.

'Sorry about messing up dinner.'

'You didn't but I'm afraid we went ahead and ate without you.'

'That's fine. I'm glad you did.'

'It's not fine.' Chrissie felt the hot tears, which she'd been building up for so long, pouring down her cheeks.

'Why not?' Now it was Lucy who sounded alarmed.

'Because that silly cow Patsy has brought someone I used to know. That's what I was trying to tell you the other week.'

'You mean Dan?'

Chrissie nodded in the darkness.

'How did you know him?'

'We were at university together.'

'Was he a . . .'

'Yes. We went out. Briefly.'

'Does that matter? Martin's not jealous, is he?'

'No. Because he doesn't know the truth.'

'And what is the truth?'

Chrissie couldn't stop crying. 'That man ruined my life, Lucy. He ruined my bloody life. And now he's come back to spoil it all over again.'

Twenty-three

Breathlessly, Patsy flopped down on the posh cream sofa with its high back and squashy silver and beige cushions with a Heals label. She'd rather enjoyed her turn. Funny really. She'd always thought party games were for snobs, apart, of course, from the very different kind of games they used to play at parties way back.

But now she could see the attraction. It made you think. And she'd rather enjoyed causing a bit of a stir with her gymnastics.

'Whose turn now?' she asked excitedly. She'd been feeling tired but those tablets – recommended by one of the photographers – had pepped her up.

Martin groaned. 'Not me. I've had enough.'

Dan patted her knee. 'See? No one else could top your act.'

She gave him a mock bow. 'Why thank you, sir.'

Mike stood up. 'I'd better go and see if Lucy's all right.'

Patsy watched him go out of the room. Cute butt. In fact, not bad looking. Not the kind of man that she would have thought someone like Lucy would go for but there you are. No accounting for taste. And as she knew all too well, you couldn't always afford to be choosy.

Suddenly she felt an acute yearning for Antony; a yearning which surprised her. Of course she liked him but she'd made it a life rule never to depend on a man. Yet she missed him this evening, even though he was still giving her gyp about those stupid kids drinking her vodka. When Maggie had clapped her hands and demanded Antony should fill in for the babysitter, she'd agreed, to placate him. But then Dan had rung for a chat and offered to give her a lift. She hadn't expected him to be asked in too, but it wouldn't do Antony any harm to hear about it.

'Antony's very late,' said Martin.

'Didn't I tell you? He rang to say the sitter hadn't turned up so he's got to stay till Maggie gets back. Blimey, I hadn't realised it was so late. Mind if you drop me back now, Dan? I've got to work tomorrow.'

'On a Sunday?' asked Martin.

Ugh! She could smell his breath from here. Patsy certainly didn't envy Chrissie tonight with a screaming brat on one side and a drunken husband on the other.

''Fraid so,' she replied crisply, edging away. 'It's a big fashion shoot at the Hilton for an American magazine.'

'Anyone famous?'

'Sort of.' She named a famous American model now living in France.

'Wow,' said Martin, lying back on the cushions and spreading his arm behind her so he wasn't exactly touching her but was close enough for her to wonder. 'Another glass of wine, Patsy?' He winked again. 'It's got a great nose and slips down very smoothly.'

'Dan, I'm ready to go.'

He yawned. 'If I stay here any longer, I'll probably fall asleep myself. No reflection on the company, Martin. If anything, it's a compliment to your excellent wines.'

Wines! Why did Dan try to impress people like this. Didn't he see how they despised him – and her – for not being one of them?

The doorbell! Antony had come after all! But to her disappointment, it was a woman's voice.

'Shit, it's freezing out here.' Jenny stamped her feet to get the ice off her boots. 'Sorry I'm late everyone but I've had the mother fucker of all days and I didn't think I was going to get here at all. Then I thought, why not?' She threw back her head, in peals of laughter. 'Someone's going to sue me, you know. I need all the friends I've got.'

She'd been drinking, noticed Patsy, although she could carry it slightly better than Martin who was still on the sofa.

'Who's suing you?' slurred Martin. 'Sit down next to me and tell me all about it. I'll get Chrissie to find you something to eat. Chrissie. Where are you? Come and look after your guests.'

Pig of a man! 'I'll get something from the kitchen,' Patsy found herself saying. 'I think your wife is looking after your kid. Sorry, Jenny, this is Dan. Dan, Jenny.'

Jenny held out her hand and Patsy took in the very pretty green jade bangle dangling round her wrist. 'How do you do, Dan?' Her eyes twinkled. 'What have you done with Antony, Patsy?'

'He's babysitting.' She eyeballed Jenny challengingly. 'Dan's an old friend and he gave me a lift.'

Jenny smiled coquettishly at Dan. 'Do you take bookings?'

Dan's eyes twinkled. 'Occasionally. Now tell me about your legal problem. Doesn't sound too good to me.'

What was it about men, thought Patsy as she wandered out in search of the kitchen, that always made them fall hook line and sinker for a pretty chest? Now, judging from Dan's lit-up eyes, they wouldn't be leaving for ages.

Irritated, Patsy pushed open one of the doors. No, that was clearly the playroom, stuffed with toys and a little television in the corner. All those toys! So much when she and Babs had had so little.

The next door revealed a utility room which was bigger than her entire flat. How much money did these people earn? The bloody room was positively gleaming with mops and a porcelain sink and a state of the art washing machine and God knows what else. Unable to stop herself, Patsy opened another door.

Wow! Some study! Patsy took in the long lime oak table with its flat-top computer screens, one at each end. His and hers. There were photographs too lining the opposite wall. The inevitable wedding picture with Chrissie in a white meringue affair and Martin looking rather nervous. Several photographs of that ugly baby (what was he called again?) and another of a much younger Chrissie and Martin, arm in arm on a boat together with Lucy and a man who definitely wasn't Mike. The dead husband? Quite good-looking. Tall. Sandy coloured hair. Eyes that bore into you. Pink shirt.

In her family, thought Patsy, no one bothered to take pictures. You were too busy trying to survive life to whip out a Kodak. Chrissie had clearly had a very different life. Take this picture of her graduation. She looked thinner in this; rather pretty.

Of course, she knew Dan had been at Durham but it had been a surprise when she'd found out he knew Chrissie. 'How well did you know her?' she'd asked after the last supper party.

He'd shrugged. 'She was a friend. That's all.'

It was a small world. No doubt about that.

Bloody hell! Opening another door, she took in the granite surfaces, huge island in the middle with wicker baskets underneath for vegetables and big racing-green cooking range. You could live in this kitchen! She certainly would. What right did that Chrissie woman have to look so miserable and harassed all the time?

The leftovers were still in their dishes but each one had cling film neatly plastered over them next to the block of knives. Should she just put something on a plate for Jenny as she'd promised or was that interfering? Oh well, she was here now.

Ugh! The feel of the meat as the cold steel sliced through, made her want to retch. How could people eat this stuff? They might as well carve a bit off their own bodies and . . .

Christ.

At first, she didn't even feel it.

It was only when the blood spurted out in front of her that she realised it belonged to her. Appalled she stared down at her left hand.

'Dan,' she called out faintly. Grabbing a tea towel, she bound it round her fingers. Almost immediately, the redness began to seep through.

'Dan!' she called out, staggering into the hall. 'Martin. Anyone. Help!'

Twenty-four

Jenny shivered as she and Dan sat in Casualty, while Patsy was being examined. It had all happened so quickly. First that terrible scene at the swimming pool last night with everyone turning green and Alicia threatening to sue. Then waking up this morning, panicking. Was the green stuff permanent? How much would she have to pay if it was? Could she go bust?

Jenny felt as though she was going to vomit out her insides. She'd worked so hard to get where she was and now someone, this Alicia, was going to bring her down through no fault of her own. She'd tried to ring her lawyer but the offices were shut until Monday. No wonder she'd got drunk last night and turned up at Chrissie's in such a state. But then this incredibly sexy, very tall, dark chap with the most incredible piercing blue eyes had opened the door and all she could do was think, bloody hell. Bloody, bloody hell.

Even more amazingly, he seemed to feel the same way. He'd got her a drink and led her to the sofa where they talked and talked and talked. It was like he'd found her G spot in her vocal chords. Only one other person had ever done that; someone she had once vowed never to see again.

Jenny had wanted Dan to strip off her clothes and still carry on talking. She told him about the crocodile and the threatened law suit; he told her about his work (wheeling and dealing from what she could make out) and how he'd grown up near Patsy and – incredibly – known Chrissie from university. And then, just as he had offered to drive her home because she'd really had too much Chardonnay to do so herself, Patsy had virtually fallen through the door, with her left hand dripping blood all over the cream carpet. What the hell had she been doing in the kitchen anyway?

Everyone had started shouting and making suggestions at the same time. But Dan had taken charge and suggested that he and Jenny should take Patsy to Casualty while Lucy sorted out some problem with Jon and Chrissie stayed with the baby.

'It's been two and a half hours,' she said, shivering again and wishing he'd put his arm around her if only for the heat. 'How much longer?'

'You know what these places are like. Could be ages. Hey, you're freezing. Have this.'

'No, I can't.'

'I insist.' He unbuttoned his dark brown suede jacket and wrapped it tenderly round her shoulders. The touch of his hands made her shiver with delicious anticipation. If Patsy hadn't been pigging out on extras from the kitchen, she and Dan could be somewhere else now.

'She was lucky not to lose the finger.'

'Sorry?' She was still mentally in bed with him. 'Oh, yes.'

Dan stretched back in his chair. 'Mind you, Patsy should be used to this by now.'

'What do you mean?'

'Well, her old man used to knock her about a bit. And her sister.'

She was shocked. 'Really?'

He nodded ruefully. 'When I was a teenager, I was always taking her to hospital. We had to pretend she'd had an accident but after a while, they got suspicious.'

'But what about Patsy's mother. Couldn't she have stopped it?'

Dan stood up, searching for change in his pocket. 'She'd gone, by then.'

'Gone?'

'Yes.' He spoke as though all this was perfectly normal. 'Scarpered. Left Patsy and her sister with the father.'

'How awful.'

He shook his head, half-smiling down at her as though explaining something to a child. 'Not as awful as it would have been if her mother had stayed. Now how about a polystyrene cup of NHS coffee to warm you up?'

Patsy had finally emerged another hour later, looking pale and even more beautiful with her left hand heavily bandaged.

'Does it hurt, love?' asked Dan tenderly.

Jenny gave him a sharp look.

'A bit,' said Patsy tightly. If it had been her, Jenny thought, she'd have been howling with pain. It was impossible not to feel a grudging admiration. 'I've phoned Antony and he's home now. He said he'd come and get me.'

'Nonsense. We'll drop you off.'

Jenny took comfort from the 'we'.

'Thanks.'

They drove back in silence; Jenny wondering whether Dan would suggest driving her back to her place afterwards or maybe going to his. She suddenly realised that she didn't know where he lived.

They pulled up outside Patsy's block. Council, thought Jenny dismissively. 'I'll walk you up,' said Dan.

'No, honestly, it's fine. Look, Antony's at the door now anyway.'

Enviously, Jenny saw him walking down to meet her; watched him envelop her in a big hug. Lucky Patsy. Poor Maggie. Why was life so complicated?

'Right.' Dan was looking across at her from his seat, his eyes fixed on hers. 'I'll take you back to your place, shall I?'

'It's quite a way.'

'That doesn't matter.' He switched on his CD player. 'I've got some great music and we can talk.'

Amazingly, they still didn't run out of conversation. But all the time, she felt tingly with expectation. 'This is nice,' said Dan approvingly, pulling up outside her apartment. 'I've always loved these Georgian conversions.'

She was so nervous that she stumbled over her words. 'Would
you like to come in?'

He looked at her without replying for so long that for a
minute, she wondered if she'd spoken at all.

'I don't think so,' he said finally.

Waves of disappointment crashed against her.

'But I would like to see you again. Here's my number.' He
handed her a card. 'Call me sometime.'

Numb, she let herself into her dark empty flat. Why hadn't
he wanted to come in? Didn't he fancy her? Why ask her to
call him if he didn't? And why couldn't he have asked her for
her number?

Fuck. Fuck.

On disappointed automatic mode, she pressed her answerphone button.

*'Jenny. It's Alan. Sorry to bother you over the weekend but can
you give me a ring tomorrow if possible. There's something urgent
I'd like to discuss with you.'*

'Jenny. This is Lily. Can you ring me please?'

*'Hi. Jenny. Steve here. Look, I might be calling out of turn here.
But I saw Jon tonight. Your sister's kid. And I think he's in a bit
of a bad way. Ring as soon you can, will you? It doesn't matter
what time.'*

*'Aunty Jenny? It's Kate. Can you give mum a ring. We had a
bit of a party tonight when she was out and she's going nuts. It
would be great if you could calm her down.'*

NOVEMBER

*Avocado delight from Bachelor Recipes, first
published 1971*

*Marguerite Patten's fabulous vegetarian casserole
('Eleanor's special version)*

Kate's magic brownies

Twenty-five

The shops had been full of Christmas stuff for ages, with excited posters exhorting shoppers to buy immediately before the world sold out. The office was getting busier too and she'd spent all week trying to arrange a plumber to sort out a tenant's shower. It was one of Maggie's tenants but she'd forgotten.

'I can't keep covering up for you,' Lucy felt like saying to her friend. But she had to. The so-called festive season was going to be very difficult for Maggie without Antony. She couldn't cope with losing her job too.

There had been times in her life, Lucy thought, when she'd felt like cancelling Christmas, especially after Luke's death. But this year, she needed to escape more than ever. And not necessarily with Mike.

When had she started to feel distant towards him? It was, she supposed, around the time that Jon had gone to Oxford and she had felt so utterly empty.

'You're bound to after all those years of looking after him.' Mike had kissed the top of her head. 'Maybe, baby, if you hadn't been there for him so much, you'd both have found this a bit easier.'

'So you think he's not settling because I over-mothered him?'

Mike had shrugged. 'Well, perhaps you have been a little over-protective. By the way, pet, someone left the light on in the bathroom. No wonder your electricity bill is so high.'

'Mum?' Sam had come in with his 'please-will-you-change-your mind' look.

'Yes?'

'Please can you change your mind about the Wattever concert? It's my last chance to get tickets.'

'Absolutely not,' Mike had said before she'd had a chance to say so herself. 'And if you even think about going without our permission, there'll be trouble.'

He'd been right of course but the look which Sam had thrown her, had cast a chill through her. If Mike carried on like this, he wouldn't just alienate himself from the children. He'd do the same with her too.

At least Jon seemed to have settled down since that last terrible phone call during Chrissie's dinner party ten days ago. He hadn't – as threatened – left Oxford. But his voice was still flat on the phone. Yes, he would say dully whenever she rang him (he rarely reciprocated), the work was OK but demanding. And yes, he'd made a few friends.

She was worried about Chrissie too. Her friend had started to say something about that man Dan but stopped, saying it didn't matter after all. But it clearly did. Then there had been all that trouble with Kate having a party without telling her. 'How could you?' she'd demanded after getting back from Chrissie's and finding beer stains on the carpet, the drawing room curtain off its rail, Chinese takeaway containers stinking out the kitchen, and empty beer bottles by the side of the bath.

'We tidied up,' said Kate defensively.

Mike eyed her coldly. 'So that's why you wanted to know what time we were getting back?'

'What's it got to do with you? This is our house. Not yours.'

'I still don't understand how Eleanor could have slept through it.'

'I told you, Mum. She had one of her heart tablets after stuffing herself with my brownies. They always knock her out.'

'What about Mr Thomas opposite? The one who complained. Did you write an apology note?'

'Yes, Mum.'

All in all, it had been really difficult after that. Maybe they needed a change of scene, especially as they'd had to cancel the Lake District trip at half term because Mike had been too busy with work.

'I'd like to go down and see Jon this weekend,' Lucy said suddenly over breakfast.

'Really?' Mike paused while buttering his toast. 'I thought we agreed not to visit again in case it unsettled him. I can't believe they only have eight-week terms. Don't they do any work?'

Eleanor eyed Mike's use of his knife. 'I think a visit is an excellent idea. Why don't we all go down on Saturday?'

'Wicked. It's so boring here without him.'

'Sam, dear, please finish your mouthful before talking.' Eleanor glared disapprovingly across the table. 'It's so frightfully common. And remember to hold your knife the right way, Kate.'

'I am, Gran.'

She was too but Lucy knew it was a comment designed for Mike. Eleanor had been here for weeks now but every time Lucy suggested gently that she must be missing home, Eleanor had reassured her that she wasn't at all, and besides she was worried about being on her own in case she had one of her 'funny turns' again.

'Saturday would be difficult to park,' said Lucy carefully, taking care not to look at Mike. 'But we could go on Sunday.'

'If you want, pet.' Mike got up from the table, despite the fact that Eleanor was still eating. 'But I might not make it. I've got a site visit.'

'At the weekend?'

''Fraid so.'

'Where?'

'Bristol. I'll need to leave early or even on Saturday night.'

Lucy felt that wave of unease again. 'That's a shame.'

'Never mind,' said Eleanor crisply. 'Perhaps it would be nice for Jon to see family, don't you think. Lucy, is there any more tea in the pot? Children, please stay where you are. It's frightfully rude to get down from the table before everyone's finished.'

Mike shut the breakfast door behind him loudly; it might or might not have been a gesture.

'Sam,' said Lucy weakly, 'Don't forget to make your bed today like I told you.'

Her youngest glared at her. 'What's the point if I'm going to mess it up tonight? Anyway, I'll only do it if you let me go to the Wattevers concert.'

'Goodness me.' Eleanor pursed her lips in disapproval. 'If your father was here, Sam, he'd have something to say about that. Lucy, aren't you going to tell him off? Really, if you don't mind me saying so, the standards in this house are really slipping.'

Lucy wanted to yell at her; ask why she didn't go home then. But if she did, it would be disloyal to Luke. Eleanor was, after all, the children's grandmother. 'Sam, don't answer back. And Kate, please help me to clear the table.'

'So are we going or not?'

'Where?'

'To Oxford at the weekend, course.'

Lucy found herself nodding. 'Yes, we are.'

With or without Mike, she added silently to herself.

'Maybe Aunty Jenny would like to come too,' she said out loud.

'Great.' Kate's eyes shone. 'Do you think Jon's friend Pete will be there?'

Every time Lucy went to Oxford, she was struck by how beautiful it was. All those wonderful buildings, each as beautiful as the other but also different in their own majestic way. University College with its imposing, almost bridal façade. Magdalen with its tawny red brick, nudging the river. Balliol with its neatly laid out lawns. But her favourite was historical New College, where Luke had gone and where Jon was now. Not new at all, really, apart from the recent extension.

Everything, mused Lucy, as the porter waved them through, has to be new once. But when exactly does someone decide that it's old? How long is the bit in between? Could she, after six years of widowhood, say she'd been a widow for a long time or did that count as merely a medium stint?

Jon had arranged to wait for them in the quad.

'Keep off the grass, Sam. Look, there's a notice telling you to.'

'Well someone stood on the grass first to put it there, didn't they? Anyway, where's Jon?'

'Maybe he's in his room,' said Jenny crisply. 'Your mother and I will go up. You lot wait down here and show Granny the gardens. And Sam, behave yourself. If I were your mother, I'd sack you!'

Her sister, thought Lucy ruefully, could handle her family so much better than she could.

'When's that woman going to leave?' demanded Jenny as they walked across the quad towards Jon's staircase. 'I'm not surprised she gets tiddly on one glass of wine.'

'What do you mean?'

Jenny's eyes glinted mischievously. 'Well alcohol affects you more when you're at a high altitude, like flying, doesn't it? And Eleanor's permanently up herself.'

'Very funny.' Lucy tucked her arm into Jenny's, feeling a rush of sisterly love. 'But she does seem to think she's superior to everyone else. It gets on everyone's nerves, including Mike who never gets upset about anything.'

'Is that why he's working today?'

'No.' Lucy felt indignant. 'He had to, anyway.'

'Look, Lucy.' Jenny's hand was on her elbow, slowing her down before they reached Jon's room. 'There's something I have to tell you. I've been meaning to for ages but it never seemed the right time.'

Something I have to tell you. The same words the police had used when they'd told her about Luke before it was all over the news.

'What?'

'It's just that, well, you know my friend, Steve? Well, he saw, or thought he saw, Jon at a . . .'

'Mum!'

Jon was already opening the door. 'I heard you coming up. Sorry, I was going to meet you outside but I fell asleep.'

Lucy took in his tousled hair, jeans which were hanging loosely round his waist and pale complexion. 'Darling, you've lost weight!'

'Stop fussing. No, don't go in. It's a mess. Can you just wait there for a bit while I grab my wallet?'

Jenny peeped inside. 'Typical squalid student room. I thought they had scouts at Oxford, unless Jon's banned his from going in. Takes me back to my first digs.'

'Me too,' shuddered Lucy.

'You were tidy! Always having a certain place for everything. I bet you never lost an essay.'

Lucy smiled. 'No, I didn't.'

She was trying not to look through the crack in the door. Jon's bed clearly hadn't been made for days. His clothes were strewn all over the floor and there was a half-empty beer glass on the ground. Lucy fought the urge to go in and pick it up.

'Mum,' called out Jon. 'I'm just finishing off something. Why don't you go back downstairs and I'll meet you outside.'

'Odd,' commented Jenny lightly. 'I wonder why he didn't want us to go in.'

'I can see why.' Lucy traced the stone wall lightly with her forefinger as they went down.

'Well, I know students are entitled to make a mess . . .'

'It's not that. Someone was under the bed covers.'

'Are you sure?'

'Quite sure. Anyway, it's what you were going to tell me on the way up, isn't it? I suppose you were going to say that your friend Steve saw Jon in a gay bar?'

'Well,' Jenny hesitated. 'I wasn't going to put it quite so bluntly but yes, actually he did.'

'I've known, sensed it, for years.' Lucy felt as though someone else was speaking. 'Jon is . . . the other way. Just like Luke was. It can be genetic you know. I've been reading up on it.'

'What?' Jenny spluttered. 'You are joking, aren't you?'

'No.' Now it was coming out, Lucy felt so much better. 'Luke told me, shortly before he . . . shortly before he died.'

'He actually said he was homosexual?'

'Words to that effect.'

'Are you sure?' asked Jenny quietly.

'Jenny, I was married to him. When you're with someone night and day you get an inkling for these things.'

'Not necessarily.' Her sister spoke hotly. 'What about all those women whose husbands have affairs and they don't know anything about it?'

'I feel sorry for them too.' Lucy was beginning to wish they'd never started this conversation. 'Shh. Here comes Jon.'

'Are you going to tell him you know?' hissed Jenny.

'Yes.'

'When?'

'When the time is right.'

They found a very pleasant tea room in Turl Street; the kind that might, hopefully, please Eleanor enough to shut her up. En route, she had insisted on quizzing Jon about all the 'young ladies' he must have met.

'I remember when your dear father was here,' she sighed over her cup of Earl Grey. 'He was always going to balls and parties and tutors' sherry parties.'

Jon carefully brushed some scone crumbs off his jumper. 'We have to work pretty hard too, Gran.'

'Yeah, you should tell Sam that,' interjected Kate scornfully. 'He doesn't do anything. He's always on MSN when he should be doing his homework.'

'So are you!' Sam stuffed a scone into his mouth. 'Anyway,

how can you say what's right and what isn't? There isn't some kind of ruler for rightness, you know.'

'Goodness,' murmured Jenny, pushing her plate away. 'That's rather profound.'

Kate smirked. 'That's 'cos he cribbed it from some brainy kid's essay to help him with history homework.'

Lucy almost choked on her mouthful. 'Is that right?'

'I was only catching up with some notes I should have taken.'

'He's lying, Mum. He paid this kid a fiver. And he got that from your purse. Ask him.'

Eleanor knitted her eyebrows, thunderously. 'Samuel, if that is true, it's stealing.'

'I didn't nick it,' muttered Sam. 'I borrowed it. I was going to tell you but I forgot.'

'Why don't you tell Jon and Mum about your French oral,' persisted Kate.

'Shut up.'

Jon smiled; the first time Lucy had seen him do so since arriving. 'This is what I've been missing. I'd forgotten how awful you two are together. Go on then, Sam, tell me.'

Sam grinned. 'Well we had this test and you had to talk in French, like. So Dave – that's Madame Davis but we call her Dave – asked what I'd done at lunchtime. And I said, "J'ai fumé avec mes amis."'

Jon erupted into giggles. 'You said you'd been smoking with your friends!'

'Yeah.' Sam shrugged happily.

'Were you smoking?' asked Lucy, not even daring to look at her mother-in-law.

'Course not. But I thought it would be fun to say I was 'cos she couldn't do anything about it. Everyone says silly things in orals anyway, 'cos it doesn't matter as long as you're speaking French. Anyway, she thinks my name is Tom.'

'And why does she think that, Samuel?' asked Eleanor icily.

''Cos at the beginning of term, when she asked us for our names, we gave her the wrong ones. Tom sits next to me.'

'I hope he's better at French than you are,' said Jon.

Sam snorted with mirth. 'No, he's worse.'

'Perhaps that explains your poor reports.' Eleanor dabbed her mouth neatly. 'Things have certainly changed since my day.'

Jenny extracted a slim silver cigarette case from her bag and Lucy experienced a brief pang. So that's where it had gone! She could remember their mother using it in the days when smoking was more acceptable.

'Mind if I go outside for a cigarette?'

'Thought you'd given up.'

'I had but your lot have made me start again. I don't know how your poor mother copes.'

'By the way, dear, I've been meaning to ask you.' Eleanor put her tea cup down. 'Is that nasty woman still suing you?'

Lucy could have sunk through the floor. Eleanor had overheard her conversation with Mike about Alicia King and she'd been forced to give her a brief outline of what had happened. But she'd told Eleanor it was confidential.

Jenny shot her a furious look. 'As a matter of fact, she is.' She slipped on her jacket. 'But it's not something I wish to discuss. See you later on everyone. I think I'll give you some time to yourselves. I'll be back at the car by five. Eleanor, why don't you take Kate and Sam round town so Lucy and Jon can have some quality mother/son time?'

Lucy wouldn't have had the nerve to have got rid of her mother-in-law like that. But now, here they were, walking round Oxford together. Just her and her strapping, tall good-looking son. One to one time was so precious when you had three children, all of whom demanded your attention. And now she had to broach one of the trickiest subjects of all.

'Everything all right?' she asked as they stood outside the Bodleian, gazing up at its magnificent dome.

'Yeah, fine.'

'Finding it easier?'

'It's OK.'

'But it's better than it was before?'

'Sometimes. Not always.'

She wanted to slip her hand into his; reassure him like when he was a little boy and had cut himself.

'Has Peter been down?'

'Yeah. The other weekend. For a party. Oh and tell Kate to stop texting him, can you? He's not interested and she's driving him nuts.'

'Where did he stay?'

Stupid question.

'In my room. With a bunch of other guys who came down too.'

'Anyone I know?'

She tried to sound bright.

'Some of them. Greg. Harry.'

She vaguely remembered them from school. Nice boys. Quiet like Jon. One had a long-term girlfriend from the girls' school.

'Was it a good party?'

'OK.'

Just say it. Come out with it. Tell him it's all right and that you understand and that all that matters is that he's your son.

'Everything all right with you and Mike?'

The question took her by surprise.

'Yes, of course. Why?'

'Well, he's not here for a start. And you haven't talked much about him.'

'He's really busy at work. I told you he had to see a site in Bristol today.'

Jon took her arm as they walked along and she clung to him gratefully. 'You know, Mum, I wasn't sure about Mike at first. It was weird, after Dad. But I do like him now. He's a decent sort of chap.'

'Thanks.' She tried to swallow the big lump in the throat. 'Jon, there's something I want to ask you too. It's about . . .'

'MUM!'

A small bald figure waved in the distance.

'Please tell me,' said Lucy, squinting against the later afternoon sun, 'that that's not Sam.'

Jon laughed. It was a strange laugh, noticed Lucy. Hollow without mirth. 'What's he done to his hair this time?'

Twenty-six

'Row, row, row the boat, gently down the stream. Merrily, merrily, merrily. Life is but a dream.'

Christ, if she sang that one more time with the mother and toddler choir, she'd go bloody nuts. Life is just a dream? More like a fucking nightmare. How the hell did she, Chrissie Richards, former HR manager, on a salary of more than 60k, come to be sitting in a cold village hall with a non-speaking milk-sucker on her knee, surrounded by women who didn't know the difference between the conditional past tense and the present?

'So he goes to me, what do you mean you don't do dirty. That's wot I'm paying you for, innit. So I go . . .'

Chrissie stood up. Tracey's voice was grating on her sanity. Any minute now, and she'd open her mouth and scream. No wonder poor bloody Sting was yelling over there in the corner.

'Is he all right, do you think?' she ventured.

Tracey glared at the interruption. 'He's just pissed off because I took his iPod off him for giving me lip.'

The kid had an iPod at his age? Chrissie walked over to him (anything to relieve the boredom), George toddling along, his hand firmly manacled to hers as though sensing her desire to run off and leave all this.

'Sting, poppet, are you all right?' She knelt next to him. The child's face had turned beetroot with hot tears running down his face accompanied by two wonky lines of green snot. Through the yells, she could just about make out the words 'Want pod'.

'Would you like a drink, sweetheart?'

Sting nodded furiously, his tiny plaits bouncing.

'Dink, dink,' demanded George. It was his first and only

word. Not dad or mum but dink. And there was still no sign of a proper sentence.

'No, not that kind of drink,' she told George firmly. 'A proper grown up drink. Look. Watch Sting.'

She dropped 60p into the box next to the drinks container and handed Sting a plastic mug. The child drained it greedily before holding it out. 'More.'

'More, please,' she corrected, topping him up. 'Here you are, George, let's try this, shall we?'

Maybe he might actually do it after watching Sting, although his manners were hardly the type she wanted imitated. Carefully, she transferred the sugar-free juice into one of many training mugs she'd bought her son. 'Let's see what a clever boy you are,' she encouraged. 'That's right. Hold the handles that way. No, George, don't wave it around. No, don't throw it. No . . .'

Sting's yells drowned the repetition of 'Row the boat'. OmiGod! The two rivulets of green snot had turned bright scarlet and were dripping all over her and the wooden floor.

'What the fuck have you done to my son?' snarled Tracey racing over.

Chrissie scrabbled through her bag for a tissue and produced a ream of kitchen roll intended for emergency nasal or anal purposes. 'Please take this.'

'No thanks.' Tracey stood up, her son in her arms, still pouring blood. 'You're trouble, you are. You can't even look after your own kid properly, let alone anyone else's.'

'Hang on. I only came over to see to Sting because he was yelling and you were ignoring him, going on about your so-called tele-sales job.'

Tracey's eyes narrowed. 'What do you mean my so-called job?'

Chrissie snorted. 'Well, giving strange men verbal blow-jobs on the phone is hardly work, is it?'

Dumping Sting on the ground, Tracey advanced towards

her. Chrissie felt sick. 'Actually, it's extremely demanding, Miss High and Mighty. And what did you do before you had your retard?'

'Retard?'

'Well, he don't talk much, does he? And he can't drink out of a mug because you're still breastfeeding him. Disgusting, I call it. I'd hate to think what happens when you shut your front door.'

A cold feeling went down Chrissie's spine. 'What do you mean?'

Tracey grinned nastily. 'Well, he's covered in bruises, isn't he?'

'He's always falling over.'

She put her hands on her hips. 'That's what you say.'

'It's true.' Chrissie looked round for support. 'They all have accidents at this age, don't they?'

No one said anything. They all stared at her, or looked down on the ground or suddenly found a need to play with their kids instead of rabbiting on about their usual rubbish.

'I'm going.' Chrissie began to gather up George's things, fighting back hot angry tears. She should never have come here in the first place. She'd find somewhere else. There had to be something; some kind of group of mothers like her. Mothers who'd had interesting jobs; mothers with toddlers who were impossible; mothers with husbands who didn't come home early any more.

'Chrissie?'

She jerked her head up. Linda, a mild mother of twins who never ever raised her voice and whose children were always beautifully dressed and well-mannered, was hovering nervously. Chrissie's heart leaped with gratitude. Someone was standing up for her!

'Yes?' she said hopefully.

'I believe you owe the kitty another 30p.'

'Sorry?'

'For the drink. You took an extra drink but you didn't pay for it.'

Chrissie picked up George in one hand and her changing bag in the other. 'That was for Sting,' she spat. 'Ask his bloody mother to pay. She probably earns enough, giving men stiffs on the phone.'

And with that, she swept out of the village hall, slamming the doors behind her.

There was an unfamiliar car in the drive when she got back. A green sports car with a beige roof and smart alloy wheels. Had Martin finally got his new work car at last?

Disbelievingly, she watched the driver open his door and get out languidly in that way she remembered so well. Dan?

'Hi, Chrissie.'

'What are you doing here?'

'No need to shout. I was just passing and thought I'd drop in. Hey, you've been crying.' His face changed immediately and he touched her gently on the cheek with his forefinger. She should have moved but couldn't. 'What's wrong, Chrissie?'

'Nothing.' Her legs began to shake. Then the rest of her. And somehow – God knows how – she found herself sobbing into his shoulder, his expensive grey cashmere suited shoulder with his arms stroking her back just as they had done all those years ago.

'Just let it out,' he murmured. 'You'll feel better then.'

But nothing could shut out George's screams. 'I've got to get him out of the car.'

'I'll do it.'

And before she could stop him, he was unstrapping George with the ease of someone who had surely done this before. Even more amazingly, George had actually stopped crying. In fact, he was gurgling with laughter, tugging at Dan's lapels.

'I have this effect on kids,' he joked. 'They can see I'm one of them. Come on, George, let's get your mum in the house and make her a nice cup of tea.'

He remembered her son's name! Stunned, she followed him to the door, fishing in her bag for the keys. 'Why have you come here?' she managed to say.

'Because I didn't like the way we left it last time,' he said quietly, shutting the door behind them.

'You mean after supper?'

'No. I mean twenty-odd years ago.'

She waved her hand dismissively. 'Forget it.'

He caught it mid-air, forcing her to look at him. 'Don't you see, Chrissie. I can't. I haven't been able to. I can't tell you what it felt like to see you again. I was bowled over.'

'You seemed pretty cool about it.'

'That was because I hid it. And because I knew you'd be there.'

'What?'

He sighed. 'Patsy told me about Antony and his friends. She described some of you . . .'

'You mean she laughed about us.'

'No. Yes. All right. A bit, I suppose. But then she mentioned you. She's good on facts, Patsy and she even mentioned your surname. And that's when I realised you were part of this supper club thing.'

'But I'd got married. My name was different.'

'I know.'

'How?'

'Because it was in the university magazine. Under the alumni news. It even mentioned Great Piddington.'

'Did you tell Patsy you knew me?' Chrissie was still trying to get her head round this.

'Not then. But I was with her when Antony rang to say he had to look after his kids and that was why I offered to pick her up.'

'So you could see me?'

'So I could see you.'

'But why?'

Dan glanced down at George who was actually playing with his bricks round their feet instead of grizzling. 'I told you. I've never been able to put that . . . that stuff out of my mind.'

Chrissie bristled. 'That stuff, as you call it, almost ruined my life.'

He put a hand on her shoulder. Scorched, she moved away.

'Believe me, Chrissie, I'd do anything I could to make up for it.'

'There's nothing.' Her eyes filled with tears again. 'Not now.'

'Is that why you were crying when you pulled up outside?' he asked gently.

'Of course not.' She stepped over George and into the kitchen to put on the kettle. 'I had to shut that out of my head years ago or I'd have never coped.'

'Then why were you upset?'

'Because of some stupid woman.'

Briefly, she told him about the playgroup mafia.

'They don't sound like your kind of people.' He lounged against the kitchen surface, watching her. 'Why don't you go back to work?'

'Because I want to be a full-time mother. It's what George deserves.'

'Doesn't George deserve a mother who can be true to herself?'

She could feel him coming up behind her; felt the heat behind her, just like all those those years ago.

'Or,' he continued, 'is it because that's what Martin thinks you should do.'

Briefly, she thought of Martin who had been a latchkey kid when his own mother had worked and who'd been determined that his child wouldn't be the same. 'It's what we both want,' she added primly.

'And do you hit him?'

She spun round. 'George? Of course I don't.'

'Sorry. I couldn't help noticing the bruises on his legs.' A shadow passed across his face. 'It happens you know. My old man was always taking the lash to me and my mother wasn't averse to it either.' He laughed bitterly. 'It's why Patsy and I have stayed close. It was normal in our kind of world.'

'Yes,' she said wearily. 'I remember you telling me.'

At university, Dan had been the socialist she'd never met before. A leading light at the student union. He even banked at the Co-Op. She hadn't realised until then that you could do that.

'So,' Dan was looking around at her Shaker kitchen, 'I see you married the right kind of man.'

'We were lucky to get together,' she said, measuring the tea into the pot.

'Took you a while, though, didn't it. Only been married for three years, haven't you? That's right. The university magazine again. I told you I used to look out for you.'

'Because of guilt,' she shot back.

'Probably. Woah, son, you took me by surprise there.' He glanced up, grinning as George rushed past. 'Quick on his feet, isn't he?'

'Very,' said Chrissie grimly. 'You can't take your eyes off him for a minute. It's the most exhausting job I've ever done.'

'You do look tired.'

'Thanks very much.'

'No, I didn't mean it unkindly. I'm just worried about you.' She handed him tea in a spotty blue Emma Bridgewater mug and they sat down at the kitchen table while George clambered over Dan, tweaking his nose and hair. 'Well don't be. What about you? Did you ever get married?'

He shook his head. 'Never found the right woman. Well, I might have done, but she didn't feel the same way.'

She had to ask. 'Children?'

He shook his head. 'I wouldn't mind them now, though.'

She snorted. 'Then have them with Patsy. You said you were close. Or Jenny. You were clearly smitten with her.'

'Patsy's just a mate. Jenny's OK. But she's not my type.' He looked at her hard. 'I made a mistake, Chrissie. And sometimes I don't think I'm ever going to get over it.'

'Look, if you've come here to . . .'

He reached across the table and grasped her wrist tightly. It hurts, she wanted to say but the sheer shock of the physical contact, rendered her incapable of speech. 'Is he good?' he growled. 'Is he good in bed?'

'It's OK,' she said.

'OK? Is that all? Do you remember . . .'

'No.' She tugged her wrist away from him. 'No. Don't you understand. I've had to black it out so I could go on breathing. For years, I couldn't even sleep with anyone else and now I've found a good man. A nice man who won't let me down. So do me a favour. Get out of my life. Now.'

George began to grizzle and at the same time, the phone began to ring.

'I'll get it when you've gone.'

'It could be important.' He picked the receiver off the hook. 'Hello, the Richards' residence.'

How dare he? What if it was Martin?

'Yes, she's right here.'

'Hello?' It was difficult to hear above George's screams. 'What? In ten minutes? Well, if you really think it's necessary but George is starting to eat more solids now so I don't really think we need help. No, of course it's not inconvenient. We'll see you then.'

'Problem?'

'That was the health visitor. She wants to see me. Please go, Dan. I've got enough to cope with, without you turning up all guilty about something that happened too long ago.'

His eyes were boring into hers. 'But I need to know if you're all right. If you can forgive me.'

She sighed. 'Yes, I'm all right but no, I don't know if I forgive you. Now get out and mess up someone else's life.'

'Don't say that.' He looked out of the window. 'Your visitor's here already. Sure you don't want me to stay?'

Chrissie blanched. 'Shit. It's Martin. Quick, go out of the back door.'

Too late. Martin's key was in the lock. 'Hi, darling.' Chrissie flew to him, planting a kiss on his cheek.

'Whose car's in the drive?'

'Hi, Martin, it's me. Remember? Patsy's friend. I left my jacket behind after your supper party and Patsy arranged with Chrissie for me to pick it up.'

Martin's face was strained. 'What? Oh, right.'

Something was wrong. Did he suspect Dan?

'Well!' Dan clapped his hands together, making Chrissie jump. George gurgled, grabbing Martin's trousers. 'Yes, little man, I've got to go, I'm afraid.' He ruffled his head. 'See you again perhaps.'

Martin barely waited until the door had shut. 'Sit down. I've got something to tell you.'

'What's happened? Oh blast, the doorbell.'

'Leave it.'

'I can't.'

She'd forgotten about the health visitor!

'Mrs Richards, thank you for allowing us to visit.'

Chrissie felt a prickle of unease. The health visitor usually called her by her first name. She was also accompanied by an older stern woman in a navy blue suit. 'Not at all. This is my husband, Martin. Darling, this is Sandra, our health visitor.'

Martin nodded curtly.

'Ah, good. This makes it a bit easier, having your husband here.'

'What do you mean?'

The health visitor looked awkward. 'I'm afraid we've received a complaint.'

'Who from?'

'We can't say at this stage. But this person felt we ought to be aware that, in her view, someone is abusing George.'

She could feel the blood rushing to her face. 'It was that Tracey from mother and toddler, wasn't it? Just because George threw something at her son. It was an accident.'

'What do you mean "abusing"?' demanded Martin.

'I mean,' said the woman in the navy suit, 'that we have grounds for believing that George is being hit.'

'How dare you make such accusations.' Martin spoke in a low dangerous tone. 'And who are you anyway?'

'I represent social services.' The woman produced an ID wallet. 'We'd like to ask you some questions.'

Twenty-seven

Fantastic Fawn Foundation. She hadn't used it before. Nice colour. Smooth. Easy to get on with. Not like this cow.

'My face feels itchy.'

The woman, an aspiring A-list actress, had done nothing but complain since Patsy had started.

'Where?' Patsy continued sponging on the foundation.

'Here. On my cheekbones.'

They did look slightly red but then again Imogen had arrived with a decidedly ruddy complexion. Patsy always found it amusing when models turned up. The professional ones knew not to wear any make-up, so the artist had a clean pallet on which to start. Yet without it, many of these girls looked quite plain.

'I think I'm allergic to that foundation.' Imogen pointed a stubby finger at the bottle. Just as well they weren't here to photograph her hands, thought Patsy, regarding her bitten nails disapprovingly.

'I doubt it,' she said carefully. 'This range is specially developed for sensitive skin.'

'Well it's doing something to mine. I can feel it burning.' The girl grabbed a hand mirror.

Keep cool. 'If you're worried, we'll take it off and start again.'

'I told you to use my foundation.' The girl looked at her stonily. 'How long have you been qualified?'

Patsy forced herself to speak steadily. 'Nearly ten years. Now excuse me, my mobile is ringing. I'll be back in a moment.'

She hadn't spoken to Antony since last night. Ever since Alice had had her vodka-fest, Antony had become colder and distant. When she'd asked for housekeeping expenses last week, he'd muttered something about being more careful. This morning he'd had left for work before she woke up. And even though she'd kept her mobile on all day, he hadn't rung.

But it wasn't Antony.

'Can you say that again?'

Patsy could feel herself burning inside as the woman at the other end explained the situation.

'No. Of course not. Yes, I understand. I'll be there as soon as I can. Yes, within the hour. And please,' her voice trembled, 'please don't do anything until I arrive.'

Still shaking, she walked back into the studio and trance-like, gathered up her handbag and coat. 'Where are you going?' demanded the model.

Patsy had almost forgotten she was there. 'Sorry, something's come up. An emergency.'

She looked across at the photographer; his back was to her as he fiddled with the lighting. 'Tell Carl he'll need to find a replacement for me. By the way, looks like you're right about that foundation. There's a bit of a rash coming on.'

She heard the scream before she reached the door. But it wasn't important. Not compared with this.

They let her in immediately.

'We had to sedate him,' whispered the nurse urgently as she walked briskly up the stairs behind her. 'I told you last time, he needs to go to a more secure unit.'

'Just give me some time with him. I'll talk to him.'

The nurse pursed her lips. 'I've already called the doctor on duty. He's on his way.'

'Please. Five minutes.'

The woman nodded reluctantly. 'Do you want someone to go in with you?'

'No.' Patsy shook her head emphatically. 'He won't hurt me.'

Not any more, she thought, slipping into the room and

shutting the door behind her. He was lying on the bed, his back to her. Sulking. Just like he used to when Mum had been around. As usual, he was wearing black. It was the only colour he'd worn since the accident.

'Dad.' She pulled up a chair. 'It's me. Patsy.'

He didn't move.

She put out a hand to touch him but then drew it back. Why bother, said the voice inside her head, after everything he's done?

'You shouldn't have done that, Dad.'

'Done what?'

At first, his voice was so quiet, she hardly heard him.

'Lashing out at the assistant like that. She was only trying to give you your dinner.'

'Don't like peas.'

Patsy sighed. 'But that's no excuse for trying to attack someone. If you go on like this, you'll get thrown out and then you'll have to go somewhere where you've got less freedom. This is a nice place. It's costing me enough.'

Silence. Stupid, stubborn old man. Why, why couldn't he see she was trying to help? How she hated him. And yet something – God knows what – wouldn't or couldn't allow her to let him go.

'Dad? I know you can hear me.'

'Babs? Babs, is that you?'

Patsy froze. 'No, you know it's me, Patsy.'

He let out a low moan. 'I don't want Patsy. I want Babs.'

'She's not here, Dad. You know she's not.'

'Then find her for me. Find Babs and I'll be a good boy.'

Patsy stood up shaking. Maybe the nurse was right. Perhaps he did need to be moved to a more secure environment. Supposing, God forbid, he hurt someone. His mind was clearly going as well as his body . . . Ugh! She could smell something. Something horrible.

'Dad, do you want the toilet?'

He turned over; his face seemed more sunk than last time. She could almost move into his eye bags. 'Want the toilet? Not now.'

He grinned and she could feel the sick rising into her mouth.

'Aren't you going to clean me up, Babs?'

'Stop it.' She wanted to shake him. Shake him until he stopped breathing. 'Stop it. You know I'm not Babs. You know she's . . .'

'No.'

His hands reached out for her neck. Just in time, she caught them. His nails dug into her hands but she forced herself not to scream out. If he knew he was winning, he'd go on. 'Don't say that. Babs is coming to visit. She rang to tell me. She's coming next week. And then I won't need you any more.'

He let go of her hands, pushing her so she fell on the floor.

'Now get out. Get out, you little tart. Like mother, like daughter. It's your sister, I want. Not you. And don't bother coming back.'

She sat, stiff with shock, on the tube home, her mind whirling with possibilities.

'Dan?'

Her fingers had dialled his number automatically like they always did when she was in trouble.

'What's up?'

'I've just been to see Dad.'

His voice sharpened. 'And?'

'He's been causing trouble again.'

'Are they going to throw him out?'

'They've given him one more chance.'

She closed her eyes, remembering how she'd pleaded with the nurse, pressing a bundle of notes – the same notes Antony had given her earlier in the week – into her hand.

'But if he does it again, he's out.'

There was a silence. 'Dan, are you still there?'

'Yes. I'm thinking. You know, Patsy, maybe that might not be such a bad idea. Perhaps he should be somewhere more secure.'

'No. You know what happened last time. It nearly killed him. He's unstable too, thought I was . . . thought I was Babs. There's something else.' She hesitated. 'I hate to ask this.'

'Sorry, Patsy, I can't.'

'You don't know what I'm going to ask.'

'I do. You need more money for that place but I've had some heavy losses this month. Sorry.'

She sighed. 'I wish you wouldn't gamble.'

'Hey, you win some and lose some. I might be able to help next week or next month.'

Too late. 'Forget it. Got to go. Bye.'

She'd have to ask Antony. The bill was already overdue, as the nurse had curtly reminded her. But if she did ask Antony, he'd want to know what she'd done with the last lot. And then she'd either have to tell him or lie or do what she used to do . . . No, anything but that.

Patsy sighed as she ran up the stairs to her flat. She was tired of making things up. Tired of pretending. Maybe she would tell Antony the truth.

'What's going on? Antony? Why are these cases in the hall?'

Her throat tightened; she felt sick. He was finally leaving her . . .

'Hi, Patsy.'

A solemn-eyed little girl was sitting at the kitchen bar, dipping a teaspoon into a jar of peanut butter. Matt was sitting next to her, eyes glued to the small television on the counter. Antony was opening a bottle of wine.

'What's going on,' she whispered fiercely. 'Why are you going?'

'Going?' he frowned.

'The suitcases. In the hall.'

'They're the kids'.' Putting his arm round her, he led her

out into the hall. 'Maggie's not well. She's finding all this too difficult to cope with. So I thought it might help if we had the kids for a few days to give her a break.'

'They'll have to double up on the sofa.'

He shrugged. 'It's only for a few days.'

'But I haven't got enough food. I'll need more money.'

'That's not a problem.' He pulled her to him. 'I knew you'd understand.'

She was torn between relief that he wasn't going and shock at the kids. 'OK. They can stay, I suppose. But you'll have to take them to school; that sort of stuff. I've got jobs lined up all next week.'

'Sure. Oh and by the way, there was a message for you.'

He handed her a piece of paper. Patsy's blood froze as she read the name. 'I've got to make a call,' she said. 'Shut the door, can you?'

She waited until it had clicked shut before punching in the numbers.

'Drydale Clinic. Nurse Brown speaking.'

'It's Patsy. I've just got your message. Is everything all right?'

'No, it's not.'

The clinical tone made her freeze with fear.

'He hasn't hurt someone again, has he?'

'No.'

'Then what?'

All kinds of scenarios were running round Patsy's head.

'When we went in to give him his supper, the door was locked.'

'But he doesn't have a key.'

'He'd pushed the bed against the door.' The nurse sounded as though she was getting pleasure from this. 'When we finally managed to get in, the window was open. Your father has gone.'

Twenty-eight

He hadn't rung. Just like the others, thought Jenny dully, pretending to tidy her desk. Somehow, she'd thought Dan was different. That interested glint in his eyes; the way he'd declined coffee because (she'd thought) he didn't want to take it too fast.

Two weeks ago now. Too long to make any excuses.

What did she do to them to put them off? Was she too keen? And why didn't she feel anything for the men who did show interest in her?

'Jenny.' Lily was hovering. 'Can I have a word please?'

That was all she needed! Lily had been acting extremely oddly for the last few weeks. Take that night when she'd left an answerphone message, asking Jenny to ring her urgently over the weekend. When she had, Lily had said it didn't matter any more. Since then, she'd been withdrawn but polite. Either she wanted a rise or else had personal problems. Well, join the gang.

'Give me five minutes, can you, Lily? I've got a couple of urgent calls to make.'

Lily shrugged prettily. 'All right.'

Jenny picked up the phone, waited until Lily left the room and then put it down again. She ought to ring her sister but it had been difficult talking to her after the Oxford trip and Lucy's revelation about first Jon and then Luke. Of course Jon was gay but she hadn't expected his mother to take it so coolly. As for Luke being gay too . . . She'd heard bereavement made you see the deceased differently sometimes, but this was plain daft.

Jenny buried her head in her hands. Work! That was what she had to do to block it out. It was the only thing she was good at. At least it had been until that bloody woman had threatened to sue. Still, as her solicitor had said when she had finally managed to get hold of him, there hadn't been a formal letter yet. 'In all likelihood, Mrs King will have contacted her own solicitor and been told there wasn't a case. Yes, I know it was unfortunate about the colouring. But as you said yourself, it all washed out.'

Meanwhile, she needed to ring Alan. He wanted her to organise some kind of winter cruise on the Tyne to celebrate his company's fiftieth anniversary. Cruises were so naff. But work was money. She couldn't afford to turn it down.

'Alan. It's Jenny.'

'Hiya, lass. How are you doing?'

His warm voice always made her feel better. He was the kind of youngish uncle that she could have done with right now.

'Fine, thank you. I've got my ticket organised for tomorrow so I'll get a taxi from the station and meet you at the office.'

'You're not getting any taxi, lass. I'll be there to pick you up.'

'Honestly, there's no need.'

'Nonsense! Us northerners are famous for our hospitality. You said you hadn't been here before. Well, I'm going to show you what you've been missing. Believe me, when you see the Quayside, you'll know you haven't lived.'

Jenny suppressed a sigh. Why was it that people from certain parts of the country, be it Wales or Scotland or the North, always had this chip on their shoulder about southerners 'not knowing what they missed'. It was almost an evangelical crusade.

'I'm looking forward to it.'

'Just one thing, lass.' Alan chuckled down the line. 'Make sure you bring plenty of warm clothes. It's a bit nippy up here at this time of the year.'

Jenny put down the phone and pressed the intercom button. 'Lily. Do you want to come in now?'

'Actually, I'm rather busy on the Macintyre account. Can we leave it?'

'Well, yes, if you want.'

'Thanks.'

Lily's voice sounded small.

She ought to ask her assistant out for a drink after work; find out what was bugging her. But not tonight. She was knackered. Her hand hovered over the phone. She could ring Dan now. Make-up some excuse. Suggest a drink. All he had to do was say no. She'd had enough rejections in her time. What was one more?

'Hi. This is Dan. Sorry I can't take your call but leave a message and I'll . . .'

Quietly, Jenny replaced the receiver.

'Er, have you got a minute?' Lily was hovering again and Jenny forced herself to smile warmly. 'Yes, Lily. Changed your mind, have you? Look, I've got about ten minutes before my next meeting.'

'No.' Lily was holding a large white envelope. 'This just got delivered by special delivery.'

Jenny's mouth went dry. Of course, it could be anything. She had lots of things that were sent by special delivery. It might be something about the cruise ships she'd been researching for Alan's jaunt along the Tyne. It might be the Christmas party information for that big bash at Syon House. It might be . . . shit. Shit.

'What's wrong?' asked Lily.

Jenny felt her chest tighten. 'It's that bloody Alicia King. She said she'd sue and she is. She claims two of her staff have been sick since the event and she's blaming that green dye.'

Lily frowned, crinkling her pretty face. 'What kind of "sick"?'

'She doesn't say.' Jenny was already punching numbers into the phone. 'But I do know that we need help with this one. Fast.'

It was a long train journey. Incredible, mused Jenny, looking out at the changing landscape, how you could actually feel the weather turn, the further up you went. They'd just got to York and already she felt frozen, despite her cashmere jumper. 'Buy some thermals,' Lucy had advised. Jenny had scoffed at the idea but now wished she'd listened.

Still, it was beautiful. She had to grant Alan that. The fields and woods seemed to go on for ever in a rugged splendour that was completely different from the softer lushness of Surrey where she and Lucy had grown up. But it still wasn't enough to take her mind off that bloody legal letter.

'I need time before we can respond to this,' her solicitor had said. 'There are various ways in which we can approach it. To begin with, I need to examine the medical reports which were enclosed and . . .'

'I looked at them,' interrupted Jenny, 'and they don't say anything specific. One of them mentions 'slight' hair loss. Well they can't sue me for much over that, can they?'

'That depends. Hair problems are tricky because they can have long-lasting effects. I once acted for a client who suffered minor hair loss after a perm which then led to serious alopoecia in the subsequent months. We also need to contact the manufacturers of the plastic toy involved. It might well be that they are liable and not you. In the meantime, I'm afraid the only option is for you to sit tight and wait.'

Jenny was incapable of doing that at the best of times. Maybe it was just as well she had this trip up to Newcastle to distract her. She only hoped Lily was capable of running the office in her absence. When she got back, she'd have to have a serious talk with her; find out exactly what was wrong.

It took about an hour of going through the notes she'd made last night for her meeting with Alan, before Jenny was satisfied. Her legs were aching. She ought to give them a stretch; maybe walk up to the buffet car to get a coffee. Bloody hell. What was that?

Riveted, she leaned towards the window. An enormous arc of a bridge stretched its arm up towards the sky. It was like nothing she had ever seen before. Proud, stunning, metallic.

'Excuse me.' She looked across at the older woman sitting on the other side of the table. 'Can you tell me what that is?'

'It's the new Millennium Bridge.' The woman spoke in a clipped Home Counties accent. 'Rather impressive, isn't it? And over there, is the Tyne Bridge.'

Jenny gazed down at the glistening water below. 'It's incredible. I hadn't realised . . .'

She stopped. The woman was smiling. 'That's how I felt when I first saw it.'

'Do you live here?'

'Only for the past ten years. It's different. Very different from Guildford where I lived before. But I'd never go back, I can tell you that. People are friendlier and the pace of life is much calmer. There's time to enjoy life.'

Time to enjoy life? Jenny had to suppress a laugh. That was one luxury she simply couldn't afford.

Alan was as good as his word. He was there, on the platform virtually waiting outside her carriage as she stepped off. How had he known which part of the train she'd be on?

'It's a big station,' she breathed, taking in the huge almost Gothic looking skylights and maze of ramps and slopes leading to a web of platforms.

'Aye, it is that.' He took her case and, touching her arm lightly, guided her through to the exit. A navy blue Jaguar was waiting by the exit. As they approached, the driver sprang out and opened the back door. 'Thought you might like to check in to your hotel first, lass. You're probably tired after the journey.'

'That would be lovely. Thank you.'

'I've booked you in at the Malmaison.'

Mmm. Rather a nice hotel if the others in the chain were anything to go by.

Meanwhile, she couldn't stop staring out of the window at a row of rundown shops which were then – as they swung round the corner – replaced with some very smart boutiques that she wouldn't have minded stopping off at. Gosh, it was cold! No wonder everyone seemed bent over in the wind. It was like being on the edge of the world.

'After we've had a spot of lunch, I thought we'd go down to the Quayside and check out the boats.'

Jenny pulled her file out of her briefcase. 'Absolutely. I've got a range of appointments lined up and I've also researched into the bands. I had another idea too. How about a themed party? Maybe with some kind of nautical topic?'

Alan was nodding. 'Sounds good. I've only got one stipulation.'
'What's that?'

'That everyone enjoys themselves. That's what it's all about.'
Yeah, yeah.

'Because,' said Alan, looking out through the window, 'there are some folks in this life who've forgotten how to do that.' He looked back at her. 'Don't you think?'

They had lunch at a nearby rooftop restaurant which, Alan assured her, had the best view of the city for miles around. The food was laid out like a painting on her plate and the scallops literally melted in her mouth.

'Sure you don't want a glass of wine?' asked Alan.
'No, thanks. I like to keep a clear head for work.'

'Well I hope you won't regard tonight as work. I've booked us in for supper at Sharrow Bay.'

'The Sharrow Bay? Where Paul McCartney proposed to Heather, depending on which magazines you read?'

His eyes twinkled. 'I take it you've never been. Good! I was hoping to surprise you. Surely you've worked out my intentions by now?'

No! Please no. He was ancient, with teeth too straight to be real. And married, don't forget.

'I'm determined,' he continued, 'that you should go back home, telling everyone how grand it is up north.'

She relaxed. 'I don't think you need have any worries about that.'

★   ★   ★

They looked at five possible boats; three weren't suitable because of the gawdy décor. The fourth was all right but the fifth really stood out. The captain had a calm professional attitude and didn't call her 'love' like the others. And the bar was sleek with plenty of room for dancing in the lounge. She checked on details like safety records and registration and the captain wasn't offended (unlike some of the others) when she asked to look at the documents.

'I think this is the one,' she said quietly to Alan as they took the stairs to the upper deck.

'I agree. Just one thing. About the band. I know you've found a couple you want to look at but a mate of my nephew – the wife's nephew actually – has recently started a jazz band and I'd like to give him a chance.'

Jenny could feel her spirits sinking. 'Are you sure? I mean I understand that you want to give him a chance but this is a big occasion.'

Alan nodded. 'Trust me on this one, Jenny.'

'Can I hear them?'

'You certainly can. On the way to Sharrow Bay tonight. By the way, lass, hope you don't mind me saying but you look a bit tense. Noticed that when you got off the train. Anything wrong?'

For a mad moment, Jenny felt like confiding in Alan; telling him about the legal letter. Even telling him about Lucy and her troubles.

'Not at all,' she replied tightly. 'Just a little tired from the journey, that's all.'

It took an hour to get to Sharrow Bay which turned out to be in the Lake District. Jenny hadn't realised there was so much wonderful countryside within an hour of Newcastle. Previously, she had just imagined it as a sprawling city with nothing much else.

'Where are we stopping to see your nephew's band?' she asked as Alan took a hairpin bend in his stride.

'We're not.' He leaned across and pressed a switch. 'I've got them on CD. Don't worry about these bends. Thought I'd take you on the scenic route. I know it's dark but you can still get some kind of an idea. These fields go on for miles. See that farm over there? No neighbours. Nothing. When they get snowed in, they can't get out for weeks. Last winter they had to have supplies dropped off by helicopter. And over there is Hadrian's Wall.'

She strained through the darkness.

'You won't be able to see it now but we'll come back another time.'

Another time? She almost said something but stopped as a rich, gravelly voice boomed through the stereo. The kind of rich gravel that sent her blood cold and hot at the same time. 'Ole man river, he can't stop turning . . .'

'I love this song,' she said, entranced. 'My father used to have the Paul Robeson recording.'

Alan nodded. 'Did your father like jazz?'

Jenny turned away. 'I believe so. But he left when we were small. I only know about the record because he left it behind.'

'When my wife died,' Alan said slowly, 'I played all her favourite music. It made me feel she was still with me.'

'I'm sorry. I hadn't realised . . . I mean I know you said your wife had been ill.'

He kept his eyes firmly on the road. 'She passed away five years ago.'

A year after Lucy lost Luke. So who was the Doris he'd referred to in their earlier meetings. A girlfriend?

'Now, see over there?'

Through the darkness, she could see light glistening on water.

'That's Ullswater. We're nearly there.'

Jenny had been to some wonderful restaurants in her time but Sharrow Bay was unlike anywhere she'd visited before. Fleetingly, she wondered what it would be like to stay in what was one of the most famous hotels in England. They had drinks in a wonderful room with the kind of squashy sofas and chairs where you could stay all day, especially if it was raining. There were even copies of *Country Life* for those couples who had run out of conversation, although with Alan this was impossible. He knew so much and came out with such fascinating facts that Jenny felt quite dim. But the most stunning feature of the room was that an entire wall was made of glass. Through it, was the lake, lit up with outside lights. It was like looking at a cinema screen.

'It's even more amazing during the day when you can see the steamers and the pine trees,' said Alan excitedly. 'I was here the other week for lunch; we could have easily stayed here instead, admiring the view.'

We? She was tempted to probe but the waiter was hovering, indicating their table was ready. 'This is amazing,' she breathed as they sat at their table in the bay window overlooking the lake.

Alan looked pleased. 'It's not easy to get these tables with a view but they know me here.'

Jenny, who rarely ate much after 6 p.m. in order to maintain her size 10, had told herself she'd just pick at the food. But everything – from the salmon to the peach sorbet to 'clear the palate' – was so delicious and beautifully presented that she actually found herself having chocolate soufflé for pudding as well.

'That was amazing,' she said over coffee.

'It is a rather special place,' agreed Alan.

There was a slight pause. 'Want to go over the details again?' she ventured.

'No. I think we've covered everything.'

'I'll send out the invitations next week.'

'That'll be grand.'

What happens now, Jenny wondered. It had been a nice meal and Alan was good company but there was something that wasn't quite right. At times she thought he seemed too friendly but then again that was probably his northern hospitality. And there were other times when he was positively distant like now, as he looked out over the lake, his face set in an inscrutable pose.

She stood up. 'Just going to find the Ladies.'

He was up in an instant, pulling back her chair. 'Of course.'

The Ladies turned out to be the kind of boudoir where she could stay all night. Rose chintz wallpaper; deep chair with magazines on a table next to it; nice hand lotion. Perfect for an escape. In some ways, she would give anything to stay up here and not go back to face this terrible, scary legal action. What would happen if it went to court? Even if Alicia King didn't win, the legal expenses could wipe her out. Everything she'd worked for, could go down the plughole just like that.

She'd better check her phone in case the solicitor had rung. Yes!

Jenny! It's me. Dan. I got a missed call from you. Listen, I wondered if you were doing anything tomorrow night? Give me a bell.'

Twenty-nine

'You can make it, can't you? Chrissie, are you still there?'

George's yells had swelled to a crescendo in the background. Heavens, how she remembered those days! Poor Chrissie. It was hard enough having three tricky teenagers but a screaming toddler wasn't something she'd want to cope with again. That reminded her. She was out of Bach's Rescue Remedy for Sam.

'Sorry. What was that?'

'You can make it, can't you? On the 15th. At Mike's place.'

'Why Mike's?'

Lucy sighed. Something was definitely up with Chrissie nowadays. When they'd met for a brief coffee the other week, she'd had the impression that Chrissie's mind was on something else.

'We're having supper at Mike's to get away from Eleanor.'

'She's not still with you?'

'I told you that when we met last week. Don't you remember? Her latest excuse about not going home is that her house is cold.'

'And I suggested you turned down your own heating so she didn't feel so cosy at your place,' added Chrissie.

'Yes,' said Lucy, relieved. So she did remember. 'Chrissie, is something wrong?'

'Why?' She spoke sharply.

'It's just that you seem rather preoccupied at the moment.'

'Well, I am, aren't I? Anyone would be with this child. I can't sleep because he won't sleep unless he's in bed with us and then he wriggles all night. So Martin gets up and goes to the spare room and I still can't sleep. And then during the day,

George either grizzles or wants to suck off me like some kind of giant leech. Look, Lucy, I've got to go. The health visitor is coming round.'

'Again? I must say, they make more visits than they did in my day.'

'Yes, well . . .' Chrissie sounded quiet. 'Actually, I wanted to ask you about that. Did you ever . . .'

'Mum, Mum! Where did you put my jeans?'

'Chrissie, can you hang on a minute?'

'It doesn't matter.'

'I'll only be a second.'

'No. That woman's going to be here soon. Ring when you have time for me.'

'But I always have time for you,' began Lucy.

Too late. Chrissie had put down the phone.

'Mum!' Kate burst in through the door. 'Where've you been? I've been looking for you everywhere. I need my jeans!'

'They're in the tumble drier. Ready in a minute.'

'I need them now.' Kate was already pulling them out of the drier.

'You can't! They're not dry.'

'I don't care. I'm going out. See you later.'

Lucy heard the door slam. Two down and one to go. Sam was still in bed which wasn't unusual on a Saturday morning although since the hair incident (her youngest had just gone into an Oxford barber's and demanded a 'number one' as part of a school dare), it was still a shock every time she looked at him. Was that one really hers? Children! Can't live without them and can't live with them. Poor Chrissie. If she thought it was bad now, wait until George got his head shaved or turned gay.

No, she wouldn't think about that now. Besides, Jon had seemed a bit happier on the phone recently. Going down to Oxford and taking him out to lunch had definitely been a good idea. It would have been nice to have had that chat about his 'sexual preferences', as one of the textbooks she was reading had put it, but as Mike said, it would happen when the time was right.

In a way, she'd been relieved. How on earth does one start that kind of conversation? 'Darling, I've been thinking. Are you gay? Because if you are, it's fine by me. And if you're not, well that's fine too.'

'Ah, Lucy, there you are! I was just wondering where you kept your cleaning materials, dear. I'd like to take a bath but there's been a rather nasty rim around it for the past few days. I would have thought it would have gone by now.'

'Really? Lucy gritted her teeth. 'Well, I'm sorry to hear that. I have been a bit behind with cleaning recently. I'll do it in a minute.' Counting to five to calm herself, she began leafing through her collection of Mary Berry books.

'Trying to find a recipe for your next supper party, dear?' Eleanor stood over Lucy's shoulder. 'I must say, I don't think very much of these so-called nouveau cuisine dishes. I always think it's hard to beat something a more traditional meal such as a roast.'

'Antony's girlfriend is a vegetarian,' pointed out Lucy.

'How very silly of her.'

'We're all entitled to our preferences.'

Eleanor sniffed. 'There are too many choices nowadays, if you ask me.'

Lucy thought fleetingly of Jon and Luke.

'Are you having dinner here, dear?'

'No. At Mike's.'

'Goodness me. Does he have the right kind of equipment to cook with?'

'Mike is very well organised. And he's been used to cooking for himself for years.'

'Really? I must say, I'd like to see his house.'

She was fishing for an invitation to supper. Lucy had felt guilty before about leaving Eleanor behind when she and Mike went out. 'Well, if you'd like to come,' she heard herself say, 'you'd be very welcome. Although . . .'

Eleanor clapped her hands together with pleasure. 'I would love that. But on one condition. You must let me cook the main course. No, I insist. It will take the pressure off you. And I must say, Lucy dear, although I hope you won't mind me saying this. You have looked extremely strained recently. I do hope nothing is wrong with you and Mike.'

'Of course not.' Lucy bristled. 'I've just had a lot on my plate recently. In fact, I've got to go into the office now.'

'On a Saturday?'

'Yes. Sorry. Maggie's been doing the early stint and I promised to take over from her. I'll be back by lunchtime.'

'If you must, dear. But don't forget the bath, will you?'

Such a cheek! And more fool her, as Jenny would say if she was here, to give in by cleaning the bath when she should be on her way to work. Sometimes Lucy wished she was more assertive, like her sister. Instead, here she was, rubbing away at the rim round the bath which showed little sign of giving in. Oh well, she'd tried. Better empty the bathroom bin while she was at it. It was one of those deep stainless steel bins where tissue and cotton wool and everything else got stuck to the bottom. She ought to line it but . . . OhmiGod!

Eleanor burst in through the door as though she'd been standing on the other side checking. 'What's wrong, dear? Oh my goodness. It's a long time since I've seen one of those. I would have thought Michael would have the decency to have wrapped it up.'

'It's not Mike's,' said Lucy faintly. 'We don't . . . I mean . . .'

Eleanor's lips tightened. 'Well there's only one other male member in the family.'

Lucy was gingerly wrapping it up in loo paper. 'I'll go and have a word with him.'

Some hope. Her youngest son was buried under the duvet

where she knew from experience that no amount of prodding would stir him on a Saturday morning.

'Sam. Listen to me.'

He grunted.

'Please!'

'Go away.'

'Look what I've found!'

He squinted open one eye. 'What?'

'It's a . . . well you know . . . a condom! What were you doing with one?' Suddenly, she remembered the party. Had she cleaned the bin since then? A wave of panic overtook her. 'You didn't . . . someone didn't . . .'

'Shut up, Mum. It was mine. It's what people call a "posh wank".'

'A what?'

'Self-use, Mum. Stop freaking out. Anyway, think how I feel when I hear you and Mike.'

Oh, God, he didn't, did he? Lucy tried to say something and failed. She'd often thought there was a real irony in the fact that although teenagers were desperate to have sex themselves, they couldn't bear the idea of their parents doing it. And as for her doing it with someone who wasn't their real father . . .

'Well, what did he have to say for himself?' Eleanor's eyes were gleaming with anticipation as she came downstairs.

She flushed. 'It was quite innocent. He was . . . er . . . experimenting. It's quite natural you know, Eleanor. Boys think about that sort of thing all the time.'

'Well!' Eleanor was pink with righteous indignation. 'Things really have gone downhill, haven't they? Just as well I'm staying for a bit, isn't it?'

Maggie looked up from her desk at Right Rentals. 'What are you doing here? It's my morning, isn't it?'

Lucy sank into a chair. 'I know but I had to get out of the house. Sam's being . . . well Sam, and Eleanor's driving me mad.

She's always there, demanding this and that. She does it in a perfectly polite way but the house just isn't my own any more.'

'Just ask her to go home.'

'I can't.'

'You're too good to her. My mother-in-law hasn't so much as rung me since Antony scarpered. Honestly. Married for twelve years, we were. Twelve years of enduring Christmases with her, remembering birthdays, taking her out for lunch. And now she drops me, just like that. She hasn't even rung her grandchildren to see if they're all right.'

Lucy was shocked. 'That's dreadful.'

'I know. And now I bet Antony's taken his floozy round to meet her. Well she's welcome to the telly that's always on and the bloody budgerigar that won't shut up and the . . .'

'Shhh, shh, it's all right.' Lucy drew her weeping friend towards her. 'It will be all right, you know.'

'Will it?'

'Yes, it will.'

Maggie blew her nose. 'What's she like? I mean I know she's pretty because I saw her but is she bright?'

Lucy floundered for the right words. 'She's definitely not stupid.'

'Do they look as though they have wild sex?'

'Look, Mags. Let's just leave this conversation, shall we? It won't help you.'

Maggie had sniffed. 'So they do then.'

Lucy tried not to recall how Antony had crawled all over Patsy, almost grazing on her. 'She seems to like him.'

'And does everyone like her?'

'What do you mean "everyone"?'

'Everyone at these cosy little suppers you've been holding with Chrissie and Jenny.'

'Well, we haven't had that many. Look, we're having a meal at Mike's next week. Why don't you come?'

'With those two?'

'I won't ask them.'

'You've probably already done so, haven't you?'

'Well, yes. But I can un-ask them somehow.'

'Don't be silly. Anyway, I'm not sure I fancy your sister's company, to be honest. She's getting worse, isn't she? Does she sharpen her tongue on those fancy nail files she carries in her handbag?'

Lucy giggled, despite herself.

'And I'm quite worried about Chrissie. I bumped into her the other day and that kid's legs were covered with bruises. You don't think anything's going on there, do you?'

'No,' said Lucy uneasily. 'She's not like that.'

Maggie snorted. 'That's what I thought about Antony. Anyway, getting back to your invitation, I might be doing something else.'

'That's great! What?'

Maggie sounded flat again. 'Don't get too excited. It's just this social group I've joined. It's not a dating agency or anything like that. Just a group of people on their own. We go to the theatre or out for a meal. That sort of thing.'

'Well let me know if you don't go. We'd love to have you round. Actually, I'm really worried about Chrissie. I don't think she's coping very well with George.'

Maggie laughed hoarsely. 'That's where we went wrong. It was all right with one but when Alice came along, Antony couldn't handle the mad frenetic pace of family life. He's a kid himself. Needs to be number one.'

'A lot of them do,' said Lucy quietly.

'Why? Is Mike like that?'

'Sometimes. He's very good at understanding my needs, although recently he's been really wrapped up in work. But he's also very good at thinking he knows what's right for my kids.'

'And he's not a father himself, so how can he know.' Maggie finished off the sentence for her.

Lucy nodded. 'I know it's unfair but I hate it when he tells them off. He had a real go at Sam the other day for not tidying his bedroom. And although he's right, I do think he expects too much of them. Teenagers are untidy and Sam's room wasn't that bad.'

'Can't be easy for him, though, can it?'

'I suppose not.'

'And you've probably got used to being on your own and doing things your way.'

Lucy fleetingly considered her habit of leaving on lights because she didn't like the dark. In Mike's book, you switched off lights when you left a room and only put them on when you went in. 'Maybe you're right.' Opening her Inbox – she really didn't want to talk about this any more – Lucy ran down the messages. 'Anything important happened this morning?'

'Two viewings and one cancellation. Oh and the cheque from the couple in Acorn Drive bounced so I've been trying to get hold of them. Mrs Thomas has finally left Abbotts Road thank goodness but no one else seems to want it.'

'Anything else?'

'Yes. What did she cook?'

Lucy looked up from the file. 'What?'

'What did this Patsy woman cook when you went over there? The night she tried to get my kids drunk.'

'She didn't try . . .' Lucy began. 'Why do you want to know what she cooked?'

Maggie looked out of the window. 'Curiosity, I suppose.'

'Well she didn't. It was all ready-made apart from the fruit salad which was so stringy that we almost choked.'

Maggie broke out into a big smile. 'Good.'

Lucy felt a wave of relief. It was so nice to see her friend laugh again.

'Maybe, when the sex has worn his course, he'll come home.' Maggie's eyes lit up. 'He always said he loved my cooking.'

'Would you take him back?'

'The kids need a resident father and I don't like being on my own. I have to have a radio on in every room, you know, so I can hear voices.' She paused. 'Wouldn't you take Mike back if he did something awful?'

Lucy hesitated, thinking about how odd he'd been recently; cold one minute and warm the next. He wasn't the type to have an affair but that's what they'd all thought about Antony.

'I don't know,' she said slowly. 'I honestly don't know.'

She could hear the arguing before she'd even got to the front door. It was Kate, yelling at someone – presumably Sam. So much for the jolly Saturday family lunch she'd planned after a heavy morning in the office.

'What's going on?' she asked lightly, taking her coat off in the hall.

Kate's eyes were flaming. 'He's broken my favourite Westlife CD.'

'Did Sam mean to?'

'It wasn't Sam. It was your boyfriend.' Kate spat his name out. 'Mike.'

Lucy went into the kitchen, hotly pursued by Kate. 'Well I'm sure he didn't do it on purpose.'

'I didn't.' Mike was standing at the Aga, stirring cheese sauce. 'But if Kate hadn't left it on the floor, I wouldn't have stood on it. I keep telling them not to be so untidy.'

'We're not.' Kate's voice kept rising. 'You ought to be more careful in other people's homes.'

'Kate!' Lucy could hardly believe what she was hearing. 'That's very rude. You know that Mike lives in both houses. When he's sold his, he'll be moving in here. I'm sure that all we need to do is reach some kind of compromise.'

Kate swigged defiantly out of a family-size Coke bottle. 'Well I hope he never sells his house.'

'"He", as you put it,' said Mike drily, 'has actually just done so. This morning.'

'Darling!' Lucy flung her arms round his neck. 'That's wonderful.'

'Is it?' growled Kate.

Mike shrugged. 'Well, I don't have to move in here. I can rent somewhere.'

'Good idea.'

'Kate. Mike. Please. Both of you.' Lucy sat down heavily at the kitchen table. 'I know this is a difficult time. But we can work this out. Kate, I'd like a word with you upstairs please. Mike, that smells amazing. I'll be down in one second.'

'Why can't we just stay on our own?'

Kate was sitting on the bed, her back to Lucy.

'Because I love him, Kate.' She went up to her daughter, stroking her hair. 'I know it's difficult for you but we have to accept it. Dad's not coming back. Do you want me to be alone for the rest of my life?'

'Suppose not.'

'I thought you liked Mike.'

'He's OK. At least I thought he was. But in the last few weeks, he's been really snappy. It's like he put on a good front for us at first and now he's showing his true colours.'

Lucy felt a twinge of unease. 'He's worried about work. Business isn't as good as it was.'

'There's no need for him to be horrid to us.'

'He isn't, is he?'

'He really snapped at Sam when you were out. He wouldn't let me make that cheese sauce, even though he knows I love cooking. And he wasn't that friendly to Jon when he rang.'

'Jon rang? He didn't tell me that. When?'

'Just after you went.'

'What did he say?'

'I dunno. You'll have to ask your boyfriend.'

Lucy sighed. 'Look, Kate. Why don't you have some time to yourself up here and come down for lunch in a minute.'

'I'm not hungry.'

'Please.'

'I'll think about it.'

Mike was still in the kitchen. 'You didn't tell me Jon rang.'

'Oh, yes. Sorry. I forgot about it when Kate had her little tantrum.'

Lucy felt a rush of irritation. 'It wasn't a little tantrum. It's a big thing for them.'

Mike carried on stirring the cheese sauce. 'Then as I said, I'll rent.'

'No.' Lucy put her arms around his back. 'I want you here. We can be a proper family then.'

He moved away from her to get the Parmesan. 'Only if we establish some proper family rules.'

'We will. Still, that's great news about the house, isn't it? How much did they offer?'

He told her.

'That's not bad. And you accepted?'

'I did. The only trouble is that they want to exchange by the end of the month and complete a week afterwards.'

'That's fast. You'll need to start selling some of the furniture.'

'We'll have to decide what we want and don't want. I thought my sofas would look good here.'

Lucy felt a prickle of unease. 'The chrome and cowhide ones?'

'They're really comfortable, don't you think? I only got them last year.'

But I can't stand them, she wanted to cry. I like my Laura Ashley chintz sofas.

'Do you think they'll go with my furniture?' she ventured.

Mike shrugged. 'We'll have to see. It's a small detail, isn't it? And like you said earlier, we all have to compromise. Now, taste this sauce, pet. I thought I'd try it out for when everyone comes over to my place next weekend. Achoo!'

'Have you got a cold?'

Mike was blowing his nose. 'No, it's that dog.'

'What do you mean?'

'I've told you before, pet. I'm sure I'm allergic to him. Must be his fur. I never used to sneeze like this.' He blew his nose again. 'That's another thing we're going to have to think about, pet. OK?'

Thirty

Neither of them felt like going to Mike's for different reasons. Martin didn't want the others to know he'd been made redundant. And Chrissie didn't want to leave George.

'Everyone else uses babysitters! We're both going to go mad if we don't have some time without him.'

'I suppose,' said Chrissie, rejecting a too-tight pair of evening trousers and wishing she had followed that baby magazine diet more closely, 'that that's why the health visitor suspected us of beating him up.'

'Look, we've been through this. They're keeping an eye on us, that's all. You can see their point. They have to, in today's day and age. And anyway, Dr Smith's on our side.'

Chrissie wasn't sure of that. After that terrifying visit from social services, she had rung the doctor in tears. It transpired that Dr Smith had already been asked to make a report. Chrissie wasn't allowed to see what was in it but Dr Smith had assured her that everyone had their best interests at heart and that, yes of course, toddlers were always falling over but being a parent could be a very stressful job.

In the meantime, the health visitor made regular visits 'just to check that everything was all right'. This made Chrissie paranoid about George falling over and getting more bruises.

'Supposing he hurts himself when we're out,' she wailed while searching in her drawer for some mascara; something she hadn't worn for months. Why bother to look good when most of your body was smeared with baby gunk?

'He won't.' Martin was holding up a shirt that he'd taken

out of the wardrobe. 'She's a trained nanny. The heath visitor suggested her. You know that. Did you iron this shirt?'

'No. Whoops.' The mascara wand slipped, leaving a big splodge under her right eye. The more she tried to rub it in, the worse it got. 'I ran out of time because your son . . .'

'The doorbell!' Martin was still in his boxers. 'She's early.'

'I'm not dressed.'

'Nor am I.'

Chrissie grabbed her dressing gown from the back of the door. 'Then I suppose I'll have to. Honestly, I wish we weren't going out.'

'So do I.' Martin pulled the shirt off its hanger. 'Where do you keep the iron? I'll just have to do this myself.'

Kim was younger than Chrissie had imagined. Very small and petite and rather pretty with dark hair, neatly pinned back and high cheekbones. No misplaced mascara there. Martin did a double-take as he came down the stairs, in a surprisingly well-pressed shirt and blue chinos.

'Thank you so much for coming,' he said, warmly shaking her hand as though Kim was a guest instead of someone they were paying to do a job. He glanced at George who was sitting in his baby bouncer and actually playing with the little figures strung in front of him. 'George has had supper although you might need to give him a bottle. I'm afraid he still likes to suck.'

'It's comforting,' said Chrissie defensively, wrapping her dressing gown around her.

Kim raised an immaculate eyebrow. 'Of course. Now there are a few things I'd like to ask, like where you keep his nappies. I believe he isn't dry yet.'

'No,' said Chrissie sharply. 'We're working on it.' She couldn't help it if George showed no signs of wanting to keep everything in, like a normal human being. 'Martin, can you show Kim where the nappies are and everything else that she'll need so I can go and get changed?'

That would show him, she thought, after all that pompous

spiel about George and his supper. Martin was absolutely hope-
less at knowing where things were round the house. In fact, he
was getting unbearable. Since being at home, he'd constantly
criticised her for everything.

If he didn't get a job soon, thought Chrissie grimly, squeezing
into the same skirt with the elasticated waist that she'd worn
last time, they wouldn't be able to pay the mortgage. And then
what would happen? There'd been a piece on the radio that
morning about one in twenty couples – or was it thirty? – failing
to pay at least one month out of twelve. Not long ago, she
would never have thought they might be one of them. But now
it was becoming a definite possibility.

'Who's going to be here?' asked Martin as they pulled up outside
Mike's house.

'Search me,' snapped Chrissie, examining her face in the
passenger driving mirror. Her second coat of mascara had also
smudged below her eyes, making her look even more tired than
she was anyway. 'Mike didn't provide a guest list.'

'No need to be rude.' Martin looked out at Mike's house.
'This isn't really what I'd expected.'

It wasn't what Chrissie had expected either. Funny, you might
know someone – or think you know them – and you get an
idea of what their home might be like. But when you actually
saw it, it wasn't always what you thought. Mike's house was a
modern semi-detached on a well-kept estate, about twenty
minutes from Lucy's. It lacks character, thought Chrissie as
they made their way down uneven stone steps without lighting.
The windows had those horrid dark brown frames and the
front garden, such as it was, appeared to be made up of small
pebbles with two large modern silver urns, containing yet more
pebbles.

'Come on in!' Mike was already at the door. 'Found us all
right then?'

She squeezed into the small hall which was dominated by a

table and neatly-ordered piles of post, marked 'To be posted' and 'To be dealt with.'

'Perfect directions,' she replied, holding out her cheek for a kiss. 'Mmm, something smells good.'

'I hope so.' Mike rubbed his hands. 'Eleanor's been helping me.' He lowered his voice. 'She's been feeling a bit low so we asked her over too.'

What a nice man! 'Perhaps you ought to start cooking now you have more time,' she said to Martin as they followed Mike through. Sitting down on a hideous chrome sofa (was it made of animal skin?), she couldn't help noticing that underneath both this and the matching sofa on the other side were piles of papers and files as though someone had tried to tidy up in a hurry.

'More time?' intercepted Mike. 'Last time I saw you, you were up to your eyes in it.'

'I still am.' Martin spoke tightly. 'It's Chrissie's idea of a little joke.'

He hardly spoke to her after that. It wasn't fair, thought Chrissie, trying to get comfortable on the brown and cream cowhide sofa which seemed to be tipped back at an angle of at least thirty degrees. She hadn't meant to let it slip out but now he'd sulk all the way home. Taking a large sip of gin and tonic – her first since George's birth – she felt a mixture of guilt and satisfaction. Sod it. Maybe it might knock him out and she'd get some sleep tonight.

'Hi.' Lucy came and sat next to her on the sofa. Martin had left a few minutes earlier to go to the little boys' room.

'He's being impossible,' said Chrissie quietly.

'Poor you. But she'll manage. She's a trained nanny, isn't she? And the health visitor recommended her.'

'What?' Chrissie had been thinking about Martin. 'Oh. Yes. Maybe.'

'The first time I left Jon, I was convinced that no one else would be able to look after him properly.'

She took another gulp of gin. 'The weird thing is that now I've left George, it's not as awful as I thought. It was the actual saying goodbye that upset me.'

'I know. Anyway, she's got your mobile, hasn't she? I'm sure she'll ring if there are any problems.'

Chrissie had been toying with the idea of telling Lucy about the social worker's visit for some days. Out of everyone she knew, Lucy would understand but it was so embarrassing. On the other hand, it would be such a relief to confide in someone.

'Actually, I was wondering,' she began. 'Did you ever . . .'

'Lucy. There you are.' They both looked up as Eleanor bustled in, replete in a grand blue and white striped apron with a Fortnum & Mason label ostentatiously protruding from the top. 'I'm so sorry to disturb you with your guests but I wonder if you could just come and help me out with a little something in the kitchen.'

She lowered her voice. 'I must say, it really is very difficult in there. Michael is rather particular, isn't he? He actually told me off for not putting the teaspoons back to back in the cutlery drawer. Still, I suppose that's what happens to a man when he's been on his own all these years.'

Lucy gave Chrissie a look which hopefully Eleanor couldn't see. 'I'll be there in a second.'

'I'm afraid dear that it's a bit more urgent than that. I'm sure Chrissie will understand. Your other guests will be here shortly. Ah, there they are. I can hear Sam opening the door.'

'Sam's here?' asked Chrissie.

'Yes,' said Lucy lightly. 'And Kate. Mike said it was high time they both earned their pocket money through doing jobs. So they're going to be taking coats and washing up.'

'What a good idea.'

'We'll see.'

She'd hoped it would be Jenny but the newcomers turned out to be Antony and Patsy. The latter had excelled herself this time in a skirt that left little to the imagination, despite the freezing temperatures outside. It wasn't terribly warm inside either, thought Chrissie, wondering if she dared ask Mike to turn on that horrible-looking three bar electric fire with mock coals.

'Hello. How are you both?' she asked coolly.

'Fine, thanks,' said Antony, kissing her wetly (ugh!) on both cheeks. He looked thinner and browner; neither suited him.

'So,' she said, draining her glass, 'what have you two been up to since I saw you last?'

Patsy looked as though she was going to open her beautifully made-up mouth and then abruptly sat down before standing up again and going out of the room.

'Did I say something?' asked Chrissie bewildered.

Antony shrugged. 'She's just a bit on edge at the moment.'

Chrissie laughed hoarsely. 'Me too.'

Antony sat down next to her. 'That doesn't sound too good. Is something wrong?'

Her eyes suddenly seemed terribly heavy. 'Not unless you count a toddler who won't sleep or eat and is always falling over with the result that he's bruised from head to toe and the health visitor thinks you're bashing him up.'

'You are joking, aren't you?'

'Nope.' Too late, Chrissie wondered if she'd said too much but Antony seemed so sympathetic, she couldn't stop. 'And then there's the little matter of a husband who has suddenly been made redundant without, unfortunately, a nice fat handout because he wasn't there for long enough.'

Antony sucked in his breath. 'But he'll get another job soon. I'm sure he will.'

'Well, nothing's happened yet. And if it doesn't, we won't have enough to pay the mortgage and then God knows what we'll do.'

'Can you go back to work?'

Chrissie snorted. 'What? Leave George with Martin? He

doesn't even know where the iron's kept, let alone anything else. I can just imagine what would happen if I did that.'

'Thanks very much.'

How long had her husband been standing there? Maybe he'd just heard the iron bit. 'I was just saying how funny it was that men found it difficult to find things,' she began.

'Absolutely,' chipped in Antony. 'In fact, there's been a book about it.'

'Is there a book about men who've been made redundant without a nice fat hand-out?'

Chrissie stiffened. 'Look, Martin, I'm sorry. I didn't mean it. It just sort of slipped out.'

'That's all right.' Martin sat down on the opposite matching sofa, a glass of wine in his hands. 'It's absolutely true. Cheers!'

'I thought you were driving,' said Chrissie pointedly.

Martin shrugged. 'Then we'll just have to get a taxi. And yes, I know we can't afford it with a dual minus income but it looks like you've had a few drinks yourself.'

'Sorry to interrupt.'

Was that Kate? Chrissie hadn't seen her for a while and she looked amazingly grown up with her flawless make-up and confident posture. Where did they make teenagers nowadays? And those jeans! There were so many holes and slashes that if she'd been Lucy, she'd have thrown them long ago.

'It's for you,' announced Kate coolly, shoving a cordless phone into her hands. 'Kim someone. Apparently she's been trying to get hold of you on your mobile for ages.'

Thirty-one

Patsy toyed with the food on her plate and for the millionth time ran through all the options in her head. He hadn't gone back to the house in Liverpool which was the first place she'd thought of. She'd immediately rung the people who'd bought it years ago but they assured her that he wasn't there. They sounded concerned and with good reason. You only had to mention her father's name in certain parts of the city and a lot of people got worried.

He hadn't gone to the cemetery either. She'd got someone up there to check that too. Or if he had, he hadn't left his usual offering of sorry chrysanthemums by the simple stone in the ground. Nor had he returned to the factory where he'd worked as a youth. That had been another favourite bolthole when he'd done this before. It was as though he felt safe there; a place before any of this had happened.

So that only meant one thing. He was out there. Trying to find out where she lived.

'More prawns anyone?' asked Mike, presiding at the head of the table.

'No thank you, Michael.' Eleanor sat stiffly wearing an emerald necklace and a black velvet dress as though she was at a ball instead of a casual kitchen supper. Too much rouge. Red lipstick when she needed a beige/pink tone.

'No more takers?' Mike sounded disappointed.

'It was lovely, darling,' said Lucy reassuringly.

Patsy almost snorted. Lovely? She didn't think anyone did avocado fans and prawns any more. Besides, those avocados had been distinctly grey round the edges.

Her father had looked grey too, the last time. There'd been something odd around his eyes; a look of desperation coupled with a certain wildness she'd seen before. She should have spotted the signs. For God's sake, she'd seen them often enough.

'Did you sort out your problem with the babysitter?' Antony was asking.

Patsy could have screamed. As if he cared. As if she cared.

'Sort of.' Chrissie, who was wearing some kind of awful elasticated skirt that made her stomach bulge, and whose outline certainly hadn't been helped by the disgusting prawn sauce, frowned. 'She wanted to know if we had a plug-in nightlight to help George get to sleep.'

'In our day,' said Eleanor importantly, 'we didn't have things like nightlights. We just put our babies down and left them to it.'

'But what if they cried?' Chrissie's voice rose in disbelief.

'We let them, dear. They soon learned. Believe me, it's much better that way. If you give in, they become a rod for your own back. Now, if you'll excuse me, I'll just go and see if my vegetarian casserole is doing.'

Mike was up in an instant. 'I'll help you.'

'Really, there's no need, Michael.' Eleanor addressed the table. 'It's my little contribution towards this evening.'

'No, really. I'd rather. You won't know where everything is.'

Blimey, thought Patsy. For a man whose house was so untidy, he was annoyingly fussy. Hope Lucy knows what she's letting herself in for. Men like Mike who'd been on their own for years liked doing things their own way. Like her father. Oh, God, what was she doing here when her father had disappeared? Maybe she ought to contact some organisation for missing people like the one she'd read about in the *Daily Mail* the other day. But if she did, would she have to give them all those details about his past? They might not want to help if she did.

'Finished?' Patsy suddenly became aware of one of Lucy's

kids hovering behind her. The boy pushed past her to get her plate.

'Careful!'

'Sorry. Oh fuck.'

Patsy stared down in horror at her white skirt which was slowly turning the colour of prawn sauce. 'You bloody idiot. Look what you've done.'

'I didn't mean to.'

'Sam!' Lucy leaned across the table. 'That's so rude.'

'Yeah, well I didn't mean to, did I? It was an accident.'

'Come into the kitchen, Patsy,' said Antony. 'We'll soon mop you up.'

She could hardly contain her rage. 'I don't want mopping up. This skirt is an original by Betty Barclay. Do you know how much it would have cost if I'd had to pay for it? It's ruined. Absolutely ruined.'

'Sounds like a lot of money for very little skirt,' joked Martin.

Patsy shot him a filthy look. The lecher had been giving her dirty looks all evening. His lumpy wife was welcome to him, she thought, reluctantly allowing herself to be led into the kitchen by Antony.

'Oh dear,' said Eleanor who was stirring something into a pan on the electric range. 'Did you spill something down yourself?'

'No,' retorted Patsy through clenched teeth. 'Your grandson spilt it when he was taking away my plate.'

Mike looked up from chopping a pepper into very small, precise bits. 'I hope he apologised.'

'No, he bloody didn't. He said it was an accident and it wasn't his fault.'

Mike's lips tightened and for a second, Patsy felt uneasy. His face reminded her of her father's when he was cross. 'I'll speak to him later.'

'I'm sure it was an accident,' she said swiftly. 'Have you got a cloth?'

'I'll make sure that Sam pays for it out of his allowance.'

'No, please, there's no need.' Her heart was pounding; Mike's face was catapulting her back through the years when anything they did, no matter how small a misdemeanour, made her father's eyes burn with a mad rage that no one and nothing could get through. 'I'm sure it will come out.'

God, she was going to go mad if she had to sit here much longer making polite conversation. 'You've dropped your tissue,' she said to Chrissie who was sitting next to her. Ugh! It was thick and soggy.

'Thanks.'

Patsy watched appalled as she slipped it though her open blouse and into her bra. What a place to keep it!

'Here we are, everyone!' Eleanor walked into the room carrying a large casserole dish in her oven-gloved hands. 'Sorry about the wait but Michael's oven is a little on the slow side.'

'I find it perfectly adequate actually,' he said stiffly. 'Let me take that, Eleanor.'

'I can manage, thank you.'

With a flourish, she set it on the middle of a table. Immediately Mike picked it up.

'The table will stain if you don't use a placement,' he said through gritted teeth.

'There isn't one,' Eleanor pointed out. 'Who laid the table?'

'I told Kate to. Lucy, get a mat. This is scalding my hands.'

Eleanor might be a cow but the casserole was delicious. Patsy couldn't remember when she'd last sat up at a table to eat a proper hot meal.

'So, Martin,' said Antony topping up his glass and handing the bottle round the table. 'Started applying for any jobs yet?'

'Yes, even though my dear wife doesn't think I'm trying very hard.'

'I didn't say that. I just commented that sitting in front of a computer screen all day wasn't going to get you very far.'

'And I told you that nowadays, that's exactly how you do get a job. Of course, you've been out of the job market now for a while so you probably don't realise that.'

God, she hated it when couples argued. That was the good thing about Antony. With the one exception, when his kids had got drunk, he was laid back. 'This casserole is well good, Eleanor,' she said, trying to change the subject. 'How did you manage to get the tofu so sweet?'

'Tofu?' Eleanor frowned. 'What's that, dear?'

Patsy prodded a piece and held it up on her fork. 'It's another name for soya meat.'

'And what exactly is soya?'

Patsy felt slightly sick. 'I thought this was.'

'No, dear. That's chicken breast. Rather good, isn't it? It came from this wonderful local butcher I found who . . .'

Patsy felt the bile rising into her mouth. 'But you said this was a vegetarian casserole!'

'It is, dear. It's got lots of vegetables in it. It's a Marguerite Patten recipe. We swore by it in the seventies.'

'But Eleanor,' said Lucy, gently, 'if it's got chicken, it isn't vegetarian.'

Eleanor looked bewildered. 'Surely you don't count chicken, do you? I mean, I can understand people not eating beef after all that terrible BSE business. And pork can be a little dodgy if you don't cook it properly. Besides, you've got to have something tasty in a vegetarian casserole. You can't just rely on carrots and parsnips, even though these are organic and I found them at . . .'

Where was the toilet?

'I beg your pardon, dear?'

'The toilet.' Patsy could hardly get the words out.

'She looks like she's going to be sick,' she heard someone say.

Patsy could feel the bits of meat rising in her throat. Chicken! She hadn't had meat since . . .

'Quick, someone. Get a bowl.'

Too late. Even as it came out, Patsy felt a wonderful wave

of relief. She was expelling it. Along with all the terrible memories of the night she had sworn she would never eat meat again. Up it came; up and out, leaving her throat with a disgusting acrid taste.

The only good thing was that she'd thrown up all over Eleanor's black velvet dress.

Thirty-two

'Did you tell Patsy you were coming?' asked Jenny casually as she slid out of the passenger seat, carefully ensuring that just enough thigh was showing.

'No.' Dan shut the door behind her and slipped his arm around her lightly. 'Thought we'd surprise her.'

In a way she'd have preferred that he'd told her. It was as though he was enjoying this; like she was part of a childish game. She still wasn't entirely sure what the relationship between Patsy and Dan was, or had been. He had, more than once, referred to the fact they had grown up near each other and she'd got the distinct feeling that this had been more than an ordinary bond. Yet Patsy was clearly an item with Antony.

'We're awfully late,' she said, rushing to keep up with him.

He glanced back, grinning. 'Worth it, though, wasn't it?'

She felt herself blushing in the dark as she recalled how he'd taken her by surprise from behind when he'd come to the flat to pick her up. 'Yes,' she said, almost shyly. The animal passion had been breathtaking. He had surprised her in so many ways and the delight he got from that had excited her even more. It had almost been enough to make her forget Alicia King and her threatening legal letters.

Dan was trying to check the house numbers in the poor street lighting. 'Here it is.' He put out a hand. 'Careful. The steps here are uneven. Hello. It looks like we're not the only ones who are late.'

In the dark, she could make out a figure leaning against the porch. A woman. With a cigarette in her hand. 'Jenny? Is that you, stranger?'

Maggie? A tight-lipped Maggie who was trying to hide the fact that she'd clearly had too much to drink.

'I'm so glad you're here.' Maggie was clinging to her, like a child. 'Lucy asked me, you know. But everyone else will be there as a couple and I'm scared. It's so hard doing this kind of thing on your own.'

She knew about that one all right. 'Dan, this is Maggie. Maggie, Dan.'

'Hello, Maggie.' Dan had this way of saying someone's name as though it was really special. 'Are you a friend of Lucy's or Mike's?'

'Lucy. Mike's friendly with my ex, you know. He left me for that silly cow Patsy. She's a real bitch and a tart as you'll see if you're ever unlucky enough to come across her.'

Jenny watched as a wave of shocked realisation crossed Dan's face.

'Sometimes,' said Dan, pressing the doorbell, 'people aren't all that they seem. I mean it sounds as though you've had a hard time but that doesn't necessarily mean that Patsy is . . . well, all those names you've just called her.'

Maggie laughed drunkenly. 'Believe me, she is. What kind of woman would persuade a man to leave his wife and kids? I hadn't realised there could be so many predatory women out there.'

Dan stiffened and Jenny prickled with unease. 'Is that doorbell working?' she asked, peering through the glass panel. 'I can't see anyone coming.'

Maggie banged the knocker loudly. 'Why don't they get a move on? It's freezing out here.'

She wasn't dressed for the weather, noticed Jenny. She herself was wearing one of the season's fashionable sweater dresses but Maggie had a thin cotton dress on, more suitable for the summer, with a flimsy maroon cardigan on top. She'd lost a lot of weight since she'd seen her last. Even in the poor porch light, Jenny could see Maggie's gaunt face was bare of make-up and her figure more like a child's as she banged the knocker like a disruptive toddler. How much had she had to drink?

'At last,' announced Dan with relief as a shape finally loomed up through the door.

'Sorry everyone. Have you been here long? Must get that doorbell fixed.' Mike, wearing a rather old pair of navy blue corduroy trousers which were distinctly frayed round the pockets, beamed at them. Then his face fell on Maggie and there was an instant look of horror.

'Maggie! Goodness. How nice to see you. Er, is there something I can do for you?'

'Of course there bloody is.' She pushed ahead of Jenny and Dan. 'You can let me in out of this perishing cold and get me a drink.'

Mike gazed helplessly after her. 'What's she doing here?' he hissed to Jenny. 'Patsy and Antony are in the lounge.'

'She thinks Lucy invited her,' Jenny hissed back.

'She wouldn't have done that!'

He shut the front door behind them and as he did so, there was the sound of raised voices.

'Oh, God,' murmured Jenny.

Dan's eyes hardened. 'Excuse me. I'd better help Patsy.'

Thanks very much, thought Jenny. 'Sorry we're late, Lucy,' she said slipping into the only vacant seat. Maggie had taken the one next to her, intended presumably for her so-called date. The table was in uproar.

'How could you have asked this bitch at the same time as me?'

'Maggie, I didn't.' Lucy was in tears. 'I asked if you wanted to come weeks ago and you said you didn't want to leave the kids.'

'So you asked that cow instead?'

'Hang on, Maggie.' Antony, who through some hapless chance was sitting on the other side of his ex, put his hand on her shoulder. 'Let's leave out the name-calling, shall we?'

'Why?' Maggie's eyes were flashing. 'She is a cow and a bitch and everything else I can think of because she took you away from me.' Tears were pouring down her face now. 'Do you know how difficult it is on my own? Do you know what it's like to look after two kids on your own without any help?'

'I've told you. I'm always there to help if you want it.'

'But with her?' Maggie stabbed the air in Patsy's direction. 'I don't want that bitch anywhere near my children. Last time she got them drunk.'

'That's not very fair,' interrupted Dan. He was standing right behind Patsy; one would think he was her boyfriend and not Antony, thought Jenny crossly. Less than an hour ago, he'd been all over her in bed and now it was clear which direction his interests really lay.

'Can I say something?' Patsy stood up, her skirt stained pink like a large blush. 'I'm sorry this is so awful for you, Maggie. But I didn't ask your husband to leave you.'

Maggie was sobbing uncontrollably now. 'Then why did he?'

'Because our marriage was over.' Antony looked as though he was going to shake her. 'It's been over for years! Patsy was just the catalyst. I'd have gone anyway.'

'Please.' Mike was running his hands through his hair. 'Can everyone calm down here for the sake of the children.'

Children? Jenny suddenly realised that Kate and Sam were there; each wearing a rather amusing version of a waiter or waitress outfit. Kate had a very short black skirt on and Sam a pair of trousers which were so big they must have belonged to Jon.

'We don't mind,' said Kate. 'It's all right, Aunty Maggie. Here, have one of these brownies. Sam and I made them to go with the coffee. Granny loves them, don't you, gran? Or would you like some wine instead?'

'No,' said Chrissie quickly, 'fetch her a glass of water.'

Too late. Maggie was already lunging for the bottle that Kate was carrying and knocked it back. 'Come on, Maggie, I think that's enough,' said Mike firmly.

'How dare you tell me what's enough?' Red wine was dribbling out of Maggie's mouth as she spoke, staining her chin and dripping down her neck. 'I can do what I like.'

'Oh dear,' said Eleanor faintly. 'This really is getting out of hand, isn't it? If you don't mind, I think I'd like to get back to my tapestry or watch that Mollie de Mille film which I videoed the other night. She had quite a chequered life too, you know.'

Lucy looked around the table in confusion. 'I can't take her. I need to be here. Can someone . . .'

'I will.' Martin staggered to his feet.

'No,' said Chrissie sharply. 'You've had too much to drink.'

'Really? I thought that being a chauffeur might be my new vocation. I mean, you told me to get a job, didn't you?'

Maggie was rising to her feet, wavering like a unsteady matchstick. 'Where's my coat?'

'You didn't bring one,' said Mike.

'Of course I did. It's bloody freezing outside.'

'Wait,' said Patsy urgently. 'You can have mine.'

'Bitch! I don't want your charity.'

Jenny gasped as Maggie slung her glass of red towards Patsy, who stepped to one side just in time. Oh, God, it had gone all over Eleanor!

'How dare you. I've already had to wipe this dress down after this young woman forced herself to be sick on me.'

'I didn't force myself,' said Patsy indignantly. 'You made me sick by putting meat in your stupid casserole.'

'Catch her!'

Maggie was shooting out of the front door.

'Where's she gone?' demanded Antony, peering into the darkness.

'I'll take the car and go left,' instructed Mike. 'You take yours and go right in case she's gone the other way. We'll find her. Don't worry.'

★   ★   ★

Dear Lucy, Sorry I spoiled your supper party. I think I'd had too much to drink. I remember now. You did say I could come but then I said it didn't matter. The doctor's changing my tablets. See you in the office next week. Love Maggie x

Thirty-three

'At least your friend Margaret got herself home in one piece,' pointed out Eleanor, putting on her Marigolds. 'Although I do think such drama was totally unnecessary. How long did you say the boys were out until you knew she was safe?'

Lucy took out a neatly folded tea towel from Mike's top kitchen drawer. 'About an hour.'

'Changing the subject, dear, I honestly don't know how Michael lives like this. It's clean enough but very untidy in places, don't you think? Have you seen the room next door? It's piled high with books and CDs! He can't possibly have time to listen or read them all. If they weren't there, you could turn it into a proper dining room instead of having to eat in the sitting room.'

'Mike loves his music and his books,' said Lucy defensively. 'He spent a long time cataloguing them, according to the artist and author.'

Eleanor sniffed. 'Well, I don't know where you're going to find space for them in Luke's house.'

It wasn't 'Luke's house' – it was hers. But it wasn't worth falling out over, especially as Eleanor had offered to help clear up after the supper party.

Mike had had to go to yet another meeting, even though it was a Saturday (this time in York) and had left them with detailed instructions on where to find the drying up cloths and other washing up equipment. When he got back, she'd have to talk to him about the dog. There was no way she was getting rid of Mungo.

'Goodness me,' murmured Eleanor, opening the fridge. What now?

'This fridge is surprisingly clean. It would almost pass the Health and Sanity regulations.'

'Safety,' muttered Lucy. 'Sorry, Eleanor but I don't get your point.'

'Well dear, he can be rather particular, can't he? He spent nearly twenty minutes instructing me on where the plates went before leaving this morning. And then he kept breaking off to talk into that blueberry of his.'

Lucy suppressed a smile as she finished loading the dishwasher. 'We all have our different ways of doing things. Besides, he's very good at getting me to sit down while he does things. It's nice to be looked after.'

Eleanor fixed her with a beady look. 'Are you saying that my son didn't do that?'

Yes. 'I'm simply pointing out that Mike is very caring. Oh, look, here comes his post.'

She picked up a couple of letters and a postcard as they came through the door, to put on the hall table. Idly flicking the card over, her heart stopped. Checking Eleanor was still in the other room, she slipped the card into her pocket, along with a half-eaten dog chew that had been there for ages.

'Are you sure you've put those in the right pile?' Eleanor, who had bustled out into the hall after her, didn't bother hiding her sarcasm. 'I must say, Lucy, I do wonder about Michael sometimes. Don't you find it rather strange that he has never married?'

'He hadn't found the right person.'

'There's no need to be prickly, dear.'

'I think it's better to wait for the right person than make compromises and marry the wrong one.'

'Do you?' asked Eleanor, her eyebrows raised. 'In our day, we were far more practical about it. And we certainly didn't indulge in the kind of dramatics which your guests did last night. Goodness me! I've never seen anything like it. Your friend

Chrissie and her husband were being extremely rude to each other. And as for that girl Patsy, well! My dress is absolutely ruined. Frankly, I think she needs a bit of meat inside her – no wonder she's so pale. And then that mix-up about your friend Maggie. How could you have invited her at the same time as Antony's new lady friend?'

'I didn't. Well I did but she turned down the invitation.'

'Well someone made a mistake. Now I don't know about you but I'm ready for a little coffee break. Shall we have one of Kate and Sam's brownies? They're absolutely delicious.'

'Not for me, thanks.' Lucy glanced at her watch. 'The children said they'd be here by now. Jon said he'd ring too but he hasn't.'

'How's he getting on now after his little teething problems?'

'I think he's all right but I haven't heard much from him.'

'Probably the best thing, if you ask me. You always fussed too much over him. Luke used to say that. Now he's eighteen, you need to give him some space. He'll be home soon for the Christmas holidays. Goodness, Lucy, these brownies really are tasty. Sure you don't want one?'

'No, thanks. I ate too much last night.'

'I have noticed that you've been putting on a little weight, dear.'

Was there no end to Eleanor's rudeness? 'I'll have to go on a diet then, won't I? Now Mike's found a buyer for the house, we've decided to get married some time next year – possibly the autumn to give the children time to get used to the idea.'

She felt a mixture of pleasure and guilt at the horrified look which flitted across her mother-in-law's face. 'Is that wise?'

'What do you mean?'

Eleanor waved the brownie in front of her face. 'Michael is a bit of an unknown entity, isn't he? I mean, what do you really know about him?'

She was impossible! 'We've been together for nearly a year. He's very good to me and the children . . .'

'You mean he's very critical of them.'

'That's just because he wants the best for them.'

'Well they don't see it that way.'

'And he's a friend of Antony's . . .'

Eleanor snorted. 'Not much of a reference considering Antony abandoned his poor wife to go off with that stupid little girl.' She put down her cup of coffee and leaned towards her. 'And have you asked yourself why he has a business meeting on Saturday when most men are home with their families? Really, Lucy, I know you don't think it's any of my business. But ask yourself if you have any doubts about Michael. And only go ahead if you are absolutely sure you are doing the right thing.'

'Where's Gran?' asked Kate when she finally turned up an hour later to 'help' (part of her waitress agreement).

'In the sitting room. She suddenly felt very tired.'

'She's gone to sleep,' announced Sam, reluctantly examining a drying up cloth as though he didn't know what it was for.

Lucy had almost finished wiping down the surfaces now. 'That's odd. Before she felt tired, she got extremely animated and worked up. Then she said she was hungry, even though she'd just had two of your brownies. I'd better go and check.'

Sam was right. Eleanor had fallen asleep. She was lying back in the chair, her cheeks slightly flushed and breathing noisily. Lucy felt her pulse. It seemed all right. Best to leave her to it. Sometimes it was easy to forget that she was in her late seventies. Lucy went back to the kitchen. 'Kate, can you wipe down those table mats? And Sam . . .' She stared with horror at the small gold glint in his left ear. 'You haven't!'

He grinned cheekily. 'I have!'

'But I said you couldn't have your ear pierced. We've had this discussion so many times.'

Sam shrugged. 'Chillax, Mum. One of my friends did his

with a needle and Bunsen burner at school. At least I didn't do that.'

Lucy began to shake with anger. 'Where did you go? I could sue them for doing it without my parental permission.'

'No, you can't. Kate signed the form.'

Kate looked a bit scared. 'He kept going on about it, Mum, and really, he's right. They're all doing it. There's nothing wrong with it.'

What was she going to do with him? 'I don't know what's wrong with you, Sam, but they'll find a word for it one day.'

'That's awful, Mum!'

Kate was right. But they made her say things that weren't her.

'So just because I have a tiny piece of metal in my ear, means you don't love me.'

'I didn't say that.'

'You meant it. Would you still love me if I had big ears or a funny nose?'

'Of course I would.'

'Then what's the difference?'

'You did this yourself.'

'Mum's right. And it looks gay.'

'That's only if you wear the stud in the right ear.'

She couldn't stand it when he argued like this. So like Luke. He used to argue interminably until in the end it was easier just to do what he wanted, whether it was painting the sitting room cream instead of white or staying at home to look after the kids instead of getting a part-time job.

'Sam,' she began.' I'm really disappointed . . .'

'Lucy?' A thin frail voice called out from the sitting room. 'Lucy, are you there? I really don't feel at all well.'

'I'd better take her home.' Lucy handed her pinny to Kate. 'You two can sort out this mess. And Sam, I'll deal with you later. Don't think you've got away with this. Just wait until Mike gets home.'

'Why?' Sam glowered at her. 'He's not my father. And even if you do ever marry him, don't ever expect me to treat him like one.'

She waited until she'd got Eleanor into her own bed and rung the doctor (who promised to come out later) before taking the postcard out of her pocket. It had been the feminine writing that had caught her attention.

How well do you really know him, Eleanor had asked.

The postcard had a picture of a stony Devonshire beach. *'Thought this might remind you of last month. Love Kerry.'*

Bile swam into her mouth just as the front door opened. Swiftly, Lucy slipped the postcard back into her pocket.

'Hi.' Mike nuzzled the back of her neck. Stiffening, she moved away.

'Hello.'

'We could go out for dinner tonight if you like, pet.' He picked up one of her tea cloths, shook it out and folded it neatly, before putting his arm around her. 'Or maybe the cinema.'

His attentiveness was cloying. 'I don't think I can. Eleanor isn't well so the doctor's coming and Sam . . . well, Sam has had his ear pierced.'

'But you told him not to. We both told him.'

The cold disapproval in his voice unnerved her. 'Yes, I know. But he's just gone ahead and done it.'

'He'll have to be punished. You'll have to take away his mobile phone and his laptop.'

'But Luke . . . Oh heavens, sorry. I mean Mike. He needs his phone for emergencies and the laptop for coursework.'

'Tough. It's time he learned who's boss here. And if you won't do it, I will.'

Oh, Lord, she'd hurt him by stupidly calling him by Luke's name. It didn't often happen but even after all these years, she still found herself doing it every now and then. She'd wanted to discuss Mungo but she could hardly do that now. She did, however, have to ask him about the name on the card but in such a way that he wouldn't think she'd been nosing through his bins.

'By the way,' she heard herself saying, 'someone rang when I was round at your place. A woman. It might have been a wrong number but she sounded a bit strange.'

'Did she give her name?'

She swallowed nervously, wishing she could lie more convincingly. But a wrong number sounded better than admitting she'd been snooping through his post. 'It sounded like Kerry.'

'Kerry?' He turned his back on her to put teabags in the pot. 'I've been getting lots of wrong numbers recently. And companies trying to sell me things too. I ought to sign up to that service that stops that kind of thing. Cup of tea?'

'No, thanks.' Her voice wobbled. 'I think I'll go up now to check on Eleanor.'

He brushed her cheek with his lips but instead of the usual tingle, she felt something almost like repugnance.

'Shall I come over later on?'

She turned away. 'Can you ring first? After last night, I'm feeling really tired.'

DECEMBER

BUENO PASTA! is now taking bookings for our
Speshial Christmas Dinners from now untill
24 December.

Only £35 a person including one glass
of house wine.

Closed 25 December.

Make speed now!

Thirty-four

'It does all sound a bit strange,' admitted Chrissie. They were sitting in her conservatory, looking out onto the lawn, waiting for a supermarket delivery which was late. She loved her garden room with its camellias and pretty wicker furniture. Unofficially, it was 'her' room and she only hoped Martin didn't decide to barge in now. How did other women manage when their husbands worked from home?

'If it was me,' she continued, 'I'd tell him that you just happened to see the postcard and ask him who this Kerry is.'

'Then he'll think I don't trust him,' countered Lucy.

'Well you don't, do you?' She heaved George onto her left breast. 'It does sound a bit fishy, you must admit. Had enough of this side, have you, darling?'

'Maggie says I ought to hire a private investigator.'

Chrissie adjusted her position so George could latch onto her other breast. 'It'll cost you. I was reading an article about it. Apparently it's not just celebrities who are doing it but ordinary women who want to know what their men are up to.'

'It seems so sneaky. He says the dog is making him sneeze, too. But there's no way we're giving Mungo away.'

Chrissie had never liked dogs, even before they'd posed a potential risk to George. Frankly, Mungo was so overweight she was surprised he didn't get carpet burn. 'Tricky, isn't it? Whoops. Sorry, darling. Did Mummy move too suddenly?'

'I'd better go soon. I'm due in at the office and then I've got to take Eleanor to my doctor for another check-up.'

'Wish I had an office to go to. Martin's driving me mad being at home.'

Lucy made a sympathetic face. 'No luck?'

'He spends all day online – it's how you get jobs nowadays apparently – but hasn't had so much as a sniff of an interview. Says it's his age.'

'But he's not that old.'

'Not to you and me but in his field they keep getting all these young kids coming in with fantastic qualifications and no ties so they're happy to work all night. Martin used to work late but then I had a go at him about being on my own with George so he started coming back early. Now he says that's one reason why they got rid of him.'

'But that's illegal.'

Chrissie smiled ruefully. 'Yes, well they couldn't cite that as a reason but it's what you call a contributory factor.'

'Have you thought of getting a job yourself?'

Chrissie felt a stab of panic as George slid off her lap and toddled off like a manic wind-up machine. 'I've been out of it for nearly two years. It's almost impossible to get back in. Besides, I couldn't leave George with a stranger. It was bad enough when we came to you the other night and the sitter kept ringing.'

'You could leave George with Martin if he hasn't got a job.'

Chrissie snorted. 'He'd have no idea! George only has to do so much as whine and he passes him to me like a hot potato.'

'But if he had him full-time, he'd learn like we all had to.'

'I'm not sure now if I could still cope with the responsibility of a proper job. Look at poor Jenny and that awful woman who's suing her. Sometimes I wonder if . . .'

Crash.

Chrissie was up before her legs knew it. 'George? NO! He's got another bump on his head. See? What am I going to do?'

'It's all right.' Lucy was stroking George who was yelling furiously, his face pink and hot. 'You can see from his eyes he's not hurt. It's only if those black bits go big that you have to worry about concussion. Chrissie, calm down. You're frightening him.'

'I can't help it.' Chrissie felt her body convulsed with sobs. 'I'm so scared they'll take him away.'

'Who?'

'Social services.' She could barely talk through the sobs. 'They're watching me. They visit us all the time to make sure.'

'Make sure what?'

'That we're not hurting him.' Chrissie reached out for George but he'd pulled away, his injury already forgotten in his enthusiasm to hurl bricks across the room. 'Because he's bruising himself, they think we're hurting him.'

'But that's ridiculous. He's a lively boy. Sam was the same. We had a season ticket for Casualty. No one ever accused us of abuse. Poor you.'

Chrissie felt Lucy's arm around her. It was so comforting. So nice to be held. Briefly, she closed her eyes and imagined what it would be like to have Dan's arm around her. No! This man had been the beginning of all her troubles. She hated him. So why did she feel so infuriatingly attracted to him?

'Have you been to see your GP?'

Chrissie nodded through her tears. 'She's sitting on the fence. Keeps asking me if I need help or if I want to go on a parenting course.'

'That might not be a bad idea.'

'So you think I'm a bad mother?'

'No! But we all need help with our kids. Did I tell you about Sam having his ear pierced on the quiet? And I'm still worried about Jon. He doesn't want me to visit but he doesn't sound himself on the other end of the phone. If I didn't have my job, I'd be in the loony bin. Honestly, Chrissie. I'd think about going back to work seriously if I was you.'

In the event, the stupid delivery van didn't get to her until 10 p.m. – *10 p.m.*! – and then it took half an hour to unload it (including a huge slab of Brie even though she'd ordered

Camembert). And she'd so wanted to get to bed early so she could . . . well, do what exactly?

It had been so long now that Chrissie felt embarrassed about even talking about it. How was it possible to let things slide so that it was months since they'd last 'done it'?

Chrissie edged closer to her husband. After George was born, sex had been the last thing she could think about. Martin had been mildly interested after the six week check but not persistent. When she'd made the usual excuses about being tired or her boobs hurting, he'd accepted it easily enough.

Then there'd been the thorny problem of contraception. She hadn't wanted to go back on the pill and when she'd tried the coil, before George, she'd had constant spotting. Since she usually had a pain down one side when she was ovulating, the best option was surely the natural method by avoiding the fertile days.

'Martin?' She rolled towards him.

'Mmm?' He was half asleep.

'I think I'm "safe" now?'

He groaned, turning away from her. 'You're what?'

'Safe. You know. We can do it if you want.'

'For heaven's sake, Chrissie. I was asleep.'

'Then wake up, big boy.' Fumbling under his pyjama top, she was willing herself to stay awake and stroke below his waist. Frankly, she'd do anything to go to sleep herself but something inside her kept telling her not to leave it any longer. 'I've just had my period so I can't get pregnant. Well, it's highly unlikely anyway.'

'Not now.' He was putting the pillow over his head, the way he did when he didn't want to be disturbed. 'Maybe in the morning.'

Half-relieved, half-disappointed, she turned away. He couldn't say she hadn't tried. George was asleep too instead of keeping his usual nightly vigil. Bit of a pity, really. She was actually feeling slightly damp.

Chrissie moved to the edge of the bed and turned over onto her stomach. Holding her crutch with her right hand, she began to rhythmically move up and down.

'Stop tossing and turning,' muttered Martin crossly. 'I can't get back to sleep.'

She froze. 'Just going to the loo.' Slipping into the bathroom, she locked the door behind her and lay face down on the carpet. So nice! She tried to imagine Martin but instantly her body stopped. How about that dishy presenter on children's television? Better. But still not right. A picture of Dan shot into her head. No! But her body seemed to think differently. God, she was absolutely dripping. She could feel him thrusting inside her, imagine him looking down at her in the dark as he used to, feel his tongue against her nipples. She was coming. She was fucking coming!

Gasping, Chrissie felt her body move below like a disembodied clock pendulum knocking inside her. Was that really her, panting? The warmth diffused through her before the wave of disgust hit. What kind of woman was she, to want a man who'd treated her as Dan had treated her all those years ago?

'Anything there?' she asked Martin over breakfast. She normally listened to Libby Purves but Martin, she'd learned since his enforced presence at home, didn't like the radio on while eating.

He didn't even bother looking up from the Sits. Vac. column of his newspaper. 'No.'

'Great. Come on, George. This cereal is really nice. The supermarket people brought it by mistake instead of the usual one you have. Just open your mouth and Daddy can pop the spoon in. Here you are, Martin.'

'What? If you can't do it, I won't be able to. Just put the bowl and spoon in front of him, like the health visitor said, and let him get on with it.'

'If I do that, it will go everywhere.'

'So? You can clean it up, can't you?'

Chrissie took a deep breath. Not a 'We can clean it up' but a 'You can clean it up'. He didn't lift a finger round here; never even made supper. What she needed was that sexy French bloke on television who went round surprising women with TLC (Tender Loving Cooking) and making them a meal at their own home.

'You know, I was thinking. Suppose I tried to get a job. Not a full-time one obviously. But a part-time one. Like Maggie and Lucy.'

'A job?' Martin looked as thought the toast had stuck in his throat. 'But who'd look after George?'

'You could.'

'Don't be daft! I'm going to have interviews to go to and then when I get a job, who'd look after him then? We couldn't afford a nanny on our mortgage. Besides, you haven't worked for two years.'

Pouring herself a cup of tea from the pot, and deliberately not offering him one, she felt a rush of anger tinged with adrenalin. So Martin didn't think she could get herself a job? Well she'd prove him wrong.

Thirty-five

Black. Pitch black. Patsy woke at around 4 a.m., unable to get back to sleep. She'd been doing this ever since the phone call from the home. Four a.m. was a wretched time, she thought, turning over in bed away from Antony so she didn't get his cold. Too early to get up. Lots of time to worry.

When she was younger, Patsy had taught herself not to worry. Thanks to her father, her mother and sister had always been bags of nerves, and she was determined not to be the same.

But ever since she'd had to put her father in a home, it had been different. She was constantly worried that he would become too difficult to handle and how she'd pay the fees. One day, when her looks faded and she ran out of Antonys to bankroll her, he'd have to go into a state home.

Patsy shuddered. She had tried that at the beginning and the stench of cabbage mixed with urine had made her throw up. Within a few weeks her father had shrunk to half the size of himself and his carers frequently 'forgot' to bring him his meals because, she suspected, he was difficult.

And now he had vanished.

4.15 p.m. No chance of sleep now, especially after Maggie's appearance at Mike's the other night. When had she started to get a conscience? The previous 'Antonys' had had wives, with one or two exceptions, and she'd never felt guilty. It took two to tango and if the man wasn't happy at home, it wasn't her fault if she was there to pick up the pieces.

But then again she had never met any of the wives until Maggie. The first time at Lucy's had been bad enough. However, she'd managed over time to erase it from her memory and blank out that desperation in Maggie's eyes, that wild look, the panic in her voice. Now, it had all come back again.

Maggie had guts and Patsy admired that. She could see Maggie's game. She'd have played it herself. Anyone looking at Lucy's appalled face would have known that she hadn't asked her friend round. No, Maggie had decided to 'make a mistake' so she could embarrass Antony. And it had done the trick. It had also made her look like the wicked other woman, something that Patsy didn't normally care about until she'd had the experience of Lucy's mother-in-law's beady eyes fixed on her across the table in acid disapproval.

Of course, running away like that was just a drama queen act. Patsy could have told Maggie it didn't work. It just made you feel silly afterwards. Even so, she was relieved to hear from Antony that the daft bitch had rung to say she'd got home safely after all.

4.35 a.m. The tree outside brushed against the window, making a noise. She'd have to get the council to do something about that. There it was again. Patsy swung her legs out of bed, admiring their shape as she did so, and went to draw the gap in the beige curtain. What was that shadow down below? Probably one of those bloody kids from the estate again. Antony had been complaining about them ever since he moved in.

It was one reason why Antony wanted to move. 'Maggie's living in the house that I worked my balls off for,' he had been saying recently. 'She can manage in a smaller place. I've taken legal advice and I'm going to suggest we sell. Then we can buy somewhere nice.'

Long-term commitment? It wasn't what she'd had in mind when she'd first met him. It hardly ever worked out. Just look at Lucy and her bloke. They weren't even married yet but any fool could see the cracks. As for their friends Chrissie and her leering husband, well she'd give them six more months max. No, she didn't want Maggie to move out. But at the same time, she couldn't lose Antony; not with her dad's fees to pay.

Looking back at his tousled head beneath the duvet, something inside her softened. 'Stop it,' she told herself firmly. 'You can't afford to start thinking like that.'

Nearly 5 a.m. now. Was there any chance that Dan might be up? Sometimes he didn't go to bed at all, depending on what – or who – he was on. Slipping out of bed, she made her way into the narrow galley kitchen, put on the kettle, took a carrot stick out of the fridge and punched in the number.

'*Hi.*' His deep rich gorgeous carefully cultivated voice made her feel better already. '*This is Dan. Sorry I'm not here but I'd really like to talk to you. Leave your name and phone number and we'll catch up soon.*'

Who was he with? A picture of Dan, lying on his stomach in bed, the way he liked to sleep at night, shot into her mind. He'd always slept like that, even as a young teenager, his right arm over his head as though to shield himself from the blows they had all grown up with. They'd all had to live with the unexpected. Maybe that was why they did the unexpected themselves.

Take the other night when he'd turned up with Jenny. She'd had to hide her shock and, if she was going to come clean with herself, her dismay. Dan and she weren't right for each other; they had proved that years ago after an unsatisfactory weekend. Sometimes, as they'd agreed, you were just meant to be friends but that didn't mean it was easy seeing him with other women.

That thing with Chrissie had been a shock, too. Too much of a coincidence in her book, apart from the fact that Dan had been with so many women, they were bound to come across some of them in later years. Even so, she'd got cross with Dan for flirting with Chrissie. It wasn't fair. 'If you do much more of that, she'll be after you,' Patsy had warned. 'Anyone can see that her husband isn't that interested in her, so she'll be desperate for some attention.'

He'd laughed her off, of course, and she could see that instead of taking her warning seriously, he rather enjoyed her reaction.

Nearly 5.30 a.m. Sod it. She'd make a cup of tea and start

early in preparation for the tough day ahead. Someone she knew from her breakfast television make-up days, had asked her to do a fashion spread for a London give-away paper. The deadline was tight – today's shoot would come out quite soon which was quite exciting really, except that with no news of her father, she couldn't get excited about anything.

'Patsy?'

There was a groan from the bed. Why was it that when men were ill, they were always dying?

'Patsy. Can you come here? I need some water. And something to stop my head throbbing. It's killing me.'

This, she thought, was why she could never get married or even live with someone permanently. But now, right now, she had to put up with it. Maybe when she found her father, she'd have to rethink things.

'God, I feel awful.'

Man flu! Although, to be fair, he was pretty hot.

'I can't believe you don't have a thermometer or Paracetamol,' he groaned. 'Maggie used to have a drawer full of stuff.'

'Then perhaps you'd like to go back to her and this wonderful first aid drawer so she can make you better.'

He put out his hand. 'Sorry, darling. But I feel so bloody awful today. And it would be when I promised to have the kids.'

'What?'

'Didn't I tell you? Got any more water there? My throat is parched.'

'Well you can't have them. You'd better ring her quickly to say you're ill.'

'I can't. It's the holidays and she hasn't got anyone else to have them.'

'Well she'll have to cancel whatever she's doing.'

'She can't do that either. She's got a doctor's appointment in London for something important.'

'What?'

'She wouldn't say.' Antony's eyes were feverish, pleading with her. 'Look I'm really sorry to ask you this, love, but could you look after them for me instead?'

'But I've got a job. At lunchtime.'

Antony leant back against the pillows. 'I'm sure I'll be better by then. If you can have them this morning, I'll take over when you have to go.'

'Hi.'

Patsy was ready for the doorbell, steeling herself for Maggie. Instead, Lucy stood there, looking tired but pretty, in a long slim-fitting pale-green winter coat that set off her blonde hair. God, how she'd love to get her hands on those cheekbones. Sienna Sunset dusted down with Gold Teardrops would be perfect for her skin tone.

'Hello. Is Antony there?'

'He's not well. I'm landed with the kids until he wakes up. Wotcha, you two.'

They stared sullenly back at her.

Lucy was shifting awkwardly on the doorstep. 'I'm not sure. I mean Maggie did say that Antony would be here . . .'

'He is. He's just in bed with a temperature so he thinks he's dying. Typical man.'

There was a glimmer of a smile on Lucy's face which was immediately replaced with the previous worried look. 'It's just that I'm not sure if . . .'

'If Maggie would want me to look after her kids.' Patsy finished off the sentence for her. 'Well put it this way. If she's not happy, she can come back and get them.'

'She can't,' piped up Alice. 'She's had to go to London. And Aunty Lucy can't have us because she's going to pick up Jon from Oxford.'

'Then it looks as though you two have drawn the short straw, doesn't it? Do you want me to have them or not?'

'Thank you. I'm sorry. I don't mean to sound rude. It's just that . . .'

'I know.' Patsy surprised herself. 'It must be difficult.' Bloody hell, what was coming over her? Was it that the kid, the girl, reminded her of her sister, with that worried look that said, what's happening to us?

'Don't worry. I'll look after them. It'll be Ribena for elevenses not vodka, I promise. Come on, I'm just kidding.'

'I'm hungry,' piped up the boy.

Lucy smiled apologetically. 'They have had breakfast but they're always hungry at the moment. Maggie says they're going through a growing spurt.'

'Well there's not much in the kitchen but I'll do what I can.'

'I want a chocolate biscuit,' whined the girl as soon as Lucy had gone.

'Chocolate biscuit?' repeated Patsy. 'You'll get fat! I might have a Ryvita or two. Come on, let's see.'

The boy had already shot off towards the bedroom. 'Dad,' she heard him saying urgently. 'Dad, are you all right? Patsy says you're dying.'

Patsy giggled. Now he really would be demanding the last rites. Well she'd give him until lunchtime and then that was his lot.

'Antony. Antony!' She checked the Paracetamol bottle she'd had to go to the corner shop for. OK, so she'd given him three tablets instead of two because he'd been so whiny but surely that wouldn't knock him out?

'Antony!' She pushed his shoulder roughly. Groaning, he rolled away.

'I've got to go to work now. Wake up or else the kids will be on their own.'

'We'll be all right, Patsy,' said a small voice from the door. She turned to see the girl, standing there forlornly clutching her teddy bear. Why had no one thought to have given her or Babs a bear like that?

'No,' she said sharply. 'I'm not having your mother saying I'm neglecting you. You'll just have to come with me to work.'

'I don't want to.' The boy was scowling.

'Tough shit.'

'Mummy says people shouldn't use rude words like that.'

'Well she's not here now, is she. So you'll just have to put up with what you hear.'

'Didn't know you had kids, Patsy,' said Vila who edited the fashion pages.

'I don't. They're my partner's.'

She'd never used the word partner before; had avoided it, not wanting to feel tied. But it just slipped out. 'He's ill and there's no one to look after them so I had to bring them.'

'Have they got anything to do?' asked the stylist.

'What?'

'Crayons, that sort of thing.'

Patsy hadn't thought of that. 'No. They'll just have to sit and wait for me.'

Vila laughed merrily. 'Kids don't do that nowadays. Now, I tell you what, you two – what are your names? – why don't you come with me and I'll find you something to do.' She glanced over her shoulder at Patsy. 'I must say, they're nice looking. I'm almost tempted to put them in the shoot.'

Patsy shrugged. 'Up to you.'

'Would their parents mind?'

'I don't know. I'll try their father again on the phone if you like.'

'Great. Yes, I rather like that idea.'

Antony didn't answer, of course. Probably flat out, dreaming of temperatures and buxom nurses.

'Did you get hold of him?'

'Er, yes. He says it's fine for me to sign the parental whatsit form.'

What the hell! He'd be OK about it and besides it would give the kids something to do rather than just watch. It would be fun. The girl was twirling around in the clothes they had given

her to try on and was actually being nice to Patsy. The boy
seemed to be enjoying it too, especially as there was a Playstation
in the corner which he was going to be pictured on during the
shoot.

'Will you make me up?' demanded the girl.

'Of course. Come on. Over here.'

Alice dangled her legs, kicking her sparkly trainers in the air,
closed her eyes and waited patiently. How sweet! For the first
time in her life, Patsy almost felt maternal. She wouldn't have
minded one like that if things had been different.

Natural Nature Foundation. 'Can I have that doll at the top
of the Christmas tree?' Alice was pointing to the huge spruce
that was going to be part of the backdrop.

'I'll ask.'

'And the presents below?'

'They're empty.'

Alice opened her eyes wide. Pale Blue Mist eyeshadow. 'Why?'

'Because they're just pretend, for the picture.'

'I wanted a Ballerina Pet doll for Christmas but Mummy
says Dad's got all the money.'

'Does she? Well maybe someone else will give it to you.'
She'd have to remember to talk to Antony about that. Ah good,
the phone. Maybe he'd had finally woken up!

'Miss Jones?'

'Yes.'

'It's Tim. From the National Missing Persons Helpline.'

Her heart pounded and she felt sick. 'Go on.'

'I don't want to get your hopes up. But we've just had some
news in. We think we might have found your father.'

'Where is he?'

There was a short silence.

'Patsy, I'm afraid you're going to have to be very brave.'

Thirty-six

Knight in tarnished armour
seeks damsel in distress.
Must love walking, good wine and dragons.
Apply box number 101.

Jenny's pen hovered over *The Evening Standard*. She'd never read these kind of columns before, but the page had been open on her desk. One woman here, was looking for Mr Write. Was the spelling intentional? She'd also added NUMP at the end. Jenny had read enough of these pages to know this meant No Ugly Men Please. Maybe she should put an ad in herself.

Anything to take her mind off Alicia King. It had all gone really quiet in the last few weeks and she'd actually allowed herself to think that the woman had dropped the idea of suing. But no, here was the letter in this morning's post from her solicitor, announcing that she was taking proceedings and demanding damages. Apparently, someone in her party claimed her hair had been affected by the green dye.

'How?' she'd demanded when ringing the solicitor that morning.

'We're not entirely certain.' He spoke in such a boring monotone that Jenny wondered if he ever got excited about anything. 'We're waiting for the report to come in.'

Jenny felt her chest tighten. 'What kind of damages is she looking for?' Inside her head, she was doing rapid figures. The business was only just breaking even; she couldn't afford to hand over thousands of pounds. Couldn't they get the money off the crocodile manufacturers?

'They're denying responsibility,' said the solicitor smoothly, 'because there's no obvious damage to the toy. Of course, we could take it further but it would be extremely difficult to prove, not to mention costly.'

But where else would the dye have come from? The best form of action, said the solicitor, was to fork out in order to avoid a costly law suit. Meanwhile, she had clients ringing and emailing all over the place, demanding this, that and the other when she didn't even know if she was going to be in business in a few months' time. Alan had phoned twice in the last hour, wanting details for the Newcastle cruise. And here she was, drawing circles round crazy dating ads.

It was all Dan's fault. Making love like that to her and then ignoring her in favour of that tart Patsy. It was enough to destroy any woman's confidence.

'Morning.' Lily, her assistant came in, wearing fashionably bright purple leggings under a short wool coat. Jenny would have given anything to have been Lily's age and able to start again. Mind you, the girl did look pale. She hadn't seemed right for a few weeks now.

'You don't look very well if you don't mind me saying.'

Lily's eyes were almost black underneath. If she wasn't so stick-thin, Jenny might have suspected she was pregnant.

'I'm fine.' Lily had her back to her, getting out some files. 'I've got the information you asked me to get together for the Newcastle event. And I've . . .'

She stopped, her shoulders shaking, her head bent. 'Lily,' said Jenny softly, going up to her from behind, 'what's wrong?'

Lily turned round and buried her head against Jenny. Her initial reaction was to recoil but then she found herself putting her arms round the young girl. 'If you don't tell me, I can't help,' she pointed out.

Lily's black eye make-up was streaming down her face. 'It's Rupert.'

'Who?'

'Rupert. You know. Alicia King's son.'

'Don't tell me he's giving you grief over this stupid case. It's none of his business. And you don't have to worry either.'

'Yes, I do.' Lily was sobbing violently now. 'He . . . he . . . did things he shouldn't at the party.'

Jenny's mouth went dry. 'What?'

Lily sat down on the chair, covering her face with her hands. 'I don't know if you could call it . . . you know . . . rape because we'd already done some stuff . . . kissing . . . that sort of thing. But then we went into the room next door and I said I didn't want to but he was so persistent and then it just happened and I haven't heard from him since.'

'Bastard,' muttered Jenny through gritted teeth. 'But you're not pregnant?'

'No but I can't get it out of my mind. I feel dirty, and I keep wondering if I sent off the wrong signals.'

'No. It's all right.' Jenny was stroking the girl's back reassuringly. 'Look, why don't you have some time off?'

'We're too busy for that.'

'I know but this has clearly affected you.'

Lily blew her nose prettily. 'I'm all right. But thank you. Shall I get that?'

The phone never stopped. 'I'll go. Hello? Alan? I was just going to call you to go through everything. Sorry, can you hang on a minute?'

She gesticulated to Lily to bring the file over and then waited until the girl left the room. 'Right. Now I've got it all sorted but there are a few things I need to run over first.'

He seemed to like the little touches she'd added like the stereo system and the karaoke set. 'Aye, people love making fools of themselves even when they can't sing,' he agreed. 'Sounds great, lass. You've obviously been working hard. Actually, I'm in London tonight. I don't suppose you feel like a bite, do you?'

No she didn't. But she didn't dare risk annoying a client.

'Love to, although I've put myself on a diet since Sharrow Bay.'
He chuckled. 'Excellent! Now, where shall we meet?'

She should have said no. She was tired and wearing a rather dull navy skirt which she'd thrown on that morning. But after the manic day she'd just had, there wasn't time to go home and change. Luckily, she always kept a fresh clean white blouse in the office cupboard for emergencies.

The Langham Hotel, he'd said. He had taste, she'd give him that, and money too. If he was a bit older, she'd suggest Lucy teamed him up with Eleanor to get the woman off her poor sister's back.

Pulling on her 15 denier tights – something else she always kept a spare of in her office drawer – the mobile rang. 'Lucy! I was just thinking of you.'

It was strange. When she thought about her sister, it was with a certain amount of love mixed with emotions too complex to unravel. But when they spoke on the phone or met, one of them always managed to irritate the other.

'Were you? I wanted to check you were all right. I haven't heard from you since supper at Mike's.'

All right. So she hadn't rung to say thank you. Naughty her. Slapped wrist. 'Yes, well, I'm afraid I've been really busy.'

'Me too. Jon's back for the Christmas holidays.'

Was that her idea of being really busy? Looking after kids who were old enough to look after themselves and having a little part-time job in a rentals agency?

'He's acting very strangely and stays in his room most of the time.'

'Typical adolescent behaviour then. I remember doing the same.'

'Maybe.' Lucy didn't sound convinced. 'And Mike . . . well I'm rather worried about him.'

'Why?' She didn't mean to sound so sharp but sometimes Lucy didn't realise how lucky she was. First Luke and now

Mike, whereas she, Jenny, couldn't seem to get anyone.

'Oh, it doesn't matter.'

'OK.'

Jenny didn't have time for these please-tell-me-even-if-you-
don't-want-to games. If Lucy was under the kind of pressure
she was, she'd understand. 'Look, sorry, but I've got to dash.
I've got a work meeting. I'll ring you soon. Bye.'

The mobile rang as soon as she ended the call. 'Yes,' she
said sharply, expecting it to be Lucy.

'I've clearly rung at a bad time.'

Yes, she wanted to say. And three weeks late too.

'Hi, Dan,' she said coolly, her heart beat racing.

'How are you doing?'

'Very well, thank you. And yourself?'

'Fine.'

Christ, this was awful.

'Look, Jenny, I know this is short notice but I wondered if
you were free for dinner tonight?'

Yes, yes, she wanted to scream. Briefly, she thought about
cancelling Alan but it would look appallingly rude and she
couldn't afford to lose his account with this legal case hanging
over her.

'Sorry,' she said. 'I'm already going out.'

'Can't you cancel?'

'No.'

'Business meeting, is it?'

So he didn't think she was capable of having a social life
without him.

'Actually, it's a date.'

'I'm hurt.' He had a teasing tone to his voice. 'I thought we
had something back there.'

'Well you didn't follow up, did you?'

'No.' There was a distinct regretful tone to his voice. 'No, I
didn't. Look, can I call you in a few days?'

'If you like.'

Had she been too cool? She did want to see him again; there was this amazing animal attraction which made her want more, especially when she heard the sound of his voice. But he wasn't reliable. Even she could see that. Was that what she really wanted at her time of life?

Jenny glanced at her watch. Blast. Grabbing the newspaper, she shoved it in her bag, set the office alarm and ran down the road in search of a taxi.

All this effort and he wasn't there. Probably had a prolapse collapse or whatever men of his age got. And to think she could have gone out to dinner with Dan! Jenny scanned the hotel bar where Alan had suggested meeting. Then one of the men turned round and smiled warmly at her. 'Jenny. Good to see you, lass. Thanks for making it at such short notice.'

He'd lost weight! That's why she hadn't recognised him. Feeling like an idiot, she slid onto the stool he pulled out for her.

'What are you having then, lass?'

She wanted to keep her wits about her. 'Just sparkling water please.'

'Are you sure?'

'Yes, thanks.'

'Got a headache, have you?'

She smiled ruefully. 'It's been a bit of a tough day.'

He nodded. Alan had a reassuring face, she suddenly realised. The kind of face that made you feel life was going to be all right.

'Want to tell me about it, lass?'

And suddenly it all came out. About the threatened law suit and how scared she was in case this woman took her for everything she had; Lily, even though she felt rather guilty about betraying confidences; and then, to her embarrassment, Dan who was totally unreliable but whom she couldn't get out of her head.

As soon as she'd finished, she regretted it. She should have been Catholic where confessions were both free and confidential.

'It's all right, lass,' said Alan as though reading her mind. 'It's good to let things out, especially to someone who, if you don't mind me saying, has probably seen a bit more of the world than you have. I have to say that if you were my daughter, I wouldn't be too happy about this Dan bloke. It's not right, not ringing a woman for weeks and then asking her out at the last minute. A girl like you deserves someone better than that but you probably haven't time to find him, with your kind of lifestyle, have you?'

She shook her head.

'And as for that poor child – Lily, did you say? Well, have you spoken to your solicitor about what she told you?'

'No. Why?'

'If you weren't so stressed and couldn't see the wood for the trees, you'd probably see it yourself. It's quid pro rata, isn't it? You've got something against this woman. If her son did do what Lily says, it's a very serious offence. And it might just be enough for her to drop the whole thing.'

They had a lovely evening after that. He made her feel, thought Jenny as she succumbed to just one glass of wine, that everything was achievable. Achievable without that terrible rush or panic to succeed which she saw in people of her own age like Martin or Antony. Of course it was easier for someone like Alan. He'd achieved what he wanted. And he didn't have money worries.

'I've really enjoyed tonight,' he said, helping her into her coat. 'Thank you very much for your company.'

'The pleasure was mine. And I think we've covered everything now for the boat cruise.'

'I think so too. I've booked you and your assistant in at the same hotel as last time. I hope that's all right.'

'It was perfect. Thanks.'

'So.' His hand rested briefly on her shoulder. 'So we'll see you next month then.'

She turned to go.

'Wait. You don't think I'm going to let you go like that, do you?'

'Sorry?'

He smiled warmly. 'We've got to get you a taxi, lass. I'd not be a gentleman if I didn't make sure you got back safely.'

The answerphone didn't have any messages. Then again, what was she expecting? Dan saying how much he had missed her and asking her out again another night?

Get real, she told herself, looking for a tissue in her handbag. There was a terrible cold going round and she felt as though she was getting one now. Then she saw the newspaper in her bag. The newspaper which had that rather interesting ad about the dragon. Something inside her made her look at it again. There was a number to ring. She'd never done this before. The instructions told her to enter the box number by the advert.

'*Hi*,' said a tinny voice. '*My name is Brian. I'm five foot eight . . .*'

She put down the phone. Five foot eight? How could he slay even a pretend dragon at five foot eight? And why was it that the only decent men around were married?

Her eyes filled with tears. No. No. She wouldn't think about that now. She'd made a promise to herself years ago. And nothing, no one, was going to make her break it.

Thirty-seven

'Mum, you haven't asked me what I want for Christmas yet.'

Lucy paused while wrapping up an end of term bottle of French wine for Sam's form teacher (the poor man probably needed it). She'd been so busy worrying about Mike and what might or might not be true, that she hadn't got the children to write their usual Christmas lists.

'How about a matching earring for your other ear?' suggested Kate.

'Piss off.'

'Piss off yourself.'

'Stop it, you two!' Mike looked up from the dishwasher.

'It's called reflective listening.' Kate smiled at him challengingly. 'You repeat what the other person says. Mum does it to us but she thinks we don't notice. It's in one of her teen-shooting books.'

Mike looked at a loss for words. 'Going back to Christmas presents, have you thought about a goat?'

'A goat?' Kate and Sam's voices both rose in horrified unison.

'Yes. You two have got so much stuff that you don't need any more. Wouldn't it be nicer if Mum and I donated some money instead to a charity that would then use it to buy a goat for children who don't have as much as you?'

Lucy nearly dropped the bottle in shock.

Kate gave Mike a withering look. 'No thanks. But you could get me a rabbit. The kind that Aunty Jenny's got in her handbag. Second thoughts, don't bother. Christmas is for family.'

'Kate didn't mean it,' said Lucy when the children had gone to school after the usual 'Where's my coursework?' and 'Who's taken my tie?', 'But Luke – I mean we – always made a big thing about Christmas.'

'Well maybe it's time to start some new traditions. Now what's this about going out for this month's supper club? I thought the whole idea was that we were going to have meals at each other's houses.'

'It is. But because of Christmas, no one was very keen to take on something extra so we thought it would be nice to go to that new Italian in town.' She glanced across at Mike who was getting ready to go out for yet another so-called meeting. 'At least it's near us.'

'That's true, pet.'

He hadn't called her that for a bit and it made her feel slightly better.

'Are Antony and Patsy coming?'

'Yes. Although I have to say, I'm still surprised you can stick up for Antony. I mean I know he's your friend but he's behaved very badly towards Maggie, you know. And now he wants to sell the house. It's not fair.'

Mike shrugged. 'It's half his, pet. But legally he'll have to be fair. Look, I've got to dash. If this meeting in York overruns, I might have to stay the night but I'll ring to let you know.'

Lucy waited until she could see his car reversing down the drive before picking up the phone. 'Hello. This is Mrs Summers speaking. He's just leaving. Have you? Thanks.'

Her heart pounding, she looked out of the window. Sure enough, a navy blue car was following Mike's car down the road. Lucy sank down on the kitchen chair, her heart beating in her throat. What had she done? And what if Mike found out?

Maggie was already in the office when she got there, looking even more unkept than usual. Her hair was sticking up in bat wings at the side and without make-up, her pale eyelashes faded into obscurity. That flimsy cardigan had holes in the sleeve and her skirt had stains down the front. Hardly the kind of image to give would-be clients at Right Rentals.

'Everything all right?' asked Lucy, dumping her briefcase and putting on the coffee machine. The rule was that the first person in did that but clearly that was something else Maggie hadn't got round to.

'Sort of. Number 5 Cumberland Avenue have decided they're not going to rent out after all.'

'But the Mitchells are just about to sign the contract. They'll be devastated.'

'They are.'

'You've told them, then?'

Maggie shrugged. 'I also told them we didn't have anything else for them.'

'But we do. There's Abbotts Road.'

Maggie ran her hands through her hair wildly. 'Blast. I forgot.'

Lucy picked up the phone. 'They're engaged. Maggie, how could you have forgotten? We've been trying to shift it for ages.'

Maggie glowered at her from the coffee machine. 'Perhaps because my husband is shacking up with a model whom I couldn't possibly hope to compete with. It tends to take your mind off things.'

'I'm sorry.' Lucy tried to put her arm around her but Maggie pulled away. 'I know it's difficult, Maggie, but we've still got a job to do. Genevieve is coming back this week and she'll want a full update.'

Maggie shrugged again. 'It's all very well being able to swan off to the States for three months but us poor buggers have got to do the boring stuff.'

'I know but . . . Mr Mitchell? It's Lucy from Right Rentals here. Look, I'm sorry about number 5 being withdrawn but my colleague forgot to mention that we do have somewhere else that might suit you. You have. Oh, I see. And you wouldn't like to see this place as a comparison, just in case? Right. Well I'm so sorry you feel like that. Please let us know if we can do anything again.'

'Maggie?' She looked around the office. Where was she? Lucy went out into the back room. Her friend was sitting on the floor, her head in her hands, weeping. 'Maggie? Please don't cry.'

Maggie buried her head in Lucy's chest. 'Patsy is so beautiful. So young. So carefree. Do you know what Antony said to me? He said she made him laugh. I could make him laugh if I didn't have so much to do.'

'I know. I know. Shhh.' Hugging her, Lucy didn't have the heart to tell her that the Mitchells were furious with Maggie for being 'offhand and rude'. They were intending, they said, to complain to the owner. That was the second time it had happened this month. If Maggie didn't get herself together, she'd be out of a job.

And what about her own problems? Mike had said he was going to a meeting. In York. What would she do if the private investigator she had paid proved he was somewhere else? Mike consistently refused to criticise his friend Antony for treating Maggie so badly. Did that mean that he, Mike, would do the same thing?

By 4 p.m. Lucy tried to send Maggie home early, telling her she could manage on her own. Frankly, she'd be less trouble. All day, Maggie had been abrupt on the phone to clients and then made a complete hash of some simple filing.

'Have you seen your doctor recently?'

'No.' Maggie glared at her suspiciously. 'Why?'

'I just wondered if you were still taking the tablets he gave you.'

'They didn't agree with me.'

'I know these antidepressants can react in different ways. I was put on various types after Luke. But it's worth persevering.'

Maggie's lips tightened. 'I don't like them. Now are you sure about me going early?'

'Absolutely. By the way, how's the new childminder working out?'

'She's OK. At least she doesn't try to get them drunk.'

Patsy was never going to live that one down and understandably too.

She waited until Maggie had left and then spent an hour tidying up the chaos Maggie had left behind her. Time to go home, she thought, when the clock got to nearly 5.30. It had been agonising waiting for her mobile to ring all day. At least work had taken her mind off it slightly but now she was on tenterhooks. Why hadn't that private investigator firm rung? Surely the man must have some news by now?

The house looked warm and welcoming when she got back, with lights filtering in from behind the drawn curtains. Whatever else you could say about Eleanor, she did know how to run a house properly.

'Hi, I'm back,' she called out as she shut the door behind her. A delicious odour wafted from the kitchen as Eleanor bustled out in a blue and white striped pinny. 'Hello, dear. How was your day?'

'Hectic.' She kicked off her shoes. 'That smells fantastic.' She gave Eleanor a wry smile. 'One of your vegetarian casseroles?'

Eleanor gave her a beady look, as though she wasn't sure if she was joking or not. 'Well it is actually but it's got more chicken in it. Children need meat to build themselves up. By the way, you really must have a word with Sam. He's been on that computer all day long. I'm sure he's addicted to it.'

She'd just add that one to the list.

'Kate's out too – again. And Jon's been in his room all day. He didn't even come down when I called him to say it was lunch.'

'You know, Eleanor, I'm really worried about him. He won't see the doctor and I'm not sure he's really enjoying Oxford. He just won't talk about it. I'm wondering if he's depressed.'

Eleanor shook her head. 'In our day, we didn't have time to get depressed. We were too busy surviving the war. Now dear, supper's ready in ten minutes and if Kate's not back by then, she'll have to go without. When we were children, we wouldn't have dreamed of being late for a family meal.'

Lucy opened Jon's bedroom door quietly. The curtains were still closed and the air smelt stale. A pair of jeans lay on the floor together with a pile of t-shirts.

'Jon,' she whispered, making her way to the bed. 'Jon. It's Mum. Do you want some supper?'

She reached out her hand to touch the shape lying on top. To her horror, it went straight through. He had left a pile of clothes there to make it look as though he was there. Her heart quickening, Lucy turned on the light.

There was a note on the bedside table.

'Mum. Don't be angry but I can't take it any more. I hate Oxford and I hate myself. Don't worry. I'm not going to do anything stupid. But I need to do something different. I'll be in touch. Please don't try and find me.'

She didn't realise she was screaming until she heard herself.

'Mum! What's wrong?'

Sam had already snatched the note out of her hand. He began to cry. 'It's because we had an argument, isn't it? It's all my fault.'

'No, of course it's not.' Eleanor had her arm around him. 'Jon's just overreacting, that's all. Look, he says he's not going to do anything stupid. I remember when your father did something similar at that age. He went off for three days and then came back as though nothing had happened.'

Lucy had never heard that story before.

'Now calm down, Lucy, and let's think who we could ring. What about that friend of his, Peter?'

She couldn't stop shaking.

'It's all right, Mum.' Sam had his arm around her.

'Your mobile!' butted in Eleanor. 'It's ringing. Maybe it's Jon.'

Numbly, Lucy pulled it out of her pocket. 'Hello?'

She moved away from the others. 'Are you sure? I see. No. No, thank you. That's all I need to know.'

'Well?' They were both staring at her. 'Was that Jon?' asked Eleanor.

'No.' Lucy couldn't feel her knees any more. She sat down heavily on the edge of Jon's bed. 'Just a work call.'

'You're still shaking, Mum. Please don't.' Sam sat next to her, holding her tightly. 'It'll be OK.'

But it won't, she wanted to say. It won't be OK. Because Mike hadn't gone to York at all. He had driven to Swanage. And he'd just checked into a hotel with a tall African girl who was, as the private investigator had put it, young enough to be his daughter. Just like Patsy. Except that she was heavily pregnant.

Thirty-eight

Chrissie sat baby George in his chair by the television. 'Don't move.' Flicking the remote control to one of the kids' satellite programmes, she thanked God, not for the first time, for the invention of the television and video machine. It was the only thing that seemed to stop her son from racing around like a toddler on speed.

The health visitor continued to visit but less frequently now. Hopefully, as Martin said, they realised that George's bruises had been accidental after all. Meanwhile, there was still no sign of Martin getting a job and, even worse, he seemed to be enjoying being at home. This morning, he had actually read George the football scores from the sports pages.

'He can't understand,' she'd snapped.

Martin had given her a hurt look. 'How do you know? Didn't you see him clapping when I told him about the Aston Villa win?'

'Pure coincidence. He just happened to bring his hands together at that time.'

'Testy, are we?'

'If I am, it's not surprising. How are we going to pay next month's mortgage? If we hadn't borrowed so much – something I advised against at the time, if you remember – we might not be in the shit.'

'You'd better not use words like that at these job interviews you're applying for.'

'So you're the expert, are you? How many applications have you sent off now? And how many replies have you had?'

He'd retorted by slamming the door and going out. That had

been two hours ago and he still wasn't back. Thanks very much, Martin, she thought. Never here when I need you.

Glancing at George, who seemed reasonably settled now, she went next door to the study and turned on the computer. She already had her old CV file; all she needed to do was update it by inserting the phrase 'Career Break'. If only that was all it had been. In truth, having George hadn't just meant a break in her career. It had also been a break in her marriage; a gap which didn't show any sign of being filled. What had got into Martin? He'd been different towards her before he'd been made redundant. Was it something she'd said? Or someone he'd met. No. That was ridiculous. Martin just wasn't like that.

It seemed as though she'd only been on the computer for a few minutes, when George began to grizzle. At first, she ignored him. Then it got too loud. 'For God's sake, can't you just shut up for a bit to let me get on?'

It couldn't be lunchtime already? Sod it. What was the point in stopping work and going to all the trouble of heating up baby food when George would only spit it out?

'Don't look at me, like that,' she said coldly. 'You're not having any more of me and that's the end of it.'

That had been one of the things the health visitor had recommended. Stop breastfeeding so George might take more interest in solids. 'Wait until he's hungry,' she'd suggested. Well she would. She'd go back to the computer and when George's fussy little stomach told him that he'd jolly well eat whatever was put in front of him, she'd start making something.

The funny thing about the computer was that when you started doing something like adding a simple phrase or two, you began to tinker with the material you already had. Her CV had seemed fine before but now, rereading it, she kept noticing little bits here and there which could, and should, be tweaked.

George's yells got louder. 'All right, all right. I'm coming in a minute.'

Where was Martin? She hoped he hadn't gone to the pub again like he'd done the other day. She'd like to go to the pub. He could have asked her. And she could keep an eye on his drinking too.

The mobile rang just as she began printing out the final version. Sod that. He probably wanted her to come and pick him up from whichever watering hole he'd found himself in. It suddenly occurred to Chrissie that this was a race. If Martin found a job first, she'd have to stay at home with George who only whined and still couldn't talk. But if she did, he could see what it was like.

There it was again! 'What?'

'Chrissie?' said a smooth voice.

Instantly, she regretted barking down the phone.

'Dan!'

'Clearly I've rung at a bad time.'

Was he referring to her previous voice or George whose yells were getting louder?

'Shall I ring back when he's settled?'

He's never fucking settled, Chrissie wanted to say. 'No, it's fine. I was just on the computer, putting together my CV.'

What did he want? And what was she doing by not cutting this conversation off. This was the man who'd almost ruined her life so why why was she babbling on about CVs?

'Actually, Chrissie, that's what I'm ringing about. Patsy mentioned that she'd heard through Antony you were thinking of going back to work. Found anything yet?'

'No. But it's early days. I've emailed loads of applications off and . . .'

'Because if you haven't, I'm looking for someone to help me. I know your background is in HR but I need someone who can handle things for me. A sort of glorified PA I suppose. I know you might think that's below you but, believe me, it's quite challenging.'

'You're offering me a job after everything that's happened between us?'

'I thought it might help.'

'I don't need your pity. And your guilt is twenty years out of date. And now, if you'll excuse me, my baby needs me. But of course, I forgot. You don't have kids, do you? So you won't understand little things like that.'

And with that, she slammed down the phone, sank her head onto the computer keyboard (erasing her file inadvertently) and wept.

Chrissie glared at Martin as he lurched through the door. 'You've been drinking!'

'So what?'

Chrissie felt like throwing the contents of George's food bowl at her husband. She might as well. Their son certainly wasn't interested. 'So I've spent most of the day looking after our baby and trying to get a job while you've been drowning your sorrows in a lunchtime pint.'

Martin shrugged, flopping down on a chair. He always said as little as possible when he'd drunk too much.

'Martin, do you hear me?'

He nodded. 'By the way, I met Kim in the pub. She sends her best.'

She dabbed some baby gunk food off her jumper. 'Who?'

'Kim. The babysitter from the other night.'

'In it goes, George. No, in your mouth, stupid, not on the floor. What was she doing there?'

'Having her lunchbreak.'

'Thought she was a nanny.'

'She is.' Martin lay back in the chair and closed his eyes. 'But even nannies are allowed time off. Like husbands.'

Chrissie snorted. The noise made George jump and burst into tears. 'Oh for God's sake, George. Stop being such a wimp.'

Martin opened one eye. 'There's no need to take it out on him. You need to get out more, that's your trouble.'

'Where do you suggest? The local wine bar? Or, let's see,

that mother and toddler for subnormal parents who phone up social services to rat on other parents.'

'Kim was saying there's a nice mother and toddler club in Amersham on Friday afternoons. They do French classes.'

'For toddlers?'

'Why not. Anyway, she suggested you came along. Said it might make you less depressed.'

Chrissie narrowed her eyes. 'You told her I was depressed?'

Martin looked uneasy. 'Yes, well she could see George wasn't easy and . . .'

'And I suppose you told her about being made redundant too.'

'Actually, she was very sympathetic.'

'How dare you tell a stranger about our problems! Now look what you've done. You've made George cry again.'

'That wasn't me. That was you.' Martin stood up. 'I'm not hanging around here if you're going to go on like this.'

'Where are you going?' Chrissie felt scared.

'To check my emails. Remember? I'm looking for a job, as you keep reminding me.'

Of course there was nothing. Either for him or for her. Only a couple of rejections, including an apologetic line from her old boss saying she was sorry but there didn't look as though any vacancies were coming up but she'd let her know if the situation changed.

The following morning, Chrissie woke up determined to be more positive. Maybe she would go to the toddler French group. Maybe . . .

'Shit.'

'What?'

Martin was opening the post. He handed her a letter, grimly. 'I thought we'd paid this.'

'We were going to, remember? But then we agreed to leave it another month.'

Chrissie stared at the credit card bill. 'But that's more than our monthly mortgage repayment.'

Martin looked sheep-faced. 'Ah, that's another thing. We had a letter about that yesterday from the broker. It's time to renew our mortgage, apparently and he can't get such a good deal.'

Chrissie sank down onto the bottom of the stairs, her face in her hands. 'How much more are we going to have to pay?'

'Another grand.'

She stared up at him. 'We can't do it, can we?'

Martin licked his lips, the way he did when he was scared.

'It's going to be tricky. But I've sent off loads of job applications and you've done the same. Do any of them look like possibles to you?'

Should she tell him about Dan? 'Hard to tell.'

Martin shrugged ruefully 'Well, we'll just have to keep trying.'

'And if we don't get anything?'

Martin looked away. 'Then we'll have to move somewhere smaller. Much smaller.'

It wouldn't be the end of the world, Chrissie tried to persuade herself, if they had to sell their lovely home. After all, there were far more important things in life like health and keeping you marriage together. She'd read about money problems affecting couples but had never experienced it herself until now. Then there was George. Babies were meant to be a blessing but this one was driving them further and further apart.

'Why can't you be good?' she hissed at her son. 'Well you'd better behave yourself here. This place is different from the last.'

'Hi, Chrissie!'

Kim virtually pounced on them as soon as they went through the village hall door. 'And little George.' She knelt down so her face was parallel with his. 'How are you doing, poppet? Chrissie, this is Marie-France. She's taking the French class today. And this is Clarissa and Camilla.'

'Would George like a carrot stick?' asked her neighbour, who'd introduced herself as Marcie, as they sat around in the circle, waiting for the French class to begin.

Chrissie shook her head. 'George isn't very good at solids yet, I'm afraid. He doesn't talk much either. Just the odd word. But my health visitor's done a hearing test and he's OK. Apparently, some children just take longer than others.'

Her neighbour spoke in a soft American accent that didn't hide her surprise. 'He doesn't like solids? How old is he?'

'Nearly sixteen months.'

'So what does he eat?' asked someone else in the circle.

'Er, he still prefers me actually.'

There was a deadly silence. 'You're still breastfeeding him?' whispered Marcie aghast.

Chrissie nodded. 'It's not my fault. He hates food. Look.'

She handed George a carrot stick. Grabbing it, he plunged it into his mouth, grinning gummily.

'Fantastic!' cried Kim as though he'd just performed an amazing act.

Chrissie could have throttled him. 'He's never done that before.'

'You know,' said Kim quietly, 'Some mothers do find it hard to break that bond. I had an employer like that once. But you have to learn to let go.'

'It's not me. It's him.' Chrissie wasn't letting this one go. 'He insists on sucking every night and my nipples are so sore that . . .'

'Shhh.' Marcie gave her a prefect-like look. 'The class is starting.'

Chrissie couldn't stop fuming. It didn't help that not only did these bloody kids eat rock-hard food but they could also talk in French. It might be single words but they could do it. George's sole English word was still 'dink' although last week, she could swear he said 'boob'.

'I do hope you'll be able to make it next week,' said Marcie, as they were all filing out at the end. 'I'm sure if you come again, George will soon pick it up.'

Patronising cow. 'Thanks. I'll see.'

'Oh, Chrissie?'

Kim was running after them.

'Yes?'

'That will be fifteen pounds.'

Fifteen pounds? For a mother and toddler session?

'It's to cover the French class.'

She didn't even have enough money for supper. They'd have to have scrambled eggs as part of her new economy drive which was why they'd had to bail out of the Italian meal with the others.

'Sorry. I haven't got enough on me. Can I pay next time?'

Should she take the job? Yesterday, it would have been unthinkable. But now . . . she'd call Lucy. She always saw things in a sensible light.

'Kate?'

'It's Sam.'

Mistaking a teenage boy for his sister was probably one of the worst things you could do! 'Sorry. It's Chrissie. Is Mum there?'

'No.'

'Well, can you give here a message?'

'No. I mean I've got to keep the line clear.'

'I see. Well I'll ring later then.'

How rude! When George was that age, she'd make sure he answered the phone properly. Looking down at her son, asleep in the pushchair, her heart melted. He seemed so sweet, lying there. So vulnerable. So good. What kind of mother was she to get cross with him? Sometimes she found herself wondering how much easier life would be if he wasn't here. Not that she wanted anything to happen – God forbid. But . . .

'There you are.' Martin was waiting for her by the door. His face was set.

'What is it?'

'The bank rang. They're not prepared to give us that overdraft.'

She felt sick.

'So what do we do?'

'I rang the estate agents when you were out for a rough valu-
ation. Even if we sell, we'll have so little left after the mortgage
and our other debts, that we might have to rent.'

Rent? But they were grown ups. Only people like Antony's
girlfriend rented. 'No!' She shoved the pushchair in Martin's
direction. 'Sort him out, can you? I've got a phone call to make.'

Thirty-nine

Black. Black with a circle of scarlet inside. A circle that was getting bigger and bigger in her head.

Patsy had never been to a morgue before. She'd heard of people having to identify friends, of course. Usually friends who'd been stupid enough to drive too fast or who'd OD'd.

And of course, she'd been to the Chapel of Rest at home. Stop. Be practical. Hard, even. It was the only way to cope.

'I can't come now,' she'd told Tim from the Missing Persons Helpline when he'd rung at the shoot. 'I've got my stepkids with me.'

She wasn't sure why she used the term 'stepkids'. It wasn't as though she was married to Antony but it made her feel better somehow. More grounded. 'I'll be there tomorrow.'

He sounded surprised, as well he might. She'd been ringing him and everyone else on the case for weeks, desperate for news. But now she'd got it, she didn't want it confirmed. Besides, she needed to ring Dan.

'Best place for him, if he is dead. Sorry, Patsy, but he's a bastard and you know it.'

'Yes but . . .'

'I know what you're going to say. That he doesn't know what he's doing any more. That he's sorry for what he did do. But that doesn't change the facts, Patsy. He's the man who . . .'

'Stop. Don't say it.' She felt sick. 'I need time for this to sink in.'

'Want me to come with you tomorrow?'

'Please.'

No point in telling Antony when she'd finally got home after the shoot with the kids. He was still asleep, snoring heavily, his face turned to the wall.

'How are we going to get home?' asked Alice worriedly.

'Your mother will have to get you.'

'She can't. She's on this medicine that makes her too sleepy to drive.'

'Well, I'll just have to take you on the train then.'

'Don't you drive?'

'Not any more.'

'Why did you stop?'

She almost told Alice to mind her own business but her little face – reminding her of Babs in a strange way – made her speak more kindly. 'I went off it. Now who wants some fish fingers before we go?'

Her head was still reeling with thoughts about her dad when they got on the train and the kids' chatter was almost a welcome distraction.

'Are you going to marry Dad?' demanded Matt.

'No. I don't think so.'

'Good.'

'Thanks,' she said wryly.

'Well Mum says she'll kill Dad if he does marry you and we don't want him hurt. She's really crazy at the moment.'

'Yeah,' piped up Alice. 'And she says you've got fag breath.'

'Shut up.' Matt nudged her. 'That's rude.'

It took ages to get there with quite a walk from the station, with the kids giving directions. She'd never seen the house before. Not as big as Lucy's but still very nice with a large front garden with conifers and a wide path leading down to a solid-looking wooden door. There was a prominent 'For Sale' sign at the top of the drive.

'Off you go then, you two.' She waited at the top of the path, to check they got in all right. There she was! Patsy turned away swiftly but not before she'd seen what a mess Maggie looked.

Rumpled hair, wild expression on her face as she gathered her children to her in a hug and glanced confusedly up at Patsy.

Patsy started running round the corner and down towards the station. What right did she have to criticise her father? She'd been just as bad as him. He might have destroyed their family but hadn't she done the same to Maggie?

Dan picked her up outside the flat the following day. Antony was still asleep after a restless night with his cold so she'd left a note. They were meant to be going out to dinner at some Italian restaurant tonight with his friends but sod that.

'You OK?'

He was looking incredibly handsome with his coat collar turned up and a cashmere sweater below.

She nodded. They'd both come so far, she thought, yet neither of them could escape their roots. No one else could understand. No one.

He squeezed her hand lightly. 'It'll be over soon.'

She didn't trust herself to reply.

The morgue looked like that place where she'd queued to get benefits in between jobs. As they checked in at reception, she could feel the bile rising in her mouth. Wordlessly, Dan passed her a tissue as they followed a girl in a white coat down a corridor and up another. She opened a door. Lining the walls were rows of deep drawers, each with a handle. The girl consulted her list.

'Ready?' she asked kindly.

Patsy nodded. Dan took her hand.

The girl pulled open the drawer. A man in his mid-sixties lay in it, his eyes closed and skin grey. He was wearing a scruffy cardigan and old jeans. No shoes, noticed Patsy irrelevantly. Fingers stained with nicotine.

Relief flooded her body. 'It's not him, is it?' she whispered as though frightened of waking the body before her.

Dan shook his head. 'No.'

The girl closed the drawer quietly. 'Like we said, he didn't have any ID but he seemed to match the description given.'

'Thank you,' said Dan, giving her one of his charming smiles. 'We appreciate it.'

It was a huge relief to be back out into the fresh bracing winter air. Dan took her arm.

'I think we need a coffee before getting back.'

She nodded, allowing him to steer her into a Starbucks.

'Just sit there,' he said kindly, indicating one of the seats while he went up to the counter. He returned with coffee the way she liked it. 'How are you feeling?'

'Shaky. Relieved. Disappointed.'

She wanted him to take her hand again but he didn't. Instead, he cupped his hands round the polystyrene cup and looked straight at her.

'Is he still dangerous?'

'He wasn't when he was on the drugs they gave him. But the effect will have worn off by now . . .'

'He doesn't know where you live, does he?'

She shook her head. 'You don't think he'd try to hurt me?'

'I don't know. He said before that he blamed you for putting him in those homes.'

'I had to!'

This time he did take her hand. 'But he's not a rational man.'

'Never was.'

'So all we can do is go on looking and chasing up leads. I don't suppose anyone from home has seen him?'

Funny how 'home' was always Liverpool, even though they both hated the memories.

'Tried that. No.'

He let go of her hand and she felt empty. 'Just be careful. That's all I'm saying.' He leant back in his seat. 'Now, changing the subject completely, I've just taken on a new PA. You'll never guess who.'

She knew that look of old. It meant 'I've done something and I'm not sure if you're going to approve.'

'Tell me.'

'Chrissie. Her husband's lost his job and she needs to get work. My PA's just left and I need someone to help. Perfect, don't you think?'

Patsy scraped her chair back, away from him. 'But she doesn't like you. She's always being rude to you. And I can guess why.'

'Why?' His eyes narrowed.

'It's obvious. I know you were at university together. You had some kind of thing with her and then you dumped her which is what you do to them all.'

He shrugged. 'Just haven't found the right woman, that's all.'

'So you're not seeing Jenny any more?'

'On and off. I've told you, Patsy. I haven't time to make that kind of commitment. What about you and Antony?'

She pushed her cup away. 'He's married.'

'That hasn't stopped you before.'

'Maybe not. But people change.'

He was looking at her intently. 'It's the kids, isn't it? You rather like them, don't you?'

'The girl reminds me of Babs.'

'The girl,' he mimicked. 'Too scared to use her name, are you, in case you get too attached?'

Patsy stood up. 'I've got to get going.'

He caught her arm. 'I don't know why you do it.'

'Do what?'

'You know perfectly well what I mean. I don't know why you prostitute yourself with a series of rich boyfriends so they can give you handouts which you then use to pay your father's home fees.'

She flinched. 'It's not prostitition.'

'Isn't it? How many well-off men have you had before Antony? Fifteen, twenty or is it more? The pattern's always the same. You don't care for them but you milk them for a while and then when they get fed up with bankrolling you, you move on.'

'That isn't fair! What else am I meant to do? I'm working as hard as I can. I'm doing my bit.'

'I know, Patsy.' He took her hand but she snatched it away. 'Listen, woman. Please. I've told you before. When I've got it, I'll give you the money. Now let me give you a lift back, now.'

'I'll get the tube.'

He put a hand on her arm. 'Patsy, you've just been to see a dead body in a morgue.'

'Go on then. If you insist. But don't talk about money or Antony. Besides, you're wrong about one thing.'

'What?'

'Antony. I do actually care for him.' She took pleasure in the pain that flitted across his face. 'And I happen to know that he cares for me too.'

Dan insisted on seeing her into the flat.

'I'm quite all right,' she argued crossly.

'You're still shaking.'

She couldn't disagree. The key wouldn't even fit in the lock.

'Let me do that.'

He took it from her and their hands brushed, confusing her. 'Want a cup of coffee?'

'No thanks. I'd better be going.'

'Sounds like a good idea to me.'

They both turned at the sound of Antony's voice. He was sitting on a chair in the sitting room, still in his pyjamas. He looked at her stonily. 'Where have you been?'

'Out,' said Patsy. 'Feeling better?'

He gave Dan a nasty look. 'While you've been having fun, I've been really ill.'

Patsy snorted. 'I looked after you, although you might not remember it. And we haven't been out having fun actually. We've . . .'

'I don't want to hear. But what I do want to know is why you had the cheek to allow my kids to be in some giveaway paper. I've just had Maggie on the phone, screaming at me. Now she says I can't have them at Christmas.'

'It was only a couple of pictures. I had to take them with me to work, didn't I, because you were too ill to look after them.'

'A couple of pictures? Maggie was furious about it when the kids told her. I'm going to ring the editor. They can't do that kind of thing without written permission.'

'I gave it to them,' mumbled Patsy.

'You what?'

'It was only a fashion shoot. And they loved it.'

'How dare you!'

Antony stood up and for a minute, she felt scared, just as she had as a teenager in front of her father.

'That's enough.' Dan spoke quietly but firmly. 'She was only doing her best.'

Antony was clenching his fists. 'What's it got to do with you?'

'Because it's true. You were ill in bed and there was no one to look after the kids so she took them with her. What else was she meant to do?'

'You seem to know a lot about my girlfriend's life.'

Dan looked at him squarely. 'We go back a long way.'

'Clearly. I know Patsy's has a chequered past but frankly, I don't need it thrown in my face. Get out of my house.'

Antony!' Patsy could hardly believe what she was hearing. 'It's not your house. It's my flat.'

'Oh, yes. That's right. I left my nice house for you, didn't I?'

'I didn't ask you to.'

'Stop it. Right now. Antony, you're bullying her. She's just had a traumatic experience.'

'What are you talking about?'

'It's my dad.' Patsy sat down, shaking. 'He's gone missing. I had to go to the morgue. But it wasn't him . . .'

She felt her body convulsing with sobs; felt someone's arms around her shoulder. It wasn't Antony.

'You said your family was dead.'

'They are.' She forced herself to stop crying. 'Apart from my dad. He's in a home. At least he was until he went missing.'

'Where is he?'

'I don't know.'

'What do you mean he was in a home? Because he was ill?'

'Sort of. He has . . . he has certain mental issues.'

'Is it a local authority home?'

She shook her head. 'Private.'

'How can you afford that?'

'It's why I work.'

Antony closed his eyes briefly. 'What a bloody fool I've been. And there I was, thinking you wanted me. It's my money you're after, isn't it?'

'No.' Patsy lurched towards him, trying to put her arms round his neck but he pushed her away. 'I promise you. It might have been like that with the others but not you.'

'The others? You mean you've been using other men like me. Breaking up their marriages?'

'She didn't break up your marriage,' butted in Dan. 'You chose to go.'

'More fool me, then.' Antony stood up. 'Well, I'm off. No, leave me alone, Patsy.'

'Are you going back to Maggie?'

'I can't do that, can I?'

'Then stay,' she pleaded. 'Please stay. At least let us talk about it.'

Antony hesitated.

'See you another time, Patsy,' said Dan quietly. She heard the door closing quietly behind him.

'Please stay, Antony,' she repeated. 'I need to talk to you. Tell you everything. Then you won't think so badly of me.'

'Go on then.'

She sat back down on the chair, drawing her knees up to her chest. 'My father was not . . . was not an easy man. He had a temper. When he was angry, you had to keep out of his way especially when he'd had a drink. But when he wasn't in a mood, he was great. Funny, warm, generous. He brought us up, me and my sister Babs, after my mother left. She couldn't cope with his moods and there were . . . there were other women too. Then one day . . .'

She stopped.

'Go on,' said Antony more gently.

'Then, eighteen years and eleven months ago, when my sister was sixteen – she was a year younger – my mother came back. My father was furious to see her and there was a terrible argument.'

She could hardly speak now. 'I'd just got back from school. He was threatening her – verbally – and she turned and ran straight out into the road. Babs chased after her. They were both hit by a lorry. My mother died immediately. My sister died two days later in hospital.'

Antony took her hands. 'My God. How awful.'

'The blood . . .' She stopped. 'I haven't been able to touch meat since. Or drive a car. Every time I think about it, I see this huge black circle in my head with a scarlet blood centre. Sometimes I think it's going to swallow me up.'

'But how can you bear to see him?'

'Because of Babs.' She spoke dully. 'When she was . . . was dying, she begged me to forgive him. So I have to. I promised.'

She sniffed, searching for a bit of toilet paper in her sleeve. 'Dad never recovered. He blamed himself. He stopped drinking but he became a recluse. He couldn't get over the publicity, you see. It was all over the papers. "Mum and daughter killed by violent dad," even though that wasn't the whole truth. People

up there are still talking about it. Thank God, I won my modelling contract and came down to London but I kept going back,
to keep an eye on him. Over the years, he's got worse and
worse.'

'And you had to put him in a home.'

She nodded. 'Recently, he's become violent. He's made threats
towards me because he blames me for putting him in a home.'

'What kind of threats?'

She looked at him, her eyes wet. 'The last time I saw him,
he said that one day he'd manage to escape from the home and
then he'd come and get me.'

She buried her face into his jumper. Cornflower blue. Wool.
Comforting damp smell. 'I'm scared, Antony. I'm really scared.'

'Don't be.'

He cupped her face in his hands. 'I love you.'

She wanted to say it. She really did. He was waiting. She
could almost smell it.

'I know.' She looked away. 'Thanks.'

Forty

The journey didn't seem so long this time in first class. It was actually quite comfortable – at least it would be if Jenny wasn't so twitchy. Perhaps she should have consulted the lawyer first of all instead of following Alan's advice and approaching Alicia King direct.

Her PA had kept her hanging on for ages before frostily announcing that Mrs King would ring back by 11 a.m. That was nearly an hour ago. Should she call again or should she ring the lawyer with the information that a still tearful Lily had given her?

Jenny poured herself another cup of luke warm tea. If only she could get rid of this horrible fog that had been engulfing her since that first legal letter, she could concentrate on her job. Tonight was really important; not just for her but for Alan. In the short time she'd known him, he'd been wonderfully calm and, well, reliable. But in the last few days, he'd been ringing her all the time, checking on details about the boat trip and even, in his last call, advice on what to wear! And she hadn't even thought about her Christmas shopping.

At last! The mobile. 'Jenny speaking.'

She barely recognised Lucy's flat, emotionless voice at the other end. A horrible flash of foreboding shot through her, just as when they'd called her about Luke. 'What's wrong?'

She listened intently, hardly able to believe it. Jon had run away. Mike had been seen by a private eye – a private eye! – going into a hotel, his arm around a heavily pregnant woman!

'Maybe there's a rational explanation for this. Have you spoken to him?'

'No.' Lucy's tone was dismissive. 'I'm waiting until he gets back tonight. Frankly, he's not important any more. Not compared with Jon.'

'But what are you doing to find him? You can't just wait there.'

'What do you expect me to do? Comb the streets? He's not likely to be around here, is he?'

'Then where would he be?'

'If I knew that, I'd be there.'

Her sister wasn't normally so brusque.

'Have you called the police?'

'Of course I have. He's got to be missing for forty-eight hours before they will do anything.'

'What about his friends?'

'I've called them. None of them knows anything.'

'Really?'

'Well they say they don't.'

Jenny's mouth tightened. 'Look, I'm on my way to the north for a client event. I'll ring when I get there. I was going to ring to say I couldn't make tonight but . . .'

'It's cancelled.'

Wasn't it strange, thought Jenny, how irrelevant things like dinner were when you had real emergencies like this?

They'd almost reached York when Jenny finally managed to get hold of Steve.

'Hi, how are you doing?'

'OK. I need you to do something for me. Remember when you came to supper at my sister's house in the autumn? You thought you recognised that friend of my nephew's from some of the clubs you go to.'

'Nice boy.' His tone was appreciative.

'Yes, well, I just wondered if you knew how to get hold of him.'

He sounded cagey. 'Any particular reason?'

Briefly, she explained.

'Right. Well in that case, I'll get onto it. Blimey Jenny, what's that noise?'

She looked out of the carriage window at the stream of people getting on. 'I'm on a train. To Newcastle.'

'The other end of the world, you mean.'

'Actually, it's very nice. Not what I'd thought at all.'

'I see.' He was clearly amused. 'Met someone up there, have you?'

'I'm here on business actually.' There was a bleep, indicating a text message had come through. 'Look, I don't want to be rude but my sister is freaking out. Can you do what you can?'

Jenny stared at the text message in disbelief. Right. Action time. Punching in the number, she worked out exactly what to say. Thank God she was good at thinking on her feet. 'Mrs King is at lunch,' announced the frosty receptionist. 'Can anyone else help?'

Her mind raced. 'Is her son there by any chance?'

'Hold on and I'll see.'

There was a silence. Had she been cut off? Should she really take this gamble if and when they put her through?

'Rupert speaking.'

'Hello. This is Jenny from Eventful Events.'

'I'm not sure we should be speaking in view of the circumstances. My mother left instructions that you were to communicate only through the lawyers.'

Her hands began to shake. 'Actually, Rupert, I've just discovered a piece of vital information which you might not want to go through formal channels.'

She'd definitely reached a nerve there.

'Would you like to explain, Miss Macdonald?'

'Well,' she paused. 'I don't want to say too much because I'm on a train and you never know who might be listening. But my assistant Lily has just told me exactly what happened on the night of the launch.'

His voice had an amused lilt to it. 'She did?'

How dare he laugh like that? Anger made Jenny take a gamble. 'You were seen, Rupert. You might as well come clean.'

Maybe if he thought there were witnesses, he might just do that.

'It was just a joke,' he said quickly.

'A joke?'

'I thought it would liven things up a bit although I hadn't reckoned on your Lily having such sharp eyes as well as a neat butt.'

'Liven things up?' she could hardly get the words out. 'Is that what you call it?'

'Well, these things can get so boring, can't they?' His voice took on a friendly edge, as though he was trying to win her over. 'I only got a couple of bottles from one of those theatre prop shops. Come on – it's not as though it was poison.'

Suddenly, it was all making sense. Rupert had actually put the dye in the water and he thought Lily had seen him! So that stuff hadn't come from the crocodile at all!

'Did your mother know?'

He hesitated, just long enough for her to know she had.

'And what about my assistant? She said you took advantage of her?'

The man across the aisle looked sharply at her and Jenny reddened.

Rupert snorted down the phone. 'What a quaint term! I can assure you, Miss Macdonald, your assistant Lily was more than keen to participate.'

Jenny hesitated. Lily herself had said she might have sent out the wrong message and Jenny knew how easy it was to do that. Far simpler to stick to the confession he'd already made.

'I take it that you will now be dropping charges,' she said firmly

'I'll have to discuss this with my mother.' His voice was still cold. He didn't appear to be scared. Supposing he denied what he'd just said. If only she could have taped this conversation.

'Well, perhaps you'd better give her this message from me. If I don't hear from her by 5 p.m. tonight, I will report our conversation to my solicitor.' She paused, remembering the text Alan had sent her this morning. 'I believe this isn't the first time your mother has tried to sue people who have done work for her. Could that be, I wonder, an attempt to get out of the bill?'

'I hope you're not threatening me.'

'Merely pointing out the facts. Goodbye, Rupert.'

Jenny was still jittery when the train pulled into Newcastle. So much had happened. The only important thing was finding Jon. That boy had always been sensitive. She'd had her doubts about Oxford from the beginning; so intense. As for Mike, well she'd always privately thought he was too good to be true, although of course she felt sorry for Lucy. Meanwhile, she had that five o'clock deadline ticking away in her head. The last thing she needed was a flipping boat trip with a client.

Alan was waiting for her, as promised, under the vaulted entrance. Slightly to her surprise, he kissed her briefly on both cheeks. 'How was your journey, lass?'

'Very smooth, thanks.' Unable to stop herself, she checked her mobile for messages as she spoke. Nothing. 'Thanks for your text. I couldn't believe Alicia King has done this before.'

He shrugged, pleased. 'Just a hunch. I got one of the boys to check it out.'

'I can't thank you enough.'

'Don't mention it, lass.'

Alan's driver glided up in the Merc and Alan shepherded her in. Leaning her head back on the leather interior, she couldn't resist closing her eyes.

'Tired, lass, are you?'

'Not at all.' She flashed him one of her 'I'm in control' smiles and opened her briefcase. 'Now, everything's set for tonight. I just want to go over one or two details to check you're happy.'

He'd booked her in again at the Malmaison which was tastefully decorated with Christmas gaieties. There was coffee and mince pies in the drawing room below, the concierge had told her but all Jenny wanted to do was lie on the wonderfully soft spacious bed. Just half an hour to rest before getting ready. She'd close her eyes for a second and then . . .

Surely that wasn't the time? She'd have to rush now to meet Alan on the boat and what was that, the alarm clock? No. The mobile. She fumbled to open it before the ringing stopped.

'Hello?'

'This is Alicia King speaking. I believe you spoke to my son this morning.'

The woman's icy tones filled her with alarm. She was going to deny what her son had said and now she, Jenny, wouldn't have any proof.

'We have decided to withdraw our complaint, providing this little matter with your employee is never raised again.'

Little matter? Jenny's hackles rose. 'I'd hardly consider your son polluting the pool and then trying to sue me for damages, to be a "little matter", especially when his mother was involved.'

There was a sharp intake of breath at the other end. 'You can't prove that.'

'No but I could try and I don't think you'd like the publicity very much. I can see the headline now. "Fashion boss's son sabotages party with green dye from a dramatics props company in an attempt to extort money." Well this is one little drama, Alicia, which you're not going to win.'

'Does that mean you are going to press charges?'

Jenny thought of Lily; poor white-faced Lily who had insisted that under no circumstances did she want to go through any publicity. Supposing it emerged that she and Rupert had made out? Even so, the woman deserved to sweat.

'I believe this isn't the first time you have tried to sue firms who work for you, is it Alicia? No, don't try to deny it. I've been doing some research.' Jenny tried not to let her nerves creep into her voice. 'We won't press charges, providing you pay a cheque for £10,000 straight into my account to cover the entire cost of the event, drop your action immediately and also sign an undertaking never to discuss this matter with anyone else.'

'Agreed.'

Wow. She hadn't expected Alicia to give in so fast on the money. 'If the cheque isn't in my account by Monday and if my solicitor hasn't received written notification by then, I will tell him exactly what has happened.'

'Very well.'

The woman put the phone down without the courtesy of a formal goodbye. She should feel ecstatic, thought Jenny, but all she could think of was Lily. The child reminded her so much of what she'd been like at that age. Innocent. Attractive. Unaware of how badly she could be hurt or lead someone on, unwittingly . . .

She punched in the office number. 'Lily? It's me. She's dropped the action. No, I didn't have to mention that. Apparently, Rupert put the dye in the pool himself and he thought you'd seen him do it, which is why he confessed. No, I know you'd have told me if you had but he thinks he was spotted so that's the important thing. Are you all right? Sure? Well, take Monday off, won't you. Yes, I'm certain.'

Her assistant should be up here with her but she hadn't the heart to ask her. She'd give Lily a few days off and then suggest she saw a counsellor. If she'd seen someone all those years ago, she might not be in the mess she was now.

Jenny had to admit it. She'd done a good job. The boat looked stunning, hung with Christmas fairy lanterns from deck to bow, while the staff, resplendent in their white uniforms, handed out canapés. The guests were filing on board, dressed in all their evening finery. And Alan! Well, Alan had completely taken her by surprise. Losing all that weight really suited him. She almost liked the spotty red and white bow tie.

'Jenny!' His eyes travelled over her admiringly. 'You look gorgeous.'

Automatically she smoothed down the long white sequinned dress which she'd found at a designer end of season sale and which set off her shoulder-length dark hair. 'Thank you.' She glanced at the guest list. 'Everyone seems to be here. I think we can set off, if you like.'

'Wonderful.' His eyes were still on her.

'Anything wrong?'

'No. Not at all, lass. I can't wait to get started. Now come with me. There are several people I want to introduce you to. You never know. You might get more business up here.'

The meal was a great success. Not only did the table look stylish with its little candles scattered over the white tablecloth but the food – salmon en croute, followed by raspberry coulis – was mouthwatering. Alan's suggestion of a local caterer who happened to be a friend of his wife's was spot on.

He was chattering animatedly, she noticed, to some important-looking man on his right but every now and then, he'd glance across as though to say 'All right?' How very chivalrous! Almost as though she was a guest.

'So tell me, what is PR exactly?' asked a gaunt woman on her left in a red dress. Jenny stifled a sigh. People were always asking her that but she had a duty to do for Alan. The evening had to be a success and if it meant making boring small talk, so be it, even though she couldn't stop herself checking her mobile every now and then in case there was a message from Steve.

The dinner was finishing now. Time for the entertainment. 'Excuse me,' she apologised to the gaunt woman in red. 'I need to check everything is ready for the band.'

The woman clapped her hands together with excitement.

'I'm so looking forward to that. I hear it's a jazz group. Is that right?'

Jenny nodded, smiling. 'I'll see you later.'

'That would be wonderful, dear. Actually, I've got a niece who's just left school. Your PR job sounds just the thing for her. Would you mind giving me your phone number?'

Jenny gave her a business card. Right. Now where was the band? She'd settled them in but now they were nowhere to be seen. Eventually, she tracked them down below, the singer white as a sheet. 'I can't stop throwing up,' he groaned. 'It must have been something I ate.'

'Here?' demanded Jenny alarmed.

'No. At lunchtime. I had a prawn sandwich.'

He pushed past her, heading for the Gents. 'Excuse me.'

Jenny faced the rest of the group. 'Are you lot all right?'

They nodded. 'We had cheese sandwiches,' said one. 'My mum always said, never have prawn . . .'

'All right, all right.' Christ, now what was she going to do?

'Can any of you guys sing?' she asked hopefully.

'We can but it's not great. Nothing like Tony.'

'Fantastic.'

She felt a hand on her shoulder.

'Everything all right, lass?'

With any other client, she'd have said yes, it was fine. She might even have phoned someone – God knows who – to be shipped over or whatever you called it to take the singer's place. But Alan's kind eyes were too much.

'Your nephew's mate's got food poisoning. No, it's all right. Not here. Somewhere else. He can't sing. I'll have to find a replacement. Just give me half an hour and I'll do it . . .'

His hand tightened on her shoulder. 'You won't find anyone lass. Not up here on a Friday night. I know you can work miracles – I've seen you – but I think even this one is beyond you.'

She stared at him distraught. 'But I've got to do something.'

'Well,' Alan began reflectively. 'I do have an idea. I'm not a hundred per cent keen on it myself but it's possibly better than nothing . . .'

'Ole man river, he can't stop rowing . . .'

Jenny sat in the lounge below deck, entranced, like everyone else. The singer's deep rich-gravel voice was totally and utterly seductive. The words of the song struck her very soul. This was the meaning of life. This was what it was all about. Love. Family. Truth. Honesty.

'He just keeps going . . .'

How did he do it? Jenny had been sceptical, not to mention amazed, when Alan had modestly suggested he sang himself. 'It's a bit of a hobby of mine, lass. Used to do it quite a lot when the wife was alive. I might be a bit rusty now but I think it will be all right.'

All right? It was mesmerising. She could listen to him for hours. The entire boat was silent, apart from the distant hum of the engine. It really was an amazing place, thought Jenny, looking out through the window at the lit-up harbour. Cold, yes. And she was grateful for her wrap. But so incredibly beautiful.

Her phone bleeped, indicating a text.

'Hv found some of Jon's friends. Lv it with me.'

What did that mean? Should she ring Lucy or would that get her hopes up unnecessarily? Did that mean . . .

CRASH.

Jenny found herself being thrown against something hard. Her head began to pound as though someone had hit her with a cosh and although she couldn't see clearly, she was aware of lights flashing. A woman screamed, after which was an eeerie silence and then a terrible crashing noise followed by a loud siren voice and a disembodied voice.

'Emergency! Emergency! Will everyone please make their way to the emergency exit as indicated.'

Someone pushed past her, knocking against her leg and she

screamed in agony. Dimly, she tried to recall the emergency procedure which the captain had run through at the beginning, although she'd been too busy to pay much attention. She'd just have to follow the crowd and try to help people on the way.

Dragging her leg behind her, Jenny clutched at the bar rail for support as the woman in red surged past her, chin in front, determinedly. Where was Alan? Memories of that terrible boat collision in London years ago, flashed through her head. Was that what had happened? Peering out through the windows, it looked as though there was a large shape out there, although it was difficult to see in the dark. The boat suddenly rocked again and someone screamed.

'Please remain calm,' came the tannoid voice. Jenny felt a sudden urge to ring Lucy; to tell her how much she really loved her. How . . .

CRASH. Something hit her head again and this time she really couldn't see anything, although she could hear people shouting; a huge crowd of them, as though they were trampling through her brain. But there was one above them. One which she could recognise even in this state.

'Jenny. *Jenny*. Where are you?'

Forty-one

The text message bleeped up on her phone as she drove into Peter's road.

'*Someone wants to view Abbotts Road on the 12th. Can't do it earlier as he's away. Insists that you show him round and not me. 1 p.m. ok with you? Maggie.*'

Lucy, sensing that Maggie would be offended by a client who didn't want her to do the viewing, texted back a tactful affirmative. Her friend's naturally blunt manner, accentuated by her marriage problems, meant that rather a lot of their customers were now asking for Lucy instead.

Jon's friend Peter lived in a small terraced house on the wrong side of the railway line. His mother had four children, of whom Peter was the eldest. His father was not the same as his brothers' and sisters' and she wasn't sure where he lived or even if Peter still saw him. The mother worked part-time in a residential home and Peter was also working now – she wasn't sure what as – after giving up college.

Lucy had always refused to admit to herself that this bothered her but now, as she knocked on the door, she wondered whether Jon had been attracted to Peter (whom he'd met at school), purely because his lifestyle was so different.

It took a long time for someone to come. Lucy peered through the cracked glass panel of the front door. It was late afternoon. Maybe Peter's mother was collecting the younger children from school. Ah, here was someone.

'Hello?'

Lucy had never met Peter's mother before. She was younger than she'd expected, in sloppy pink tracksuit bottoms with a small silver stud in her nose. But it was her face that really struck Lucy. It was the kind of face you could immediately trust. Kind, open, friendly eyes.

'Hello.' Lucy hovered awkwardly on the doorstep. 'I'm Lucy. Jon's mother.'

The questioning look on the woman's face immediately cleared. 'Of course. I can see the resemblance now. I'm Shelley. Sorry about the door. One of the children was playing football. You know what kids are like! Please, come in.'

Lucy found herself in a small narrow hallway. But it was warm and light; from the top of the stairs, she could hear music and in the room next door children's laughter and the background hum of the television.

'Any news of your son?'

'No.' Lucy bit her lip. 'That's why I'm here actually. I spoke to Peter when we first found Jon had gone but I wanted to see him in case he could remember anything that might help.'

'Course. I'll just get him.'

As Shelley ran up the stairs, Lucy couldn't help thinking that if it had been her, she would probably have just yelled. A tall youth with three earrings on one lobe lolloped down the stairs, his lopsided fringe flopping over one eye in the same way that Jon wore his.

'Hi, Mrs Summers.'

He spoke straight at her, without avoiding her eyes. If he was hiding anything, he was doing a good job of not showing it.

'Please,' she said awkwardly. 'Call me Lucy.'

'Why don't you go into the lounge,' said Shelley. 'I'll ask the little ones to move.'

'No, really,' said Lucy quickly. 'I don't want to disturb anyone. I just needed to talk to you to see if you could think of anything that might help me find Jon.'

He shrugged. 'Not really. I've told you everything.'

'Have you heard from him?'

'Nope.'

'Tell you what,' said Shelley brightly. 'Take a seat on the kitchen stools here and I'll leave you to it.'

Lucy perched on the edge with Peter opposite. The kitchen was clean and bright with funny postcards on the fridge and the smell of coffee. No arguments. No stepfather. No visiting granny who did everything different in her day. She could see why Jon had chosen to spend more time here than at home.

'Look, Peter. I need you to be honest here. I'm scared. I don't know where my son is. I know he didn't like uni. I know he missed you.'

He shifted awkwardly in his seat.

'I also know he's gay,' said Lucy softly.

Peter gaped. 'You do?'

'I've known for a long time. Call it a mother's instinct if you like. I tried to talk to him about it but there was never the right time. Is that why he's gone? Because he missed you at Oxford?'

The boy nodded. 'Partly. But he also hated the whole set-up, like. The course. The other blokes. That kind of thing.'

'So where is he?'

'I really don't know. Honest. I'm as worried as you are. He texted me to say he was going away for a bit cos he didn't want to go back to Oxford.'

'But if you're . . . if you're close, wouldn't he want to be with you?'

Peter's eyes flinched. 'That's what I thought. But I think he's confused. Needs time to think.'

Lucy could hear Shelley moving around upstairs. 'Does your mum know?' she asked softly.

'About me, you mean?'

She nodded.

'Yeah, sure.'

'And she's OK about it?'

'Says we've each got to be what we are like.'

'But Jon was scared. Scared of what I'd say?'

Peter nodded and Lucy felt sick with guilt. What kind of mother was she, that her son couldn't confide in her any more?

'Look, Mrs . . . I mean Lucy. I really want to help, like. I could give you a list of the places we used to go to. Clubs in London. That kind of thing. I can come with you, if you like.'

'Thanks.' It was a start. 'Anything. Anything that you think might help.'

'I want to come too,' said Sam in a small voice.

'You can't.'

'Home's like boot camp. Look how you wouldn't even let me go to the Wattevers concert. No wonder Jon ran away.'

'Shut up, Sam. These clubs won't let you in anyway.' Kate was already getting on her jacket. 'If anyone's going, it's me. You'll stand out like a sore thumb, Mum, even if you have got Jon's weird friend with you.'

'Shh,' hissed Lucy. 'He's waiting by the door. And I'm sorry Kate but you're not going. I need someone here to man the phones in case we get news.'

'Gran can do that,' spat Kate.

'No, she can't.' Lucy tried to keep her voice low. 'She might get it wrong.'

'Get what wrong, dear?' asked Eleanor taking out her earphones.

'Nothing.'

'Mum's going to try and find Jon in some London clubs and I want to go too,' pouted Kate. 'You'd let me, wouldn't you, Gran?'

'In my day, dear, we had tennis club dances. Not like the kind of clubs you've been telling me about. Well if you do go, Kate, dear, can you leave me your iPod? I hadn't realised how clever it was. Have you tried it, Lucy?'

'No.' Lucy could have shaken her mother-in-law. 'I've had other things to think about.'

'That reminds me, dear. Isn't Michael back yet?'

'No.'

'Goodness me. I don't remember Luke working so late. Still if you're happy about that, dear . . .' She let her voice trail away meaningfully. 'You'd better come here, Mungo, and let Gran give you a stroke. When Michael gets back, you'll be banished to the utility room again. What are you going to do about Mungo and Michael's allergies when you get married, Lucy?'

'Eleanor! My son has gone missing. Frankly, Mike's allergies are the last thing I can think about. If he gets back, tell him to heat something up in the microwave.'

It had been years since she'd been to anything remotely like a club. In her day – God, she was sounding like Eleanor – they'd called them discos. They'd started off by driving to Soho Square and parking down one of the side streets.

'We'll try this one first,' said Peter, leading her down a basement. A girl was on the door, wearing a leopard skin wrap cardigan and a skirt that barely did the job. She glanced at Lucy curiously.

'Hi.' Peter seemed far more relaxed here than he'd been in the car. 'We're looking for Jon. You know? The friend who usually comes here with me.'

Lucy winced.

'Have you seen him? It's important, like.'

The girl shrugged. 'I don't think so, mate, but it's difficult to tell.'

Lucy could see her point. Peering inside the door, she could see . . . well what could she see? Smoke, the outlines of bodies, the smell of cigarettes and drink. The overpowering juddering music which made her feel dizzy just to hear it.

Peter gave the girl a small photograph. 'Can you pass this around? There's a number on the back to contact us.'

Why hadn't she thought of that? And where had he got the picture from?

'Jon gave it to me some time ago,' said Peter, as though reading her mind. 'I got some photocopies done.'

'Thanks, Gary. See you around.'

Gary? Lucy looked back, desperately trying not to stare. Only then did she realise the girl in the leopard print was actually a boy.

It wasn't until they'd ruled out the fourth club that Lucy really began to have doubts. When Jon was little, she knew exactly where he was. Why hadn't she appreciated that more? Now he could be anywhere. In a bus shelter, dossing down for the night on a cardboard box in a London street, on a train heading for heaven knows where, lying in the gutter somewhere . . .

Peter touched her arm gently. 'He'll be all right.'

'How do you know?'

'Because Jon wouldn't do anything stupid.'

'Running away was pretty daft, wasn't it?'

'He'll come to his senses soon.'

She could have hugged him. How wrong she'd been to label this boy as a social misfit who was wrong for her son. She could see now that he was genuine. Kind. Thoughtful. But if that was the case, why hadn't Jon told his friend where he was going.

'Did you have an argument?' she demanded. 'Is that another reason why he went?'

Peter sighed. 'I wanted him to stay at Oxford. Finish a year at least and then see how he felt about it. I said I'd wait for him but he was worried I'd find someone else. But he wanted to leave and us to get a place together so he could concentrate on his music.'

It was beginning to make sense now. 'So it wasn't just that he thought I'd disapprove?'

'No.' He looked at her protectively. 'Does that make you feel better?'

'A bit.'

He held out his arm and she tucked hers in his. It was comforting, especially in the cold.

'I always knew he was gay,' said Lucy suddenly.

He tightened his hold. 'How?'

She smiled wistfully, remembering Jon as a little boy. 'There was just something different about him. I could never really put my finger on it. He was sensitive too, although of course a lot of boys are without being . . .'

'That way inclined,' he finished for her.

She nodded. 'But it drove Luke mad. You never knew him, did you?'

He shook his head.

Lucy's mouth tightened. 'He had very set views on life. On everything. He didn't like it when Jon fussed about things. Even as a child, his shirt had to be done up a certain way. He didn't like sport. He wasn't what Luke considered to be a man's boy. So I didn't say anything. And then, after Jon's father died, there never seemed to be the right time. I tried, once, a few months ago, to talk about it but somehow it just didn't happen.'

He stopped and looked down on her, his eyes full of sympathy. 'Don't beat yourself up.'

She had this crazy urge to bury her head in his shoulder but this wasn't the time to tell him that Luke's unforgiving re-action had probably been because he had been 'that way inclined' himself. Suddenly she could see why this understanding boy and his warm family had such appeal for her son. 'I can't help it. I really can't.'

'I understand. But my mum says there's no point in trying to change the things we can't. We can only try to change the things we can.' That made sense. They were outside another club now. 'Why don't we try this one,' he added kindly, 'and then think about going back?'

As they approached the entrance, there was a tall man in a heavy black overcoat, hands in his pockets. He looked up as they came towards him and began walking towards them. 'Lucy! There you are!'

She could hardly believe it. 'Mike?'

'I got home just after you left. Kate gave me a list of the clubs you were going to. I've been round some of them to try and find you.' He looked at Peter, and Lucy's hand tucked in his arm.

'This is Jon's friend,' said Lucy coolly.

'I'll go into this one on my own, shall I?' said Peter.

She waited until he'd gone down the spiral stairs into a noisy basement. 'Mike, please go. I don't want to see you right now.'

'Pet, what are you talking about?'

'Don't "pet" me. I know what you've been up to.'

He hesitated, just for a second, but it was enough. 'What do you mean?'

'I had you followed. That's right. By a private detective.'

'What?'

'That's right.' Lucy felt sick at the look on his face. 'So I know about your girlfriend or rather your girlfriend's baby. I presume it is yours? How could you have done it, Mike. How could you?'

She started beating his chest with her fists but he caught her wrists. 'Is that what you really think?'

'You've been cold and distant to me for weeks. Snappy with the children. And . . .'

'It's because I've been worried out of my mind.'

'Join the club.'

'Look, pet, I know it's awful about Jon. But please, you've got to listen to me about Kerry.'

'I don't want to hear her name . . .'

'Lucy.' He grabbed her hand, pleadingly. 'Please listen to me. I can explain everything.'

They had to wait until they got home and Lucy had dropped Peter off. Kate was still up.

'Did you find him?'

'No. Any messages?'

'One but I left it on answerphone. Nothing to do with Peter.' Kate narrowed her eyes at Mike. 'Back now, are you? Granny thinks it's very odd that your meetings go on for so long. I'm off to bed now.'

Mike waited until she'd gone upstairs and then turned to Lucy. 'Do you want a drink?'

'No. I want to know what you've been up to.'

'Fair enough.'

He sat down on the opposite chair. 'I should have told you when we met but to be honest, I was scared it would put you off. What happened doesn't show me in a very good light.'

He took a deep breath. 'When I was a teenager, I fell in love. With a girl called Denise. We went out for six months and then she broke it off.'

He stopped. 'This is the difficult bit. I bumped into her some time after that and she was pushing a baby in a pushchair. I asked if it was mine and she said it was. So of course I offered her some support. I even said something about moving in and helping to bring her – it was a girl – up but she didn't want any of it. I went back to her house the following week but she and her family had moved. No one seemed to know where they'd gone.'

Was he telling the truth? Luke had lied to her. Mike could be doing the same.

'You were a teenager. We all did daft things.'

'No but this was different. She hadn't wanted to . . . to have sex.'

She stiffened. 'You didn't force her.'

He shifted in his seat. 'No but I knew she'd had too much to drink. Don't look at me like that. I know I was wrong. I feel terrible about it. Why do you think I don't drink now? I took a vow that day I saw her with my daughter. But it still didn't help. I could never forget that I had a child whom I might never see again.'

'Is that why you never married?' asked Lucy suddenly.

'Partly. And also because I hadn't met anyone I could feel committed to, until you.'

'It must have been hard for you, being with my children.'

He nodded. 'I know I've been a bit tough on them but I kept thinking that my daughter would be about the same age as Jon.' He smiled ruefully. 'And of course, like many people who don't have kids of their own, I had my own ideas on how to bring them up.'

'And the girl in the hotel . . .'

'Was Kerry. About two months ago, I got a letter from her.' He smiled softly. 'Her mother emigrated to Australia but before she went, she finally told Kerry my name and she tracked me down.'

'How do you know she's telling the truth?'

Mike smiled ruefully. 'Because if you saw her, you'd see.'

Was this really the African girl the private detective had seen? She was on the point of asking when she realised that if she waited until they met, she could see if Mike was really telling the truth. 'What does she want? Money?'

Even as she spoke, Lucy berated herself for being small-minded. The girl had lost her mother. Of course she needed to find her father now – provided Mike was her father.

'No.' Mike spoke in measured tones. 'She wanted to see me because she'd found she was pregnant herself. She doesn't want money but she would like to be part of a family now. The boy who got her pregnant, doesn't want to know.'

'Poor thing.'

She said it half-sarcastically but Mike didn't seem to realise. 'Exactly.' Mike's eyes glittered with hope. 'So I told her I was getting married and I said that once I'd explained the situation to you, I was sure you'd welcome her in.'

'She's not living here!'

'I didn't say that. But I'd like her to visit every now and then. But look, this can wait. The most important thing at the moment is finding Jon. And we'll do that. I promise.'

She looked up at him, seeing a different man from the one she'd been so in love with. 'Why didn't you tell me before? I'd have understood.'

'Would you?' He looked sadly at her. 'You've changed too, Lucy. We seem to be snapping more at each other. Maybe it's Eleanor. Or perhaps we're both scared of making a commitment.'

Mouth dry, she nodded.

He took her hand. 'But it will be all right now. I promise.'

'No more secrets?' she asked.

He stroked her cheek with his finger. 'No more secrets. Now come on. Up to bed.'

'I'll check the answerphone first.'

'Lucy? You don't know me but my name is Alan. I'm a client of your sister Jenny. I wonder if you could ring me as soon as possible. It's rather urgent.'

Forty-two

'Jenny. Jenny, can you hear me?'

She was falling, weightlessly through air. But she wasn't scared. Someone – she couldn't see who – was there to catch her.

'Jenny!'

Someone was taking her hand. It felt like Lucy's. When they'd been little, their mother had always instructed her older sister to hold her hand when crossing the road. She'd resented that, just as she'd resented so much about Lucy. The way she did better at school. The fact she was prettier and more popular. The boyfriends she'd had . . .

'It's all right, Jenny.' The hand that was stroking hers suddenly didn't feel like Lucy's any more. It was a male hand. Strong. Hairy. Firm. Rather like . . .

'No!' She tried to sit up but something – something attached to her legs – seemed to be in the way. 'Leave me. I told you. I never want to see you again. It's not right. It's not fair on the others.'

Someone was smoothing her forehead now. 'It's all right, Jenny. You go back to sleep. Your visitors will come back later.'

She had no idea how much time had elapsed before she woke up again. Where was she?

'It's all right, Jenny. You're in hospital but you're going to be fine. You've hurt your leg and you got concussed but they say there isn't any more damage.'

'Lucy?' She tried to put out her hand but everything throbbed. Her sister was sitting on a chair next to her bed, stroking her hair as she spoke.

'It's me, Jen, it's all right.'

Lucy. And Alan too. It was coming back to her now. The boat. The noise. The crash. Her head . . .

'Are you all right?'

He beamed. 'I am now that you're awake.'

'Did anyone get hurt?'

'Amazingly not. We're very well equipped in these parts, you know. People might think the north is the other end of the earth but we know how to do things up there.'

'Yeah, right, like crash a boat.'

'Nice to see you've retained your sense of humour.'

Jenny lay back on the pillow. 'My head hurts.'

'That's not surprising.' A nurse was bustling in. 'I told you both not to stay for more than a couple of minutes. I'm afraid I must ask you to come back later.'

'No.' Jenny made a grab for her sister but her eyes were on Alan. 'Please don't go.'

'Don't worry.' Alan spoke first. 'We'll be back later.' He dropped his voice. 'As soon as that old dragon lets us, anyway.'

She wasn't sure when they came back exactly. But they did so separately. Lucy first.

'Jenny, I was so scared. I can't believe it. I mean, I heard it on the news and I should have put two and two together because you'd said about the cruise but I didn't and . . .'

It was all coming back now. Jon had disappeared. And from Lucy's appearance, he was still missing. Her sister's eyes were black underneath from smudged mascara and her clothes crumpled as though she'd slept in them.

'Any news on Jon?'

'No.'

She and Lucy might be chalk and cheese but her innate sisterly intuition told her there was something more. 'And Mike?'

Lucy looked away. 'Tell you later. It's Jon I'm really worried about. Sorry, you don't need this in your condition.'

'Don't be silly.' Jenny touched her sister's arm lightly. 'I'm your sister. Look, I wasn't going to tell you this but just before . . . before the crash, I got a text from Steve. He knows where some of Jon's crowd hangs out. He's going to make enquiries.'

'We've already done that and we haven't got anywhere.' The panic in Lucy's voice was rising. 'I went round some of the clubs.'

'You did?' The thought of her sister going into a smoky nightclub, let alone a gay haunt, would have made Jenny laugh if her head hadn't been throbbing so much. 'Who with?'

'Jon's friend and Mike.'

'Good for him. Mike, that is. I didn't realise he had it in him.' She was getting tired now. 'I'm really sorry. But I feel terribly sleepy.'

'Of course you do. Lucy ran her hand lightly over her fore-head. 'I'll be here when you wake up.'

'No.' Jenny was so tired she wasn't even sure the words were coming out. 'Do me a favour. Go back and help look for Jon. He's more important.'

'No. I can't.'

'Of course you can.'

A deep male voice cut in. 'Of course you can do what?'

'Alan,' she murmured sleepily. 'Talk to Lucy, please. Make her go home.'

When she next woke, she felt a little better. Gingerly, she turned her head. There he was, sitting on the chair that Lucy had been in not long before. 'Has she gone?' she asked.

Alan nodded. 'Poor woman. What a terrible thing to be going through, although I must say, your sister is very stubborn, despite her sweet exterior. She left firm instructions for me to stay by your side in case you need anything.' He grinned. 'Instructions which I'm very happy to obey, by the way.' He looked slightly more serious. 'There's something else, too. They told your sister that you'd be well enough to go home in a couple of days. She wants you to go back with her. And no, before you tell me you're perfectly able to look after yourself, trust me. You won't be able to do much with a leg like that for some weeks.'

'But Lucy's got her own problems,' she protested. 'I can't impose on her.'

'Exactly,' cut in Alan deftly. 'That's why I'm suggesting you stay up here with me, as my guest, in one of the spare bedrooms. I have a housekeeper, Doris, who will be delighted to have someone else to fuss over. And I'd be delighted to have your company.'

So that's who Doris was! 'But what about my work? When you run your own business, you can't just take time off like that.'

'Can't you?' His eyes softened. 'I did when my wife died. No one is indispensable, Jenny. If you dropped down dead tomorrow, someone else could take over. Besides, you've got Lily. Taking charge might be just what that girl needs to help her move on.'

Which is how, three days later, she came to find herself waking up in one of the most comfortable double beds she had ever slept in with an original walnut headboard, softened by creamy white lacy pillow cases, an antique rose bedspread, a side table with a pile of *Country Life* and – heavens – a selection of her favourite upmarket glossy women's magazines.

Just as she was taking in the elegant curtains (Colefax & Fowler if she wasn't mistaken), and matching chest at the bottom, there was a knock on the door. A kindly, amply-covered woman in her late fifties or possibly early sixties came in, bearing a tray with a blue and gold bone china teapot and matching cup and saucer.

'I haven't woken you up, have I, Miss Macdonald?'

Jenny felt as though she had stepped back in time to a character out of one of Mary Wesley's novels where heroines spent their days being looked after in country homes and house parties. 'No, not at all. And please, call me Jenny.'

She vaguely remembered Doris introducing herself when

she'd arrived last night from the hospital, although she'd been so tired and so unused to having her right leg in this awful heavy plaster cast, that she hadn't taken much in. All she could remember was being amazed by the incredible scenery when Alan had driven her away, out of the city centre, and out towards Corbridge where he lived. She had had no idea that it could be so green, so ruggedly beautiful and so . . . well, so unashamedly honest. Rather like Alan.

'Alan says there's no rush to get up. You can have breakfast in bed if you like or, if you want to come downstairs, use the phone here to ring and Alan will come and help you downstairs.'

She glanced at the covers hiding Jenny's plaster cast leg. 'I broke my leg once, riding. It's not until you do something like that, that you realise how much you rely on it. Never mind. It will mend soon enough, providing you don't do too much.'

But that's exactly what she had to do. Too much. It was what she always did. What she loved doing. What she had to do, to shut the past out of her head. But how could she tell this nice Doris woman that? Instead she said, 'What lovely curtains. I love the way this bedroom is furnished.'

Doris looked pleased. 'That was Caroline. Alan's late wife. She was an interior designer.'

'I hadn't realised.'

Doris nodded. 'Had her own business, she did. Alan was very proud of her.'

Jenny floundered for the right thing to say. 'It was so sad. I mean, about her dying quite young.'

'Aye. Only in her fifties, she was. Still, Alan's getting much better now. He's moving on at last.' She gave Jenny an odd sort of look. 'His work helps of course. Always was a workaholic, his wife used to say. But you can't use work as an excuse forever, can you?'

'No,' said Jenny quietly. 'You can't.'

'Now,' said Doris more briskly. 'If you need any help getting dressed, use the phone. It's an internal one. My number's 1 and Alan's is 2.'

Before even attempting to get out of bed, Jenny rang Lucy. She'd already had several missed calls from her sister on the mobile. 'Any news?' she asked, pre-empting any polite preamble.

'No. Mike's still looking round clubs with Peter. Your friend Steve rang a few times but no one knows where he is.'

'If something awful had happened, someone would have called you. You said he had identification on him.'

'Yes. That's what I'm banking on. Jenny, I feel so awful at not having stayed with you. Especially at Christmas.'

'Don't be daft.' It came out more brusquely than she'd meant. 'None of us are going to feel like celebrating this year. Anyway, I'm living the life of Riley here. Alan's being a perfect gentleman and, get this, he's even got a housekeeper. If I didn't have so much happening at work, I could almost get used to it.'

'Well ring me tonight. Look, Jenny, I don't mean to be rude but I've got to get off the phone in case there's news.'

Of course! How could she be so selfish?

It was a real struggle to get showered and dressed. She'd never thought about it before but now she felt truly sorry for people who couldn't function properly all the time. Eventually, however, she succeeded, although the image that stared back at her from the oval mirror in the enormous Georgian armoire, looked decidedly less groomed than her old London self. She hadn't been able to style her hair properly without her precious hair straighteners. And although Alan had arranged for her stuff to be brought over from the hotel, she couldn't be bothered to put on her full make-up.

Eventually, she was ready to phone. She'd rather get downstairs on her own but remembering those steep mahogany stairs from last night, there was no way she'd make it.

There was a knock on the door within minutes as a genial-looking Alan, wearing a cravat and checked shirt, half-opened the door. 'Sorry, I know you rang for Doris but she's busy sorting out lunch so you've got me instead. Besides, I reckoned you might need help down the stairs.'

'Thanks.'

'Right. Now trust me, the best way to do this is like this. That's right, lean on me. Now, one step at a time. No rush. Fantastic.'

Somehow they got to the bottom with less trouble than she'd feared. 'You're very good at that,' gasped Jenny, as he helped her onto a chair in the sitting room.

He looked modestly pleased. 'Ah well, I had plenty of experience with Caroline.'

He'd never mentioned her name before. It was usually 'my wife'.

'She did a lovely job with the house,' commented Jenny looking round. The sitting room – one of several, she suspected from the size of the place – was elegantly but comfortably furnished with a sage green carpet, deep chairs that you just sank into and small Georgian walnut and mahogany side tables with little silver frames and china.

'Doris told you, did she?' Alan looked out of the French windows onto an immaculate lawn. From where she was sitting, Jenny could see an iron arch leading onto a walkway of lavender bushes. 'Caroline loved this house. It's one of the reasons why I could never leave it. But it's too big for me really. It might have been different if we'd had children but sadly that never happened. Still, I have my work and my friends. We're a very friendly lot up here. And there's a great golf course near here. Do you play?'

'Fraid not. I did have to play once at a client do and I nearly scraped half the green up with my iron or whatever you call it.'

'Right,' said Alan firmly. 'Then I'm definitely not taking you to my club. I'd be thrown out.'

She giggled.

'Changing the subject, I presume there's no news on your nephew or you'd have said something.'

She shook her head.

'That's too bad. Sometimes I wonder how parents cope with the responsibility.'

'Me too,' chipped in Jenny.

'You've never been tempted then, by motherhood?'

He said it so kindly that it didn't seem like the intrusion it sounded. 'I would have if the right person had come along.'

'And that never happened?' Alan looked astounded. 'But you're such a lovely woman. I can't believe it.'

'Well,' said Jenny slowly. 'There was someone once. A long time ago. But he wasn't available.'

'Married,' said Alan quietly.

She nodded, not trusting herself to speak.

'So you did the right thing?'

She'd been asking herself the same question for so many years, that she wasn't sure now. 'I tried to but . . . well then it ended anyway.'

Alan stood up. 'Life's not simple, lass, is it? Now, I'm going to leave you to your magazines and Doris is going to bring coffee in shortly.'

She suddenly realised that there was another pile of magazines, like the one upstairs, on the table near her. 'You're spoiling me.'

'Am I?' He seemed pleased. 'Well, maybe you need it. I've seen you racing around like a dervish, trying to kow-tow to all your clients. Maybe this leg wasn't a bad thing. You're going to have to rest now. And you could always use the time to think.' He tweaked his yellow paisley cravate. 'Now I'm afraid I'm going to have to go into the office. But I'll be back for lunch. Will you be all right until then?'

'Absolutely.' Jenny laid her head back on the chair. How odd. Part of her was itching to get on the phone to clients, yet part of her felt so tempted to close her eyes and just daydream. 'See you later.'

*   *   *

It was amazing, thought Jenny, how easy it was to fall into a new routine. You went along with your old life, not imagining it could be any different, and then suddenly one day something happened to change it all and you had to get used to doing things differently. At first, it seems impossible but then, as the days and weeks go by, the new becomes more familiar and you can't imagine going back to the old again. Except that of course, she had to.

Since she'd been here for – what was it now, just over three weeks ? – nothing dramatic had happened at work, thank goodness. No terrible disasters, apart from a conference which Lily had organised at a place called Brook House, not realising there was a Brooke House too, not far away. A couple of delegates, who didn't read their invitations properly, had gone to the wrong place and the client had been a bit narked but otherwise everything was all right. And not a squeak out of Alicia King.

Meanwhile, Alan was a very attentive host. Nothing was too much trouble. Her clothes appeared, as if by magic, washed and ironed. The supply of magazines was constantly replenished. In the evenings he persuaded her to play chess with him – something she hadn't done for years and which, to her amazement, she actually enjoyed. Bloody hell, he'd be getting her to play bridge next!

'I'll have to teach you to play Dirty Scrabble,' she teased.

'What's that?'

'It's where you use rude words instead of polite ones. Lucy and I used to play it with her husband when he was alive. One evening, the children came down and were really shocked!'

'Sounds great although we'll need to hide it from Doris.' He winked. 'She gets shocked quite easily.'

They'd had the nicest Christmas Day she'd ever had. Very peaceful with Doris joining them for lunch. Corbridge, she'd discovered, was absolutely charming with its stone houses, ranging from cottages to grander places like Alan's. As for the shops . . . well, she could have happily spent days here, browsing round the tasteful designer fashion outlet, reputed to be run by a well known former London model, and the kitchen shop and the deli and the art gallery.

'This is lovely,' she said over lunch at one of the ivy-clad pubs in the village where Alan had taken her one day. 'So civilised.' She patted her stomach. 'When I get back to London, I'm going to have to go on a diet. I don't normally stop for lunch.'

Alan poured her a glass of wine and then himself. 'I hope that when you are back in London, you'll come back to visit. There's so much I want to show you which is difficult at the moment, with your gammy leg.'

'I'd love to.'

There was a short silence. 'More wine?'

She giggled; recently, she was finding herself doing that more and more. 'You've just given me some.'

'So I have.' He gave a mock sigh of exasperation. 'That's what happens when you get to my age.'

'You don't look it,' she said suddenly. 'I mean, I don't know how old you are of course but you look quite young and . . .'

She stopped, conscious she was treading on tricky ground. Alan was a client, she reminded herself. He'd offered her a refuge out of sheer chivalry.

He laughed. 'Thanks very much. I'll take that as a compliment, shall I?'

'That's what it was intended as,' she said, still confused. 'It just sort of came out the wrong way.'

'Actually, I find it rather endearing.' He glanced down at the menu. 'Now, shall we order? I can recommend the salmon.'

They didn't get back until tea time. That was another thing, thought Jenny amused, as she sat in the front seat of Alan's Merc while it purred up the drive towards the house. She had never ever had 'tea' in London. But now she was becoming quite used to Doris coming in with a tray and a slice of fruit cake around 4 p.m. Not that she could eat anything after that delicious lunch but . . .

'Hello. Looks like we have visitors.' Alan glanced at the little sports car parked in front.

Jenny took one look at the green car with its beige sun roof and felt sick. Maybe she was mistaken, she told herself urgently. There were probably lots of other cars like that around.

Alan held out his arm as he always did when Jenny was getting in and out of the car. She leant on it gratefully and they made slow but steady progress towards the door. Doris opened it before Alan had time to find his key.

'There's someone here,' she announced importantly. 'A friend of Jenny's apparently.'

'Well he's got a very nice car. I remember having something like that when I was a young man.'

Doris raised her eyebrows. 'He just wants us to tell him he's still young but we'll ignore him, shall we? Anyway, I've put your visitor in the small sitting room.'

Clearly she didn't consider him eligible for the large one, thought Jenny. With her crutches, she made her way across, Alan beside her.

A man rose up from the chair. He'd grown a thin beard along his jaw line which made him look older.

'Hello, Jenny.'

She nodded curtly. 'Alan, may I introduce Dan?'

He was the perfect gentleman. Didn't ask questions. Merely left them to it, making polite excuses about having 'something to do'.

Jenny didn't feel nearly as charitable. 'What are you doing here?' she hissed as soon as they were alone.

'Lucy told me about your accident and, as I was going to be in the neighbourhood, she asked me to bring up some of your stuff and your Christmas presents since you're apparently staying up here for a while. I gave them to that woman.'

'Her name is Doris.'

'Is it now.' He looked around. 'Nice place your boyfriend's got.'

'Alan isn't my boyfriend. He's a friend who's . . . who's giving me a base until I'm more mobile. A reliable friend.' She couldn't help adding that bit. At least he had the grace to look abashed.

'Yeah. Well, I'm sorry about that. I was never great on commit-ment. But we had a good time, didn't we?'

'Did we?'

'Oh come on, Jenny. I didn't think you were the stuffy kind. You told me. You like fun. I like fun. So we had fun.'

'Well maybe I've changed now.'

'Maybe we all have. Look, I've got to go. I only called in because Lucy asked me to.'

'Very kind, I'm sure. What are you up here for, anyway? Another blind date?'

'No. I'm here to find someone. As a favour for someone else, actually.'

'So you do think of other people sometimes?'

'Yes, Jenny. I'm not as selfish as you think I am. No, don't bother getting up. I'm sure Doris will see me out.'

Alan didn't come down until some time after Dan had driven off and when he did, he was carrying a pile of papers. 'Afraid I've got to do some work before supper so we won't be able to have our usual game of chess.'

Jenny felt a pang of disappointment. 'That's all right.'

'Nice to see your friend, was it?'

'He's not a friend.' She hesitated, not wanting to lie. 'Well, he was. Briefly. But not now. He just came to drop off some of my clothes which my sister had given him.' There was an awkward silence. 'I suppose I ought to be thinking about getting back to London in a few days.'

'Whenever you're ready.' She'd never heard Alan sound so cool before. 'My driver will take you.'

'No. Really. I can get the train.'

'Jenny.'

'Yes?'

'Sorry. I'm behaving badly. Ridiculous I know but I didn't like that boy. There was something about him. Bit of a wide-boy, if you ask me.'

She smiled weakly.

'Seriously, Jenny, I don't want you getting hurt.'

'I'm not. Not really.'

'But you are. Don't you see? I noticed it the minute I met you. I've been hurt too but in a different way but I could still spot it. Don't go, Jenny. Don't run away again.'

'Again?'

He was standing so close to her now that she could almost have reached out and touched him.

'Well that's what you've been doing, isn't it, Jenny? Running away. For most of your life, from what I can gather. I'm not sure what you've been running away from but don't you think it's time to stop?'

The lump in her throat was making it hard for her to speak. She'd never told anyone about this. Ever.

'I don't know if I can.'

'Then talk to me, Jenny. Tell me about it. It might just help.'

She sank down on the chair, leaned her head back, closed her eyes briefly and then opened them. He was still looking at her. Waiting. So kind. So understanding.

'All right,' she said finally. 'It's not a pretty story. But this is what happened.'

JANUARY

Chicken with organic carrots
(in blue bowl with cling film on top)

Plain yoghurt

Bottled breast milk
(for emergency)

Pear crumble

`Shepherd's pie`

Ginger and Orange Marmalade 2003

Forty-three

It was the start of a new year – after a dire Christmas at her mother's – coupled with the sudden realisation that she was doing George more harm than good by being a stay-at-home-mum, that finally made up Chrissie's mind about working for Dan. Something had to stop, she told herself, after snapping at her son for refusing to eat breakfast and then realising her throat felt sore.

But on that first day, she'd woken up sick with fear at leaving George. 'He'll be fine,' Martin had said irritably as she fussed round, making endless lists. Oh, God. George looked so adorable, sitting in his highchair, quietly for once. He was actually blowing her kisses. Who'd taught him to do that?

'I'm not sure I can do this,' she said sitting down heavily.

'We've already discussed it.' Martin, still in his pyjamas, was putting on the kettle. 'One of us has to work and, Christ knows, he's paying you enough. That man must be rolling in it. More money than sense.' He gave her an odd look. 'I still don't know why he's offered you a job.'

Chrissie swallowed the wave of panic in her throat. 'Because I'm worth it?' Perhaps she should have told Martin about Dan but now she'd left it too late. Besides, what could she say? This was the man with whom she'd had a brief, passionate affair with at university and who . . .

'Where did you say his trainer mug was kept?'

Did this man actually live with them? 'In the cupboard to the right of the sink,' said Chrissie through gritted teeth. 'If you can't find the trainer mug, you'll never manage. Where's his lunch?'

Martin put a finger to his chin and gave a mock 'I dunno' face. 'Er, in the fridge.'

'Congratulations.'

He took a mock bow. When had they learned to be sarcastic with each other? When had they stopped laughing? When had they stopped making love?

'Chrissie, you're going to be late.'

She still didn't want to go. 'What are you going to do today?'

Martin yawned, sipping coffee. 'Haven't decided yet. Go to the park, maybe. Dash off a few more CVs before going for a walk. I'm rather looking forward to it actually after years of being incarcerated in the office.'

She snorted. 'It's not that easy, you know. You have to watch him every second. Take your eyes off him and he'll be pulling something off a shelf or bumping into a table. And don't be surprised if the health visitor turns up unexpectedly.'

'Just go.' Martin was sounding irritated. 'Bringing up kids isn't rocket science. We'll be fine without you.'

Fine without you? So she'd spent every minute of her day and most of the night too, looking after an ungrateful little ball of kinetic energy that zoomed from one room to the next, creating havoc in its wake. And suddenly someone else tells you they can do it just as well if not better.

She slipped on her working jacket, a designer number from the days when she'd been able to afford Patsy Seddon. It used to be loose but now she couldn't even do it up. *Fine without you.* The words still resonated round her head. Well, they'd see about that.

Dan's office was a forty-minute drive away in North Harrow, on the third floor of a building which looked unpromisingly grey from the outside. There was no name on the door; nothing that gave away the kind of business he was in. What was she doing here?

'Hi,' Dan mouthed at her, opening the door, phone tucked

between his neck and shoulder without his usual Bluetooth. He waved at her to sit down at a desk, laden with papers. So, in fact, was every other available surface. She glanced at one document headed 'Confidential' on which was balanced a half-empty cold mug of coffee with the word BOSS-Y on it.

Ten minutes later, Dan was still on the phone. This was so boring! Her fingers were itching to tidy up this unruly mass of documentation, confidential or not, even if it was just to put it into neat piles.

'Wow. I'd forgotten what colour the desk was,' said Dan when he finally came off the phone.

She gave a satisfied look at the almost tidy surface. 'I felt I ought to be doing something while you were busy.'

'That's great. You didn't see my Bluetooth, did you? I put it down somewhere.'

'Here.' She produced it with a flourish. 'What else would you like me to do?'

'Well, let's see. You could start a proper filing system if you like and of course the phones will need answering.' He sounded very vague for someone who, judging from his new BMW, flashy watch and designer clothes, must be making money from somewhere.

'Can you explain exactly what it is that you do?'

Dan picked up the phone again. 'Oh, you know, a bit of this, a bit of that. I do a bit of share dealing and recently I've been dabbling in property. I've also started importing . . .'

Quite what he'd started importing, she didn't find out because he began speaking and the second line rang. 'Hello. Dan Green Enterprises,' she said unsurely.

'Dan there?' demanded a gruff male voice.

'I'm afraid he's busy. Can I take a message?'

There was a click as the caller disconnected. Clearly not.

Dan was permanently on the phone until nearly lunchtime, when she finally got a chance to talk to him.

'You know, I still don't really know why you gave me this job.'

'Don't let's go through all that again.' Dan was frantically leafing through a bundle of papers. 'Frankly, I didn't expect you to accept after . . . well, after everything.'

'Ah, so you offered, thinking I'd turn it down.'

'For God's sake, Chrissie, I can't go into psychological stuff now. I'm trying to find something.'

'What?'

'It's a shares certificate. You wouldn't know which one.'

'No need to be tetchy. Do you mean this one?'

He glanced at it. 'No. But I've been looking for that one too. Thanks.'

'Pleasure. I might have fifteen years experience in HR but I also know how to be organised.' She shuddered at the desk in front of her. 'You know that meeting you've got today? At 4 p.m.?'

He looked at her suspiciously. 'Have you been reading my diary?'

'Of course I bloody have, Dan. I'm your over-qualified PA. Remember? PAs check their bosses' diaries to make sure they haven't forgotten something. How long's the meeting due to go on for?'

Dan stared at her as though she was bonkers. 'I don't bloody know, do I? One hour. Two.'

'There's no need to be rude. If it's two hours, I'll try – no promises, mind you – to get this other lot cleared. Then we might be able to get somewhere. Whatever happened to your previous PA? She should have sorted this lot out.'

'Ah.' Dan adjusted his glasses. 'Probably best not to talk about her.'

'You slept with her, didn't you?'

He shrugged.

She moved away, in disdain. 'You haven't changed, have you? I thought you were going out with Jenny?'

'Jenny?' He waved a hand dismissively in the air. 'We saw each other a couple of times but that's it.'

'And what about Patsy?' Her eyes narrowed. 'You two seem very close.'

'We go back a long way. But she's going out with Antony, isn't she? I'm a single man. I can do what I like. Now for Christ's sake, Chrissie, just get on with your work without asking any more questions, will you?'

So she had. Somehow (in between trying to get hold of Martin on his mobile to check everything was all right), she had tidied up the desk and other work areas. Gosh, she'd forgotten how satisfying it was to get things shipshape. In an office, you sorted something out and no one – let alone a small cannon on unsteady toddler legs – would chuck it on the floor or smear baby food on it.

'Blimey!' Dan ran his hands through his hair, whistling appreciatively. 'That looks so much better.'

She tried not to show her pleasure. 'Good.'

That night, when she got home, Martin reported triumphantly that George had not only eaten the whole of his lunch but had also had a nap afterwards.

Chrissie could have screamed. 'Didn't you read my instructions? Now he's had a nap, he won't go to sleep tonight and then I'll be up while you're conked out.'

'It wasn't a long nap. Only about twenty minutes.'

'The length is irrelevant! They only need a five-minute power nap to give them enough energy to yell through to the next morning.'

'You sound as though they're another species.'

'Well, they are, as you'd have found out if you'd spent as much time with them as I have.'

'You should listen to yourself.' Martin was looking at her as though he hadn't seen her before. 'Your face is creased up with anger. There's no need to get so uptight. And you're upsetting George.'

Chrissie scooped up her son from the playpen, cradling his soft cheek against hers. Pushing her away, he held out his arms to Martin. How could he change affections after such a short time? 'Go to Daddy then, if that's what you want. I'm having a bath.'

'Don't be long. Supper's ready.'

Chrissie nearly fell down the stairs. 'You've cooked supper?'

'Well, not exactly. I got something from Marks & Spencer. It looks really tasty.'

'A ready-made meal? But we're meant to be saving money.'

'It was extremely reasonable, actually. And I'm sorry to tell you that George didn't like your pureed chicken with organic carrots.'

'But you said he ate his lunch!'

'Loved it.'

She came down the stairs slowly. 'Martin. What did you give him to eat?'

He looked slightly awkward. 'Pot Noodles. In fact, he liked it so much that I've stocked up.'

'So how's hubby managing without you?'

It was the following day and Chrissie was typing something onto the word processor. Something about jute and import duties. 'Oh, you know.' Briefly she thought of the furious argument they'd had over the Pot Noodles. 'All right, although it's not the same as me being there.'

'I'm sure it's not.' Dan shuddered. 'I couldn't think of anything more emasculating than having to stay at home, as a bloke, looking after the kid.'

She bristled. 'Actually, I think it's very manly. I admire Martin for doing it.'

'I hope you've told him so. I know it's none of my business but I've heard you on the phone to him, Chrissie, and I can tell you that if a woman spoke like that to me, I'd tell her where to get off.'

'You're right,' retorted Chrissie, pressing the Print button. 'It is none of your business.'

'By the way, any news on Jon?'

'Jon?' Bother. She should have printed two copies.

'Lucy's son.'

'What about him?'

'Haven't you heard? He's gone missing. Been gone for weeks actually. No one knows where he is. Lucy and Mike are out of their minds, apparently. I'm surprised you didn't know.'

How could she have been so selfish? She'd been so bound up with her own problems that she hadn't had time to ring Lucy since . . . since when? Around the time the Italian restaurant meal got cancelled. Poor Lucy! She'd always wondered about Jon. Lucy always said he was the child hit hardest by his father's death. She'd go round straight after work and if Martin complained about her being late home, it was too bad. Serves him right for having his mobile off.

It was only a short drive to Lucy's house from Dan's office. Eleanor opened the door looking, as usual, very elegant in a neat little beige jacket over navy blue linen trousers.

'Chrissie, dear! Do come in.'

'Actually, I wondered if Lucy was here. I've only just found out about Jon and I wanted to see if there was anything I could do.'

'How kind.' Eleanor sighed. 'I don't think so, thank you. Lucy is out with Michael. They spend all their time now following up leads and going to these dreadful clubs in case Jon is there.' She sighed. 'The police are meant to be looking too but one never really knows how seriously they take it. It was the note, you see.'

'Note?'

'The one that Jon left.' Eleanor led the way through to the kitchen. 'He said he needed time to find out who he really was. So as the police say, it's not as though he had suicidal intentions or anything like that.'

'How are the other children taking it?'

'Well, it's calmed them down a bit. Coffee, dear? I've just

made a pot. They're so shocked that they're behaving for once. In fact, they're upstairs doing their homework. And Sam actually used protection when he went skateboarding the other day – I've managed to make him wear a hat, you know, which is more than his mother could. Frankly, I think Lucy's place is here with the children instead of being on some wild goose chase. I don't know, Chrissie, I really don't. In my day . . .'

'Oh, for God's sake, stop going on about what it was like in your day!' Chrissie heard herself saying. 'Of course Kate and Sam are shocked. It's terrible for them. But instead of criticising Lucy all the time, it would be more helpful if you told her what a good job she's doing.'

'Well!' Eleanor looked up startled from the coffee pot. 'I've never been so insulted in my life. I don't criticise Lucy all the time . . .'

'Yes, you do. I've heard you. And you're always talking about Luke which can't be easy for Mike.'

Eleanor sat down with a soft thud. To Chrissie's horror, her eyes were moist. 'I can't help it. I need to talk about Luke. If I didn't, everyone would forget him. I know he might not have been the best of husbands but he was my son. Imagine how you'd feel if anything happened to George. It doesn't matter how old they are. They're always your babies.'

Chrissie pulled up the seat next to her and took the older woman's hands in hers. 'I know. I'm sorry. It's just that it's difficult for Lucy and now, this, with Jon, well it's dreadful. I don't know what I'd do if anything happened to George. I'd rather something happened to Martin, actually . . .'

She stopped, shocked by what she'd just said.

'Really?' asked Eleanor sharply.

'Well, obviously, I wouldn't want something to happen. But if it was a choice between Martin and George, I wouldn't hesitate. Well, it's natural, isn't it?'

'I'm not sure, dear.' Eleanor had calmed down now; it was Chrissie who was distressed. 'I noticed at that dinner that things were a little tense between you and your husband. Milk, dear? Of course, what you said didn't really help, did it?'

'What did I say?'

'On the baby alarm. I wasn't there but I heard Lucy talking about it. Not that I was eavesdropping but . . .'

Chrissie felt a cold sweat breaking out down her back. 'Baby alarm?'

Eleanor took a sip of black coffee and sat back, her eyes sparkling, almost as though she was enjoying this. 'Apparently, you were talking about sex.'

'Sex?'

'Yes. Something about there being only one person who'd ever "done it for you", I believe that was the expression. And that since that person – you didn't say who – no one else had been able to "turn you on". I believe that had been another phrase.'

A dim recollection of warbling onto herself while feeding George at Lucy's first supper party flashed through her mind. No! The alarm couldn't have been on! No wonder Martin had been so distant and cold since then. But why hadn't he said anything? Was it because – oh, God, she felt sick – because he had someone else and no longer cared?

'I didn't mean it. Well I did in one way.' She hesitated, wondering herself why she couldn't seem to forget that huge physical magnetic pull between them even though she knew Dan was all wrong, mentally and emotionally for her. 'But not now. It was so long ago. It's Martin I love. Heavens, Eleanor. What am I going to do? Shall I tell him I know?'

'Definitely not.' Eleanor laid a cool arm on her hot one. 'It will just lead to an argument.' She appeared to be thinking for a moment. 'No. What you need to do is woo him again. Dress yourself up.' She eyed Chrissie's black skirt disapprovingly. 'Take particular care with your make-up. Look after him and make him nice meals.'

'That's difficult. I've had to go back to work. He lost his job.'

'I heard.'

'So he's looking after George and he's meant to be making supper.' Chrissie grimaced with disdain as she recalled last night's limp spaghetti, the texture of which wasn't dissimilar to certain of her husband's nocturnal body parts.

'Well, you must surprise him! Come home with something you've bought. Or else stock up the freezer. Who are you working for?'

Chrissie wriggled uncomfortably. 'Dan. A friend of Patsy's. I used to know him. At university.'

Eleanor's eyes darkened. 'And was he the one you referred to when you were overheard?'

Chrissie nodded miserably. 'I don't even like him. Not any more. But he did things to me that . . . I've never felt that physical stuff with anyone since then. It's all such a mess, Eleanor. I've been carrying the guilt around with me for years and now it's come back to haunt me.'

'It can't be as bad as all that, dear.'

'Oh, but it is. There's much more.'

Eleanor put an arm around her. 'Then why don't you tell me all about it?'

Afterwards, Chrissie felt so much better. Almost light-headed as she drove home. Eleanor might have her faults but she was a savvy old bird. Her tips on how to seduce Martin almost made her feel enthusiastic.

'Hi,' she called out, entering the hall. 'I'm home.'

A wonderful smell wafted out from the kitchen, along with the sound of tinkly laughter. Dropping her handbag, Chrissie marched in. Kim was sitting in her place at the table and Martin was talking animatedly while George, in his highchair, was swapping carrot sticks with another kid next to him.

'Chrissie!' Kim beamed at her. 'How was work?'

'Busy,' said Chrissie, looking daggers at Martin. 'I told you to be careful with carrot sticks. He gags on them.'

'Actually, he's been fine,' chirped Kim. 'Very good for their teething, you know.'

'That tooth finally came through today,' glowed Martin as though he'd propelled it out himself. 'Clever boy, aren't you.'

'Wee.'

'What did he say?'

'*Oui.*' Martin glowed. 'We've just been to the French class again. George is really picking up the hang of it, thanks to Kim here.'

Kim shrugged. 'Oh, I can't take all the credit. George is a very bright boy.'

Chrissie began to unbuckle George to give him a cuddle but he pushed her away.

'He's tired,' said Kim sympathetically. 'It's been a long day what with French club and the picnic in the park.'

'Picnic in the park?' Chrissie couldn't stop the acid from creeping into her voice. 'How nice for you all. Well, if you'll excuse me, I'll just go and change.' She threw a look at Martin. 'Someone has to earn some money around here.'

She waited until the door shut and then braced herself as Martin came up the stairs. 'Was that necessary?'

'Yes.' She turned away so he wouldn't see her flabby post-natal stomach as she squeezed into her jeans. 'Any fool could see she's after you.'

'After me?' He snorted. 'And what about Dan? How do you think I feel about you working for your ex-boyfriend?'

'He's not . . .' she began.

'Don't lie.' He looked away from her as though unwilling to have any contact, either visual or physical. 'I didn't say anything because I was waiting for you to tell me the truth. But I heard what you said about . . . about no one else being able to "turn you on", as you so eloquently put it, since him. We all heard, on the alarm. How do you think that made me look? And then suddenly, your ex-boyfriend turns up out of the blue. Bit of a coincidence, isn't it?'

'Martin!' Panicking, she reached out for him. He pushed her away. 'Martin, I didn't mean it on the alarm. I was just rambling. But why didn't you say anything?'

Something gave in his eyes. 'Because I was scared. I thought you still liked him and I didn't . . . I didn't want to lose you, Chrissie. Things have been different between us since George was born and, I don't know, I get worried about us sometimes.'

She flung herself into his arms and this time, he didn't push her away. 'I know it's been different but Lucy says it's natural after a baby. We've just got to adjust, that's all. And as for Dan – well, I can't stand him. Yes, I had a thing with him at uni but that was over years ago. I don't know why I said what I did. I don't know why I say half the things I do nowadays.'

'But you're working for him.'

'Yes, because we need the money! He means nothing to me, I promise you.'

He looked at her harshly. 'Do you promise on George's life?'

'Absolutely.'

She could see something move in his eyes; he knew she'd never lie about that. Chrissie's heart fluttered with gratitude at the possibility of a reprise. Thank God he didn't know the whole sordid story. Maybe she ought to do what Eleanor had suggested. She clutched his arm. 'I've got an idea. Please listen to me. It might sound crazy but it could just work.'

Forty-four

Golden yellow with a hint of treacle brown. She'd always thought you just bought pear crumble instead of making it, until she'd seen Australian Bruce make it. Patsy had vague memories of tinned rice pudding when her mum had been home but later, when it had just been her dad, 'afters' had disappeared along with the waft of her mother's soft good night kiss. 'Tea' was usually fish and chips wrapped up in *The Sun*.

So why was she now weighing out flour and sugar like some bloody Nigella?

'It's comfort cooking – although knowing you, you won't eat it,' Dan said when he popped over unexpectedly again. Sometimes she didn't know how she'd cope without him. He'd even driven up to Newcastle to see if her dad had gone to one of his sisters (he hadn't.) Now he was sitting down, looking almost amused as he leafed through the *Cookery For Beginners* book she'd found at the Oxfam shop. 'Shouldn't you be stirring those pears before they burn?'

'Piss off. I had another demand from the home today.'

'How much?'

She named a figure.

'But they lost him.'

She winced. 'I still owe them. Don't worry. I'll find it.'

'You mean, ask Antony.'

She scraped a bit of burnt pear from the bottom of the saucepan. 'I can't. All his spare money goes on Maggie and the kids.'

'So your golden goose isn't performing, eh?' He looked amused. 'Time to move on, then, I presume.'

'No. How the fuck does this mixer work? I'm meant to "rub" the butter and sugar together. Can't I just do it with my fingers?'

'You'll spoil your hands.' He showed her how to push the whisk attachment into the mixer. 'If Antony hasn't got enough money to sort out your father, he's no use, is he.'

She turned on the machine and a spurt of butter and sugar leapt out. Shit. 'That's not fair,' she shouted over the noise. 'I don't just want Antony for his money.'

'Really?' He pressed the Off switch. 'I thought that was the whole point. It was with the others.'

He was right. It had been but Antony was different. Memories of how he'd held her, comforted her, rocked her when she'd told him how scared she was of her father finding her, flooded back. Apart from Dan, she'd never been able to talk to a man like she could talk to Antony. He made her feel special. Not cheap.

'I love Antony,' she said softly. 'But I feel bad about Maggie.'

Dan laughed. 'Am I hearing right? First, our Patsy, who never commits, declares herself to be in love. Then, after years of shagging married men, she suddenly develops a conscience. And now, on top of everything else, she's making pear crumble. Are you feeling OK, Patsy?'

'Shut up. No, I mean it.' She waved her wooden spoon at him. 'I don't want you in here any more. Just get out.'

There was a movement against the window. 'What was that?'

'The wind.' Dan spoke irritably. 'I don't know what it is with you women. Maybe it's your hormones. Nice one minute and unpredictable the next. Chrissie's the same.'

She was still cross but curious too. 'How's she getting on?'

'Quite well actually.' Dan looked smug. 'She's more efficient than anyone else I've had for a long time. And it's quite a nice feeling to know I'm helping out.'

She stared at him stonily. 'From what you've told me, and I'm not entirely sure it's the whole truth, you bloody well should be "helping her out" to make-up for the past. Well don't go and jump on her. She's got a husband and a kid.'

'I have no intention of doing anything like that.' Dan picked up his leather jacket. 'Blimey, it's windy out there. You ought to get the council to do something about those trees. Those branches are going to scratch the window. Good luck with the crumble and Antony. And let me know if you get any news about your dad. By the way, why aren't you at work?'

'Tomorrow's shoot cancelled. Will be in touch.'

They hadn't even had the decency to call. But the text said it all. Her scrap with Francesca over the pink blusher, coupled with the model whom she'd left mid-session, last year, when her dad had needed her, had led to a sharp decrease in bookings. The complaint that Maggie had lodged against the magazine which had run pics of the children hadn't helped either. Now the editor was refusing to use her again. If things didn't get better, she wouldn't be able to fork out the rent on this place. Still, at least she still had some work today.

Patsy poked the soft surface with her finger. Why wasn't the crumble cooked yet? It felt squidgy rather than crisp. Bugger. She had to leave now and she'd so wanted to surprise Antony. Maybe she should turn up the oven. She'd be back by 3 p.m., max, and then it would be ready.

Crazy really to worry about a crumble when her dad was still out there. Still wandering round in the cold, his trousers loose round his waist. Probably no coat. How would he cope in this weather?

She was late for the session. Only a bit but enough to rile the beauty editor who had a reputation for being sharp. 'Sorry,' said Patsy, getting out her make-up bags. 'I had a crumble in the oven and it wasn't ready.'

The beauty editor snorted. 'Come on, Patsy. Your idea of cooking is to buy a pack of low-fat yoghurts from Waitrose.'

'People can change.' Patsy delved in her bag for the eye pencil she needed.

'Not that much. Now, look, this is a before and after. We've made the case history look as grim as possible but she used to be a well-known model. Not that you'd think it now. Still, do your best, can you? We need her in twenty minutes for the cameras.'

Patsy wished the beauty editor's voice wasn't so loud. The 'case history' as she put it was only sitting in the cubicle next door. She might have heard her. Patsy popped her head round. 'Hi, I'm Patsy. Ready now. Sorry to keep you waiting.'

'Patsy?' A tall woman with doe eyes – shadows underneath – and shoulder-length mousy hair smiled at her. 'It's me. Marigold. Remember?'

Marigold? Not the same Marigold who had done so much for *Vogue* when Patsy had just started out? She'd been lovely to her, unlike some of the other haughty models. The last time Patsy had seen her, Marigold had been pregnant and about to get married to some bloke who was rolling in it. But now look at her.

'How are you doing?' she asked, as Marigold brushed her cheek.

The woman's eyes flickered. 'Oh, well, you know. Up and down. But not too bad considering.'

Patsy sat her down and started cleansing her face with cucumber wipes. 'Considering what?'

'Didn't you hear? It was in all the papers. Justin went off with someone else. His secretary, can you believe?' She laughed hoarsely. 'From what I can gather, she made a beeline for him. I suppose she was after his money. Well, she's got it now and him. They got married last month.'

Magic Matt Age-Concealing Foundation base. 'I'm sorry.'

'Thanks. The worst of it is that I really didn't think he'd ever do anything like that. And the girls are in a terrible state.'

'How old are they?'

'Twelve and ten.'

Same age as Alice and Matt. 'Are they very upset?'

'Of course they are. It's the worst thing to happen to kids at that age. This secretary is little more than a teenager herself. I just hope she realises, one day, the damage she's done.'

Patsy's hands shook. Shit, she'd have to re-do that eyeliner. Fumbling in her bag for the wipes again, she knocked her other handbag onto the floor, spilling the contents all over the floor.

'Ready?' asked the photographer, coming in.

'No,' snapped Patsy.

'Tut, tut, no need to get ratty.' The photographer bent down to help her pick up the contents of her bag. 'Ooh, here's a good-looking boy. Is this your other half?'

'No. It's a friend's son.'

'So what are you doing carrying around his picture?'

'Because he's missing, that's why. And his mother has given them out to anyone in case they come across him.' Right. She'd found what she was looking for. 'Give me ten minutes and we'll be there.'

It would have taken a miracle to have got Marigold back to her former state, thought Patsy after the session, when she'd packed up her make-up and set off to meet Antony for a drink as arranged. The wear and tear on her face from what had happened to the poor woman could never be repaired. Not even with all her magic sticks.

And this was exactly what she was doing to Maggie.

Patsy turned into the tube station and peered closely down at the man sitting on the corner with a blanket draped over his knees and a dog, wearing an incongruously jolly red and white spotted scarf round his neck.

'Gis us a quid, love.'

Hurriedly, she dropped a coin into his lap and ignoring his 'Thanks, miss', hurried off into the bowels of the station. He was nothing like her father but she couldn't help checking everyone she saw or passed in the street who might just be him. She only hoped, thought Patsy, stepping onto the escalator, that if her father was in the same position, someone, some-where, was dropping a pound coin into his lap too.

'Any news on your dad?' asked Antony when she joined him in the wine bar.

'Nothing.'

'Well, try to put it out of your mind just for a bit. What do you fancy? The usual?'

She nodded.

'This is fun, isn't it?' He looked at her apprehensively, as though seeking reassurance.

It had seemed a good idea at the time. A drink after work. Just the two of them.

He picked up the bar menu. 'Want something to eat?'

'I've made supper. Well, pear crumble.'

'Really? You made it yourself?'

'Well what's so amazing about that?'

'Nothing. It's just that . . . well . . . you don't normally . . .'

'Was Maggie a good cook?'

'Well yes but . . .'

'And what do you think she's eating tonight?'

'I don't know. Patsy, what's this all about?'

She took a large gulp of vodka and lime. 'I'll tell you what she's eating tonight. Nothing. Sodding nothing. Probably just like my dad, for different reasons. Maggie won't be eating because she'll be feeling sick. Sick because another woman has stolen her husband. Me.'

'Look.' Antony put his arm out. 'This isn't easy for either of us. But I've told you. I'd have left her anyway. You were the catalyst. No, don't look like that. Patsy, please, where are you going?'

'Home. My home.'

He gave her a strange look. 'I know what this is about. It's not Maggie, is it? It's because I can't give you so much money any more. I saw that final demand this morning. I suppose you've found some other bloke to bankroll you now.'

She hesitated. 'Yes. That's right. I'm sorry, Antony. Now just go back to your wife, will you? Try to make up for what you – we – have done.'

Patsy walked briskly through the estate and up the stairs to the flat. She was used to telling lies so why did that one hurt so much? Wasn't it easier for him to see her as a complete bitch? At least that way, he wouldn't be moping over her and he might actually turn things round with Maggie.

Those bloody supper parties had made her see things in a new light. All those couples had something in common. They had families. Families who fought with each other but who loved each other. Just look at Lucy and her missing kid. They were all trying to help each other. The only family she had was Dan.

Her fingers closed over the mobile. It could be so easy. He'd sort out that bill somehow. He'd love her if she let him. But she didn't love him. She didn't feel that attraction for him that she had for Antony. She couldn't . . .

Funny. The door was open. She was certain she'd closed it. And there was a smell of burning. Fuck. Dashing into the kitchen, she opened the oven door. Clouds of black smoke billowed out. She shut it quickly. It was then that she heard it. A sort of squeal. As though something – an animal? – was trapped in the sitting room. The curtains were closed, though she could swear she'd opened them that morning.

'Dad?' She saw him as soon as she switched on the light; a dishevelled, wild-eyed man in a dirty blue anorak, standing in the middle of the room holding Maggie by the throat with one hand and her kitchen knife in the other.

'Any closer, Patsy my girl, I'll kill you and this woman.'

'Help me,' whimpered Maggie.

Patsy's mind raced. Her mobile was still in her pocket in the kitchen. Talk. Keep them calm.

'How did you know where I lived, Dad? she said, forcing her voice to sound steady.

'It was on the notes. In the home. When I got here, I found her trying to get in through the window.'

'I wanted to see where you lived too.' Maggie's eyes flashed defiantly, despite the grubby arm round her neck. 'I wanted to know where my husband was and I wanted to talk to you. Properly. Not like last time. I wanted to tell you exactly how you'd ruined our lives.'

'I know.' Patsy's legs shook. 'I'm sorry.'

Maggie looked as though she was going to spit at her. 'A bit late for that, isn't it?'

'Maybe not.' She turned to her father. 'Put that knife down, Dad. And let Maggie go. She's not going to hurt you. She's a mother, for God's sake.' She took a deep breath. 'Like Mum.' Another breath. 'Like Babs could have been, one day.'

It was a gamble. A huge one. Unable to breathe, she watched his thick arm relax around Maggie's neck and slowly release her. Maggie ran across the room and towards the door.

'Come on, Dad,' said Patsy softly. 'I've got a nice crumble in the oven.'

His mouth twitched and she tried not to look at the gap between his teeth which hadn't been there last time.

'When did you last have a decent meal, Dad?'

'Dunno.'

'Where have you been? You've worried me sick. I've been looking for you.'

'You have? Where?'

'Everywhere. The Embankment. Christ, everywhere you can think of.'

'Why?'

She was getting closer now. A thick globule of saliva was dribbling down the side of his rough mouth. 'Because I love you, Dad. You know I do.'

Maggie was inching towards the door. Patsy stood with her back to her, so her father couldn't see.

'Then why did you send me to those fucking awful places?'

'Because you had to go somewhere, Dad, after . . . after what happened. And they were nicer than the first home. Remember?'

'Where's your mum? And your sister?'

He was rambling again. On good days, she reminded him of the stark truth. On bad days, like now, she humoured him.

'Out, Dad. They're out.'

Maggie had gone now. She only hoped she'd gone for help.

'Come on, Dad, sit down, and I'll bring you the crumble. It's really nice, Dad. A bit burnt but it's hot and good for you.'

Slowly she lowered him into the armchair before dashing back into the kitchen and plonking a large spoonful into a bowl before he moved again. 'Here you are, Dad, eat this.'

'Grace.'

'What?'

His eyes glared at her. 'We need to say grace first.'

My God. She'd almost forgotten. Her father had always made them say grace at table before they so much as dared to look at the food on the plate. On the rare occasions when they'd tucked in first, he'd beaten them.

'For what we are about to receive, may the dear Lord make us thankful.'

The words came out automatically – amazing after all these years! – as she held his large, cold, callousy hand in hers, trying not to recoil from it. As soon as they finished, he thrust his hand in the bowl, scooping the food up in to his mouth.

'Use the spoon, Dad.'

Ignoring her, he continued to shovel it in so fast that the crumble began to dribble down his unshaven chin. Patsy made to wipe it but he flinched as though she was going to hit him. 'Is that what they did to you in the home, Dad?' she asked softly.

He nodded with milky eyes. 'If you didn't eat it, they'd slap you sometimes. Then you wouldn't get anything next time round.'

'Well you're all right here, Dad,' she said softly. 'Now why don't you lie back in the chair and have a nap.'

He did as he was told, closing his eyes. Patsy covered him with a blanket. Within a few minutes, he was snoring deeply.

'Dan? It's me.' She whispered fiercely down the phone. 'Get over here. Fast.'

Forty-five

'Is that all you're eating?' Mike eyed her spoonful of mince disapprovingly.

'I'm not hungry.'

It had been like this ever since Jon went. Her stomach rumbled with hunger but how could she eat when she didn't know if her eldest son, her first born, was doing the same?

'Remember the note,' Mike said, as though he knew what she was thinking. 'He just needs some time alone.'

'Shh,' she said. 'Here they are.'

Kate and Sam streamed in, arguing fiercely over television channels. 'It's my turn to choose after tea.'

Kate regarded her younger brother with disdain. 'No, loser, it's mine.'

'I'm not a loser. Tell her, Mum.'

'Kate, that's not very nice.'

'Shut up, Mum.'

'Don't be rude to your mother, Kate.'

She shot Mike a withering look. 'That's my business not yours. And what's this?'

She regarded the bubbling shepherds pie in the middle of the table, with contempt. 'That's Jon's favourite. Why are you making it for us?'

'It's Wednesday,' said Lucy quietly. 'I always make shepherd's pie on Wednesdays.'

'Well I don't bloody want it. Not if Jon isn't here.' Kate pushed her chair back and stormed off.

'You're not going to let her get away with that, are you?' demanded Mike.

'She's upset.' If he had kids — really had kids and not just some child who had turned up out of the blue, like a late Christmas present, claiming to be his daughter — he'd understand.

'Well I'm upset too, on your behalf. By the way, Kerry rang. This probably isn't the best time but she'd like to meet you and . . .'

'You're right,' Lucy cut in curtly. 'It isn't the best time.'

Her eyes wandered to the pictures on the wall. When the children had been little and brought home their drawings, beaming from school, she'd framed them. Luke had scoffed at her for that ('the house will be overflowing by the time they're at secondary school') but they meant so much to her. Reminders of their childhood; of happy days when they'd sung on the way home from school, when she'd known exactly where they were. There was a picture of a house with an over-yellow sun by Kate. And there was a tractor — at least she thought it was a tractor — which Jon had painted when he was about six. She swallowed hard.

'Mum.' Sam's voice, this time at its usual pitch instead of the artificially deep tone which he'd been affecting recently, broke into her thoughts. 'Is Jon coming back tonight?

'No.' she hadn't meant to sound sharp. 'Why?'

Sam looked puzzled and for a second she could see the child he really was instead of the difficult fifteen-year-old who so desperately wanted to be the same age as his older siblings. 'Because you've laid the table for five, not four.'

So she had! It had been an automatic thing. Something she had done after Luke had died and then again, after Jon had gone to uni. 'Silly me,' she said lightly. 'Finished everyone? No, don't bother to clear. I'll do it later.' She stood up. 'I've got to show someone round a property. Won't be long. Mike, don't forget your tablets.'

This was exactly why she needed to work, she thought, pulling up outside number 7 Abbotts Road. Much as she loved her family, there were times when she had to escape. Besides, January was a busy time for the lettings agency. They were always deluged with requests from husbands or wives who had finally decided to leave their families after the rigours of Christmas. Maybe this was one of them. Walking up the path, keys in her hand, Lucy saw a tall well dressed older man in a suit, waiting by the door. They needed to find a tenant; the house had been on the market for weeks, partly because of the difficult access at the side. Mrs Thomas had also been right; those noises in the attic were still there despite assurances from the environmental company that there was nothing in it.

'Mrs Summers?'

His face seemed vaguely familiar. Shaking hands with him, she noted his lined face and slightly thin top lip. Probably in his late sixties or even early seventies. Maybe he was renting to be nearer work if he was still working or perhaps he needed to be closer to a 'lady friend'. Lucy had seen it all before.

She took him into the front room, her hand on her mobile just in case there was a problem. Both Lucy and Maggie were used to showing single men around but there was something about this one that wasn't quite right.

'As you can see,' she said looking round the bare floorboards and cold-looking sixties fireplace with boring beige tiles and a Cardinal Red hearth. 'It's unfurnished but it could easily be made into a comfortable home.'

The man looked out of the window, his back to her. 'I'm not interested in the house, Lucy. It's you I've come to see. No, don't ring anyone. I'm not going to hurt you.' He turned round, smiling sadly. 'Don't you know who I am, Lucy?'

She felt scared.

'No. Should I?'

He handed her a card. 'Jim Macdonald. Engineering Consultant.'

'That's right, Lulie. Remember how I used to call you that

when you were little? I'm your father. I gave a false name to your girl in the office or I was afraid you wouldn't see me.'

No. No. She stared at him. This man with the cold eyes and thin upper lip was her father? It had been so long since she'd seen him and yet there was something about the look in his face, the way he spoke, his knowledge of her pet name which only he had used . . .

'I don't believe you.'

'Thought you might say that.' He pulled a brown envelope out of his pocket. 'Take this. Read it later if you like. There's enough evidence in there to make you realise I'm telling the truth.'

'But how did you find me – and why?'

'Chance, actually. I am looking for a house to rent in this area because of work commitments. I happened to spot some editorial about your agency in the local paper with a picture of you and your name. I couldn't believe it.'

'But you left us.'

He shook his head. 'I'm not proud of that. How is your mother?'

'Dead.' Lucy began to shake. 'She never got over you going. Nor did Jenny.'

'She's why I left. You didn't know, did you?' He laughed hoarsely. 'Well of course, your mother wouldn't have told you. Jenny wasn't my child. Your mother was in love with someone else but he let her down. Like a fool, I didn't realise for a few years.'

'Jenny isn't your daughter?' Lucy felt her mouth speaking on its own, like a ventriloquist's dummy. 'You're lying.'

'Am I? Take a good look at your half-sister. You might have both inherited your mother's blonde looks but in nature, you were chalk and cheese unless, of course, that's changed.'

Lucy leaned against the wall for support. 'Get out. Please. Now.'

'Sure?' He held out his hand. It was knarled and slightly

grimy as though used to hard manual work. 'I thought we could get to know each other. That's why I went to all this trouble.'

'I want you to leave.'

He shrugged. 'As you wish. Just one thing. I'd rather you kept this to yourself. I have a family of my own and I wouldn't want this to cause any trouble.'

'Don't worry.' Lucy eyed him disdainfully. 'You won't be hearing from me again.'

'By the way,' he added. 'I'd get that roof checked out if I were you. Looks like you've had magpies nesting there.'

The documents – a copy of her birth certificate and a yellowed newspaper clipping of her birth announcement – proved what he had said. Lucy sat in the car outside her house, unwilling to go in. She ought to tell Jenny but if she did, it would destroy her mentally. Jenny had idolised their father. She couldn't do that to her, especially as there was no way now their mother was dead, of finding out who her real father was.

'Lucy?

Mike was knocking on the car window. 'Why are you sitting there?'

She got out slowly, handing him the brown envelope silently. 'You'll never believe what has happened.'

Lucy lay in bed, listening to Mike gently snoring. Those anti-histamine tablets which the doctor had prescribed for his allergy to Mungo seemed to be knocking him out. 'I agree it's not the right time to tell Jenny,' he had said earlier. 'Maybe later but she's got enough to cope with at the moment.'

Poor Jenny. And poor Mum. She must have loved Jenny's father very much to have taken such a risk, only to be let down. Funny really. Her mother had done exactly what Antony had, yet she still felt sorry for her. Perhaps she should try and see Anthony's viewpoint too. Besides, what did 'let down' mean exactly? What exactly did that mean? Had this other man been married? Had he had second thoughts about taking on a woman with two children; one of whom wasn't his own? She'd just about fallen into an uneasy sleep when the phone rang. Jumping, she knocked the alarm clock off the side table. 3.12 a.m.? Surely that man hadn't got her private number?

'Hello. Who is it?'

Silence.

'Jon?'

'No, it's Peter.'

The disappointment took a few seconds to register. 'Have you had some news?'

'Jon's just rung me.'

'Where is he?'

'Er, that's the thing. He doesn't want me to tell you. He just asked me to ring you and say he's all right.'

'But I need to see him!'

'He's worried you might get mad about leaving Oxford.'

'But I won't. I told you that.'

Peter was hesitating. 'But he thinks your . . . he thinks Mike will influence you and that you'll try to get him to change his mind. He just wants to stay where he is.'

'Who is it?' Mike was awake now, propped up on one side, listening intently.

Lucy ignored him. 'Peter, you've got to help me. Just think how your mother would feel if she didn't know where you were. You've got to tell me where he is.'

'I'm sorry. I can't. I promised.'

'But is he all right? What's he doing for money?'

'He's got a job.' Another pause. 'Not the kind of job you'd expect him to get but he's all right.'

Lucy was fighting back the tears. Her son. Her eldest boy. He didn't want her to find him because he distrusted Mike. This was her fault for bringing a stranger into the family. 'Peter, can you ring him for me? Tell him that Sam and Kate miss him. We all do. Just tell him that it doesn't matter about Oxford. All we want is for him to come home.'

As everyone said, at least they knew now that Jon was OK. 'He'll come back when he's ready,' said Jenny irritatingly. Sam and Kate were less forgiving. 'Doesn't he want to come back and see us?' demanded Sam, his eyes deep with hurt.

'I think he's a selfish bastard,' said Kate.

Lucy glanced at Mike. He hated bad language and was always criticising the kids for their liberal use of forbidden words. 'I agree with you,' he said.

'Maybe,' said Eleanor, looking up from her tapestry, 'Jon is having a nervous breakdown. His father was a very sensitive man, you know, Michael. Of course, in my day, people just pulled up their socks and got on with it.'

'Granny,' said Sam, turning up the television at the same time. 'Why weren't you at dinner last night?'

Eleanor flushed. 'I was out dear. What did you have?'

'We had Mike,' quipped Sam. 'He always seems to be here nowadays.'

'Sam!'

'It's all right, Lucy. I can handle it.'

'Now, now, you two.' Eleanor looked up from threading her tapestry needle. 'With all this trouble about Jon, we need to hang together as a family, not argue. Sam, dear, do turn the volume down or we won't hear if your brother rings.'

'Look,' said Mike later when they were getting ready for bed, 'I know this isn't great timing with Jon but I had another phone call from Kerry today. She really wants to meet you.'

Why, Lucy wanted to say. What's it got to do with me?

'I know how you feel,' said Mike gently, rubbing his finger lightly down her back so her spine tingled without the permission of her head. 'But it would mean a lot to me. Just as it meant a lot to you when you introduced me to the children. And yes, before you say it, I know it seems odd to think of her as my daughter. But you know, every day, it seems less weird to me and more natural.' His face shone. 'I never thought I'd feel like this. But now I can see what it's like. To have a child, I mean.' He drew her to him. 'You're going to really like Kerry. I know you are.'

Eleanor, of course, made a huge fuss. Not only did she bake an impressive Victoria sponge drenched with warm raspberry jam and icing sugar on top (just like the cakes her mother used to make, thought Lucy, her mouth watering), but she also took to the house with the Dyson with religious zeal.

'In our day, we took pride in running a house, like you girls run your careers. Those dog hairs are everywhere and poor Michael's nose is still running, isn't it, despite his new tablets. I hadn't realised he was allergic to animals. That's going to be tricky, isn't it, if you ever get married? Of course, you could always carry on being lattes.'

Kerry was due to arrive at tea time. Even the kids were excited.

'Well you can't blame them,' pointed out Chrissie when she'd rung for a consoling chat. 'I mean it's pretty rich, isn't it? I'd never put Mike down as the type to have skeletons crawling out of his woodwork. Makes you wonder about people, doesn't it?'

'Yes,' agreed Lucy faintly.

'Of course, I don't mean those kind of skeletons,' added Chrissie hastily. 'Mike's a decent bloke and anyone can have a child without knowing it. I've often thought that was quite tough on men. Mind you, it'll be interesting to see how he handles it. I mean, don't take offence, but Mike can be pretty fussy, can't he? I wonder how he'll manage changing nappies when he's a grandad. Lucy, are you still there?'

'It doesn't seem right that everyone's so excited when Jon isn't here,' said Lucy quietly.

'I know. It stinks. Frankly, I'd kill George if he ran off.'

'Everyone keeps saying that at least I know he's safe.'

'Doesn't take away the pain, though, does it? Are you mad at him for not wanting to come home?'

'Hurt, rather than angry. What kind of mother have I been that my own son doesn't want to come home?'

'You've been a very good mother,' said Chrissie firmly. 'Jon needs to discover himself, that's all. In fact, I'd say that the very fact he has the strength to do that means you've done a great job as a mother.'

'Do you?'

'Yes, I do. Now look, Lucy, I'm really sorry but I've got to dash. Dan's due back in the office any time and I've got to finish something before he returns.'

Chrissie had become far more self-assured, thought Lucy. More like the old pre-George Chrissie. She could imagine now how good she'd been at her old job. An HR manager needed all kinds of skills; being good with people, able to judge characters, capable of having the balls to tell someone when their work wasn't up to scratch, even firing them if necessary.

Everyone seemed to be moving on, instead of her. Her meeting with her so-called father seemed like a dream. She'd thought about him so much in the past but, in a way, it was easier to find he was nothing like she'd remembered. Put him out of your mind, Mike had advised as though it was a triviality.

'She's here!' someone called.

Mike's daughter was here and her eldest son wasn't. This would never have happened if she hadn't allowed Mike into her life. Suddenly, she felt an unexpected gust of anger. 'This is your fault, Luke,' whispered Lucy. 'If you hadn't got yourself killed, none of this would have happened.'

Lucy came into the sitting room after everyone else. At first, she could barely see Kerry through the kids and Eleanor who were surrounding her, talking animatedly. Seeing her, they drew back. It was all Lucy could do not to gasp with surprise. She'd tried, countless times, to imagine Kerry in her head but nothing really came to mind. She certainly hadn't expected this.

Kerry was – there was no other way of saying this – a very pretty dark chocolate colour. Despite her height, she was extremely slim, apart from her protruding stomach which looked as though someone had stuck a lump of clay on it. This was made all the more obvious with her short ribbed top which exposed a large midriff gap.

But it was the rest of her which took Lucy's breath away. Her long bare arms (even in this weather) were covered with tattooes and so too were her shoulders! Her deep black hair, plaited in tiny braids, was streaked with green stripes and she had a collection of small silver studs in her nose as well as a brace of hooped earrings down both sides.

Yet her eyes were exactly like Mike's – the same, laughing chestnut brown – and she had his nose. The cheekbones, she realised with a pang, must have been her mother's, chiselled as they were with breathtaking definition.

So this really was the woman that the private detective had seen, which meant Mike had been telling the truth. No wonder Eleanor's eyes were out on stalks.

Kerry eyed her unsmilingly, as though knowing just what she was thinking.

'Hello,' said Lucy. She half put out her hand and then, feeling this was too formal, took it back again. 'You found us all right then.'

'Yeah.' She put a piece of gum in her month. 'Lee dropped me off.'

She spoke as though Lucy should know who Lee was.

'Is he, er, your baby's father?'

'No.'

There was a short silence.

'Well,' said Mike, with over-forced jollity, 'who'd like some tea? Eleanor has made an amazing cake.'

And I've made some cucumber sandwiches, Lucy wanted to add, petulantly.

'No, ta. Lee and I had dinner late. We're not hungry. 'Sides, I don't want to put on any more weight with this thing inside me.' She looked around. 'Nice place you've got here.'

'Do you want to come and see my room?' Kate was almost tugging her by the hand. 'Come upstairs. I love your hair. Where did you get it done?'

'Lee did it for me.'

'Is he a hairdresser?' enquired Eleanor.

'He's trying to be one.'

Was it that difficult?

'Great nose studs,' observed Sam. 'Mike and Mum went mad when I got my ear done.'

'Why?'

Lucy couldn't hear the reply as they went up the stairs but she could guess it.

Left alone in the sitting room, she glanced at Mike.

He shrugged. 'It's bound to be awkward at first.'

'Are you sure she's really yours, Michael?' Eleanor's well-modulated tones rang out into the air so loudly that Lucy dived for the door to shut it.

'Yes,' he said shortly. 'She's shown me the birth certificate and before you say anything you shouldn't, Eleanor, her mother was born in Ghana. Look, I know she isn't what you were expecting and I probably should have filled you in. But to be honest, I wasn't sure what you'd think and . . . sod it. She's my daughter. Take it or leave it.'

Lucy reached out for his hand. 'I understand. I do. Really. I feel the same way about Jon and the others. They might not be what I thought they would. But they're my kids. Just like Kerry is your daughter.'

He smiled gratefully at her.

'Well,' clucked Eleanor, moving towards the tea table. 'In my day, we wouldn't have dreamed of turning up like that and claiming to be someone's daughter. Let's just hope she doesn't encourage Sam and Kate to have any of those awful heart pictures on their arms. In our day, only the navvies had them. Now, if no one is going to have some of this sponge, I'm going to have a piece myself. Oh, Mike, I forgot to tell you. The estate agents rang. Something about the buyers for your house. They want you to ring immediately.'

Luckily the estate agents hadn't quite closed for the day. Lucy could hear Mike talking urgently on the phone in the hall. Upstairs, the music got louder. Someone was thudding on the floor.

'Everything all right?' she asked as he came back into the room.

'Yes. Well, I think so.'

He looked apprehensive.

'The buyers haven't pulled out after the damp report then?'

'No. They're happy with the guarantees. In fact, they want to exchange this week and have a short completion date.'

'What do you mean by that, Michael?' asked Eleanor, dabbing her mouth with a napkin.

Was it impossible to have a private conversation in this house?

'I mean,' said Mike, looking searchingly at Lucy, 'that they want to complete the week after that.'

Lucy's mind began to circle wildly. 'The week after next? But that hardly gives us any time to sort things out.'

'I don't want to lose them.'

'No, of course not.'

'I could go into rented accommodation if you want.'

Lucy became aware of Eleanor holding her breath. 'Don't be daft,' she said putting her arms around him. 'We want you here.' She looked at Eleanor over Mike's shoulder. 'To be one happy family,' she said deliberately.

Eleanor snorted and cut herself another piece of cake.

'Great,' said Mike, blowing his nose. 'Down, Mungo, down.

Pet, put him in the utility room can you, while I ring the removal firm to sort out dates.'

'Don't forget the storage company too.'

'Well, if Jon's not coming back for a bit, we could save money by putting some of my music in his room. And I was thinking that one of my sofas would look rather good in here, next to your flowery chair. What do you think?'

Forty-six

If the situation had been different, she'd almost be tempted to stay. Lily had managed very well but recently there'd been a certain note of panic in her voice which Jenny recognised all too well. This wasn't the kind of business you could do on your own. She wasn't being fair on the girl.

'Would you like some more toast?'

Alan passed her the silver toast rack and she wondered whether he'd noticed that the jar of marmalade which Doris had put on the table that morning, bore a handwritten label, reading: *Caroline's home-made ginger and orange marmalade. 2003.* Was that a subtle message from Doris and, if so, what exactly did it mean?

'No, thanks. You've spoilt me so much that I've put on nearly four pounds.'

He beamed at her. 'Suits you, if you don't mind me saying it.' He patted his sides mockingly. 'And there I am, losing weight.'

'That suits you too,' she said rather too fast. 'I don't mean you needed to but . . .'

'Come on, Jenny.' His eyes twinkled. 'We agreed to be honest with each other. I think we both knew I needed to get a bit trimmer.'

It was true. After her tearful confession the other night, they had agreed how important it was not to hide things.

'About that – the honesty bit. Are you sure you don't think badly of me?'

He held her eyes in his. 'I told you. We all do things at times that we shouldn't.'

'Did you?' She glanced at the silver-framed photographs of his wife on the mahogany sideboard.

'I was never unfaithful. But I didn't spend enough time with her and she was lonely.' His voice faltered. 'So there were times when she found other amusements.'

She hadn't expected that. 'Did you mind?'

'Very much so. But I never said anything. Too scared, I suppose, in case it rocked the boat. None of them lasted. Including her.'

If she could have got up more easily, she'd have hugged him. 'I'm so sorry.'

'Don't be. Sometimes life has its compensations.'

'But I still don't know what I should do to make up for what I did.'

Alan stared out into the garden, reflectively, regarding the lavender walk and trellis. 'I can't advise you on that one, Jenny. All I can say is that one day, it will just come to you.'

Maybe, it really was time to go home now. Her leg was doing well, according to the private consultant whom Alan had insisted on her seeing. And she had to get back to work. Yet at the same time, it was so comforting taking time out, as her sister had put it on the phone. She'd also miss Alan. Miss their talks and their chess games and their walks with her limping along on crutches. Miss the pretty shops in Corbridge where she was just beginning to get to know people.

'You could always stay.' Alan's voice cut in over the break-fast table.

'Sorry?'

'Well.' He buttered his toast carefully. 'If I'm not incorrect, you were thinking of going, weren't you? Back down to London.'

She nodded.

He stood up and began to walk towards her.

Jenny held her breath and studied the silver coffee pot in front of her carefully.

'You could always stay here with me,' he repeated, standing behind her.

She couldn't move.

'Unless of course, you're missing that young man.'

'No.' She swung round in her chair. 'You know I'm not. I've told you. He means nothing.'

He was squatting on the ground next to her, on her level. His face was closer to hers than it had ever been. His eyes were kind. Searching. 'And what about me? Do I mean anything to you, Jenny?'

Before she could speak, his hands were cupping her face and his mouth was on hers. Soft but firm. Intentional. Meaningful. This man knew how to kiss! Before she knew it, Jenny found herself responding hungrily. This was ridiculous! Alan was almost old enough to be her father. Well, maybe a young uncle. Yet she hadn't felt her body reacting like this since she'd been a teenager.

Finally, they broke off breathless. Alan wobbled and then fell over. Jenny burst into laughter. He grinned ruefully from the carpet. 'Clearly not as young as I was!'

'Don't say that.'

They both stood up, him helping her steady herself. 'Well, now you can accuse me of taking advantage of a woman with a gammy leg.' He took her hand. 'I meant it about staying.'

Yes. No. Shit, how was she to know? She'd made so many mistakes about men in the past, that she no longer trusted her judgment.

'I'm not sure. No, please don't look like that. What I do know is that I need to get back to London. Lily needs me. My business needs me.' She stroked his cheek. 'And I need time to think.'

She tried to sleep on the train but it was impossible. Too much was going on in her head. Besides, the train was packed. She hadn't realised so many people came up and down to the north. Did they commute? Did they have long-term relationships too?

At the station, Alan had awkwardly kissed her goodbye on the cheek, close to her mouth, and confused, she'd hugged him back, burying her face in his warm woollen coat.

'Don't keep me in suspenders for too long, lass,' he'd joked.

Now, despite the pile of magazines and emails from Lily which she'd intended to go through on the train, all she could think about was the man who had stood on the platform, pulling funny faces at her through the window, and waiting until she couldn't see him any longer.

It only took three hours to get to King's Cross. She could easily come back at the weekend, as he'd suggested. 'Or I'll come down to you,' he'd added.

She'd rejected that idea too, explaining that if she was going to have time to think properly, it was no good if they met up again so soon. Now, as she headed for the taxi rank at the side of the station, still heavily reliant on her crutches, she wondered if she'd been too hasty. One of the porters was kindly pushing her luggage next to her but how was she going to manage when she got to the flat? She should have taken Alan up on his offer to drive her down.

Then she saw it. A notice bearing her name. *Ms Jenny Macdonald.* It was being held up by a man in chauffeur uniform. A man whose face she recognised.

'Miss Macdonald?' He recognised her too. 'Mr Alan asked me to meet you. He thought it might be easier than you getting a cab.'

'Thank you.'

It was all Jenny could do not to whip out her mobile and thank Alan too. It was so typical of him; so thoughtful and generous. But she mustn't. She needed this time and distance. She'd already make one mistake. A bad one. And she couldn't afford to make another.

Someone had been into the flat and tidied up. There were fresh flowers on the table and fruit in the bowl. Also a note.

'Welcome back. Ring when you're home. Supper's in the oven. Missed you. L x'

Jenny opened the over door. A fish pie – what an amazing

smell! – bubbled merrily away inside. There was only one thing missing. Someone – and not just any old someone – to share supper with and natter about the day.

The following morning she took a cab to the office. Not long now until the plaster came off, thank heavens, and she could drive again. Lily was already at her desk.

'Hi!' Lily's eyes were sparkling and she looked more like the girl Jenny had originally hired. 'Welcome back. It's so good to see you.'

'You too.' Jenny slid into her seat. The desk with the bouquet of lilies on it, her drawers, the files . . . they were all as she remembered it. So why did she feel this flat, dull sense of anticlimax?

'Lovely flowers, aren't they?' bubbled Lily. 'They arrived just now.'

Jenny opened the card. '*Miss you*,' it said simply. '*A*.'

Jenny felt a warm surge running through her, followed by a sharp pang of guilt. Screwing up the card, she flung it into the bin. She didn't deserve to be missed by anyone.

'Something wrong?' asked Lily, frowning.

'No.' Jenny switched into office mode. 'Now I need you to update me, Lily, on everything that's happened while I've been away.'

By the end of the day, she was exhausted. What was wrong with her? It was only 6 p.m. Before she'd hurt her leg, she would have kept going until much later. Resting wasn't always a good idea because it fooled the body into thinking it could slacken. Well she wouldn't allow herself to do that. She needed to keep going, to block out the thoughts.

'Come round for supper,' Lucy had bubbled on the phone when she'd rung during the day. 'I've got so much to tell you and I want to hear all about the north.'

She spoke about it as though it was the other end of the earth and Jenny felt, on behalf of Alan, a slight frisson of irritation. But supper wasn't a bad idea – she didn't want to eat alone again – and she did genuinely want to see her sister.

'I'll come and get you, shall I, after I finish in the office?'

It was a source of aggravation to Jenny that Lucy finished work at 4 p.m. 'Wish I finished that early.'

'It's in my contract.'

Lucy's hurt voice cut her. Well done, Jenny, she told herself. Only back a couple of hours and you've already put your foot in it.

Poor Lucy. Jenny felt so sorry for her all through supper. There was Mike, hanging on every word of his so-called daughter who was telling Lucy exactly why she should allow Sam to get his various orifices pierced and Kate to have green stripes in her hair. Eleanor was conspicuous by her absence. She'd joined some kind of social group apparently. Well at least that was one blessing.

The only light relief was Mungo who kept trying to work himself off against the table leg. 'Is that dog of yours on Viagra?'

'Aunty Jenny!'

Lucy, she noticed, kept glancing at Jon's empty chair. Reaching for her sister's hand under the table, she squeezed it gently. In return, Lucy gave her a sad, grateful smile. It wasn't fair, thought Jenny angrily. If no one else was going to do something about it, she jolly well would.

The following morning, she rang in sick. 'I thought you'd come back too soon,' said Lily alarmed. 'You will take it easy, won't you?'

She didn't need to make excuses. After all, she was the boss. But it was safer for everyone to think she was at home. 'If my sister calls, tell her not to come round. I need to rest.'

The taxi company, whom she was probably funding single-handed with all the business she was giving them, said they could take her. She only hoped the little squirt was at home. She also hoped Kate wouldn't squeal on her. It had taken £50 to appeal to her niece's sense of indiscretion before she'd parted with Jon's friend's address.

Right. They were here. Jenny limped up to the door of the small terraced house. She had to knock three times on the glass panel (no bell or knocker) until he opened it.

'Yes?'

'Remember me?' She forced her way in past Peter. 'We met once. At my sister's. I'm Jon's aunt.'

Alarm flitted across the kid's face and she felt a glimmer of hope.

'Please, I promised Jon not to tell Lucy where he is.'

Jenny caught him by his collar. 'Yes, but you didn't promise not to tell me, did you? Now you'd better spit out the address or I won't be held responsible for what I'll do next. And believe me, I'm not like my sister. I can be very, very tough when I want to be. Get it?'

What a wimp! He'd caved in almost immediately or was he just relieved to be forced? 'I didn't want to upset Lucy,' he had said. 'She's a nice woman.'

'She is.' Jenny glared at him. 'But this is the best way, believe me.'

The taxi driver was still waiting outside, meter ticking. 'Where now, love?'

She gave him the address, on the south side of the river. It wasn't exactly a salubrious area. Peter had said that Jon was working at a bar in the evening to pay the rent. If that was the case, then hopefully he'd be in the flat now.

No reply, although it might help if there was a doorbell instead of a door flap which served as an inadequate knocker. Jenny peered despondently up at the squalid block of flats, before returning to the taxi.

'How long do you want me to wait, love?'

'Another half an hour, if you don't mind.'

She didn't want to be stranded in this part of London. God knows how she'd get another taxi round here.

'It'll cost you.'

'I know.'

'Waiting for someone special are you?'

'You could say that.'

Leaning back in the seat, she closed her eyes with exhaustion and tapped the plaster on her leg which was beginning to ache.

'Don't suppose this is him, then. Not your type, I wouldn't think love, if you don't mind me saying.'

She leapt up. A tall gangly boy with a floppy fringe was walking disconsolately along the pavement with a Spar carrier bag in his hand.

'Jon?'

His pupils were big. Had he been taking something?

She shook him gently by the shoulders. 'Jon. It's me. Aunty Jenny. You've got to come home.'

He broke away from her.

'No. I can't.'

'Why not?'

'Because Mum . . . she'd be so ashamed of me. I've let her down. Oxford . . .'

He couldn't even get a full sentence out.

'Look, Jon. You've got to listen to me. Your mother's ill. She's ill because she thinks you don't want to see her. Don't do this to her, Jon. Come home with me. Please.'

FEBRUARY

Safari supper!

Prawns in lime and ginger (with a splash of vodka)

Vegetarian goulash with mushroom and almond couscous

Bombe

Wensleydale cheese

Forty-seven

She'd worked out how to do it a couple of weeks after starting. Despite her best efforts, Dan's office was still a tip. Every time she tidied up something, he messed it up again. Maybe he and George should spend some time together. But it did mean that a few missing papers here and there would easily pass unnoticed. Besides, he was hardly there at the moment.

It started when he'd received that phone call from Patsy. He suddenly went very quiet when she'd asked if he was all right. 'Yes,' he muttered as he grabbed his wallet and tore out of the office. 'Don't you want your jacket?' she'd called out after him. 'It's freezing out there.' But he'd gone.

Something was definitely going on. He didn't get back that day and when he returned the following morning, around lunchtime with a packet of sandwiches each (far more thoughtful than the old Dan had been), it was only to ensconce himself in his small office and make more furtive phone calls. The rest of the week – and the next – was the same.

'I wonder if Antony knows Dan's having an affair with Patsy,' she asked Martin one evening over dinner when George, miraculously, was already asleep.

'Are you sure about that?'

She picked at her food. Being busy at work – and not being within constant reach of the kitchen biscuit tin – had done something to her appetite and she'd actually lost a few pounds, even though no one else had noticed. 'Pretty certain.'

Even if she hadn't been, the relieved look in her husband's eyes as he tucked into a spaghetti bolognese which she'd made late last night would have been enough to have justified her theory. Martin appeared to have believed her when she'd promised – sworn – that Dan meant nothing to her any more. It was true too. Sometimes, when she watched him in the office, frowning down the phone or scratching his armpits, she couldn't understand how much he had affected her. And why in God's name had she held a torch for him for so many years after it had ended, thinking that he was the only man who could really get her juices going, as Jenny would say?

It really was too easy to paint the past like a rosy picture. OK. So he had been amazing in bed. But out of it, he was a heel. Just look at how he was carrying on with Patsy. She only hoped to God he hadn't told Patsy about what had really happened at uni. If he had, she might tell Antony, who'd tell Mike, who'd tell Martin . . .

Chrissie could hardly breathe when she allowed herself to consider that scenario. She ought to confess to Martin but every time she tried to steel herself, she felt sick with fear as she pictured his reaction. 'Honesty isn't always a good idea in a marriage, dear,' Eleanor had warned and Chrissy was beginning to think she might be right.

Meanwhile, with Dan out so much, she set herself the task of doing what Eleanor had suggested, under the pretext of sorting out the massive mess and establishing a proper filing system. It took her nearly five days before finding what she needed.

'I need £500,' she announced to Martin when she got back that night.

He laughed. 'Where are we going to get that from?' He was giving George fish fingers and broccoli for tea. Somehow, he'd managed to convince their son to eat proper food; uneasily, she wondered if that was Kim's influence.

'We'll have to borrow it.' She cupped his face in her hands. 'You've got to trust me on this one.'

'I don't know.'

'Fine.' She picked up George who immediately starting crying and dumped him angrily in his father's arms. 'Here. Take this. Clearly he doesn't want me. I'm going upstairs to have a shower.'

He was waiting when she got out, wrapped in a towel. His eyes travelled briefly to her chest and then up again. Something hopeful fluttered inside her. Did that look mean he wanted her? It had been so long but every time she tried to make a move, he made an excuse.

'That five hundred quid,' he began. 'Are you sure you can make as much money from that as you say?'

She took a deep breath. 'Pretty certain.'

'Let me get this straight again. Dan . . .' He paused and she could tell he didn't like saying his name. 'Dan told you to buy some shares in his name in a company that he thinks is going to do well.'

'Fantastically well,' she corrected.

'But instead of buying shares in his name, you're going to buy them in our name.'

She nodded. 'Correct.'

'And what's to stop him suing you or going ballistic?'

'I know too much.'

'About his business?'

'Of course. What else?'

'Nothing. It just sounds a bit too easy, that's all.'

Easy? It was what she was entitled to after everything that man had put her through.

'Sometimes, Martin,' she said said, putting her leg on the side of the shower and gently smoothing last birthday's Chanel 19 body lotion into it, 'the smartest plans do seem easy.'

She looked up at him. He was definitely looking at her legs. 'George is quiet.'

'Yes. He's gone to sleep.'

How did he do it?

'Feel like an early night?' she asked softly.

'I've still got the ironing to do.'

'I'll do it.'

'No. The deal was that you went out to work and I ran the house. You go to bed if you want. I'll be up later.'

Jenny was predictably blunt when she called. 'Sounds to me like he's having an affair. All the signs are there. Avoids sex. Makes excuses for coming up late. Hangs out with pretty nannies.'

Chrissie felt sick. 'Martin's already said there's nothing going on between him and Kim. Besides, he isn't like that.'

Jenny laughed. 'That's what we all think until it happens.'

She shouldn't have rung her, Chrissie told herself; she should have phoned Lucy instead who would have been more encouraging and sympathetic. But she hadn't liked to burden her friend when she had so much to cope with herself. 'Jon still hasn't come back then?'

Jenny snorted. 'Don't tell Lucy but I made his mate tell me where he was and I went all the way across town to some grotty flat in South London to get him to come home. Little sod refused. Said he needed to "find himself". That's another male phrase you want to watch out for.'

'Poor Lucy. And Mike's moved in, I hear.'

Jenny laughed. 'You should see it! Eleanor's walking around with a permanently pinched face, moaning about Mike's music which is stacked up in boxes all over the place. Lucy's lovely home is a real mess. She's putting a brave face on it but it's not easy. And she's so hurt about Jon.'

'What about you? It must be a relief to be home.'

'Yes.' Something in Jenny's voice faltered. 'But it's very beautiful up there.'

'This man, Alan. He sounds very nice to have looked after you like that.'

'He was. How are you getting on with Dan?'

There it was again. That guarded tone in her voice.

'Oh, all right. His office is in an awful mess.'

'He came up to see me in Corbridge, you know.'

'Did he? Why?'

'Said he was in the area. Look, Chrissie, I know it's none of my business and I also know you knew him at university. But I'd be careful of Dan. I really would. Don't trust him.'

Chrissie could have laughed out loud. 'Don't worry. I won't.'

A few hours later, Chrissie checked the screen. She had done it! Strange. She didn't feel that huge rush of elation she had expected. Just overwhelming relief, coupled with apprehension.

'Everything all right?'

Dan's voice made her jump. She hadn't thought he'd be back so soon. He leaned over her shoulder, rather too close, and she moved away, watching his eyes narrow.

'What's this? You were meant to have bought those shares in my name. But they're in yours. What the fuck . . .'

'Dan.' She stood up, her back towards the door, ready to run if needs be. 'I needed the money.'

'I know you do. That's why I gave you this job, for Christ's sake.'

'But I need more money. And you owe me.' Her voice faltered. 'For what happened.' Her voice came out firmer now. 'And before you think money can make up for it, it can't. But it can help right now. So if you do something or if you try to say I've abused my position, I'll tell everyone what happened.'

'I'm not going to.' He was stroking his chin, half-smiling. 'I'm impressed, Chrissie. You've got balls. In fact, as long as you promise not to fleece me any more, I'm prepared to keep you on here.'

'No thanks.' She was already gathering up her stuff. 'I've made more money through those shares than I could earn in the next year here. Good luck with this chaos, Dan. I only hope you find someone to sort it out. And by the way, don't be surprised if Antony somehow gets to hear that you're having a little thing with Patsy.'

He laughed drily. 'Haven't you heard?'

'Heard what?'

'Antony's gone back to his wife.' He stuck his hands in his pockets defiantly like a small boy pretending not to care. 'So frankly, what Patsy does with her spare time is entirely up to her.' His eyes narrowed. 'Got it?'

She should have known. If she'd got back at the usual time, she would have missed it. But she was early. So it was no surprise, really, that Kim's pert little convertible Mini was in the drive.

She opened the door quietly, closing it gently behind her. There was the sound of laughter from the kitchen. How cosy. Just like last time.

'Hello,' she said coolly, putting her keys on the hook. 'Any chance of a cup of tea for a woman who's just got in from work?'

Kim leapt up. She was wearing a short skirt with thick black leggings underneath. Her make-up was immaculate. 'I was just going actually but the pot's still full. Shall I pour you a cup?'

'No thanks,' retorted Chrissie, purposefully ignoring her husband. 'I'm perfectly capable of doing it myself in my own kitchen.'

'Chrissie,' began Martin.

'What?' She shot him a furious look.

'I really was just going.' Kim was putting on her jacket.

'Goodbye then.'

Martin waited until the door had shut. 'That was very rude.'

'Was it? Well I think it's very rude and disrespectful to be entertaining other women in my kitchen when I'm out.'

George started yelling.

'Now look what you've done.'

'What I've done! Typical. You always blame me for everything. Well, things are changing now. I've left my job, so we're both going to be at home again.'

'Left your job?' Martin's mouth hung open. 'How are we going to manage?'

She waved an email confirmation slip in front of him. 'Because I've just made a substantial amount of money in buying and selling shares that I should have traded in Dan's name. Just like I told you.'

'And what's he going to do when he finds out?'

'He already knows.'

'So what's he going to do?'

'Nothing.'

'Why?'

She shrugged.

'This doesn't make sense.' He grabbed her arms. 'You've got some kind of hold over him, haven't you? That's why he's allowed you to do this. What is it, Chrissie? Tell me.'

'Don't be silly.' She wriggled out of his grasp.

'I don't think you're telling me the truth.'

'And I don't think you're being honest with me, either. This Kim woman. You find her attractive, don't you?'

He hesitated. 'Well of course she is but . . .'

'Fine.'

'No. No. Chrissie, you've got it wrong. I don't fancy her. Yes, she's attractive but I don't want her. I want you.' His hands cupped her face. 'But you've changed, Chrissie. First with the baby and now with this job. And this shares thing. It doesn't make sense. Why do I get this feeling you're hiding something from me?'

Now. Now was the time to tell him. She held her breath. 'I'm not. He . . . Dan . . . he just felt sorry for us. Of course he was a bit cross about the shares but he said . . . he said he knew what it was like to be skint and that if it helped us, it didn't matter.'

'Honestly?'

'Honestly. Besides, he's really involved with Patsy at the moment. I'm not sure what's going on there but he's spending a lot of time with her. And apparently Antony's gone back to Maggie.'

'Bloody hell. Can that work?'

'I don't know.' She searched his face. 'But it is possible to start again, isn't it?'

'Maybe. I don't know.' Why wouldn't he look at her? 'I don't know anything at the moment. Watch George, can you? I'm going to check my emails. See if any of my job applications have come through. If you're going to be at home, I'd better get back to job-hunting.' He gave a half-smile. 'Your ill-gotten gains will get us out of this mess for a bit but one of us still needs to be working.'

Forty-eight

She'd known Dan would sort it out. He always had done. Ever since they were kids when her father used to threaten her and fifteen-year-old Dan would go round to the house and tell him that if he so much as laid a finger on Patsy, he'd go straight to the police.

And two weeks ago, he'd done the same again. He'd settled Patsy's father down in a chair (Dad had suddenly gone very quiet, as if he realised what he'd done) and persuaded Patsy that this time things had gone too far. Then he'd rung the GP who'd taken one look at Patsy's father and set the wheels in motion.

The result was that he was now in a secure 'nursing home', drugged up to the nines. It wasn't what she'd wanted but, as Dan said, they didn't have any choice now.

'Come and stay with me for a bit?' Dan had suggested.

For a minute, it had been tempting. Dan's flat was a converted loft apartment overlooking the Thames, with cream walls and glass-topped furniture. She'd want for nothing. Apart from integrity, that was. And colour. When she closed her eyes now, she could see purple. Nothing but purple. She'd read somewhere that purple stood for healing. Was she being healed now? It didn't feel like it; not with the pain of Antony's absence.

God, she missed him. She missed the way he nuzzled her breasts. The way he listened to her as though she had something worth saying. She missed his bad jokes. And she missed the way he accepted it when she felt too tired for sex instead of accusing her of not fancying him like so many of the others.

He'd left messages, of course. On her mobile. On the answerphone at home. But she'd ignored all of them. She had to give him a chance to get back with Maggie. She'd only spoken to him once and that was the night her father had been taken away.

'I know about it,' he had said. 'Maggie told me. She's with me now.'

'Is she all right?' she'd asked urgently.

'A bit shaken.'

'Has she called the police?'

'No.'

'Why?'

'Because it would mean admitting that she broke into your flat.'

Thank God.

'Patsy, are you all right. I'm worried about you. I miss you . . .'

Stop right there.

'I've got to go. Look after Maggie.'

And she'd put the phone down. Had she done the right thing?

Who knew. But every time she closed her eyes, the purple was still inexplicably there.

She threw herself into work. It was what she'd always done when things got too much. With her brushes and what she laughingly called her magic potions, she could shut out the rest of the world.

'You're on top form,' Niall, the photographer, commented admiringly after she'd transformed a rather dowdy middle-aged mother into a stunning 'After' for a makeover feature. 'That woman looks amazing. I might even ask her for her number.'

'You can't,' snapped Patsy. 'She's married.'

'Whoa there. I didn't mean it. And since when did you get so moral?'

She pushed past him. 'Fuck off.'

'Boyfriend problems?' he called out.

Patsy shut the door behind her. She was doing a series of magazine makeovers on ordinary readers, desperate for tips and advice. It made Patsy feel as though she was doing something useful instead of taking away other women's husbands.

She never used to worry about this before. But then again, she'd never got close to any of the wives before. Not like Maggie.

Her mobile rang. 'Ant' said the screen. She switched it off just as Niall knocked on the door and opened it before she had time to reply. 'Ready for the next one?' he asked. 'Or are you still in a strop?'

She took a deep breath.

'Ready.'

'Good.' He lowered his voice. 'You're going to need all your skills for this one, believe me.'

'Shh.' Patsy glowered at him. 'She might hear you.'

'I doubt it.'

Niall stood to one side as the next makeover came in.

Patsy stiffened.

It was Antony.

'How did you know where to find me?'

'Dan told me.'

'Dan?'

'I got his number from Chrissie. He was surprisingly helpful actually.'

She turned her back on him, pretending to rearrange her brushes. 'Well he shouldn't have been.'

'I miss you, Patsy.'

'You've got a wife who needs you.'

She felt his hands on her shoulders and shook them off, moving towards the window. Outside people were scurrying around on the pavement. People who lived ordinary, honest lives.

'She doesn't want me. Says it's too late.'

A glimmer of hope fluttered somewhere inside her. White with a tinge of pink round it. Instantly she squashed it.

'Then try a bit harder. You owe the kids.'

'I have tried. But Maggie isn't stupid. She knows I don't love her. I told you. Our marriage had been dead for years.'

She snorted. 'That old excuse. So I suppose the children were immaculate conceptions?'

'No. There was a time when it was all right but it wasn't like us. You and I have something special. Real chemistry.'

She picked up a lipstick, pretending to examine it. Cupid Red.

'But I only want you for your money. Remember?'

He was so close to her she could feel the heat. 'I don't think that now. I just didn't realise why you needed it. You should have told me, Patsy. I'd have understood.'

She laughed shortly. 'No one can understand. No one. You wouldn't believe me if I told you everything about my dad.'

'Try me.'

'No. I don't want to think about it.' She turned round. 'And I don't want to think about you any more, Antony. Go back to your wife. Try a bit harder.'

'It's him, isn't it? Dan. You're having a thing with him, aren't you?'

She looked at him squarely. 'Yes. That's right.'

His eyes flinched. 'How could you, Patsy. How could you go from one man to another, just like that?'

The purple had gone now. Just black. 'It's what I've always done,' she said simply. 'Now go, Antony. Please.'

Forty-nine

It was way past George's bedtime but she didn't want him to go; not when she'd only just back from work and needed to see him. To her delight, he was actually playing a sorting brick game with her when Martin, who'd gone to check his emails before supper, came in.

He was holding a print-out in his hand. Immediately she knew it was good news.

'You've got an interview?'

'No.'

'A job offer?'

'No. But you have.'

'But I haven't applied for one.'

'Then you'd better read this. It's from Bicky Biscuits.'

She couldn't believe it.

'They want me back!' She looked up at Martin, her eyes shining. 'My old job. They're offering it back to me. The other person didn't work out.'

'Do you want to do it?'

'Yes. Of course I do.'

'But you gave it up in the first place because you wanted to look after George.'

'Well he doesn't seem that bothered about me, does he? Great mother, I've been. He hasn't had one accident since you and that Kim woman have been looking after him.'

Martin briefly put his hand around her shoulder. 'Kim hasn't been looking after him. I have. And those accidents weren't your fault. George is like a wound-up toy. He barges into everything. Kim says so . . . Sorry. I mean . . .'

'Stop. Please.' Chrissie looked longingly at the email. 'If I went back to work, you'd continue to look after George and I'd miss out.'

'You mean, you'd be constantly wondering if Kim and I were up to anything.'

'No. Yes. I don't know. Well, you can see my point, can't you?' She looked away, embarrassed. 'You never want to make love to me and . . .'

'That's because you see it as a duty.'

'No I don't. I want to.'

'Do you?' He began to stroke her hair.

'Of course I do. But you don't find me attractive any more because I'm fat after George and . . .'

'You're not fat.' He stroked the outline of her breasts. 'You're gorgeous.'

'Really?'

He drew her to him.

'Really.'

She could feel him hard against her as they lay down on the carpet.

'Not here,' she giggled.

'Why not?'

'The Teletubbies might see us.'

'Sod the Teletubbies. Anyway, it's a video. It will keep him quiet for a bit.'

His hand slid down the back of her new Sloggies. 'Are you sure?'

'Absolutely.' He was undoing her blouse. 'Come on, Chrissie.' He grinned. 'You know nanny always knows best.'

By the end of the week, she had almost got the pastry right. It wasn't doughy like the first time. Nor so thin that it fell to bits when she lifted it from the floured board and onto the flan dish Patsy had bought from Ikea.

It was the first cookery dish she'd ever bought. When she

brought the apple pie out from the oven, it looked so good that she almost didn't throw it away. Golden brown, oozing with liquid. But what else could she do with it, she thought, as she scraped it into the bin. There was no one to eat it. Not here in her lonely flat. And the last thing she felt like was eating it herself. No, the comfort was in making it; proving to herself she could do the impossible.

She'd have to empty the bin now. The hot mixture had seeped through the liner, just like her father had been leaking when she'd been to visit him yesterday. The stench had nearly made her retch but, she had to hand it to them, the staff were very good at cleaning him up. They were good at sedating him too. He hadn't even known she was there.

'Is it necessary?' she'd asked the impossibly young doctor.

'At the moment, yes. But believe me, we'll continue to monitor the situation.'

They seemed to know what they were doing; more than the other places. And as Dan said, what else could she do?

Actually, there was something. Rinsing her hands, after the bin, she unfolded the letter on the side which she'd read so many times that she knew the wording off by heart.

Dear Patsy, We are delighted to offer you the post of makeover manager on our cruise liner, The Ocean King. Please contact our personnel office to make final arrangements.

It went on to give salary details but Patsy had merely skimmed those. The money side wasn't important. Not any more. What did matter was that she would be able to go far, far away.

What was that? It sounded like a knock on the door. Why hadn't they used the bell? Patsy stiffened, her hand on the mobile. Another knock. Please God, not her father. A third knock. She peered through the peephole and then opened the door disbelievingly.

'Maggie?'

The woman nodded. Pale. No lipstick. Straggly eyebrows. Smudged mascara. Was she trolleyed, like last time? If she was, she was hiding it well.

'You'd better come in.'

They perched on her kitchen stools, facing each other. Maggie had curtly refused coffee. The smell of the discarded apple pie hung in the air.

'Antony's not here,' began Patsy awkwardly.

'I know. He's with the kids. I expect you want to know what I want.'

Patsy nodded.

'Do you love him?'

Red. Brilliant red.

'No.'

Maggie leaned forwards furiously. 'Then how could you have considered breaking up a family if you hadn't loved him?'

That wasn't fair. 'I did. Love him, that is. But then I realised . . . when I met you. And when I talked to someone who'd had the same thing happen to her. I started feeling guilty.'

'Bit late for that, isn't it?'

'Yes. I know. Sorry.'

Maggie snorted. Silence.

'I don't love him, you know.' Her eyes were challenging Patsy.

'Then why do you want him back?'

'I don't. I did. But not now. I'm getting used to being on my own and so are the kids.'

Patsy felt sick. 'But you've got to take him back.'

'Why?'

'Have you found someone else?'

'No. But if I had, it wouldn't be any of your business.'

'But Antony's living with you, isn't he?'

'No.' Maggie looked away. 'He's staying with friends; Lucy and Mike. You've met them, haven't you, with your little supper parties.' She glared at Patsy. 'Do you have any idea how hurt I felt about them? Lucy's meant to be my friend but because Mike is Antony's, I didn't get invited.'

'I'm sorry,' mumbled Patsy.

The letter fluttered off the side. Maggie bent forward to pick it up, glancing at it.

'That's right,' said Patsy quickly. 'I'm going abroad to work.'

Maggie shrugged. 'It won't make any difference, you know. I don't want him back. I despise him for what he did. It wouldn't be the same. I've got friends who've tried it. The trust has gone.'

Purple. Just a flash. But purple nevertheless.

'What will you do?' asked Patsy gently.

'He's letting me have the house. At least he's not going to sell it now. I suppose it helps, him having money. That was one of the attractions for you, I suppose?'

Patsy let that one go.

'Why did you come round?'

'I'm not sure, really. Lucy said I shouldn't. But I wanted to see you properly. Talk to you. Find out why you did it. Now I can see.'

'See what?'

'That you love him. You might pretend you don't but I think you do. And he loves you.' Maggie stood up. 'That's why I couldn't take him back.'

'Stop.'

Patsy touched her on her arm.

'What?'

Maggie glared suspiciously at her.

'This is going to sound crazy.'

'You mean like father, like daughter?'

Patsy flinched. 'I'm sorry about that. He's not right. But there's a good reason for it.'

'Please, spare me.'

Good cheekbones. Eyes that needed defining.

'Maggie, there's something I want to ask you.'

'What?'

'Have you ever had a makeover?'

'Now I know you are mad.'

'Because I could make you look beautiful. Really beautiful.'
Maggie stared at her. 'What the fuck are you talking about?'

'It would help, you know. Show you a new you.'

Patsy picked up her make-up bag. 'Please. Let me show you
just a couple of tricks.'

Maggie stepped backwards, pulling her mobile out of her
bag. 'Don't touch me or I'll call the police.'

'I'm not going to hurt you.' Patsy held out her hands pleadingly. 'But if you're going to start life on your own, you could
do with a bit of help. Take your eyes for a start. Brown Kohl.
That's what you need.'

'So you mean I'm a mess? Thanks very much.'

Maggie headed for the door. 'You know, my husband's
welcome to you. You're crazy. Just like your father.'

Maybe she was right, thought Patsy, sitting in the darkness.
Making apple pies and throwing them away. Trying to do a
makeover on the woman whose life she had ruined. Perhaps
her father wasn't the only one to go over the edge. But then
again, was it surprising after everything that had happened to
her in life?

There was a click at the door. Only two men had a spare
key. Patsy closed her eyes. All evening, she'd been waiting for
this. Hoping. Wondering.

Purple.

Red.

'Patsy?'

His voice was soft, muffled in the darkness.

She didn't reply.

'Patsy.' His voice was in her hair, stroking it, caressing it like
her hands. 'Patsy, say something.'

She could sense his face searching hers in the dark, his lips coming down on hers.

Oh, God. She couldn't help herself.

'You know we're meant for each other,' he said, breaking away. 'Don't you?'

She nodded. And then slowly, very slowly, she lifted her lips to his.

'I love you, Patsy.'

This time the words – words which she'd never been able to say to anyone before – slipped out before she could take them back. 'I love you too.'

Fifty

'A safari supper?' repeated Lucy doubtfully. 'I don't know. I honestly don't feel like entertaining at the moment.'

'You won't be,' interrupted Chrissie. 'Well, only briefly. The whole point of a safari supper is that we all go to each other's houses to have one course. It's to celebrate my new job and . . .'

She stopped.

'What else?' asked Lucy intrigued.

'Oh, nothing really. But it's such a relief to know we don't have to sell. Do you know, Lucy, I hadn't realised how much I'd missed work. And I seem to get on better with George because I'm not with him all the time, if you know what I mean.'

Oh, but she did. Lucy would have given anything not to have had Eleanor and Mike there all the time. She couldn't think. And even though the house was really quite large, there simply wasn't space for them all; not with Mike's stuff. He'd wanted to put some of it in Jon's room but she'd been furious at his insensitivity, pointing out that one day her son might choose to come back.

'Who else is coming to this safari supper?' she asked, playing for time.

'Jenny. Obviously not Patsy since Antony has gone back to Maggie.'

'He hasn't!'

'But I heard he had.'

'He asked her to take him back but she wouldn't have him.'

'Good for her.'

'You didn't hear what happened then with Patsy's dad?'

'No. What?'

The word 'dad' made Lucy shake again. She hadn't heard from her so-called father since, but every time the phone rang, she felt shaky. How dare he think he could just come back into her life after leaving them all? She would die rather than leave her own children.

'It's a long story. OK, Sam, I'm coming. Look, sorry Chrissie, I'll have to ring you back. Can I let you know about the supper when I've had a word with Mike?'

She honestly didn't feel like it. In fact, she didn't feel like anything but she had to make an effort for the kids' sake. 'Why can't we go and see Jon?' demanded Kate who was making more brownies.

'He doesn't want us there at the moment,' Lucy explained carefully.

'Gran says he's having a breakdown.' Kate was eyeing her accusingly.

'Well, he's not. He just needs time alone.'

Even so, Lucy felt uneasy. It was exactly what she was wondering herself but if Jon wouldn't allow her to see him, how could she arrange medical help? The only consolation was that Jenny had insisted he seemed quite controlled. Not like someone who was losing it.

'Gran says that Dad had a breakdown.'

Thanks, Eleanor.

'Well, that's not exactly true. But your father did sometimes have some rather . . . rather black moods.'

Kate was wrinkling her face questioningly. 'What do you mean?'

How could she tell her? How could she describe those horrible cold phases when she couldn't get through to him and when everything was her fault?

'Well,' she began carefully. 'The oil business is very competitive. Your father was always aware he had to be good and he didn't like it if things weren't the way he wanted.' Had she said too much? 'Still, we all have our moments, don't we? Now, have you finished your homework?'

'I told you I had. But Sam hasn't. He's in the bathroom again, dying his hair or rather, what's left of it.' Kate grinned. 'Fluorescent green this time.'

'But I told him. I said he wasn't to do that again.' Lucy began running up the stairs. 'That child will drive me mad.'

'Oh and Gran rang.' Kate called up the stairs after her. 'Said she was going to be late again so don't bother about supper.'

Mike stretched out on his chrome and cowhide sofa, blew his nose and patted the seat next to him. 'Come and sit here, pet.'

She'd rather have stayed in her comfortable Laura Ashley chair with its pretty chintz cover. It wasn't just the chair. It was the nagging feeling that had been growing for some months but had now escalated since Kerry's appearance in their lives. The feeling that Mike simply didn't understand what it was like to be a real parent. If he did, he would realise how upset she was about Jon. He wouldn't, with a dismissive wave, say that at least they knew Jon was all right; that he wasn't lying in a gutter somewhere; that he would come round in his own time.

He draped his arm around her, drawing her to him. 'I think the safari supper's a great idea. We could ask Kerry. I'd like the others to meet her.'

'I thought you didn't believe in children being at adult parties,' she pointed out.

'Kerry's hardly a child, pet. Hey, what's up. You're all jumpy this evening.'

It wasn't just this evening, she wanted to point out. It was ever since Jon disappeared.

'Nothing.' She edged away.

'Come on. I can tell.'

'If you really want to know, I keep wondering where I went wrong with Jon. Did I push him too hard to go to Oxford? Was that why he freaked out?'

'He pushed himself to go there.' Mike started stroking her hand. 'He wanted to be like his father. You told me that.'

'Yes but I must have done something wrong, mustn't I?'

'No. It's not easy being a parent. I'm beginning to see that now.'

This was too much. Lucy jumped up. 'Oh, please don't give me that. You've no idea what it's like to be a proper parent. Just because some girl has turned up out of the blue, claiming to be your daughter, you suddenly think you know what it's all about. Well you don't. You don't know what it was like to stay up all night with her when she was ill as a child. You weren't there when she needed help with homework. And you sure as hell weren't there when she got pregnant.'

Mike was very still. 'That's true.'

'What's more, you have no idea how difficult it is for my children to have you here.'

There. She'd said it.

Mike stood up. 'I'm sorry. I know it's not easy on them.'

She couldn't stop now. 'It's not easy on me either. I've been used to being on my own. I've had . . . had to cope with making all these decisions single-handed. I love you, Mike, but I'm not sure I can live with you.' She couldn't stop now. 'And I hate your sofas.'

'Really?' He was looking at her strangely. 'Well I don't like that lipstick you're always wearing. I'm sorry to tell you, Lucy, but pale pink doesn't suit you.'

He was going now. Towards the door. She'd driven him away, like she'd driven Luke away. Mike, who never lost his temper, was leaving her.

Just as Luke would have done, if he hadn't got himself killed.

Fifty-one

Yes of course she was in, said Maggie. She didn't have a hot date tonight. That was last night. This was said so matter of factly that Lucy wondered for a minute if she meant it. Come on round, insisted Maggie. You sound dreadful.

Maggie, on the other hand, looked a lot better. It had only been a week since she'd last seen her in the office but something about her seemed different. She seemed more composed and she was wearing new jeans with a snug fitting pale blue cashmere jumper. 'From that second-hand designer place,' she said airily. 'The good thing about my new model diet is that I can fit things I couldn't do before.'

'Model diet?'

'That's right. Very simple, really. You just fail to notice when your long-serving husband falls for a Page Three model. Then you feel so sick that you don't want to eat anything. It's all right. You can laugh. I'm getting used to it now.'

'You've done your eyes differently, too,' observed Lucy.

'Yes. Well I went to one of those make-up demonstrations at Debenhams. Now, what's all this about Mike?'

Tearfully taking out a tissue from her pocket and scattering dog chews at the same time, Lucy told her. 'I'm sorry,' she said when she'd finished. 'It should be me comforting you; not the other way round.'

'Nonsense. It's nice to be on this side of the fence for once.' Maggie poured her a large gin and tonic. 'Do you know what I think?'

'What?' Lucy felt nervous.

'I don't think it's easy for either of you. You've both been on your own; both used to your independence. You're scared he's going to end up like Luke.'

'You promised you wouldn't tell anyone,' cut in Lucy.

'I won't and I haven't. And he's probably worried about taking on your kids.'

'So what do we do?'

Maggie jingled the ice in her glass. 'You follow your womanly instinct. That's what I did when Antony wanted to come back. I knew it wasn't right but I didn't know it until he asked me. You're on the edge of that precipice now and only you can decide whether to take a step back or jump.'

'How did you know it wasn't right?' asked Lucy curiously.

'Because I could see from his eyes that he didn't love me any more. Something had gone and I couldn't bear to be second best. Besides, I'd already found out that the kids and I could manage on our own. It's not easy but it's possible.'

'Have you met someone else?'

'I've met lots of people. I've joined this group called Social Friends. It's not a dating service. It's just a crowd who meet up for different events like going out to dinner or the theatre. It's made me realise I'm not the only one in this situation.' Maggie leant forwards, her eyes sparkling. 'I nearly forgot. We were out last night, at a restaurant, and you'll never believe who I saw?'

Lucy was still thinking of Mike. 'Who?'

'Eleanor! She was with an extremely attractive grey-haired man.'

'Eleanor? Are you sure?'

'Positive. When she saw me, she blushed and tried to hide her face with the menu. But it was her all right. And before you try telling me that maybe he was her accountant, I can assure you that not many accountants hold their clients' hands in public! By the way, Chrissie rang me about that safari supper which I thought was nice of her, considering I've been left out for most of your cosy little dinners. No, don't say anything. I know Mike and Antony are thick as thieves. Anyway, as I told her, you can count me in. I'll do pudding.'

With any luck, thought Lucy, as she let herself in, Sam and Kate had gone to bed. There was a light on in the kitchen. Someone was cooking. There was a smell of bacon and eggs in the air.

'Mike?' She felt both relieved and apprehensive. 'I thought you were still out.'

'I was.' He gave her a quick squeeze before returning to the frying pan and flipping the eggs over. 'I went out to get some bacon. We didn't have any and I fancied a bacon sandwich.'

'At this time of night?'

He smiled ruefully. 'An old bachelor habit.'

'Aren't you cross with me?'

'Cross? Why should I be cross?'

'Because . . . because of what I said.'

Deftly he flipped the egg over with the spatula, depositing it on top of the bacon. 'You only said what we'd both been thinking. But you were brave enough to come out with it. You're right. I'm not a proper parent, although I have to say that Kerry turning up is the most amazing thing that's happened to me, apart from meeting you. And yes I do find your children difficult, especially when Sam tells you to Foxtrot Oscar. But pet, you come as a package. I love you, so I love Kate, Sam and Jon too.' He drew her to him. 'We'll get through this, I promise you. It might seem strange at first but love is full of compromises.'

'What about the pink lipstick?'

He nuzzled her hair. 'I just didn't like to tell you before.'

Briefly, she thought of all the things she and Luke should have said to each other. 'But we must!'

'All right. We can make a list! It will be great fun.'

She looked up at him, wonderingly. 'You're amazing.'

He shook his head, laughing. 'I don't think so, pet.'

'No,' she insisted. 'You are. Luke was such a control freak that he would have gone . . . well he'd have gone crazy.'

'Well, we each have our own way of doing it. Now I'm going to do something really awful.'

'What?'

'I'm going to eat my bacon sarnie in the sitting room in front of the late night footie. You don't mind, do you?'

She shook her head in relief. 'That's fine, providing I can leave the light on in the kitchen. You know I hate dark rooms.'

'Touché.'

'By the way, Eleanor's got a gentleman friend according to Maggie, who spotted them at some "do" for singles. Not that she mentioned it when she rang earlier to say she was going to be late tonight, so I didn't let on. Instead, she was going on about her recent tests at the doctor which showed those new heart tablets are suiting her. I'm also cross with Jenny because after years of telling me I'm too soft on the kids, she now says I shouldn't have told Kate she couldn't go to that all-night party because if we don't give her some "freedom", she'll do what Jon did and . . . what's happened to the sofa?'

She stared in disbelief at the gap.

'Oh, that.' Mike looked a bit embarrassed. 'Actually, Eleanor pointed out that my cold got worse every time I sat on it. Maybe it was the cowhide that was setting me off. So for an experiment, I got Sam to help me put it in the garage.'

'So it was the sofa and not Mungo that gave you your allergy?'

'Looks like it, pet. But I'd have got rid of it anyway. I could see you didn't like it.' He patted the side of her Laura Ashley chintz chair. 'This isn't what I've have chosen myself. But it's growing on me. Now come here. Forget the kids for a minute and snuggle up.'

Fifty-two

The phones were ringing when Jenny got into the office. 8.30 a.m.! In the old days, before the accident, she'd been here at 8 a.m., if not earlier. Lily was already there, thank heavens, phone against her ear as she sent an email at the same time. She smiled at Jenny.

'I'm afraid she's in a meeting at the moment. Can I ask her to ring you back?'

Not for the first time since she'd been back, Jenny marvelled at how much Lily had changed; being in charge had done wonders for her assistant's confidence and made her far more self-assured.

'Thanks.' Jenny poured herself a large cup of black coffee. 'I take it that wasn't anyone important?'

'Just the company that's booked us to do the summer regatta. It's all sorted. They just wanted to go over a couple of details but they can wait.'

Sometimes she wondered who was running her business. Don't be daft, she told herself. You've got to delegate more. Remember what Alan said. You can't do it all yourself. No one can. That's why you have to have people you trust.

'Did Westlake settle that invoice?'

'Finally.' Lily made a face. 'But not until I'd sent them three reminders and then they had the gall to talk about cash flow. I told them we had a business to run too.'

Jenny was scrolling down her emails. 'I hope you didn't put them off.'

'I was firm, that's all. And if they don't come back, it will give us more time for customers who pay when they should.'

She'd been like that at Lily's age, Jenny remembered. Keen. Hungry for work. Indignant when people didn't do what they should. Taking it for granted when they did.

'Anything wrong?' Lily was looking at her.

'No. Why?'

'You just look a bit tired, that's all.'

That's because she was. Tired of all this. Tired of chasing clients for work and money. Tired of getting up in the morning and seeing cars blocking the street instead of lawns with lavender beds.

'I'm fine.' Jenny briefly scanned the latest email from Alan before deleting it. 'Absolutely fine.'

There were three messages flashing for her on the answerphone when she got in.

Not yet. Kicking off her shoes, Jenny peeled off her office suit and slid into a pair of designer jeans and wrap-round cardi with her flat gold loafers. Pouring herself a large glass of Chablis, she put a Gourmet Sunkissed-Tomato Pasta Meal for One into the microwave. Just three minutes later, she was sitting on the sofa, tray on her lap, catching up with the latest recorded episode of an American comedy which she always loved.

So why didn't it seem funny any more? Was it because the characters seemed to be getting old for their parts, just like she was for hers. What exactly did she want out of life? Alan had asked her that after she'd made her confession. She'd laughed. 'What I want is something I can never have,' she'd said.

'What's that?'

'To wipe the slate clean. Start again. Make sure it never happened in the first place.'

'You can't do that,' he'd said seriously. 'But you could start to make amends.'

Now, lying back on the sofa and watching the American stars grappling with situations that were even more ridiculous than hers, she wondered if that was really possible. It would be so nice to have forgiveness; to be able to live with herself again.

Who was she kidding?

Reaching over for the answerphone, she pressed the button.

'Hi, Jenny. You might not remember me but you called a few months ago. It's Brian. The er, tarnished knight. I've been away in the States. Fighting dragons. That's a joke actually – well, the dragons bit . . . But I'm back now and if you feel like a drink or . . . well a drink, then feel free to give me a ring.'

She'd forgotten all about those crazy weeks when she'd actually rung some of those blind date ads in the newspaper. She must have been insane. Still, he didn't sound as bad as his voice message had, all those weeks ago.

Second message. *'Hi, Jenny. It's me. Just checking you're all right. I haven't heard from you for a few days. Listen, we're having a safari supper this Saturday. Chrissie wants to do it and it might be fun. Sam, stop that right now. Sorry, Jenny. Do you want to be in on it? You could do the starters if you like. Ring me back and let me know.'*

What the fuck was a safari supper?

Third message. Click. She hated that, when someone rang and didn't leave a voicemail. Now she'd wonder who that was. Alan? Dan?

A burst of canned laughter shot out from the screen, making Jenny look up. 'Suits you when you laugh, lass,' Alan used to say.

But it was easier, wasn't it, when there was someone to laugh with. Slowly, Jenny picked up the phone and dialled the number.

Half an hour later, she was sitting on the edge of the sofa, nervously waiting for the doorbell and wondering if she was overdressed or underdressed. Sequinned jeans with a black velvet t-shirt. Too much cleavage? Maybe she should change.

Too late. There was the doorbell. She could pretend to be out. No, that wasn't fair. She took a peek through the spyhole. Not bad. Slightly tousled hair, largish nose, navy blue blazer over cream chinos. Hands in pockets.

She opened the door. 'Hi.' She paused.

'Hello.' He put out his hand, shaking hers rather formally.

Instantly, she knew this was a mistake. His handshake was limp. His palms felt clammy. He was wearing trainers under the chinos and he had a small gap between his two front teeth.

They hovered awkwardly on her doorstep.

'Would you like to come in? That is, before we go out?'

'Yes. Thank you.'

This was going to be painful. 'What would you like to drink?'

'Squash would be great.'

Squash? She hadn't bought a bottle since she was about eleven.

'I'm afraid I only have the hard stuff.'

He didn't even smile. 'Water will be fine.' Sitting on the edge of the sofa, he wiped his glasses and put them back on. 'I've booked the table for nine. Thought it might give us time to talk, to get to know each other. It's really great that you could meet up at such short notice.'

She handed him a tumbler of water and poured herself a large gin with even less tonic than usual. 'Tell me,' she said, taking a slug. 'Why did you call yourself a tarnished knight?'

He shrugged. 'A friend in advertising suggested it. Thought it might make me stand out.'

What a berk. 'So what do you do?'

He puffed out his chest. 'I'm an accountant.'

You'd think he could count the spaces between his teeth then and get them fixed.

'What do you do?'

'I own an events company.' She could see he was confused. 'We put on parties and social occasions for companies.'

'So you're in the entertainment business then?'

She could feel herself being filed.

'Yes. I suppose so. Look, about dinner . . .'

'Yes?'

'I was just wondering.'

His face fell. No, she couldn't do this. It wasn't fair. She'd got herself into this mess and she'd just have to see it through. Quick, think of something. 'I was just wondering if I was a bit over-dressed.'

His face lit up. 'You look great.' He produced a large white handkerchief from his pocket and wiped his brow. 'Phew. For a moment there, I thought you were going to say you didn't want to go. The last one did that to me. To be honest, that's why I took my time coming back to you after your message. I mean I did have to go to the States but I could have rung sooner. Gosh, I'm rambling, again, aren't I? My ex used to hate that.'

'Did she?' asked Jenny brightly. 'Do you mind if we leave now to see if we can get an earlier table. Only I'd quite like to get back before eleven. I've got an early start tomorrow. It's a bit complicated. I mean complicated.'

Dinner was excruciating. Never again, vowed Jenny as she listened to his unending stream of complaints about why people didn't get their tax returns back on time. He didn't even give her a chance to speak when she did think of something to say about figures. Memories of Alan listening to her views and then expressing views on something that she felt exactly the same way about but had thought she was the only one to do so, came into her head.

Even Dan, unreliable Dan, had been more interesting.

'So, tell me, what are your hobbies?' he asked, hand on chin, gazing at her across the table.

What a clot. Funny, the old her would have been irritated by Alan's old-fashioned language but now, in his absence, she found it almost endearing.

'I don't have time. What about you?'

She could tell from the way he puffed out his chest that he'd been waiting for this question. 'I'm into the Second Life,' he said, leaning forwards.

Oh, Lord, she'd landed herself a born-again Christian.

'No, not that.' He laughed nervously. 'It's a computer game. Well, more than a game. Thousands of people do it. I've devised this online character that lives the kind of life I've always wanted to live. I – he – interacts with other people's online characters. Last week, I went paragliding. Online, that is. I'd be a bit too scared to do it in real life. Afters?'

'Sorry?'

'Would you like anything else?' He scanned the menu worriedly. 'I wouldn't mind one but I need to check it doesn't contain nuts. I'm allergic, you know.' He grinned, toothily. 'Just the smell of a nut can kill me. I have to be really careful with sweets.'

Pudding, she wanted to scream. I call it pudding. Only a few weeks ago, she had accused her sister of being 'snobby' for correcting one of the children over that. What was happening to her?

'I'm fine, thank you.' She shook out her napkin. 'If you don't mind, I really ought to be getting back. That was very nice.'

He insisted on driving her home and then, because he couldn't get a space near the flat, on walking her to the door.

It was only when they got close that she realised someone was waiting by the security doors.

'Jenny!'

Alan stood up.

'I'm sorry. I tried to ring you but . . .'

He looked at Brian who'd had the cheek to put his arm around her shoulder.

'I apologise. I appear to have come at a bad time.'

'No.' Jenny angrily shook off Brian's arm. 'No, it's fine. This is, er, Brian. Brian this is Alan. Brian was just going.'

'Was I?'

'Actually, I think I'll come back another time.' Alan was already walking towards the road. She could see his driver sitting in the front of the black Merc.

'Fuck.'

'I beg your pardon.'

'I said fuck, Brian. Look, I'm sorry. Thanks for the meal. But it's not going to work, is it? Good luck with the others.'

'But I thought we really had something there.'

She was running now. As fast as she could towards the car. The engine had started. It was rolling away, snaking between the other cars. Through the green traffic lights.

'No!' Tears began to stream down her cheeks. 'No.' It was too late now. She'd hurt him and she'd hurt herself too. 'How fucking stupid.' If it wasn't for her leg, she'd stamp her foot. 'How bloody fucking stupid can I get?' Feeling a pair of hands on her shoulders from behind, she angrily shook them off. 'And you can fuck off too, you and your bloody armour.'

'Armour?' questioned an amused voice. ''Fraid I left that at home, tonight.'

'Alan!' She swung round. 'But you've gone. In the car. I saw you.'

'I told the driver to go back. Said I wanted to walk. But then I saw you coming after me. What have you done with the boyfriend? And what's this about armour?'

'He's not my bloody boyfriend. I got him out of the paper. He described himself as a tarnished knight, looking for a damsel in distress.'

He chuckled. 'That old line. You're reading the wrong newspaper! Look, I'm sorry for turning up. But I did leave a message, saying I was coming down and wondering if I could just drop in. So when I didn't hear from you, I thought I'd do it anyway.'

'Thanks.' She sniffed. 'I'm glad you did.'

'Hanky?' He handed her a blue and white spotted one. She blew her nose gratefully.

'How's the leg?'

'Fine.'

'Mine isn't.'

She looked down alarmed. 'What have you done to it?

He made a funny face. 'It's like this. Ever since you left, it's been going all wobbly on me. It won't stand up properly. But now I'm here, the other one has started wobbling too.'

She tried to read his face.

'I've missed you, Jenny. I've really missed you.'

'I've missed you too.' This was ridiculous! He wasn't her type. Yet she had missed him; she really had.

'I know there's an age difference. And I'm aware you usually go out with different kinds of people like that tarnished knight and that Dan charlatan who turned up . . .'

'How do you know he was a charlatan?'

'Trust me. I could tell.' He was drawing her to him now. 'But I think we've got something, don't you?'

'Possibly.' She could hardly breathe.

'I mean, that kiss.' He was so close now she could see his breath in the cold air. 'That kiss was really something, wasn't it?'

'Maybe.' She looked at him teasingly. 'But perhaps we should try it one more time. Just to make sure.'

Fifty-three

In the end, they had decided to have the first course at Chrissie and Martin's, mainly because Jenny's place was too small. There had been, thought Chrissie hastily laying the table, so much to-ing and fro-ing and changing of mind about who should have which course, that she'd wondered if her idea had been rather daft.

But now, arranging some daffs in the middle – so wonderful that it was almost spring! – she was glad she had. It would be nice to see Lucy again; she'd been so busy at work that they hadn't had a good natter for weeks. And she was dying to hear all about Jenny's new man who was, Sam had assured her when she'd bumped into him in town, 'wickedly ancient'.

The kids were coming too, ostensibly to keep an eye on George if he woke and also to help with washing up. That had been Mike's idea. 'They need to learn to earn their pocket money,' he'd pointed out. Funny. At the beginning, when Mike had first been around, Chrissie had thought he was too hard on the kids. But now, maybe because George was growing up, she could see that children needed guidelines.

George hadn't had a whiff of breastmilk for weeks now. Sadly, it meant her boobs weren't so impressive but he seemed perfectly happy on whatever the rest of them were eating. Sometimes Chrissie wondered why she hadn't been firmer earlier on. But it was so difficult to see things clearly when you were in the thick of it.

'They're here!'

Martin was calling out from the kitchen which looked out over the drive. He'd volunteered to do the cooking; it had been one of the new-look arrangements they had drawn up when Chrissie had got her old job back. He'd proved to be a surprisingly good cook, if a little over-imaginative at times. Frankly, she had doubts about tonight's menu.

'Hi!' Lucy gave her a gentle kiss on both cheeks. She looked almost beautiful, thought Chrissie. Very floaty in that pretty voile skirt and more peaceful than she'd seen her for a long time.

'How are you?' asked Chrissie quietly.

Something flickered in Lucy's eyes. 'I'm learning to come to terms with it. Jon wrote to me last week, you know. He said he was sorry about not being able to come home yet but that he needed this time to think. I suppose I just have to give him that.'

Chrissie squeezed her hand in sympathy. 'And what's it like now Mike's moved in?'

Lucy's eyes sparkled. 'Actually, it's lovely. The kids seem to have accepted it much better than I'd thought and even Eleanor hasn't been too difficult.'

'Still with you, then?'

'Yes.' Lucy gave her a meaningful look. 'Mike says we've got to talk about that one but we're putting it on hold for a bit. Oh, look, here's Maggie, and Jenny's car behind. Kerry's coming later, I'm afraid.' She tugged at Chrissie's sleeve. 'There's something I must tell you quickly, before they come in . . .

'I must say,' said Maggie, chewing her prawns in lime and vodka thoughtfully, 'you've lost some of that baby weight, haven't you Chrissie?'

'Yes.' Chrissie tried not to sound offended. Maggie had always been one to speak her mind and being on her own clearly hadn't softened her. 'There isn't time to binge-eat now I'm in the office.'

'It's me that's put on weight.' Martin patted his stomach ruefully.

Maggie gave him a sharp look. 'Well as long as you're not drinking so much.'

'More croutons?' Chrissie handed the bowl round the table, hoping to change the subject. She could see Martin was smarting. Maggie could be so tactless!

'Thanks.' Maggie helped herself. 'And have you had any more problems with that health visitor?'

Chrissie stiffened, darting a 'how could you tell her?' look at Lucy who promptly shook her head.

'No, Lucy didn't tell me. It was Eleanor actually.'

'That was meant to be in confidence.'

'Hah,' said Mike, topping himself up with Chablis. 'Don't ever tell that woman anything in confidence. She'll promptly put it in the paper.'

'She split on me about watching the Late Night Sex programme,' piped up Sam. 'If she'd gone to bed when she should have done, she'd never have found out.'

'Anyway,' continued Maggie. 'Talking about putting it in the paper, your health visitor has been reprimanded. Haven't you read about her? Apparently she kept accusing all these poor mothers of beating up their kids when they'd just had ordinary bumps and bruises. Obviously got a bee in her bonnet, she has.'

'I can't believe it!' Martin thumped the table. 'I've a good mind to take action against that woman.'

Jenny shuddered. 'Don't talk about legal stuff to me.'

'But it's all right now, isn't it?' asked Lucy alarmed. 'I mean you sorted out that swimwear woman, didn't you?'

'Yes. But to be honest, it's put me off the whole thing. I don't get a kick out of my work any more.'

Maggie gave Jenny a knowing look. 'Where's this new man of yours then. Does he really exist?'

'Yes, he does, thank you very much. I told you. He'll be here shortly.'

Mike glanced at his watch. 'I'm surprised Kerry hasn't arrived yet. I hope nothing's happened to her.'

Chrissie felt tempted to point out that he was always the first to tell Lucy she was fussing unnecessarily, when she was concerned over the kids. Clearly now he had an instant one of his own, he could see the other side.

'Interesting prawns by the way,' said Maggie.

'They're great.' Kate helped herself to more. 'What's in the sauce?'

'Vod . . . I mean lime,' said Chrissie quickly. 'Martin did them.'

'Ah, yes, I forgot you were cook and nanny rolled into one now,' said Mike jokingly. 'What's it like?'

Chrissie groaned inside. Now he'll really get into a humph. She also felt a bit sick. Funny. She used to like prawns but these tasted odd with that awful vodka sauce. She only hoped Martin had defrosted them properly.

Martin stretched back in his chair. Had he had too much to drink again? She'd caught him having a second glass while he was cooking and now he'd had a third at the table.

'Not bad. I'm not saying I'll do it for ever, mind. But for the time being, I'm quite happy to let the wife go out to work.'

'That was . . . quite inventive,' said Lucy, dabbing her mouth with her napkin. 'George is very quiet.'

Chrissie stood up. 'I'd better go and check him.'

'No.' Martin put out his hand. 'let him sleep. If you disturb him, he'll wake. Kate's going to stay here to babysit, aren't you, while we go onto Maggie's. It is you next, isn't it?'

'It certainly is. When you're ready everyone.'

Martin picked up the car keys.

'I'll drive,' said Chrissie quickly.

He looked as though he was going to protest and she braced herself for the usual 'You think I've been drinking again' accusations again. But then his eyes softened. 'You're right.' He squeezed her bottom briefly. 'And don't worry. I'll only have one more glass tonight.'

Fifty-four

Jenny had brought a ready-made tomato and green pepper salad as a contribution to Maggie's meal and an apology for not having everyone at her place because her apartment was too small for everyone.

The truth was that she didn't want anyone in it. Her home was hers as far as she was concerned and she didn't want Martin or any of the others, Lucy excepted, snooping round.

In fact, she'd have bowed out of this safari scenario if Alan hadn't thought it was a great idea. 'It will give you a chance to introduce me to your sister,' he'd said. And now he was late, tied up in a last-minute meeting. She'd texted him with directions on how to find Maggie's but he hadn't replied. The others, she thought ruefully, inverting a steaming bowl of couscous onto a plate, would gleefully assume she'd been stood up.

Maggie's house was different from the last time she'd been here. It seemed more colourful and almost studenty with those floaty gauzy curtains that were no more than chiffon draped around poles on top. She had Indian sequinned cushions on the sofa and big bean bags on the floor. And there were lamps everywhere with different coloured light bulbs inside. There was a smell of something – possibly rose and jasmine – from some floating candles on the side dresser and in the kitchen where they were working. The whole effect was soft and relaxing.

'Like it?' Maggie smiled at her.

'I do. You've made some changes.'

'I had to. To preserve my sanity. It's not easy when your

husband walks out after nearly twenty years of marriage for some bimbo, you know.'

Jenny began to chop the parsley nervously. 'I'm sure it isn't.'

'Do you know, that woman – I refuse to say her name – had the audacity to come and find me. Said she was sorry and then she offered to make me up.'

'Make you up?'

'Yes, with her witchcraft pallet. What a bloody cheek! And did you hear about her photographing the children – my children – for some giveway paper. I've never been so angry in my life.'

'You said she was sorry.' Blast. She'd cut herself slightly with the knife.

Maggie snorted. 'Bit late for that, isn't it.'

'But Lucy said . . . I mean I heard that Antony wanted to come back.'

Maggie wiped her hands on a cloth. 'Do you honestly think that would ever work? When someone has a thing with someone else, the trust goes. So do all those intimacies that you share from day to day. You don't laugh together any more because nothing seems funny. You can't watch a film with sex in it because you wonder what he did with her. And as for having sex together again, well, I couldn't even think about it. He might be sorry but he should have thought about that before he started the whole thing. Personally, I think women who have affairs with married men should be stoned.'

'That's a bit harsh, isn't it?' Jenny picked up the bowl of couscous. 'Where do you want me to put this?'

'Delicious,' said Mike enthusiastically. He'd been more relaxed, noticed Jenny, since that daughter of his had finally turned up and was sitting next to him. 'Er, what is it?'

'Vegetarian goulash with couscous,' Maggie said smartly, as though she'd been waiting for the question.

'Is there something else with it?' asked Martin, helping himself to more than his share of couscous.

'Martin!' Chrissie made an I-told-you-not-to-put-your-foot-in-it face at her husband. 'Have you turned veggie then, Maggie?'

'I'd been meaning to for years but Antony always liked his meat.' She raised her glass. 'Bit ironic don't you think, that now he's got both a wife and a mistress who are non-carnivores.'

'Has he gone back to her then?' Jenny couldn't help herself, despite Lucy's warning look.

'Oh I expect so. You lot probably know more than I do.'

There was an uncomfortable pause. 'Er,' said Mike finally, 'I believe he might have done.'

'Oh, look,' said Lucy with relief. 'Someone's turned up. It must be Alan.'

'No.' Jenny's heart rose and then sank at the same time. 'It's not his car.'

'I don't believe it,' said Mike, looking through the window. 'It's Eleanor. With a man.'

'Good evening, everyone!' Eleanor beamed at them, kissing them all on each cheek and almost suffocating Jenny with a wave of hearty perfume. 'I'm so sorry we're late. This is Walter, everyone. Walter, this is my family together with some friends.'

A rather small shy-looking man with thin grey wiry hair and wearing a dark grey suit and tie shook their hands formally.

'Don't you live opposite us?' said Mike.

'I do indeed. Number 9. I came to live with my son last year and he can't seem to get rid of me.'

Eleanor laughed politely, as though she'd heard that one before.

'Why don't you come and sit down,' said Maggie. 'We've only just started.'

'Hang on,' said Jenny quietly to her sister as they took their seats. 'If that's the bloke from number 9, wasn't it his son you were trying to fix me up with last summer? The one that was meant to come to dinner but didn't.'

'That's right, dear.' Eleanor leaned across the table. Nothing wrong with her hearing, thought Jenny. 'Walter told me all about it. In fact, that's how we got together. He and I happened to be gardening one day – Lucy's garden is far too much to cope with on her own, don't you think? – and he started chatting over the hedge. I think you had a lucky escape there, Jenny. Walter's son Gary is . . .'

'Now, now Ellie. We said we wouldn't mention that.'

Ellie? Jenny tried not to giggle. Across the table, she could see that Lucy was trying to keep her composure too.

'I've brought you a little present, Lucy. It's just a jar of pickles that we bought today from a sweet little tea room.'

Jenny couldn't help it. 'Looks like someone's ancestor.'

Lucy unsuccessfully stifled a giggle, caught Jenny's eye and started off again.

'What an interesting thought. Now how are all you young things doing? Chrissie, did you take my advice on those shares?'

'What shares?' asked Jenny sharply.

Chrissie flushed. 'Just a tip that Eleanor passed on.'

'And Martin, dear, I do hope you're managing all right. What is it they call you nowadays? Homely husbands, isn't it?'

'Househusbands, actually,' he said stiffly.

Eleanor fluttered her eyelashes and looked down on Walter. 'In our day, that sort of thing just didn't happen, did it?'

'No, Ellie, it definitely didn't.'

'I don't think it's anything to laugh about, Jenny,' said Eleanor sternly. 'When we were young married women, we ran the house and our husbands went out to work.'

Jenny watched Martin top up his glass.

'Well I think Martin's doing a great job.' Chrissie's voice cut into the silence. 'In fact, he's far better at looking after George than I am. And from what I hear, I'm not sure you did such a fantastic job with Luke when he was a kid.'

Eleanor went white. 'Well! After all the help I've given you . . .'

Maggie sprang up. 'The doorbell. I'm sure I heard the doorbell.'

Dear God, if you exist, thought Jenny, please may this be Alan.

As soon as she opened the door to him, she felt better.

'Sorry I'm late, lass.' He drew her to him; the warmth of his body made her feel so good. She didn't even mind the 'lass' bit.

'Come on in and I'll introduce you to everyone.'

He looked nervous and Jenny laughed. 'They won't eat you. In fact, they don't think you exist.'

They were all sitting round the table, looking up expectantly and Jenny's heart lurched for Alan. 'This is Alan. Alan, this is Eleanor, Lucy . . .'

She went round the table in turn.

'We were beginning to think Jenny had made you up,' announced Eleanor crisply. 'Poor girl doesn't have much luck with boyfriends, do you, dear?'

'That's not fair . . .' began Lucy.

'Well if it is, I'm extremely grateful,' said Alan firmly. 'It means that the others have left me with a chance. Now tell me, Eleanor, I believe you come from Cornwall. I knew that part of the world when I was a boy.'

She had to hand it to him, thought Jenny. A younger man would have taken offence; might even have been rude. But Alan was positively charming the old bird who was hanging on his every word.

'You knew the Lancasters?' Her eyes were nearly popping out of her head. 'They had some wonderful parties.'

'They did indeed. My parents were invited every year and then of course they would come up north in the autumn for the shoot.'

Maggie managed to collar her on the way out to the kitchen. 'He's nice. A bit older than I'd thought. But nice. And he really likes you.'

'I really like him too.'

'That's just as well, lass.'

She hadn't realised Alan was behind her. 'I wasn't eavesdropping, mind. I just came out to help. Have you told everyone yet?'

Jenny wavered. 'Not yet.'

'Told us what?' repeated Maggie as they went back into the dining room.

'Has someone got some news?' Eleanor's eyes sparkled excitedly. 'Oh, good. This dinner party was in danger of getting rather dull.'

Everyone looked at Jenny, including Alan. This was crunch time. This was when she had to be true to herself.

'I'm moving,' she said quietly.

'Moving?' Lucy's jaw dropped. 'But you didn't tell me.'

'Where are you going?' demanded Chrissie.

'To the north.' She glanced up at Alan who slipped his arm around her shoulders. 'Just outside Newcastle.'

'How wonderful!' Eleanor clapped her hands. 'You know, I think there's a great deal to be said for a woman to marry an older man. So much more stability, don't you think? Will you ask the Lancasters to the wedding?'

Alan cleared his throat. 'Actually, Eleanor, Jenny says we couldn't possibly get married because we talk far too much and have great sex. Married couples can't usually do either, let alone both at the same time.'

Jenny burst into fits of laughter. But Lucy was looking at her, hurt, across the table. Why didn't you tell me, she was asking silently. I'm your sister. Didn't I deserve to know first?

'Sorry,' she mouthed.

Lucy looked away and her heart sank. She should have said something first. Another bloody cockup.

'Sssh everyone. Isn't that my mobile?' Chrissie looked wildly around. 'Where did I put it? Look, it's on the floor. Mind your foot, Martin. You're going to tread on it. Hello? Yes? What? Kate, please speak slowly. I can't understand what you're saying.' She looked wildly at Martin. 'I said this would happen. I said he'd choke on those bloody carrot sticks you gave him or climb over his stair gate again. I said he'd fall down the stairs and knock his head and then social services really will take him again and then . . .'

'Chrissie, what's happened?' said Martin urgently. 'Please, give me the phone. Kate, now just calm down and tell me what's happened. Really. You're sure? Yes, we'll be right there.'

His hands were shaking and sweat was breaking out in little beads on his forehead. 'You're never going to believe this.'

The whole table was silent.

'George has said something. Not just one word but a whole sentence! He can talk! My son can finally talk! There's nothing wrong with him after all! Isn't that fantastic?'

'Is that all?' muttered Mike. 'I thought something awful had happened.'

'Dad!' Kerry dug him in the ribs. 'I hope you're not going to be so unsympathetic when your grandchild is born. It's scary stuff you know when you have a kid. I'm really nervous about it.'

'Don't be.' Lucy put out her hand and squeezed Kerry's lightly. 'We're here for you.'

'Of course, in my day,' boomed Eleanor, 'children learned to talk when they were ready. We didn't make a fuss about it. Personally, I blame all those so-called development books by people like Sheila Kissinger. She ought to have stuck to politics like her husband.'

Maggie snorted. 'It's Sheila Kitzinger, actually, and she has nothing to do with Henry Kissinger. Anyway, I thought her books were great.'

'What did he come out with?' asked Alan. 'What did George actually say?'

'That's the thing,' said Martin beaming. He put his arm around Chrissie. 'You're never going to believe this, love. He said "Want Mum."'

'No,' gasped Chrissie. 'Really? You're not just saying that?'

'No. I'm not.'

'I'm not sure I'd call that a whole sentence, dear. In my day . . .'

Chrissie leapt up from the table. 'I've got to go. I have to hear George say it myself. Sorry, Lucy, we'll come round later.' Tears began to roll down her face and Jenny felt hideously embarrassed for her. If this was what it was like having kids, she didn't want it.

'Dad,' said Kerry, 'I feel really tired. Would it be all right if I stayed with you and Lucy tonight?'

'Sure,' said Mike quickly.

He hadn't even asked Lucy, noticed Jenny, although of course her sister was nodding her agreement. Did Mike realise how lucky he was to have someone like her? Not every woman would take kindly to a missing daughter turning up out of the blue.

'So we're off again?' asked Alan as everyone began to get up.

''Fraid so.' Was he getting bored with all this? 'Perhaps this wasn't such a great idea.'

'Nonsense.' Alan began to clear the table, despite Maggie's polite protests. 'I'm rather enjoying it.' His eyes twinkled as he pulled her to him, whispering in her ear. 'The only thing is that I'm absolutely starving after that vegetable stuff. Any chance of stopping off somewhere on the way to your sister?'

Fifty-five

Just as well she'd bought some cheese as well as making pudding, thought Lucy as she got back to the house before the others. Maggie's vegetable dish had looked very pretty but Mike was a meat and potatoes man.

He'd offered to drive Kerry back here in her car. It was incredible how well-balanced and frighteningly independent she was, although today the poor child did look tired. They'd have to put her up in Jon's room for the night since Eleanor had taken over the spare room.

'Hi, we're back.' Mike came into the kitchen and kissed her softly on her neck as she unwrapped the Brie, putting it on a pretty Portuguese plate which she and Luke had bought on holiday years ago. 'Sure it's all right about Kerry staying?'

How could she say no when Mike, unlike her own father, was trying to be a responsible dad? 'Of course. Jon's bed has clean sheets on it. Can you find her a clean towel from the linen cupboard? Oh, and there are some spare nighties in my chest of drawers.'

'It's all right.' Kerry yawned, her mouth open. 'I don't usually wear anything in bed.'

Mike looked embarrassed.

'Well, if you're sure,' began Lucy. 'Would you like a bath?'

'Too tired.' Kerry yawned again, revealing a wide array of fillings. 'Maybe in the morning. Mind if you don't wake me? I could do with a lie in. By the way, Lucy, I hope you don't mind me telling tales but there's something I've got to tell you about Kate.'

'What?'

Kerry made a funny face. 'If I were you, I'd take a careful look at what she's putting in her brownies.'

'You don't mean that . . .'

'I'm afraid I do. She told me – silly girl thought it was funny. She didn't put in too much but I told her how daft it was. Says she won't do it again but I just thought I ought to tell you.'

Lucy's mouth was so dry that her tongue stuck to the roof. 'Where did she get it from?

'You two of course.'

'What?'

'The medicine cupboard. She just helped herself.'

'Hang on a minute, Kerry,' said Mike evenly. 'What exactly do you think Kate is putting in her brownies?'

'Bach's Rescue Remedy. Couldn't you taste it? It's brilliant stuff and I couldn't help seeing you've got a few bottles.'

'They were for Sam,' began Lucy weakly.

'Well, maybe you'd better put them away. Kids at that age . . . there's no knowing what they might do, is there, Dad? It's really cool to be able to say that!' Grinning, she planted a kiss on Mike's forehead. 'Well, ta ra now. Better get some sleep. See you later.'

Mike waited until she'd gone up the stairs. 'I thought –'

'So did I! You don't think that's why Eleanor fell asleep that time, do you?'

'Could be.'

'Oh dear. That's awful.'

'So why are you smiling?'

'I'm not. It's really serious. It's just that Eleanor kept saying how nice they were. Thank heavens she wasn't ill.'

'We've still got to talk to Kate. But look, about Kerry. I know she isn't what you expected. But she's not what I expected either.'

'She's your daughter.' Lucy's head was still reeling with the implications of Kate's cooking. 'When you have kids, you love them unconditionally whatever they say and do.'

His arms circled her back. 'I'm beginning to learn that. I wish the others weren't coming back to us now.' He looked down on her meaningfully. 'I could do with an early night.'

'Me too.' She broke away regretfully and took out the pudding she'd made earlier.

'What's that?'

'A bombe.'

He raised his eyebrows. 'I know things are a bit tense but is that necessary?'

'Very funny. It's ice cream with sorbet inside. No, don't do that.'

Mike was cutting himself a wedge of Wensleydale. 'But I'm starving!' He wolfed it down hungrily. 'Actually, I've just had a great idea. Maybe if we all went veggie, we could persuade Eleanor to go home.'

'I've got a funny feeling that she might never be going back,' said Lucy. 'Look.' They both peeped through the window at Eleanor and Walter who were standing in the porch, locked in each other's arms.

'Let's just hope it lasts,' said Mike ominously. 'Frankly, I'd pay him to take that woman away. As far as possible.'

'What do you think of Alan?'

'Well, pet, he's not what I expected to be honest but I like him. He says what he thinks and he clearly adores your sister. As for her, well I think she's finally realised there's a lot to be said for a solid, reliable man who makes her laugh.'

'Exactly what I think.'

He put his arm around her. 'That's because we're on the same wave-length. Hang on. The two love birds have finished snogging and Eleanor's looking for her key. Looks as though the others are arriving too.' He gave her a playful slap on the bottom. 'Perhaps we ought to play another of our after-dinner games to chivvy things along. How about your Dirty Scrabble?'

★ ★ ★

'Sam! Kate!' She hadn't been expecting them but now here they were, pushing their way past Eleanor and heading for the kitchen.

'We're starving.'

'Excuse me,' said Eleanor haughtily. She looked to Walter for back-up. 'Young people nowadays are so rude. In my day, we wouldn't have dreamed of pushing past our elders.'

'I'm sorry.' Lucy flushed. 'Kate, apologise.'

'Sorreeee. Mum, we haven't got any bacon in the fridge.'

'This isn't some kind of midnight canteen, you know,' said Mike firmly. 'Your mother is in the middle of a dinner party. You can't just expect food on demand.'

'Why not?' Sam was munching crackers. 'This is our home. Not yours.'

'Sam! That's very rude.'

'Why? It's true, isn't it?'

'Hi, everyone.' Chrissie breezed in, bearing a potty in one hand and a striped bag containing enough baby stuff for a week's holiday in the other. Martin was close behind, holding a very awake George. 'Hope you don't mind but I couldn't bear to leave him so we brought Kate and Sam back with us. Listen! He might say it again. He's been doing it all the way over here. Go on, George. Want Mum.'

George grinned toothily.

'They never do it when you want them to.' Maggie ruffled her son's hair affectionately. 'Mind you, I couldn't stop you lot talking. Sorry Lucy, I had to bring them too. My babysitter blew out.'

'We could have a kidsfest in the tv room,' said Sam bringing out another giant packet of crisps from the larder.

'Good idea.' Jenny was leaning against Alan and he was, Lucy noticed, stroking her arm quietly. 'We can get rid of you lot.'

'Thanks very much.' Kate had made a pile of toast. 'Actually we don't want to be near you either.'

'Come on, sweetie.' Lucy watched as Jenny pulled her niece towards her for a hug. 'You know I didn't mean it.'

'Why don't us adults go into the dining room,' said Mike. 'Then we can have pudding. I'm starving too . . . I mean it would be nice to have something else to eat.'

'Kate,' added Lucy sharply. 'I want a word with you later on. About your brownies.'

'It's Mungo you ought to have a word with, Mum. He's just wolfed down all that Brie you left out. And he's been sick on the sofa.'

The bombe had managed to invert itself properly and everyone complimented on her it. 'It's really very easy,' said Lucy modestly. She could hear the kids laughing and arguing in the room next door; it reminded her of the days when all three had been at home and Jon had been the leader of the gang with the younger ones hanging on his every word.

'What do you think, Lucy?'

'Sorry?'

'Do you want to play an after-dinner game?' Mike patted her knee. 'You were miles away, weren't you?'

'Yes. Sorry. What kind of game?'

'What about shag, marry or die?' suggested Martin. 'You have to think of someone and everyone says which one they'd rather do.'

Eleanor leaned forwards. 'Could someone please explain how a carpet fits into this game?'

'Ouch, Chrissie! Er, it doesn't really, Eleanor. Shag means . . . OK, how about truth or dare? I haven't played that since I was a kid.'

There was an uneasy silence.

'I'd rather play charades,' said Chrissie meaningfully. 'By the way, Lucy, did I tell you George was learning French? Which language does Sam do?'

'The one with "F" words in it,' quipped Jenny. 'Come on, Lucy, don't look like that. I'm only joking.'

'Stop changing the subject.' Martin drained his glass. 'Come on, everyone. Let's give it a whirl. I'll go first, shall I? Eleanor, truth or dare?'

Eleanor giggled. Was it that second glass, wondered Lucy, or was it Walter's presence? 'What do I do?'

'You tell him which one you want and then you either have to answer a question truthfully or do a dare,' said Walter patiently.

'Ooh dear, I'm not sure. Dare. No, truth. No dare, please.'

Martin's eyes twinkled mischievously. 'I dare you to sit on Walter's knee.'

A gasp went up from around the table. 'Oh, no, I couldn't possibly. No, really, Walter. Have I got to? Oh dear, how embarrassing. At my age too!'

Lucy watched speechlessly as her mother-in-law clambered onto his knee. The poor man looked as though he was going to vanish under the weight of lace and black velvet. 'Right!' Eleanor looked as though she was sitting on a throne. 'Is it my turn now? Michael, truth or dare?'

'Er, truth.'

'Did you enjoy Maggie's goulash and couscous?'

'Er, yes.'

'No, Michael!' Eleanor was tapping her side plate with the cheese knife like a headmistress. 'I overheard you telling Lucy that it made you feel sick. Didn't you? If you don't tell me the truth, I won't be able to trust you again. And nor will my daughter-in-law.'

'That's not fair,' began Lucy.

'All right. Sorry, Maggie. It just wasn't my sort of thing, that's all.'

'Fine.' Maggie's tone could have sliced through the bombe like a knife.

Mike shifted uneasily. 'Eleanor, truth or dare?'

'She's been done,' interrupted Jenny. 'It's got to be someone else.'

'Pity. I was going to ask her when she was leaving,' muttered Mike. 'All right, Maggie. Truth or dare?'

'Truth.' Maggie narrowed her eyes and Lucy felt apprehensive at the visible tension between the two.

'Were you,' said Mike slowly, 'about to leave Antony anyway before he left?'

'Mike!' said Lucy, shocked.

'No, let me answer.' Maggie was looking straight at him. 'I was considering it, yes.'

'Why?'

'That's two questions,' cut in Chrissie. 'It's not allowed.'

'Because I didn't love him any more. I'd never loved him. But I was scared of being on my own.'

'And did Antony know that?'

'I think so.'

'So maybe we should all try and see both sides of this.'

'That's enough.' Martin was speaking now. 'Maggie, your turn.'

'OK.' She took a deep breath. 'Chrissie, truth or dare?'

'Dare.'

'Coward. I dare you to eat up the rest of that bombe.'

'I can't. I'm on a diet. You know that.'

'Then it will have to be truth then.' She took a deep breath. 'Those bruises that George had. You said they were accidents. Is that true?'

The room went silent.

'Yes.'

'Sure?'

'There was one.' Chrissie's voice wavered. 'Just the once. He wouldn't stop yelling.' She glanced across at Martin helplessly. 'I didn't mean to. It just happened. I pushed him. Hard. Across the room. And he fell against the wall. That's how he got that egg on his head.' She covered her face with her hands. 'Now they'll take him away from me.'

'No.' Lucy had her arm around her, glaring across at Maggie. 'How could you ask such a question?'

Maggie shrugged unrepentantly. 'Sometimes it helps to get these things out.'

'Does it?'

'Yes.' Jenny heard her voice ring out clearly as she twisted her green jade bangle nervously. 'It does. Look, I know it's not my turn but can I ask Lucy something?'

Lucy felt slightly sick. She'd sworn to herself that the discovery that Jenny was a half-sister wouldn't affect their relationship. But every time she realised how different they were, it all seemed to make sense.

'Lucy, were you aware that Luke was unfaithful to you?'

'That's ridiculous.' Eleanor's haughty voice cut in. 'My son would never look at another woman.'

'Maybe not another woman.' Lucy's mouth was dry.

'Are you saying my son was a homosexual?'

Lucy swallowed hard, remembering how disinterested Luke had been in sex. It had been a miracle that Sam had come along at all. 'He told me, before . . . before it happened that he'd done something terrible. Something unnatural.' She looked sadly at Eleanor. 'You must have wondered yourself. He could be so sensitive, like Jon. That's why he was good at his job.'

She paused for a minute, reflecting. Luke had worked for a big oil company and had built up a reputation as a capable businessman with heart. At his funeral, she'd been amazed at the number of letters from colleagues who described how he'd given them advice on all kinds of matters ranging from homesick employees to those who'd been hurt or bereaved by the terrible accidents which occasionally happened on rigs.

It was only at home that he showed his true colours.

'It's not true.' Jenny's voice cut in. 'You got the wrong idea about Luke. You always did, he said. But he used it as a smoke-screen so you wouldn't guess.'

Lucy felt a knife of ice slicing through her. 'What are you talking about?'

'When he said he'd done something terrible, something unnatural, he was talking about us.' Her sister looked white.

'Us?'

She'd never seen Jenny look scared before. 'Him and me. Luke loved me, Lucy. And I'm ashamed to say that I loved him too.'

Jenny saw Lucy looking at her as though she was seeing her for the first time. No, her eyes were saying. No, this isn't true.

Christ! Jenny twisted her green bangle so it pinched her skin.

'I'm sorry,' she mouthed.

'Now that really is ridiculous . . .'

'Shut up, Eleanor.' Jenny's eyes were fixed on her sister's. 'I'm so sorry, Lucy. I've wanted to tell you for years. I didn't mean it to happen. Neither of us did. But I couldn't go on any longer, not telling you the truth.'

She wanted to get up. Run away and scream. But her legs were buckling beneath her, exactly as they had when Luke had told her at the wedding reception, just after marrying Lucy that he really should have married her. Nothing had happened for ages after that but there'd always been that smouldering undercurrent of intent between them, even though she'd known how wrong it was. And then, finally, she had given in. It hadn't quite been rape; not like Lily. But she'd resisted, knowing it was wrong. Maybe she just hadn't resisted hard enough . . .

'It didn't last long . . .'

Wracked with guilt, she'd vowed to herself never to see him again. 'You can't do that,' he'd pleaded. 'There's got to be some way. Let me talk to Lucy.'

'No!' She had held Luke then by the wrists, hard, and made him promise, absolutely promise, never to breathe a word to her sister. That's why he got on that light plane in Brazil. He must have known about the safety record out there. Knew, as the inquest had later revealed, that the plane was due to go in for emergency works later that day and should never have been allowed to fly first. And then they'd brought Luke's body back on the plane and she'd had to act the role of concerned sister-in-law instead of bereaved lover.

'Stop!' Mike was standing up. She was twisting her bangle – the only gift that Luke had given her – so hard that it hurt. 'Lucy doesn't want to hear any more. I think it's best if you leave now, Jenny. Just go.'

Fifty-six

'You must have suspected something,' said Mike gently as they got into bed after everyone had finally gone off home.

'No.' Lucy felt as though someone else's words were coming out of her mouth. 'I knew they got on well and they were always laughing and joking together. When he died, she was devastated but I thought that was because she was upset for me.'

'I know you said you didn't want to talk about Luke's death but do you think it would help?'

'I told you. He'd been sent out, at a moment's notice, to Brazil. There had been an accident – on an oil rig – and he had to make sure the company wasn't responsible.'

'So he was just doing his job.'

'Well, yes. But I think he deliberately put himself in danger.'

Realisation dawned in Mike's face. 'Because he was having an affair with your sister?'

'Half-sister.' She bit her lip. 'Like I said, just before he left, he told me he'd done something awful but that he'd explain when he got back. We had a terrible argument.' Lucy buried her wet face in the pillow. 'That was the last time I saw him. Now I realise he knew I'd never be able to cope with . . . with him and Jenny. So he deliberately put himself in danger by getting on a plane with a poor safety record because he didn't care about living any more. If that hadn't worked, he'd have found another way to have ended it all.'

They were both silent for a few minutes.

'And this theory you had – the one about him being gay. Did you really believe it?'

Lucy shook her head. 'I didn't think he was actively . . . you know. But there are a lot of men out there – you must see that – who are almost like women-men. Sometimes, at work parties, there would be the odd comment from other people. I remember one man coming up to him and straightening his tie which made me feel uneasy. And as I've told you, he wasn't that bothered about sex.'

She paused, remembering. 'It was one of those things I couldn't bring myself to talk about in case it wasn't true and I annoyed him. He might have been sensitive but he could have a terrible temper when he wanted.'

Mike stroked her hand comfortingly. 'Maybe it was a smoke-screen on his part, to hide what he was really doing. Pet, there's the phone again. It's probably Jenny. You'll have to answer her calls sometime.'

'Not yet.'

He reached out for her in the dark, 'I'd never be unfaithful to you. You know that.'

She held onto him, nodding silently.

'Try to sleep.' He stroked her hair. 'It will be all right. You'll see.'

'I shouldn't have told her. Should I?'

Alan held her tightly under the covers.

'I don't know, lass.'

'But I want to tell her why. How it happened. Now mum's gone – and dad's probably never coming back – we've only got each other. And I've ruined it.'

'Give her time. She'll want to know herself.'

'Is that how you felt about your wife's relationships?'

'Oh, yes. I wanted to know every detail.'

'And did that make it better?'

His silence screamed through the silence.

'Alan, did it make it better?'

'I'm afraid it didn't, lass. Sometimes there are things that are too big to undo.'

★   ★   ★

'I didn't mean to hurt George.'

'I know.'

She felt Martin wrap his arms around her as she nestled her back into his naked chest.

'It was months ago. Before I went back to work. I just got so frustrated.' She turned round to face him in the dark. 'Does that mean I'm a bad mother?'

'No. Everyone gets frustrated. I do, too. But it's better now, isn't it?'

'Yes.'

'I can't believe that about Jenny and Luke, though.'

'I can.' She sighed. 'I might not have known Luke but there's always been something sharp about Jenny. If I was Lucy, I'd never forgive her.'

'I'd forgive you for anything.'

Was this a trick? 'Would you?'

'Well almost anything.'

She was tempted, so tempted to tell him. Confess about the abortion she'd had at uni after sleeping with Dan and tell him that that's why she panicked so much about George; in case something awful happened to him as her 'punishment' for getting rid of the first baby. But Eleanor's words kept ringing in her head. 'There are some things a woman has to keep to herself,' the older woman had warned.

'Why?' murmured Martin, turning towards her. 'Are there any other confessions you want to make?'

She thought of George asleep in his bed at last. She thought of Martin and how they'd finally got their marriage back. And she thought of poor Maggie on her own. What good would it do, all these years later, to tell her husband about something that had happened when she hadn't been much older than Jon?

'No,' she said reaching out for him. 'Nothing at all.'

'I do apologise for calling so late but I wanted to know you were all right after this evening.'

'Thank you, Walter. That's very courteous of you.'

'Don't be too upset about your son.'

Eleanor wiped her nose with her handkerchief at the other end of the line. 'Luke didn't . . . didn't do those things. That wicked girl was telling a pack of lies.'

'I was wondering . . .'

'Yes?'

'Well, you said the other evening that perhaps you'd outstayed your welcome and maybe it was time to go home.'

Eleanor glanced at the bags by her bed which she'd just finished packing. 'Yes, Walter, I'm afraid it might be.'

'Could I drive you back? I thought maybe you could show me the area. Perhaps I could stay for a while. We could share the cooking, that sort of thing. Just to see how we got on.'

'Do you mean we could live together?'

'Does that shock you?'

'Yes. It does. Thank you, Walter. I'd rather enjoy that.'

'Sam!'

'What?'

'Are you asleep?'

'Not now.'

'Mum and Aunty Jenny were having a row.'

'No, they weren't.'

'Well Mum told Aunty Jen to go and that she didn't want to hear her excuses any more.'

'Shit. Maybe she won't get me those Wattevers tickets now.'

Fifty-seven

The doorbell went before anyone else in the house was up. Lucy was sitting in her dressing gown, nursing a mug of coffee and thinking.

'Please.' She tried to close the door. 'I told you, Jenny. I don't want to talk about it.'

'But I do. I've got to, Lucy. Please. You're my sister.'

Jenny pushed ahead and went into the kitchen, putting on the kettle. She always did that, thought Lucy, annoyed, as though she owned the place.

Jenny's face was tight. 'You know that Luke and I got on well . . .'

Lucy put her hands to her ears. 'Stop. Please.'

'We were just friends. OK, so we'd meet up for drinks without telling you but it was just to talk. We could talk and talk . . . And when it finally happened, well it was only the once.'

Lucy stared ahead.

'We'd had too much to drink. It was after one of Chrissie's parties. You were putting Sam to bed and we were down here and . . .'

'You did it here?'

Lucy felt sick.

'Once. Like I said. And afterwards, I felt terrible. So did he.'

'How could you? You're my sister.'

'I know.' Jenny clutched at her. 'I'm sorry.'

'You were always jealous of me, weren't you?' Lucy's eyes flashed. 'Always jealous because I did better at school.'

'No. Yes. Sod it. All right, I was. I thought you had every-thing handed to you on a plate. Dad loved you more than me

– no, don't deny it. It was obvious. You had the children. You had Luke. And now you've got Mike.'

'That's because I've made choices. We all have choices.'

'Yes but some of us have more than others, don't we? Look, Lucy, I'm sorry. I'm going up north with Alan later today. Can I ring you next week?'

'I don't know.'

'Please.' Jenny made to kiss her on the cheek but Lucy turned away.

'Just leave me alone for a bit, can you?'

Ten minutes later, the doorbell went again.

'Haven't you got the message?' demanded Lucy. Then she stopped. 'Jon? Jon!'

She drew him to her, breathing in his smell, holding her first-born in her arms. 'Thank God you're back. I've missed you so much.'

'I've missed you too, Mum.' He looked ruefully at her, dragging his guitar in behind him. Apart from the filthy jeans and torn jumper, he looked almost the same. A little thinner and his hair was shorter but he could almost have walked in through the door as though he'd come back from getting a pint of milk. 'Mum, I'm sorry I upset you but I had to get away to think.'

He looked around. 'I never thought I'd say this but it's so nice to be home.' Picking up his guitar, he gave her another hug. 'I can't wait to see my room again.'

'No, Jon, wait . . .'

Too late. He was already bounding up the stairs, guitar in hand, and in through his door before she could stop him.

'Who the fuck are you?'

For a minute, she thought it was Luke; that same furious angry shout that had scared her so much when he lost it. There was a female-sounding cry of surprise. Jon strode down the stairs, pushing past her. 'Great,' he yelled. 'I'm only out of here for a few weeks and you let my room out to someone else.'

'Wait, Jon. Let me explain. Please don't go.'

He already had the front door open.

'Don't you dare go!'

They both turned round. Kerry was standing at the top of the stairs, presumably naked under the duvet she had wrapped round her although her bare shoulders revealed another fretwork of tattoos which Lucy hadn't noticed before. 'Your mum has been through hell and back. And if you go, I'll fucking well run after you, even in my condition. I'm fast, you know.'

Lucy could see Jon staring at her, struggling to control himself. 'Would someone please tell me who this . . . this person is?'

'I'm Mike's daughter.'

Jon snorted. 'Mike's really got his feet under the table now, hasn't he? Putting his daughter in my room.'

'It was just for one night, Jon,' said Lucy hastily. 'Kerry's got her own flat. Well, she's renting one. It was too far for her to go back to so I said she could sleep in your bed.'

'Is that the truth?' His eyes searched hers.

'Yes, I promise.'

'Don't worry. I'll be out of there in a couple of minutes and then you can have your room back. Didn't think much of your posters on the wall, anyway. Oh, shit . . .'

She sank to the top of the stairs, her arms wrapped round her knees.

'What is it?'

Lucy was by her side in seconds.

'It's nothing.' Kerry started shaking. 'Probably what the midwife called Brixton Hicks.'

'Branxton Hicks,' corrected Lucy gently. 'Are you having contractions?'

'Have been since yesterday, on and off.'

'Since yesterday?'

Jon groaned. 'Great. That's all we need.'

Had her son always been so selfish? 'Jon, go and ring the

doctor. You know where his number is. In my address book by the phone. Kerry, have you got your midwife's number on you? And Jon, when you've done that, ring Mike please. And Eleanor.'

'Oh, God.'

Lucy had her arm around Kerry's frail shoulders. 'Is it getting worse?'

Kerry nodded, her eyes closed. 'Feels like I want to push.'

'Surely not?' Lucy began to panic. 'That's too soon.'

'Not necessarily.' Eleanor's voice boomed out across the hall. 'I thought something might be going on when I saw Jon turning up. Nice to see you're back, dear. Now perhaps you'd like to help your poor mother. Have you any idea what you've put her through? Still, that's what sons are there for. Remind me to tell you about something your father did once. Kerry, I want you to lie back, yes on the landing, so I can take a look. No, don't protest. I may not be a nurse but I had Luke at home and . . . Oh. Good Lord.'

'What?' said Lucy and Kerry together.

Eleanor put her hands to her mouth. 'I believe, unless I'm very much mistaken, that I can see the head!'

Fifty-eight

Thank heavens the doctor had come so fast! Lucy couldn't believe she had actually helped to deliver a baby. It almost, but not quite, took her mind off Jenny. Kerry was now tucked up in Lucy and Mike's bed, sun streaming through the pretty chintz curtains, and beaming at the baby in her arms. Lee, who had arrived shortly afterwards (his mobile had been off) was sitting in his dirty overalls on the edge of the bed, his arm draped round Kerry.

'Isn't she beautiful?' breathed Mike. 'So tiny! Are you sure she's meant to be that small?'

'I remember Sam being that size,' said Jon wonderingly.

'Me too.' Kate nudged him. 'Titch.'

'Shut up.' Sam pushed her back.

'Mind you,' said Kate, 'I'm glad you weren't born at home. All that blood.' She shuddered. 'There's no way I'm ever having sex again!'

'What?'

'Only joking, mum.'

'No she's not. She told me she'd done it with that bloke in the sixth form . . . Ow, Kate. Shut up.'

'Well if you do it again, you'd better take precautions,' said Kerry, sharply. 'You're too young to handle something like this.' She looked down at the sleeping bundle on her body. 'I'm not even sure I can. Supposing she stops breathing?'

'She won't.' Eleanor smoothed down the coverlet. 'All new mothers worry. Of course in our day, we had our own mothers nearby to help out. But you've got us.'

'I have?' Something hopeful flickered in Kerry's eyes and

Lucy felt a pang. She hadn't been fair. All this girl wanted was for someone to love her, just like the rest of them. A vision of Luke and Jenny shot into her head and angrily she brushed it away.

'Of course you've got us.' She stroked the side of the baby's cheek, wondering at the soft velvety feel. 'We don't live far away. And we'll always be there for you.'

'But your friend Chrissie . . . You said she found it hard to cope with a baby. Supposing I do too?'

'Chrissie just needed to sort herself out,' said Eleanor crisply. 'She had certain issues to deal with. And no, Lucy, don't look at me like that. I wouldn't dream of divulging the details.'

'I wasn't going to ask,' spluttered Lucy. Chrissie had confided in Eleanor? How much – and what – had she told her?

'Hi. Sorry to just drop in but I wanted to drop off a present for the baby.'

'Rubbish.' Lucy shepherded her in. 'You wanted to find out what was happening.'

Chrissie dumped George on the ground and he zoomed off into the house like an electric car. 'Well you must admit, it was a bit dramatic! I can't believe that stuff about Jenny and Luke. She was drunk, wasn't she? That story about Luke couldn't possibly be true.'

'Yes she was drunk and yes it was true.'

'Wow! No wonder you two are always so prickly with each other.'

'It's not just that.' She'd spent all night analysing it and now she spoke on remote, having worked out the whys and whens of something so terrible that surely it was happening to someone else and not her. 'It goes back a long way. She was always jealous of dad and me being close.'

'Has she called?'

'Yes.'

'But you don't want to talk to her.'

'No. Besides, I've got enough to cope with. Jon's back, you know.'

Chrissie looked concerned. 'How is he?'

'At first he seemed really pleased to be back. Now he's got itchy feet again. It turns out he's made some contacts when he was away and has got about five bookings in clubs over the next few months.'

'That's great.' Chrissie squeezed her arm. 'Look, I know it's not Oxford but you've got to let them do what they want. Listen, I've got some news. I'm pregnant. Yes, really! It must have been the time when we . . . well, anyway, I am. I wasn't expecting it because my periods still hadn't got back to normal. And I think giving up breastfeeding had something to do with it. Isn't that exciting!'

'Well . . . yes.'

'I know what you're thinking. You're worried I'll find it too much to handle. Well Eleanor says that when I have number two, I'll be too busy to panic as much as I did with George.'

'But what about your new job?

'I'm not giving that up! I love it. I've already spoken to HR – well I am HR, aren't I? – and they're opening a crèche. So the baby and George can go there. I expect Martin will have found a job by then.'

'That's amazing.' Why couldn't she sound more enthusiastic?

'You think I'm going to hurt this one too, don't you?'

'No but . . .'

Chrissie caught her arm. 'I didn't mean to. I don't know what came over me and I'm so ashamed.'

Then why did you do it, Lucy wanted to say. But at the same time, she knew exactly why. As Mike had said in bed last night when they'd been discussing it, sometimes a part of you does something which the rest of you would never contemplate. But there's nothing you can do to stop it because by the time you try, it's too late.

'Does Martin understand?'

'Yes but . . .'

'But you didn't tell him the whole truth.' She dropped her voice. 'You didn't tell him about the abortion.'

Chrissie stared at her. 'Who told you?'

Whoops. 'I'm afraid Eleanor did. But I haven't told anyone else.'

Chrissie hung her head. 'I couldn't tell him. You see why, don't you? He might leave me if I did and I think I'd die if that ever happened.'

Lucy put her arms around her, hugging her tight. Maybe Chrissie was right. Maybe it was best not to know everything. If only her so-called father had never told her about Jenny and if only Jenny had never told her about Luke, she might still have a sister.

Fifty-nine

Maggie finished washing up. Last night had been weird. She'd thought it was just her life that had been turned upside down in the last year. It just went to show.

'OK, you two?'

The kids, hooked by some crap on television, nodded without turning round.

Funny. Not so long ago, she'd have felt that familiar wave of panic; that sickness at being alone with just the children for company. But after she'd told Antony that no, she wouldn't take him back, she felt a sense of power. A slight regret too, to be honest. But as Eleanor had said after supper last night, there was no going back now. And sometimes not knowing what was in store was exciting. Rather like knowing someone, somewhere, was cooking you a mystery dish and all you had to do was wait for it to turn up.

In the meantime, there were things to do. Maggie punched the numbers into her mobile. 'Hi. Is that Sue from Social Friends? It's Maggie. About the barbecue on Saturday night. I'd love to come if there's still a space left.'

'Hi.'

'What are you doing?'

'Eating.'

'What?'

Dan swallowed his mouthful. 'A takeaway.'

'Want to come over here for a bite?'

'Is Antony there?'

There was a brief silence. 'Yes.'

'No thanks then.'

'I wish you wouldn't be like that.'

'Like what?'

Patsy's voice was low and urgent down the phone. 'Look, Dan, I'm sorry. But we weren't right for each other. I love Antony. And I'm not breaking up his marriage any more. Maggie doesn't want him back,'

'How's your father?'

'OK. Seems quite happy actually in the new place.'

'Good.'

'How about tomorrow? We could meet then. Antony's got a late meeting. Not that . . . well you know. Just as friends.'

'Just as friends?' Dan rolled the words over in his mouth, testing them. 'Sorry, Patsy. I'm taking someone out to dinner.'

'Mum, look at this.'

Jon pushed a printed-out email in front of her nose.

'It's some modelling agency. They got a picture of me from that girlfriend of Antony's who showed my picture to some photographer and they want me to come in for tests. Isn't that amazing?'

'Yes,' said Lucy cautiously, 'if that's what you want to do. But I thought you were going to concentrate on your music.'

Jon fiddled with his hair in the mirror. 'I can do both, can't I? Look, I'm going out now. See you later.'

'What time will you be back?' Mike asked.

'Why? Are you cooking instead of Mum?'

'No. I just think it's courteous to let her know what time you'll be back.'

'It's all right, Mike . . .'

'No, I think we should know.'

'After supper.' Jon stared at him challengingly. 'If that's all right with you.'

Lucy waited until the door had slammed. 'I wish you wouldn't be so hard on him. I don't want to drive him out again.'

'Nor do I. But he can't ride rough-shod over us, like his father did to you.'

Lucy winced.

Mike put his arm around her, pulling her to him against the Aga. 'I know you don't like talking about it but why did you stay with Luke, when he made you so unhappy?'

'I was scared of being on my own. I know that sounds pathetic but the children were young.'

'So why do you feel guilty about loving me? It's not as though we met before he died.'

She nestled her head in his shoulders. 'It's a weird kind of guilt, partly because I don't feel I deserve such happiness. You make me see life in colour, you know, whereas before it was just black and white. But I also feel guilty because I'm putting more strain on the kids by introducing someone who isn't their father. And I'm scared. I trusted Luke at the beginning. How do I know you wouldn't do the same to me?'

'I wouldn't. And I'll also try to be more understanding with the kids. I'm not going to promise it will be easy. But I'll do it on one condition.'

'What's that?'

He smiled down on her. 'I want us to set a date. A wedding date so we can start a new life together and find a home that we can do up together. I think it's time, don't you? Because, whatever you say, you do deserve such happiness as you put it. And so do I.'

'Everything all right, dear? You look as though you're miles away.'

Lucy jumped. She hadn't noticed Eleanor coming in.

'Sort of.' She began tidying the newspapers and magazines on the table. 'I've got a bit of a headache. There's been so much going on.'

'I know.' Eleanor took her hand. 'That's what I wanted to talk to you about, dear. Can we sit down? I must say, I'm very glad you persuaded Michael to get rid of his awful settee.'

'I didn't. He . . .'

Eleanor patted the seat next to her. 'Now, dear. What I wanted to say was this. I was extremely shocked by Jenny's so-called confession the other night, although we all know she'd been drinking so it couldn't possibly have been true.'

'Actually, Eleanor, I wouldn't be surprised if Luke had other affairs too.' Lucy paused, thinking of all the people Luke mixed with in his job.

'Well I expect he did, dear. No, don't look like that. Luke's father did the same and very hurtful it was too. But men think through their trousers and in my day we understood that if we wanted to keep our nice homes and comfortable existences, we just had to put up with it.'

'That's not what I believe,' said Lucy unsteadily.

'Ah well, that's up to you, dear. But what I did want to say is that I've been observing Michael over the last few months and if you want to marry him, I won't lodge any more objections.'

Lucy wondered if she'd heard her right. 'That's very kind of you, Eleanor, but even if you did . . .'

'You see,' continued Eleanor as though she hadn't spoken. 'I've been re-awakened.' She flushed slightly. 'Walter has reminded me what it's really like to be in love. I haven't felt like that since Cedric.'

'Cedric? But I thought George was Luke's father.'

'He might well have been, dear.'

'Might have been?'

'We didn't make a fuss about that sort of thing in my day, Lucy, provided no one got hurt. What was I talking about? Ah, yes. Cedric was my first love. I couldn't marry him because he didn't have enough money. But I never forgot him. Never.' Her eyes grew misty. 'I often wonder what became of him.'

'And has Walter got enough money for you?'

'There's no need to sound so disapproving, dear. Do you know what my mother used to say? "Don't marry for money but marry where the money is." Sensible, don't you think? Anyway, Walter has asked me to marry him. Isn't that nice? I'll be right next door so I can help out with the children, although we will be spending part of the year abroad. Walter has a house in Tenerife, you know.'

Lucy was still trying to absorb all this.

'There's just one other thing, dear.'

There was more?

Eleanor took her hand again, stroking it lightly. 'I do think you ought to forgive your sister. When you get to my age, you know, you realise that family and health are the only really important things in life. I learned that when you took me in. No, don't say anything. I know I was an intrusion at first, although I like to think I've helped out a bit. So do think about what I've said, dear. You wouldn't want to lose your sister forever, would you?'

MARCH

Second helpings?

Sixty

'What do you think then?'

'About what?' Lucy looked up from her pile of paperwork which was inexplicably covered with dog hairs even though Mungo had only been in the office a couple of times when Genevieve was away.

'You haven't been listening, have you? Have you even gone over those figures? I don't know what's got into you, Lucy. You're so distant nowadays.'

'Sorry. Run it past me again.'

Maggie sighed. 'It's like I said. Genevieve wants to sell the business, right? Now with the money Antony's giving me and a bank loan, I could put in half. You said you had enough for yours and if we knock Genevieve down a bit, we can take on the lease and run this business ourselves.'

Three months ago, Lucy would never have thought Maggie was capable of running to the supermarket let alone running a business. But she felt different now, she'd explained, now she knew where she was. It had taken time, granted, to accept Antony really loved that woman. She still refused to use Patsy's name but finally she could see it was time to move on.

'So shall we make her an offer?'

It had been a long time since she'd seen Maggie look so excited and hopeful. This was just what she needed and, as Mike said, a new project might just be what she needed too.

'Yes!' She felt a frisson of excitement running through her. 'Go for it.'

*   *   *

Sometimes, she felt as though she'd wandered into a different world. She was even getting used to waking up in Alan's arms with the sun streaming in through the curtains. She could change them if she wanted, Alan had said, but she didn't. Somehow she sensed that Caroline wasn't a threat and even Doris, despite the marmalade, seemed to approve of her, having offered to take her out riding when she was better.

It was amazing, too, how easily she had slipped into the way of life up here. People had time to talk; to go out for tea. It was like discovering a rather old-fashioned side to herself which she hadn't realised existed.

She'd decided not to work for a bit but one of the designer shops in a smart suburb of Newcastle had asked her to draw up a press release. Then another had commissioned her to organise a fashion show. 'Great, lass,' Alan had enthused.

There was just one thing missing.

'I hear congratulations are in order.'

Chrissie, who had picked up her office phone expecting the usual lunchtime call from Martin, froze. No need to ask who the caller was. She'd recognise his voice anywhere.

'A new job and a new baby on the way!' He sounded almost amused. 'That's going to take some juggling.'

'I'll manage.'

How could she ever have held a candle for him?

'You're not very talkative. Busy are you?'

'Very.'

'I only rang to say goodbye. You'll be pleased to hear I'm going to France. I've bought a small château near Perpignon and I plan to work from there.'

'Good luck,' she managed to say.

'And good luck to you too, Chrissie.'

★   ★   ★

Yellow. A lemony yellow with a border of blue. No carpets. Posh beech floorboards with an American fridge in the kitchen. And four bedrooms!

'Do you like it?'

Patsy did a twirl in the middle of the room. 'Like it?' she said, eyes shining. 'It's wonderful.'

She draped her arms around his neck, gently pulling him towards her; needing to smell his skin.

'She'll see us,' whispered Antony, referring to the estate agent who had tactfully withdrawn into one of the two spare bedrooms which, they'd already agreed, would be perfect for the children at weekends. The guest room would, theoretically, be for her father. Patsy wasn't ready yet to admit he might never be well enough to come out. Besides, she'd been pleasantly surprised at how caring the staff were at the new home. 'Things have changed in the last few years,' the matron had told her kindly. 'I'm sorry you and your father had such a bad experience before.'

Antony turned to her. 'So shall we buy it?'

Buy it? Move in together? Commit herself to one man? Something she had always thought she could never do.

'Shall we?'

He needed an answer. She owed him that. And she owed it to herself too.

'All right.' Lemon yellow was one of those colours that made you feel good. She shrugged happily. 'Don't mind if we do.'

Tomorrow was her sister's birthday. She hadn't sent a card.

Heaven knows, she'd tried but every 'Sister' card she'd looked at gushed with wildly inappropriate pleasantries. Lucy sat at the kitchen table, cupping her hands round her hot chocolate, remembering how their mother used to make them Ovaltine every night at bedtime. She and Jenny would sit at the table while their mother fussed around, tidying things away and checking they'd done their homework. Where had their father been? Working late, their mother had always said. It was only when she'd been older, long after he'd left, that Lucy had questioned it.

When, on the rare occasions, Dad had come home before bedtime, he would ruffle her hair and ask how her day had been. Then he'd quiz Jenny on why she hadn't done better in her maths test or what she was doing wearing nail polish when she was only thirteen.

'I can never do anything right,' Jenny used to mutter under the bedcovers at night in the small bedroom they shared next to their parents.

It wasn't surprising that as soon as she could, she left home, choosing to go straight to work instead of university as Lucy had done.

'Look after your sister,' their mother had said towards the end. It was their mother's death soon afterwards, which had brought them together; the shock of suddenly realising it was just the two of them. They'd both been so used to their mother's heart condition that somehow they'd assumed it would be all right.

And she'd tried. She'd really tried, despite their differences. Conscious that they were Jenny's only family, she and Luke (how ironic!), always kept their home open to her; often invited her round for Sunday lunch; made her godmother to each child.

How could she have been so stupid?

How could Jenny have done what she did?

'I loved Luke very much but he could be extremely selfish,' Eleanor had said sadly before leaving last month.

Yes, he could.

'You have two choices, dear. You can forgive her and pick up the pieces. Or you can continue ignoring her calls and then, one day, find it's too late to make up.'

★   ★   ★

Dear Luke,

I know now.

Jenny told me. Last month, actually, but it's still sinking in. I can't believe you did what you did but at the same time, it's a relief. It explains so much. It wasn't my fault you didn't find me attractive . . . it was because you wanted someone else. Someone whom you could never have, without tearing apart the family.

I'm angry with you, Luke. It's taken years for that anger to finally seep through and I don't know why. Maybe it's because I felt so guilty before. I always thought it was my fault you insisted on going on that plane. My fault, because of that horrible argument we had when I said I'd stopped loving you.

I'm sorry I said that. What I really meant was that I'd stopped loving the person you'd become. I wanted the old Luke back; the one I'd met all those years ago, before things went wrong. Why did they go wrong, Luke? Was it because we married too young, without really knowing what we were like ourselves, let alone what the other was like?

Your mother suggested I wrote this letter. She said it might help to write down my feelings. Someone told her to do the same, apparently, after your father died. I thought it was a daft idea at first but actually, this is helping. You shouldn't have led Jenny on like that. She was too young and vulnerable. But I forgive you, Luke. I forgive you because your behaviour has shown me it wasn't all my fault and so, finally, I can forgive myself.

I know you'll never be able to read this. But in a funny way, I feel as though you're doing just that, over my shoulder. You're raising your eyebrow in the way you always did when someone did something you disapproved of. And you're telling me that I must be crazy to write to someone who's been dead for years.

Maybe you're right. But I think Mike would understand. Yes, that's right. I've met someone else now. I waited for years after you'd gone before I started seeing anyone and, in fact, he was the first. Antony – you remember Antony? – introduced us.

Mike's very different from you and we've had our teething problems. But I think the children (and even your mother) are beginning to accept him.

I'm going to go now, Luke. But first I'm going to tear this letter up into little bits so no one else reads it. I hope you're all right, wherever you are.

Love Lucy x

Sixty-one

Mike had gone to bed by the time she'd come up. The light was still on but his back was facing her. Luke used to do that while she sorted out whichever child had woken up. But he would also have turned out the light and then got cross when she woke him up getting into bed.

Slowly, so as not to disturb Mike, Lucy climbed into bed. Immediately, he rolled over, taking her into his arms and stroking her back.

'I didn't want to wake you.'

'You didn't.' He nuzzled her hair. 'Is Sam back?'

'Yes, although he's still going on about wanting a tattoo like Kerry's. Kate's just got in from walking Mungo. Jon's still on the computer, organising gigs. And Kerry rang to say she's got the baby to sleep at last. Chrissie's white music tape seems to have done the trick.'

Mike stretched out luxuriously, draping an arm around her. 'So the whole family is safe.'

She thought of Jenny and her father who hadn't seemed like her father, although at least he hadn't tried to contact her again. 'I suppose so.'

His hands continued to stroke her back, rhythmically. 'Have you thought any more about what I said?'

'Yes.' She closed her eyes, wondering if she had the courage to say what had to be said.

'And?' He was nervous; she could hear that.

'I wondered . . . I mean I thought . . . I wasn't sure but I did think that . . .'

Mike sat up, looking down at her, uncertainty etched all over his face. She reached up and put her arms around his neck. 'I agree. July would be a nice time to get married.'

'Phew! For a minute, I thought you'd changed your mind.' His mouth came down on hers, hard and meaningful yet soft and considerate at the same time. She could feel his hand reaching underneath her nightdress and she moved away.

'What's wrong?'

'Nothing. Well, there is but it's nothing to do with us.'

She felt herself getting out of bed. 'There's something I've got to do. I'm sorry. I'll be back in a second.'

'You can make the phone call here, if you like.'

'How did you know?'

He kissed her, handing her the receiver. 'Because I understand you better than you think. It's Jenny's birthday tomorrow. You're still desperately hurt but at the same time, you feel you should forgive her because she'll never know her real father.'

She nodded. 'Exactly.'

'Want me to leave the room?'

'No.' She snuggled up next to him, nervously punching in the numbers.

'No answer?'

'No.'

'Try again.'

'I'm not sure. It's very late. Perhaps . . .'

The phone rang in her hands. Lucy stared at it.

'Answer it,' said Mike softly.

'Hello?'

Jenny's voice, so familiar, sounded worried yet defensive at the same time. 'Did you just ring?'

Lucy took a deep breath. 'Yes. I wanted to wish you happy birthday for tomorrow.'

'Thank you.' Jenny was quiet. Distant.

'I haven't sent a card, I'm afraid.'

'It doesn't matter.'

'I didn't know what to put.'

There was a silence. Then they both spoke at once.

'Are you happy up –'

'I'm so sorry, Lucy.'

One day, she'd have to tell Jenny about their father – her father. But not now. 'I haven't rung to talk about that.'

'You haven't?'

'No.' Lucy took a deep breath. 'I rang to ask you something.'

'What?'

In the old days, she'd have taken offence at the abrasive 'What?' Now, she suddenly realised, that brusque manner was a mask for her sister's guilt.

'I rang to ask whether you and Alan would like to come down to supper next week. A sort of late Christmas and birthday combined.'

'Are you sure?'

'Quite sure.' Lucy nestled into Mike's arms. It wouldn't be easy but Eleanor had been right. Family was the most important thing in life. Even a family which didn't share the same blood and genes.

'Shall we say Saturday? About eight o'clock? In fact, why not come for the weekend?'

LEFTOVERS

'Whotookthesalmonoutofthedishwasher?ThatAustralianbloke ntellysaysyou'remeanttocookitthatway.Antonydidyoudothis? Antony! No. Don't . . . don't stop. MMMM, that's luuvly . . .'

'Hi Pete. It's me, Kate. Remember? I've emailed you a few times but I expect you've been busy so I'm leaving a message. Mum and Mike are going on their honeymoon next week and we're having a party while they're away. I just wondered if you wanted to come.'

Tattoo parlour. Come on in and see what we've got! ID not necessary.

Dear Lucy and Michael,

Walter and I are having a wonderful time in the Maldives. I didn't realise how much you can do when you're not doing anything. In my day, holidays were really rather boring compared with this. Love to the children. So sorry we'll be away for the wedding.

Best wishes,
Eleanor and Walter

SENSUAL . . .
'Mum, have you been playing Dirty Scrabble again?'

'George, will you stop saying that naughty word? Honestly, sometimes I wonder why I taught you to talk. Martin, can you hurry up? He's going to be late for the crêche and I've got my antenatal appointment.'

'Wattevers tickets! For the Easter holidays! Thanks, Mike. That's naked.'

Special Delivery. Contents: one pair of garnet earrings

Dear Lucy,

I know you'll recognise these. Mum gave them to me before she died but I want you to have them. Something borrowed and all that . . .

'Who's eaten all that Brie in the fridge? Mungo? Oh, God, he's been sick again . . .'

Still trying to lose those post-Christmas pounds? Follow our Family Diet, exclusive to *Charisma* magazine!

Mum's Wedding Cake Recipe
(Note: I've included this one in my recipe book in the hope that one of you girls will need it one day! It was passed down to me by my own mother – Granny B.)

Two pounds of mixed fruit
Two pounds of butter
Four pounds of flour
12 fresh eggs
Three generous tablespoons of brandy
One dash of luck
A large dollop of love